About the Author

Patrick Barrow was born and grew up in London. After university, he pursued a career in media and public relations including spells with the Daily Telegraph and the BBC and contributes to various on-line publications. A keen student of history and current affairs, he is also a sports lover, most particularly rugby and cricket. Patrick now lives in Kent with his wife, Lucy, and two children. 'Bang out of order' is his first novel.

Bang Out Of Order

Patrick Barrow

Bang Out Of Order

Olympia Publishers
London

www.olympiapublishers.com
OLYMPIA PAPERBACK EDITION

A CIP catalogue record for this title is
available from the British Library.

ISBN: 978-1-80439-413-7

This is a work of fiction.
Names, characters, places and incidents originate from the writer's
imagination. Any resemblance to actual persons, living or dead, is
purely coincidental.

First Published in 2024

Olympia Publishers
Tallis House
2 Tallis Street
London
EC4Y 0AB

Printed in Great Britain

Dedication

This book is dedicated first and foremost to my wife Lucy − my own Rachel − and 'trouble' from the moment I laid eyes on her. Also to my children for whom no love is enough. As it should be. And to my wider family.

Acknowledgements

I have been 'about to write a book' for many years. Done it now. My thanks, as ever, to my wife Lucy for the time, space and, frankly, insistence that allowed this to happen. There has always been a crowd, a small one, I grant, saying "you should write a book, you know?" The voice of my conscience answered. Thanks to all of you. To Pat Goodwin. Twist to the tale.

It was the year of explosions. That's how he remembered it. Detonations. In post boxes, on trains, on shop shelves and under cars. They erupted seemingly every day. The newscasters grim as they flickered black and white on the early evening news and announced the latest. The deaths, the dismemberment, the ashen-faced injured, blood mingling with the brick dust and plaster as they sat disbelieving on a kerb or on the step of an ambulance. They had been blown up but were still alive. They didn't know which they could comprehend less.

He remembered two firemen in their old-fashioned helmets, blue serge coats and heavy boots shovelling − shovelling − remains into two bags. London, Belfast, where he couldn't recall, but there it was; black and white and red all over. The news.

And his mother's friend. A nurse the night someone chucked a bomb through the window of a pub full of soldiers. He remembered her. Vaguely now.

Other explosions too. His father's. The easy switch from jolly charmer to raging bullshit. Sunday lunches running down the wall, fists raised, fists used. The punches to his mother's arm as she drove, the maudlin moods and misunderstood genius. The lies and confections, the gathering storm. Add alcohol and stand well clear. Who was in for it this time? Not him, never him. Even when the police came, he'd lie calmly. They'd eye him suspiciously of course. They knew. The broken bannister, the crumpled faces, the tension oozing from the walls along with the wine from a thrown glass.

Then the bang that changed everything. The slammed front door. Even in a world of explosions, it echoed with the clarity of a single rifle shot. She'd gone. And left them.

Where that had left Sean Christopher was where he stood now. On a high hill overlooking London. The new increasingly

11

overcoming the old in height and in light and in prominence. An old bronze general staring silently over the river from his plinth while the aviation lights atop the skyscrapers winked cheekily back like upstart urchins taunting a Chelsea Pensioner.

It was autumn. The leaves were turning and the conkers poked their shiny noses through heavy shells of fading green. They were parting slowly, preparing to drop their off-spring onto the pavement. A silent bearing down.

Years ago, there would have been gangs of children throwing sticks into the branches to try and harvest them for playground duels. Nobody played conkers any more. The horse chestnuts remained unmolested by string and experiments with ovens and vinegar. Only the pavement awaited. "There's a moral there somewhere," he thought, "Heads they win, tails you lose."

General Wolfe still bore the shrapnel scars of a mistimed German bomb. Down there, beyond the Canaletto façade of the Naval College and the grim brick face of the old power station, was that they'd been aiming at; the river and the docks.

Christopher thought of the conkers. Change in a nutshell. How many times had he looked down at that view? When he was a kid and the park had been his playground and refuge, joy and solace, running down to the Cutty Sark pier on a yawning Seventies Sunday when all that was open was the tourist ice cream stand and the old ship herself, looking forlornly at the water from her dry dock and her Scottish figurehead looking for a fight.

He thought of London then, mid-rise and soot-faced from four-star engines and dirty diesels. The bike rides out into the melancholy flat lands where the clank, clank, clank of the pile drivers sank the footings for the flood barrier.

And he looked now. At the shining towers of Canary Wharf

where the lights twinkled like stars in the East, a distant robot train on the light railway, the apartments running east and west down the river's banks and a cruise ship, vast and white, slowly navigating its tourists towards a hard Victorian stop just below Tower Bridge.

Somewhere, he thought, somewhere between that past and this present lies the riddle and its answer. He straddled both, knew that city, knew the jaded old cow under that all that make up and knew she never really changed.

Christopher and the general were looking at an old friend who had somehow defied the ravages of time; familiar but unrecognisable. They both looked without seeing. The man forever scanning the horizon for a lost city because in it he might find a lost woman.

Darkness was closing in. Of mood as much as anything else. And Christopher hated that. He was not maudlin by nature and so tried to deny the slow seep of past woes much ingress. God knows he'd seen enough misery to know its corrosive effects.

He looked up at the statue still looking sternly out across the Thames and on into the great city as though he could see up every street and down every alley. Because Christopher was, just, still a detective and because an old police TV series catch phrase came unbidden to mind, he winked and said: "Keep 'em peeled[1]."

He was smiling to himself as he walked back towards his car. Below, London illuminated like a thousand fishing boats on a coal black sea. They were, for the moment, for the first time in a long time, at ease with each other.

Christopher was stillness amid the buzz and bustle of the incident

---

[1] The catch phrase of Shaw Taylor who presented Police 5, a TV programme engaging public help to solve crimes.

room. He wasn't working on an investigation but, on the verge of retirement, he could increasingly afford to sit and simply immerse himself in a life he was about to leave.

It was an almost cinematic experience. The images running in front of him, imprinting themselves indelibly on his brain as he ate metaphorical popcorn and connected the various plot lines, identified the main characters and judged them sympathetic or otherwise.

Christopher could feel himself vanishing. Like a solitary viewer in the cinema as the lights first dimmed, then blackened and only the screen's luminescence and the green word 'Exit' stood out starkly against the dark.

His presence in the room was amiably tolerated. He'd been around a long time and was popular, if always slightly apart, from the teams of detectives that came together in intense bursts of energy and then broke up again as a crime was either solved or a trail went so corpse cold that resuscitation of a case was impossible.

They'd tease him good-naturedly about being lucky. Out. Safe. Pensioned. And Christopher was, after all, a handy source of reference with all his years of experience banked, logged and filed. He drank it all in like a traveller about to enter a desert. These last few weeks would have to sustain him across the lone and level sands. 'Look upon my works ye mighty and despair![2]' He thought.

"One last look, mate?" His boss. Old friend. Surpasser and master. They'd been through school and then the college at Hendon together. Marched out, passed out together, white-gloved and focused on keeping in step in front of the Union flag and a picture of the Queen.

---

[2] It's about the ephemeral nature of power.

He'd done better, strode quicker. If Christopher had always been the better instinctive policeman, Francis, Peter Francis, had trumped him with political nous and the ability to find himself in the right pub at the right time back when coppering had been a beery occupation and favours were swapped after hours and on a trip round the optics with a tired landlord wishing they'd all go home.

If it were true that villains had a habit of running out of the back door and into Christopher's arms, it was a fact that Francis always remembered the kids' names and had just the right quip for any occasion.

For all that, they got on. A ying to the yang, they'd cleared each other up after a wade in the messy moral margins of criminal investigation. They'd seen the worst the world had to offer and helped each other summon four a.m. courage in the aftermath when the ghosts came out from under the bed and the demons rattled from inside the wardrobe. Best of all they'd helped each other resist that most corrosive of police assumptions; that because all villains are people, all people are villains. Somewhere, they retained a sense of humanity and held it safely between them.

Christopher emerged blinking from his film. "Something like that, boss." He smiled easily up at Francis. "Got something for me?"

"Think so." Answered Francis, unusually tentatively, and dropped a case file into his friend's lap. A file. Intriguing in itself. Old, manila, the definition of analogue in a computerised world where the Police National Computer (PNC) was Watson to HOLMES, the major investigation system. Where had he got it from? These weren't stumbled across, these harkings back.

Christopher glanced at it. Historical. Well, he'd expected

15

that though it wasn't really his remit. He looked up at his boss who was watching him keenly, pensively. Was this just to give him something to do? He scanned his old oppo's face trying to find some kind of clue. Was there an uncharacteristic malice there? Faint jealousy of a man who was on the verge of his pension but didn't have the decency not to hang around and make a show of paid up idleness. No. It wasn't in him and, anyway, his old mate wasn't far behind. Slightly younger, better connected but still coming into the final bend.

Francis winked at him. Not his usual matey, 'let's have another,' cheeky boy wink. Complicit, cryptic, almost willing him to understand something. Christopher knew faces. Honest, dishonest, the ever-shifting blend in most of us. The dead-eyed Satans he'd interviewed several murders in, remorseless and amoral. The shocked disbelief of the one-punch killer and the 'fuck off, copper.' defiance of the truly nasty villain, refusing in the face even of a lengthy stretch to acknowledge the authority of the law. For the moment, anyway. But he could see only his friend in front of him. Same as ever.

"Take a look," he said. "Might interest you." And, as though reading Christopher's mind, added smilingly: "Give you something to do, anyway. Cluttering the place up and rubbing it in. Do something while you still can." And he wandered off before Christopher could interrogate the quip.

Swivelling his chair round to face the empty desk he'd parked at, Christopher opened the file, noting it smelt of must, pulled on the glasses that aged him ten years every time he glanced professorially over their top, and began to read.

The mid-Seventies in London were a blast only for the IRA and lit up only by the blazing heat wave of 1976. Christopher remembered both for different reasons.

He remembered the endless sunshine of a summer that lasted from May to September. Each day an endless roaming of London's parks and swimming pools at Greenwich, Charlton and Eltham. There was the river too. He and his brother and a dare to swim in it, climbing down the slime green stairs of Greenwich pier and into the muddy swirl of the Thames.

A memory, snapshot clear, of waking from a somnolent sun-induced study to take a catch at school cricket, the hard red ball inches from his face and the last grass on Blackheath savannah brown in the heat. Congratulations from his teammates on a courageous 'grab' close to the bat and the ball at terminal velocity. His teacher winking at him as if to say, 'you woke up just in time.' Christopher smiling back at a secret shared; his instinct for self-preservation.

Christopher smiled again at the brief and ancient glory.

Less so at the change in mood come evening. His father in from town, overweight and sweating from the commute, the taint of alcohol on his breath and his mother trying nervously to please. Cold drinks and quick supper to the form stretched out on the sofa. Tick, tick, tick, boom!

Which is what the file dealt with.

In 1973, the Irish Republican Army (IRA) acted on a crude calculation. That a bomb in London was worth thirty in Belfast. It was an equation based on an easy algebra where x was the number of high-profile targets, y was the density of population and their sum, as future Prime Minister Margaret Thatcher would later describe it, was 'the oxygen of publicity.'

The terrorists sent active service units (ASUs) to England. The first of these attacked the Central Criminal Court at the Old Bailey in the City of London, injuring over 200 with one man dying of a heart attack.

The gang was arrested trying to flee England by plane shortly after the explosion and with security forces on full alert.

The IRA learnt quickly and changed tactic, activating a cell later known as The Balcombe Street Gang to maintain a sustained campaign of atrocities and all the while based in England. For fifteen months, it succeeded.

Pubs where soldiers gathered, top London restaurants and hotels, up-market shops like Harrod's and Selfridges, all were bombed or machine gunned as were mainline London stations at Euston and King's Cross.

Nor did the gang confine themselves to London, bombing pubs in Birmingham and Guildford before being eventually tracked down to Balcombe Street in London where, after a siege lasting several days, its four main members were arrested in December 1975.

The attacks had reached a crescendo of one every three days in the previous year. By the time the cell was apprehended, nineteen people were dead and hundreds injured.

Christopher paused for a moment, lifting his glasses off his eyes and rubbing them to clear his head as much as his vision.

He glanced down again, the file went on in this vein for some time. Each page outlined a new horror, a fresh tragedy and he was uncertain as to why Francis had handed him a file containing a brief history of the IRA's activity in mainland Britain.

All this had been wrapped up long ago without ever going away. Sporadic up-surges of sectarian violence in Northern Ireland now ran cover for the terrorist-turned-gangster unemployed of the old paramilitaries. Occasional trials of junior British Army soldiers, still pursued long after the IRA had welcomed its convicted back into the welcoming embrace of warm hearth and warmer mythology. Warnings from the intelligence services that the heart still beat in the old beast of Irish grievance even as Britain's erratic memory failed it.

Christopher was trapped somewhere between boredom and curiosity as well as the knowledge that said his old friend had implied some greater import than merely revisiting the memories of exploding shop fronts and imploding lives.

He got up, got coffee and got started once again. And then he found it. A file within a file.

An attack on a commuter train in 1979. The Provos had attacked the transport system before. Sometimes at tube stations, sometimes at major terminuses but rarely the trains themselves. The file documented a previous attempt at Cannon Street, the station in the heart of the City of London, the capital's historic financial quarter, in which there had been an explosion on an empty train which had just disgorged its passengers from the stockbroker belt town of Sevenoaks in Kent, south of London.

This had been different. A bomb padded out with the hallmark ball bearings designed to cause maximum carnage had detonated on another train from Kent via south east London just as it pulled in to a packed platform six at London Bridge, another gateway station to the City and West End of London.

Christopher screwed his eyes tight shut. He remembered it. The evening horror show on the news. Bodies laid out under the tatters of their own bloodied coats on the scorched paintwork of platform six. Firemen handing pieces of human out of the tortured metal of the carriage, great piercing sharps of steel pointed skyward, outward. The newscaster talking over the faint background screams of disbelief and pain and the dull, shocked silence of death.

He remembered it.

Twenty-seven bodies laid out on the platform. The legless, the armless, the blind, the distraught being manoeuvred past them by ambulancemen, doctors, off-duty nurses from nearby Guy's Hospital, their focus on the now blinding them to the horror that would return later. In the night. In the years hereafter.

He remembered the faint concern, hope perhaps, that his father might have been on that train. He had glanced repeatedly at the front door that day. Not because he might come through it but because he might not. And besides, it was the day his mother had left. The Yale bouncing out of the latch with the force of her departure. A terminus reached and the bomb gone off.

Christopher forced his attention back down onto the file.

He studied each page itemising name, age, injuries, cause of death. The flat facts of medical observation reducing evisceration, decapitation, mutilation to the vocabulary of unemotional science. Exsanguination. Amputation. London Bridge station.

Christopher reached the end, still feeling that he was missing something. He checked back.

Twenty-seven bodies. The police report said it. The weary hand of an exhausted doctor signing off death certificates said it. The firemen matching pulp to torso, torso to limb said it. Twenty-seven. Thirteen men, ten women, four children being taken to out-patient appointments at Guy's or heading to the City of London School.

And yet. He read the notes again. Only twenty-five had ever arrived at London's mortuaries. At Guy's and nearby St Thomas's, in other places where bodies were quickly taken in a desperate attempt to avert the public's gaze and clear the bottle-neck station for use, only twenty-five had faced the unseeing indignity of tagged toes and their relatives' descent into

20

inarticulate, lifelong heartbreak.

He flicked again through the pages. Twenty-five single page descriptions of slaughter. One person to a page. Two missing. A man and a woman. Had they fallen out? The file was old enough for the papers simply to have disintegrated, weakened or been casually discarded in an office move.

All the other pages were securely fastened. Still strong and backed by card dividers.

He looked through the entire file again just to ensure that they hadn't been slipped back in out of place. Nothing. No explanatory note, no questioning memo, no exhortation to investigate. Just two numbers that didn't tally and no explanation as to why nor indication that anyone had noticed.

Christopher looked up quickly, deliberately. He wanted to find Francis' eyes and find them unguarded and yielding a clue. He failed. Francis was deep in conversation on the other side of the room. His face the usual blend of encouragement, purpose and the ability to put people at ease. They all fell for it, colleagues and villains alike. Not that it was entirely an act. Francis had just long ago understood that the sun worked quicker than the wind in stripping people of their armour but that didn't make him less steely of purpose.

He waited, reading the rest of the file to see if there was something else, some other discrepancy or call to action that he'd missed. There was nothing either obvious or cryptic enough to excite his detective's curiosity.

"The mysterious case of the miscount at the morgue." He muttered to himself. An old case, a cold case, a no case at all case. It seemed nobody had noticed up to now. Is this really what Francis wanted him to eke out his time with?

He looked over. Francis was still locked in conversation.

Current affairs. And Christopher felt suddenly felt like very old news.

It wasn't until later that evening that he finally slung the file down on his boss's desk and himself into a chair.

"What's this about, Pete?" He asked. With nobody around they fell easily into the informality of long mutual acquaintance. "Missing persons? Long missing persons? The Night of the Living Dead? No body of bleedin' evidence. Have I done something wrong?"

Christopher wasn't aggressive, more baffled. And suddenly very weary. "I take it I'm looking at the right thing, am I? I counted 'em all out but didn't count them all in again? And where's that file from?"

Francis looked at him appraisingly then rubbed his eyes as if trying to clear the day from his vision. He exhaled all other concerns and focused on his friend.

"Well, the file came from Central Warehouse. I sent that new probationer over for it. Mandela Way, I thought, but she ended up traipsing half way round south east London. That's where we spend our money now, you know. State of the art filing systems.

"If it isn't written down, officer, it didn't happen." They chorused a defence barrister's refrain.

"Anyway, I asked her to get it because I was summoned to one of those 'don't forget about terrorism' meetings the other day and, unusually, Ireland was topping the bill. Made a change, Catholics and Protestants rather than Muslims. Someone's God is always great.

"Lest we forget, they gave us a potted history of what they were capable of back in the bad old days. You can only imagine what they could get up to now.

"Naturally, they're most concerned about public transport and they used the London Bridge bombing as an example.

"I remember it," said Christopher.

Francis glanced at him but didn't break stride. "Well, I got talking to a fella after whose old man was in Special Branch at the time. Said his dad always claimed that they never really knew how many had gone skyward, mass confusion at the time.

"25 against 27?" asked Christopher.

"Spot on. Southwark nick, the Transport mob and he ended up falling out over it, though there was nobody really in outright command in the immediate aftermath. Shit and bullets everywhere and some of these poor bastards simply unrecognisable, covered in a blanket while the medics moved onto the next.

"So eventually, they round up as many doctors, nurses and ambulance service people as they can track down and all of them say the same thing. It was chaos. They either miscounted or were distracted or somebody duplicated someone else's work. It was the 70s too, people didn't have easy communications or the sort of established procedures we have now. Plus, you had the added complication of good Samaritans and medics rushing over from Guy's to try and help.

"They finally concluded it was a mistake. Until an old ambulance driver sidles up and says that he and a mate had just picked up a body to move it the morgue when it got up off the bloody stretcher and staggered off. Woman. Scared the shit out of the pair of them. They were about to chase after her when they got whistled up by a doctor and, by the time they got back to that part of the platform, she'd gone.

"That still leaves one more," said Christopher.

"It does. A man. What happened to him, or whether he even

23

existed, remains a bit of a mystery. Every morgue and hospital in London was checked and the ambulance service all re-interviewed.

"The only clue was a cabbie who remembered some bloke standing in the middle of Tooley Street covered in blood and trying to hail him. But that could have been anybody. Suited and booted but dishevelled. The cabbie offered to take him to a hospital but he didn't want to go. Got belligerent. Worse, got belligerent in an Irish accent, so the cabbie told him to sling his hook. The driver found a uniform and told him what had happened but it was never pursued beyond a scribble in the copper's notebook. Trail ends."

"Well, minor mystery but why send the Plonk over to pick up the records and dump it onto me?" asked Christopher.

Francis eyed him again, ignoring the archaism.

"How long have you got left, Sean? Three months? Not long enough to get involved seriously in anything new that comes up, too long to kick about counting down the clock.

"For three months you've got a badge and my writ. Why not take a look? And here's why; you'll haunt yourself forever if you don't. You're a long time retired."

Christopher was taken aback.

"Oh, I'll live," he said. "Am I missing something?"

Francis erupted: "Christ, Sean you're a fucking detective! Have a think, would you! All the time I've known you, you've nursed a bloody melancholy. You're a bright bloke, good company. When you were young you represented the Met on half the available sports teams, the girls all loved you and you opened the batting with the chief constable. But you stalled, let's be honest Sean, you stalled. Fuck me, you could walk through a monastery and find a pickpocket. The most natural copper I've ever met, yet you're about to call it a day as a mid-ranker with two commendations and nobody waiting at home.

Why? Because, there's always been a distance, Sean. Some part of yourself with your mind elsewhere and nobody allowed in. You once told me that nobody is allowed a sad song when they're past 28. Well, you're still singing old son. Very quietly, humming perhaps, whistling between your teeth but the melody is why your mother walked out on you and where she went that was so great she could leave you with your old bastard of a father. Abandonment issues or some old naus the criminal psychologist could tell you about if you hadn't chatted her up then not finished the job.

Mate, I've known you too long. Finish this now. Answer it while you still can." Christopher looked baffled.

"Look, Sean, it's the only clue you've ever had. That train came in from Dartford via Greenwich. It stopped at Maze Hill. Nearest station to where we lived when we were kids and it came through on the same day she left.

"I know she was covered in snot and tears but the description of that woman who got off that stretcher. well, it's close enough to tickle my interest if not yours. You've got nothing to lose and everything to gain."

He flung the file back at Christopher. The tension was palpable. To break it, Francis broke into a *faux* New York accent: "Get out on the streets detective!" Christopher couldn't help but smile. He pulled an imaginary gun from a shoulder holster. And both men avoided the stand-off..

The encounter had been a bruising one. Christopher reran it in his head as he drove home. He mulled it again, knowing he would be no kind of company, as he cancelled his date for the evening and cogitated every word through a long evening and sleepless night.

The conversation had reached deep into his consciousness and stirred to the surface the darkest of mud. It smelt.

It smelt because so much of what Francis had said was true. He felt disappointed by that truth, a life come up short when the promise had been so great. And he felt infantilised by a flaw created in childhood and which his adult self had been unable to repair.

The truth. He was defeated. Or at least unvictorious.

He was a good-looking man still. The athleticism of his youth hadn't yet deserted him either and his good humour combined potently with the faint tang of melancholy to intoxicate women who wanted the handsome man with the easy smile and were convinced they could cure the injured boy they scarcely concealed.

They were wrong. So he remained alone.

His police career too had suffered the curse of potential. Of talent misdirected and distracted. It was all right but it could have been more. 'How many centuries has talent scored?' as Christopher often quoted about those marked by the hoodoo of easy gifts, mischievously bestowed.

He had the awful realisation that somewhere on whatever Olympus, the gods were watching and laughing at him. And a pantheon of benign goddesses had failed to save him from a great celestial tease.

Christopher sighed into the darkness. The bed still smelt faintly of its last visitor and the memory tortured him with false comfort.

Other memories too. The hope that she would come back. The realisation that she wouldn't.

His father's descent even further into hell whence he emerged possessed. The raging, the lies, the perverse accusations coughed out like malign ectoplasm, seeping through the ear and materialising in despair.

The fists and belts and ever on the alert. The time he'd woken in the night to find his father looming over him with a broken bottle claiming some imagined slight and hissing dire threats of scarred retribution.

His siblings' frightened tear-stained faces, jumping with each slam of a cupboard door or shattering of a cup.

How Christopher had taken, like a prisoner, to wearing his trainers all the time in case he had to fight. Christopher could feel that fight coming as could his father. Young lion, young stag, young upstart. Nature demanded that showdown.

'You'll never be big enough,' was the taunt. Chest-beating. Till the day Christopher was.

He exhaled again, briefly tempted to drink. But the same vanity which kept him fit and a natural revulsion of self-pitying drunks easily talked him out of it. He remained lying on the bed until, eventually, sleep came palliatively to his agonised soul. Christopher felt it dying inside him and let out a choking sob of pain before darkness saved him from the enduring shame of being a man and crying in the night like a child.

He awoke late. It wasn't a problem. Francis had effectively rendered him a free agent. In his hours of sleep, the spirit of what he was had been at work. Restorative, curative, nourishing.

Christopher had never gone down easily. He was a man of a certain place and certain generation and both were intolerant of what they still, if perhaps quietly now, thought of as weakness. Overnight they'd had him in his corner and whispered in his ear as they worked on him. Even if it hurt he was getting off his stool again.

For a brief moment, he contemplated making Francis his opponent. But Francis was the opposite. He'd given him a chance at redemption, however slim a chance.

He had a series of coincidences, some question marks, a file, history and a few living witnesses who were either senile, forgetful or some combination of both. Chuck in his old mate's intuition and his own gifts and experience and he had enough of a broth to stir. Just.

Whatever, Francis had given him renewed purpose. He felt it surge up through him and inwardly thanked old friendships and loyalty. Christ, they were rare enough. Making a mental note that he owed him 'a good drink' at some point, he also thought of his old games teacher, a reflex catch and a burnt grass cricket match. "Woke up just in time." He smiled to himself. It had begun.

It was always the hard bit. Starting. The more so as there wasn't the urgency and, yes, exhilaration, of being at the heart of a big new case with an assistant commissioner shoved in front of a camera to 'reassure' the public with a carefully scripted monologue of determination sprinkled with just enough compassion. Proceeding in a westerly direction but in a caring way.

No, Christopher was moving backwards and into territory that unnerved him. *Terra* too bloody *cognita*. A career in the force had taught him that it didn't do to dwell.

Then there were the practicalities. Starting with the obvious fact that he could hardly secure the crime scene. If crime there was. He had to remind himself of what he was investigating. Not an old bombing from a terrorist war of yesteryear but the disappearance of a woman.

Chances are she wanted to disappear. There was more than a chance she was dead or sat somewhere barely able to remember her own name. A chance too that her reinvention was complete and happy. Or that her twilight years, they must be by now, were haunted by the regret of steps it was too late to retrace.

Chance. Christopher knew its place. Turn another corner and a girl escapes a murder. Check a bloke with false number plates and he turns out to be the Yorkshire Ripper. He'd always been a lucky copper and Christopher was softly singing Sinatra's prayer for that fickle lady to stick with him as he climbed into his car and drove towards Greenwich and back in time.

442 Foyle Road sat about half-way down the slope of a suburban street which, if you followed its gradient would naturally lead down to the Thames but defied river geography by bumping into Humber Road.

Like most of the houses there, 442 was Victorian and semi-detached. When Christopher had lived there as a kid, there had been a bomb site a little further down on which he and his friends had played 'war' for hours among the bramble and old bricks. There was a modern development there now.

At the top of the hill and over the road had been prefabs, a quick-fix solution to post war homelessness for the bombed out, still inhabited in the 70s and, at the bottom, allotments behind a long fence of green railings. Both similarly developed.

Christopher looked up and down the street, the cars closely parked. Electric, expensive, the eco-conscious status symbols of the young and comfortably off. The street had once hosted everyone from coppers to a hippy commune, a classical musician and the family of deaf mutes who had lived a few doors down.

He remembered their fluttering hands and the noises like aquatic mammals, happy and self-contained in a pod of mutual understanding.

The boy and he had played hours of 'three and in' against a garage door and Christopher remembered feeling a sort of shame at their contented dignity while his own home raged and tore like a disturbed child.

He doubted many of the old neighbours and nodding acquaintances would still be there but he was going back to basics, knocking on doors but only in the expectation of young stay-at- home mothers, a baby on a hip and a vegan lunch on the go. They'd shake their heads, their willingness to help and desire to please running full tilt into the fact they simply weren't there.

A large Mercedes pulled up on the other side of the road. An old man stared from the rear window, his eyes wide with a nameless fear as though the very size and power of the vehicle was something he couldn't comprehend. His mouth was half open.

A middle-aged man descended from the other side and walked round to help him from the car. An elderly woman joined him. Her hair, possibly a wig, was lustrously auburn and she wore large glasses and thick make-up of which the most striking feature was lipstick. It was simply a replacement for the lips of which age had deprived her. She had painted on a mouth.

Christopher watched their struggles, the old man's repeated attempts to step down from the huge car defeated by thighs so weak they shook with each failed attempt to rise. The young beat copper in Christopher walked over the road and reached into the rear of the Mercedes, taking the man under the arms and carefully lowering him to the ground where a wheeled frame was quickly placed in front of him by, he guessed, his son who thanked him in the begrudging terms of a man embarrassed by his own physical ineptitude.

The old man smelt of medicine and something else. Something Christopher knew well. He smelt of being inside too long; of institutions, of despair, of the dread of another day and the fear of another night. He smelt of imprisonment.

The woman, meanwhile, eyed him silently. Eyed him with the frankness only lovers, children and the elderly possess. Then, as her husband shuffled with glacial slowness towards the kerb, the son beside him, she suddenly said: "Sean." Not a question but a statement of emphatic recognition with no emotion beyond, perhaps, a satisfaction that her random access memory had provided an answer to a puzzle destined to torture her through the long hours of watching her husband sit slack-jawed and frightened in a chair.

In this at least she had the drop on Christopher whose mind's eye could not see through the layered years to see a younger woman familiar to him from childhood.

"Glenda," she said. "Glenda Le Poirier," she said it strongly. Clearly. Her eyes sharp behind the glasses and with the same emotionless certainty with which she'd said his name a few seconds before.

Christopher stifled an urge to laugh. Facetiousness had long been a weakness. But he had a vague memory of finding the name funny as a boy and now all he could conjure was a 1950s burlesque act emerging through the blue fug of her own fag. The make-up didn't help.

"Hello Glenda. Of course. How are you?" she continued to survey him sternly as though the question was an artful trap. Something inside gave a little and she sighed simply "Burdened." She gave an eye roll towards her house where her son had almost got her husband to the door. It wasn't entirely clear which of them she meant. Either way, Christopher sympathised.

Glenda invited him in. He didn't particularly want to accept but the prospect of knocking up doe-eyed recent mothers smelling of organic baby food held no appeal. He nodded. She was probably his best chance of some kind of lead and, besides, some part of him felt for her.

Inside, the house had the dustless tidiness of a place only two people simply waiting could inhabit. Vladimir and Estragon[3]. "Nothing happens. Nobody comes, nobody goes. It's awful."

Her son, Christopher had placed him as Ben, regarded him with undisguised hostility. Once, he had been an unremarkable boy, his bedroom over-stuffed with the compensatory gifts of only childhood. He had existed on the fringes; thin legs, thick glasses, last to be picked, always in danger of relegation.

Obviously, he had had some sort of later blossoming as Christopher gleaned he had gone to work among the shining towers of finance visible now over the river on the Isle of Dogs.

Christopher could tell the compensation wasn't over. Ben sported a beard now. A façade of masculinity betrayed on shaking hands. They were veal calf soft. He was well-dressed but formless for all the tailoring. As Christopher talked with his mother, Ben's interjections were loaded with a brittle self-regard.

Years in the force had taught him that a certain sort of middle-class professional wanted to maintain a kind of 1950s relationship with policeman in which they indulged the flat foot as a necessary periphery to whom they gave smiling indulgence, their clumsy enquiries directed only through the help of people who really knew. People like them.

---

3 They wait for Godot - the title character who never appears. Hope is always deferred.

Ben, he at first thought, was among 'them.' But he realised it was more. It was personal. Christopher couldn't quite place why. Their acquaintance had only been passing. Perhaps that was it. Who knows the prism we're viewed through, what emblem we become in someone else's sub-conscious?

"Do we ever get over it?" he asked. As much of himself as the man smouldering opposite.

Pleasantries and history exchanged, Christopher took the opportunity to ask: "Glenda, do you have any recall of the day my mother left?" He wanted to add detail such as 'It was the day of the explosion', 'it was hot' but he knew people's desire to please in these circumstances and wanted to supply no false memory for her to construct a premise to do so.

She wasn't the sort though. Glenda shook her head unhesitatingly. No pretence even at the effort of casting her mind back. "No Sean," she said "We all felt for Christie, you know that. And for you. Especially after she'd gone. But I didn't see her, nor hear from her."

The room fell silent. Cristopher simply nodded, wincing slightly at the mention of his mother's name as he remembered her fleeing into various houses along the road when the punching and the screaming and the lies whirled to a *djinn* of such proportions that she could no longer contain her fear of the devil. Glenda's had been sanctuary more than once.

Her husband sat there, silent, wide eyed, seeing God knows what.

Ben filled the void. A fleeting glint of malice illuminating his face. "I saw her." Christopher looked at him. He had such experience of liars, of the worst of human nature, that he saw into souls. Ben was used to being in charge and suddenly found he wasn't, Christopher's glance was searing, so much so that for a moment Ben almost physically recoiled.

"I did." He was quieter now. Less sure of himself. He sounded like a schoolboy with his ear between the headmaster's thumb and finger. He tried to free himself with a low swinging blow.

"She was obviously upset but that happened so often I hardly took any notice."

Christopher let him talk, you don't spend a lifetime as 'pig' and 'filth' and bite easily.

"She was walking up the hill. I'd seen her upset before but this was anger, fury." I didn't even say hello. I remember it because she was normally kind but she went past without even a glance. I mentioned it to mum but by the evening we'd all been distracted by the bomb."

Glenda glanced at Christopher and gave an imperceptible shrug. She knew as well as he did what she was looking at. "Burdened."

The bomb. He hadn't mentioned it. Ben had added the direct connection. Again, he let him talk. Christopher had the feeling that if he asked if she had turned right, he would say left as a reflex.

"I watched her. I watched her because she was different. She had her arms folded across her chest and her purse in her hand but even at my age I could see she was going somewhere. It wasn't aimless escape. She got to the top of the road, didn't pause, turned right towards the park. That was it."

It was Glenda who filled the distance between Christopher's stare and her son's almost shamefaced admission. "Ben," she said with the patient weariness of someone who dealt occupationally with an ungrowable child, "Are you sure that what you're telling Sean is true? It was a long time ago."

All he could do was nod. And, for reasons that Christopher couldn't begin to fathom, that boy had tears in his eyes.

He wandered the hill knocking on doors. Where he got an answer at all, it was largely as he'd expected. Too young, too recent to offer any helpful snippet of memory, false or otherwise.

Christopher hadn't overreacted to Ben's remembrance of things past. He let the account digest. If true, it suggested a direction of travel, though the streets and interconnected paths would have easily allowed her to roam at will, return to a point, stop and weep on a park bench, London spread out before her like a dog at her feet, looking up at her sorrow. The variations were almost infinite.

What caught Christopher's curiosity was the assertion that his mother had been walking in angry purpose, almost as in pursuit of a plan, an exit plan.

At only one door did he receive dawning realisation and a warm welcome — but no help.

For the moment, all roads, the only road, lead to London Bridge. If she'd turned right and her way out had indeed been through the heart of the capital, it was, as Francis had divined, almost certainly via the railway station at Maze Hill. As though mounting a reconstruction to jog public memory, he followed her footsteps past Vanburgh Castle and down past the long eastern wall of Greenwich Park to the station.

At Lewisham nick, Europe's largest purpose-built police station, Francis was having an attack of conscience. The road to hell was paved with good intentions and he had the vague feeling his conversation with Christopher had laid the groundwork and poured the tar.

Unusually for a man who used good humour and *bonhomie* to smooth a path, he had allowed exasperation to blast his way to the point and he regretted it. The more so because he hadn't heard from Sean since and he felt too guilty to try and call him.

"Fuck," he exhaled and leant out of his office door.

Rachel Scott had joined the force later than usual, a convert from the corporate world. Both factors made her a mature entity who intrigued her fellow officers. She was bright, more than capable of handling office politics and brought commercialism's can-do energy to whatever she did.

Used to handling C-suite egos, she blended charm and steel with men and sisterly diligence with women.

Like most floor-crossers, Scott had sought something more than the empty pointlessness of corporate snakes and ladders but had dismissed the usual haven of teaching on the basis of wondering whether she was made of more than lesson planning and the weary angst of a staff room.

What she was made of was an intriguing alloy. Her sharp intelligence, tendency to sharper dressing and an indefinable sexual allure – her confidence perhaps? – attracted and repelled in her new surroundings in equal measure.

Both men and women were either unnerved or suspicious. She was an introduced species. Red where she should be grey. Exotic where she should be plain. Capable, too capable, of thriving in the environment but the native creatures didn't recognise her scent.

For that, she remained a woman apart. Too often she'd find herself despatched to the outer reaches of the Met's empire. Away for a day on something marginal. It was Scott who had been sent in search of the file for Francis on the station bombing. Anyone else would have given up rather than traipse from one facility to the next. She hadn't.

Her it was who caught his eye when he emerged shamefacedly from his office. "Rachel, have you heard from DSI Christopher lately?" she shook her head.

"Do me a favour, track him down. I've put him on something and he may need a hand. Stick with him until it's resolved, will you?"

Scott agreed enthusiastically. Not that she had a choice but it had to be a step toward.

Francis walked back into his office. He wondered briefly it was fair to introduce the woman to Christopher's psycho drama.

"Fuck it," he thought to himself. "They're both one step beyond. They'll get on like a bloody house on fire, she'll learn and he'll have help. Cracked in no time." But even as he sat down he had misgivings. "Christ, you can't do right for trying."

Christopher was heading north and west on a train from Maze Hill to London Bridge. It had been rolling in just as he'd arrived so he'd had no time to run the station through his memory. He vaguely remembered some football punch-up from the early Noughties.

Coppers pouring in to intervene in one of the last staged outbreaks of organised hooligan violence. A fight by arrangement. The local side, just down the line. Charlton Athletics' finest in a tear-up with Southampton. The last wave of a dying dragon's tale at a spot a distance away from police stations. What a way to spend a Saturday. A second-class return, second class football and a beer bottle in the face.

The train rolled on through Deptford on London's oldest railway line. A Victorian wonder that vaulted the city's south eastern suburbs on flying brick arches.

When he was young, the arches had been filled by dubious garages and the old houses backing onto the line had shown their filthy backsides to the trains. The trains. Fifties slam- doors smelling of cigarettes and wet raincoats. He had had a schoolfriend with a talent for finding dirty magazines under the blue-green tartan bench seats. They had laughed themselves to tears on trips 'into town.'

Now, the trains were clean and modern and from the point of view of Christopher's old friend, disappointingly free of pornography. The passengers insulated themselves from each other with earphones. The stations were clean, concrete and modern. The terraced housing they passed had scrubbed brick and fresh paint and the new flats, block after block of them, shone orange and grey in the autumn sunlight.

The old street corner pubs, huge and institutional, were closed or something different. No more working men from docks or works. The old biscuit factory housed only graffiti and the foundry was flats adorned with flags of identity. Gay pride. A Welsh dragon. The EU's circle of stars. A football team.

Millwall rolled by. Christopher remembered it from his early days coppering. Extra money to police the most notorious crowd in England. "No-one likes us, we don't care." The defiant working-class pride taunting a besieging world from its last bastion.

Christopher was no romantic. The pubs had been hostile, the estates dangerous and run down, a displaced and redundant people left to rot after their purpose had expired had descended into a hateful anger. "Let 'em come, let 'em come, let 'em come, let 'em all come down to the Den." "Come and have a go if you think you're hard enough!"

Modernity was working even among old London like creeping vegetation. In many places it had long since overwhelmed. Sometimes it had beautified and in other places strangled a distinct character both for better and for worse. Somehow he had to reach into that undergrowth and pull out a piece of the past.

ACAB – All Coppers Are Bastards – someone had scrawled across a gantry as they rolled into London Bridge. He found it vaguely reassuring. Some things never changed.

A clear view across the span of Tower Bridge emerged briefly to his right and, at that point, Rachel Scott rang.

They met in a small café in railway arch just near the southern end of the bridge, London Bridge, the historical crossing between Southwark and the City, medieval heart of London and now home to one of the world's great financial centres. The incongruity of old street names like Pudding Lane and Cornhill amid the towering modern architecture of global money moving.

The café was unusual in not being a chain and their conversation was muffled by hisses of steam from the espresso machine and shouted sandwich orders.

Christopher was taken aback but not entirely displeased. This was a lonely investigation that took him to dark places and to undertake it solo was to drip acid on his soul. Scott was plainly very bright and her enthusiasm infectious. Her company, if nothing more, was welcome.

For her part, she was out of the office and the unmistakable feeling that she was tolerated but nothing more. Christopher did not give her the same impression though, as he spelt out precisely what it was they were trying to do, her heart fell a little.

Christopher had presented it as a tying off of ends. A missing duo from an old incident attracting the attention of a tidy minded superior. He hadn't disguised the personal element, nor had he over-egged it.

Scott surveyed him trying to see how much of this was a purely personal quest. She noted the still handsome face and the easy conversation. If he was damaged, haunted or obsessive, it didn't show in broken veins or hollow eyes.

She sipped contemplatively on her coffee as he talked. He was reassuring. The confidence of an old hand who had resisted being jaded. Scott knew already that she would learn from him, that for the first time she was being treated open-handedly and that he had some notion that her unexpected help was to be reciprocated.

Christopher, meanwhile, was feeling thoroughly ashamed of his 'Plonk' comment. The old police slang for a female officer had been made partly to test the boundaries with Francis but also served as a gentle reminder of the longevity of their relationship. He could tell already that she would be an asset and that, like him, she sat a little apart.

The partnership was a boost to both. He thought of the City over the river, its investment banks and insurance houses, traders and stockbrokers. "It's the sort of thing they'd say," he thought. He glanced up to see Scott studying him. Seriously. Intently. Christopher smiled at her and she looked away.

There was nothing to be found at the railway station. Christopher had hoped to find some ghost, some spiritual infusion of its very brick work that would betray the presence of a woman so desperate that she would walk out on her own children and leave them trapped in the pandemonium from which she had engineered an escape.

He was, he realised, hoping that somehow outrage would betray outrage. That the bomb and her, he groped for a word and alighted on one he shrank from and then embraced, 'desertion' would vie to turn each other in. Each so disgusted by themselves that they hid one behind the other, like kids, or footballers, each claiming the other did it first.

But modernity had bulldozed the bricks, illuminated the dark corners and laid fresh, light concrete over the exhaustion of the past. The geography was the same but London had done what it does best, absorbed and moved on. Layer upon layer, it buried its secrets, elevated its glories and ran towards its future.

In a way, he was glad. He didn't want to feel like a child in a graveyard. Desperate to see, yet frightened to behold. If there was an exorcism to be done, it would not be here. Instead, Christopher boarded a train back towards south east London, nestling into its seat, letting London hold him in its arms, until the rocking sent him into a gentle doze.

At the same time, Scott was heading back to Lewisham with orders to find a room, read the file – which Christopher had handed to her at the café – and unearth as much history and coverage of the '79 bombing as could be found.

She was excited to be doing something, intrigued by Christopher and faintly disturbed. What manner of man he was eluded her, fascinated her, beckoned her on. Scott mirrored him in thinking of ghosts. She felt like the hapless girl in a supernatural thriller, driven to explore the unearthly noises in the attic and, while all sense said to run, she was instead lowering the ladder and switching on a torch.

Christie Christopher. O'Donnell before she'd met him. Convent educated, one would have thought the Devil was obvious to her.

But temptation comes in what we wish for and what Christie wished for was escape.

Escape from the narrow confines of a life bordered by the near horizons of a family one generation away from rural Ireland. Escape from ecstatic martyrs, melancholic history and stolen kisses that went no further. Escape from Sunday Mass and her father hovering outside the social club until the doors opened for the itchy first pint. Her mother doting on a young parish priest called Kevin, secretly hoping he'd surrender his vocation for Christie and confessing it, to a different priest of course, every Tuesday evening.

What Christie wanted was simple. She wanted to open her mind, open her legs and open her vista. She wanted London and a guide to its Sixties temptations. A naïf, she backed her natural vivaciousness and charm to see her through. She was attractive, blessed with the dark-haired Irish looks of Armada myth and men liked her. Men it was who trapped her, from Jesus to Joseph, Jesuit to Geordie – her loving but limited father – and men it was who would set her free.

And with that, the Devil took the form of man.

Jonty Christopher was a liar. A prince of lies. He wasn't Jonty for one thing. That was a corruption of his second name, plain old John. But Jonty had with it the smack of the upper middle-class nursery, a decent public school and lively fielding in the deep. Jonty was the son of a diplomat, a senior soldier or a private banker.

John was none of these things. But that didn't prevent him from hinting, suggesting or outright claiming it. And he had a long habit of forming friendships on that basis, dissolving them – often on the pretext of some contrived grievance – just as unmasking loomed.

Professionally, his life was similar. A roller coaster ride of talking his way in, then flouncing out one step ahead of a summons to the managing director's office. What he actually did for a living remained a matter of considerable conjecture and covered a gamut from gun runner to freelance journalist, trades that few understood, often came masked by independence from identifiable organisations, had a vaguely raffish air of romance but were all entirely false.

In fact, when employed, he wandered the world representing companies of a certain colonial British heritage. Companies which believed a man whose own father had been a diplomat, a senior soldier, a private banker and who often traded in places where to be British and confident was sufficient.

It helped, of course, that he believed his own lies and that each often came burdened with just enough truth to bear cursory scrutiny, especially when supported with a smattering of quickly acquired regional facts for which airport book shops and long flights were particularly useful.

For Christie, for Sean, for his siblings, life was a support act for the latest contrivance. It required a certain agility and, for Sean, a lifelong lesson in the way of the fabulist that would serve him well in the interview rooms of the future.

That his father's personality was a house with many occupants, the cloud and sun of many moods passing constantly across his mind and meeting regularly, frequently, in terrifying storms of raging self-pity, hatefulness and cruelty was also, at least professionally, a boon.

Sean knew people's temperament, could read intent even before they themselves knew. Like snatching for that hurtling cricket ball of childhood, it was a matter of self-preservation.

But for Christie, lured in as she was by the appearance of

metropolitan sophistication, the demon preserved his best face for the early years. The ugliness of torment would be saved for later, for when the magic had been spoken, the enchantment woven and Christie had signed her soul, her innocence and her salvation away to marriage and pregnancy.

Then came the price. In the beatings and the drink. In the rages and the public humiliations. In the secrecy and the perverse calumnies against anyone more dignified, more successful, against anyone happier.

The returns from the illusory world of business class travel, unmerited respect and hotel living were the most difficult. The void filled with the reality and it was too awful to behold. Jonty was an East End chancer with a borrowed accent and an education in long haul paperbacks. And, at home, he was that again. Nothing special.

There were the children, baffled, confused, frightened. There were the quick, tear-stained flights to neighbours, the longer evacuations to relatives. The solution was obvious But Christie never took it. The cheques slipped to her for a planned retreat. The concerned faces giving counsel while all the time knowing it would never be taken. A wistful acceptance that she had shaken hands with the Devil and couldn't let go.

Sean it was who would, eventually, cast him out with the bell, book and candle of three things learned at a 70s inner London boys' school where each day was a battle for physical supremacy. Do it first, do it hard, do it till they stop. But when Christie walked out, that reckoning was still in the future.

He was raging again. Christie's mother had just died. She wasn't giving him enough attention. "I wouldn't put up with this when I travel." He wanted some new whim. Sardines, no, kippers. It was breakfast time. "Not like this, not laid out like fuckin corpses!" He slung the plate across the room at her. She was a 'whore's whelp.'

Christie finally broke.

Even Jonty knew he'd gone too far. Her expression of cold fury was mythological. She slammed out of the house, ignoring the boy from over the road who smiled at her as she stalked blindly past him. Medea's anger was unknown to her. But the cost was her children.

Donal O'Driscoll had not got out in time. He'd tried but he'd been wedged in by the sheer press of commuters travelling into London Bridge station. He was dressed in a suit bought from Burton's in which he was distinctly uncomfortable but it helped him blend in with the office workers of the City as they headed towards London Bridge and used it to cross the Thames or changed for Cannon Street in the Square Mile itself and only a single stop away.

From the West of Ireland, he'd been suckled on tales of British cruelty real and imagined and raised with the belief that 'between the famine and the Crown' his countrymen had been cut down by a far-flung regime of religious and cultural persecution.

He had moved seamlessly from sympathiser to activist. Crossing the border into the north where he could 'take the fight to the enemy' and British forces on the streets of Belfast, Derry and in the Armagh bandit country between the province of Ulster and the Republic.

Without the distinctive accent of the north and with no history among the politicos and backroom bars of the Falls Road, O'Driscoll had not immediately been accepted. The Irish fear of informants ran too deep.

Slowly he had proved himself. Small errands had led to bigger ones. Arms smuggling had led to arms use. Until, one day, O'Driscoll had found himself with a gun and with a British Army patrol in his sites. He had not hesitated. Moreover, he had kept his head when the storm of return fire from the army's powerful SLR rifles had started to dismantle piece by piece the pre-fabricated flats from which he had fired.

As the troops advanced in short, sharp darts up the street toward his hiding place and then, more quickly behind the cover of a six-wheeled Saracen armoured car, he had made good his escape through the bin alleys and back yards, keeping his gun, and with only barking dogs to say they'd seen him.

After that, O' Driscoll's elevation had been quick and he had found himself sent to mainland Britain with an active service cell.

Now, looking like one of them and one of the sort of Brit he despised the most, O'Driscoll was set to die among them. He had boarded the train at Dartford, the beginning of its run into London, sliding an executive briefcase packed with ball bearings and explosives under one seat and then shifting to another to distance himself in case of discovery.

His plan had been to get off at Deptford, the last stop before London Bridge, and let the timers do the rest.

By Deptford, O' Driscoll was trapped. The previous train had been cancelled and nobody was leaving. More and more people squeezed themselves onto the service, leaving him wedged on a seat by its central aisle with his face just in an inch or so from the pencil skirted behind of a City secretary.

He thought, briefly, of fighting his way out claiming he was feeling unwell but he didn't want to attract attention to himself nor did he want some helpful guard delaying the train while he received attention on the platform. Worse, had anyone seen him deposit his briefcase they would try and pass it to him, hand over head over hand over head.

O' Driscoll became angrily obsessed with becoming 'an own goal.' It was not infrequent for the IRA to blow themselves with their own bombs either during their construction or their planting. He could imagine the grim smile of consolation among some Brit security agency at his fragmented departure from the world and all fuelling the myth that Paddy was a bit thick.

By London Bridge, he'd decided to gamble on a hasty departure, forcing his way through and claiming he was about to vomit before seeking refuge in the toilet block between platforms.

The train creaked to a halt outside London Bridge station. It always did. A notorious bottle neck, a delay on a previous service would leave later services queueing on the approach, waiting to be given a platform.

Pressed shoulder to shoulder, face to face, crutch to crutch, the ancient heaters trickling warmth into the carriage, people shifted, groaned, exhaled and sweated. None more so than O'Driscoll.

He looked up to see one man had managed to fold the pink pages of his *Financial Times* to handkerchief size proportions, the column only inches from his face as he tried to read in such a confined space. The page touched the back of a woman's hair and she flicked at it as though an insect had alighted.

The carriage jolted, moved, slowly, at first nothing more than a crawl, a down train passed in a squeal of wheels and a flash of sparks. His own picked up speed, slowed again and then, finally, eased onto platform six.

"Jesus!" he suddenly shouted. "I'm sorry but move will ya, I'm going to be sick!" People hurried to get off, leaning out of the slide down windows to release the handles on the outside of the carriage, the doors swinging open along the length of the train almost in unison as it came to a halt with people spilling out onto the platform like milk from a popped carton.

"Oh, for God's sake let him out!" It was the man with the FT. O'Driscoll noticed a Savile Row suit and a public school drawl, the whole thing such a bore as he pronounced the final word 'ite'. O'Driscoll took a brief, savage satisfaction in what was about to happen and launched himself out onto the platform as his fellow passengers pressed back to let him by.

He rushed to the lavatories, swimming up-stream against a tide of humanity, trying to gain distance between himself and his own murderous intent. 'Out of order' was the last thing he saw before the world disintegrated and went black.

Despite Ben Le Poirier's assertions, Christie had no plan as she left her own home and walked with an aimless determination, jet fuelled by anger and pain, up the street.

She knew only one thing; that she could endure no more. Her departure had, of course, been to leave his presence. To reduce proximity. To make it stop. Her directed, hard-paced stride up the hill was the dissipation of fury but also of disappointment which, for one moment, as she had looked at the latest meal hurled at her, she genuinely feared was going to crush her. If not actually to kill her, then to do something worse. To drive her to her knees, to reduce her world to a cowering blackness. To send her insane.

Insane. The Devil's sentence. From despair to the end. Another soul to the collection. If the plate had hit her, well so much the better, but it wasn't the point. It was to demean her efforts, force her to kneel. Clean. It. Up. A corrupted genuflection, the sobs racking her shoulders, her hair hiding the tears.

Christie felt her right hand move to bless herself. An old habit. She thought of her forebears for whom religion and superstition had blended against the innumerable hazards and moral jeopardies of life. The banshee in the chimney, the temptation in the lad, the blight in the fields. A shawl pulled tight like an armoured helm and the sign of the cross wielded freely to fight off all evils.

She stopped herself. It hadn't worked then and it wouldn't work now. Her mother had gone. Her father clung on. Disappointed and far from home. She knew the feeling. Such promise. The bright lights and the bright man. How quickly it had ended. The premature pregnancy. Not one but quickly two. And then it had started. The first blows, the perverse accusations, the denigration and the brooding drinking sessions. At least then he had apologised in the morning.

Shame. All was shame. His shame. Thick-tongued and guilty. Her shame. Fool. Coward. The shame for those children, three of them now. How could she have done this to them?

Worse, how could she feel like she did. That they were the nails that kept her fixed to this bloody suffering. Christ, would it never end, this slow plod through misery?

Christie kept walking blindly. Her breathing slightly laboured by her pace up the hill and the rage within. Eventually she stopped. She felt like a child that had run away and, having got as far as the end of the road, felt she should hide behind a pillar box for a while and see if anyone came after her. He'd be waiting, of course, for her to come back beaten. Smug and dictatorial. Learnt your lesson? The kids' anxious faces, hammering her to the home.

She had arrived at the station as if by wind-blown drift, the energy of anguish still coursing and the need to feel, if only for a moment, that she had done something, taken action, finally mobilised.

Christie bought a ticket to London. A single. A small act of defiance that, deep in her heart, she knew she would rescind. How could it be otherwise? She indulged vague plans of contacting a relative, borrowing some money. Running, fighting, something. But they were just handholds on fantasy.

Agitated, she walked on to the platform, barely noticing that it was unusually crowded. She wasn't a regular commuter. A guard edged his way along and replaced the previous train's destination board with a new one, sliding it into a metal slot mounted on a post; Greenwich, Deptford, London Bridge, Waterloo East and Charing Cross.

He then returned to the booking office and, over a tannoy, apologised for the cancellation of the previous service, his distorted voice bouncing off the surrounding buildings. Christie was heedless, her mind a-race with plans half-formed, regrets half-articulated and a life half-lived.

She pushed her way on board as the train halted. A smoking carriage. The blue haze curling around her head in serpentine coils as she shouldered her way in. London calling: siren to waifs, strays and turn-agains looking for gold-paved streets. She was calling back and knew it, "London help me, London save me." The city had to her always seemed like salvation and, as the train laboured away from Maze Hill, cigarette smoke in her hair, a purse clasped to her chest and the pain she could scarcely bear, Christie was running towards its open arms.

Two carriages away, Donal O'Driscoll watched in disbelief as more and more people pushed, squeezed and argued their way into his compartment. Nobody left. Inevitably, somebody, a woman, shouted; "Could you move down, please!" She was irritated, more so when her plea was greeted with groans, rolled eyes and outright mirth. "You surely jest?", someone shouted back. O'Driscoll didn't laugh. He had an increasing feeling he was about to become an own goal and that wasn't funny.

Rarely for Rachel Scott, she was beaten. She had approached Christopher's research task with her usual diligence. Between internet searches and calls to the archives of all the major newspapers, she had become an accidental expert in the IRA's campaign of terror against mainland Britain and the London Bridge bombing in particular.

The table in the room she had commandeered at Lewisham nick was covered with newspaper cuttings, photocopies and photographs. Not strewn. Covered. It wasn't her way to mine among a slag heap hoping for a diamond. Instead, Scott had delved systematically and thoroughly into each and every bit of coverage. Each snippet of reportage, each column inch of commentary, read, highlighted, summarised and, in frustratingly few instances, stuck by magnet to the whiteboard wall that filled one side of the room.

One double page spread – a DPS she had learnt they called it in the newspaper world — helpfully pictured each of the dead including several blank frames in which a simple question mark had been inserted. Most of those, Rachel had established, had later been identified and she had filled in the details by hand. The newspaper still showed twenty-seven frames plus a further three with photographs of suspects based on the speculation of 'a security expert.'

On top of her files and her piles lay bookmarked academic works pulled from Amazon, specialist publishers, university

51

libraries and think tanks.

Her laptop was open. On it, she had viewed sparse and grainy YouTube footage and, later, digital files sent to her by the archives at the BBC and ITN, the only contemporary domestic television news broadcasters.

She had noticed the sombre, deadpan reporting. No embellishment, no freneticism, no attempt to inject into the unthinkable any further drama than was already stretched out on the platform.

She had been shocked too by what they had been prepared to show, far more than a modern audience would tolerate and, unheralded by warnings or cautionary advice, the pictures had simply told their own ghastly story.

Rachel sat back. Her hope was that the footage would serve the purpose of the now ubiquitous CCTV and show faces, reveal identities, suggest some pattern of events in the immediate and confused aftermath. Because of that, she had asked for unedited footage as well as broadcast news.

What she had seen had horrified her. Faces flayed, limbs shredded, the pulping of living flesh by the ball-bearings and nails packed with the bomb and released with massive force by the explosion. What was it the military called it? 'Fragging'.

It must, she conceded, take a special kind of detachment to hold a camera steady over the rag doll corpse of a child, hair still blonde atop the blood red and bone white of an utterly destroyed body. Rachel wandered what haunted the cameraman's dreams. She fought to control herself, even at distance of time and without the smell and gelatinous reality of body matter, she still struggled. God knows what it must have done to whoever stood there tightening the frame on a snapshot of such horror.

Worse still, her efforts had revealed very little beyond

context and colour. Not just the blood and gore but the monochrome seediness of a run-down London only just fighting its way back to post-war modernity. Rachel had the feeling that of she reached into the footage and put her finger on the right spot, everything would simply collapse. London Bridge is falling down.

Christopher came in. She was sat back in her chair, back arched and the heels of her hands pressed to her eyes in an attempt to clear mind and vision. Christopher glanced round the room, taking in Scott's methodical efforts and the images on her screen. "Bit much?" he said.

She took her hands down and nodded back, not entirely trusting herself to speak. "Come on," he said, "Fresh air and a pint."

All her corporate instincts wanted to decline. For her, drinks were still post-work and political, not an afternoon breather and inspiration. She looked at the cuttings on the table, still so many to look at. More than that, Rachel suddenly realised that she wanted to walk with this man. She smiled at him and nodded again.

The brief interlude in a nearby pub was a pleasant one. Scott filled Christopher in on what little she had so far gleaned from media and other reports. In essence, that the discrepancy in numbers of dead had gone unnoticed but that the journalistic need for a figure had been satisfied and the news had moved on.

In fact, there had apparently been no media curiosity regarding that aspect, though it had received a mention *en passant* in the BBC documentary series *Panorama*. It had been assumed a mistake had been made in the confusion and, having seen the footage, Scott was increasingly inclined to agree.

Christopher simply nodded impassively. She noticed it. A certain emotional disengagement which she found baffling. For all his apparently coincidental interest in the current case, she was unconvinced that his personal connection to it could not be the driver for his involvement. She had expected at least some level of emotional intensity but picked up none except, perhaps, a wistfulness.

It was he who moved the conversation away from their investigation. He didn't play the old hand though he did give her colourful pen sketches of various characters at the station which had her laughing out loud.

Christopher was easy with her and she liked that. He proved to be witty and a mine of obscure facts which he presented in such a way as to make her uncertain whether he was teasing her or not. Though he showed an interest in her previous life, he never probed so far as to make her feel that she too was under investigation. She couldn't decide whether he was, in fact, a master interrogator waiting for her to come to him unguarded, or simply polite enough to enquire but not interested enough to pursue.

Either way, an hour or so passed quickly and they made to leave, crossing the busy road towards to the police station and then another, quieter one from which side streets ran.

It was from that direction that she came. Christopher, his instincts attuned by years to the unusual, to the disturbing, saw her first and was walking hard towards her before Scott too caught the flurry of movement to her left.

The woman had emerged from a terraced house at the run. She was naked except for a pair of turquoise briefs. Only when she was several yards into the street, did she cross her arms over her bare breasts either through sudden realisation or discomfort.

Either way, deprived of the use of her arms, she visibly slowed which seemed to panic her and she again dropped her arms to run better.

Moments later, two young girls emerged from the same house. One still a child and in obvious distress, the other, probably in her mid-teens dressed in a star-spangled jumper and pink fluffy slippers chased after the woman down the street; "Mum!" She kept shouting "Mum!"

Scott pulled off her coat, noticing that Christopher had simply let her run straight past him, and, like a farmer's wife gathering in an errant goose, allowed the naked woman to run into it. "It's all right, love, police, It's all right." She soothed, surprised at her use of a colloquialism she rarely employed. The woman struggled briefly and almost as the darkness covered her, went dead still, her children arriving with her seconds later.

Scott looked for Christopher. A man had emerged from the same house. Bare-chested, his shaved head disguising premature hair loss and his torso a canvas for tattoos in every variation. He wearing track suit bottoms and huge, pristine trainers. Like him, they were over branded.

He looked at the woman clinging to Scott, her bare legs showing from beneath the coat and started towards them before noticing the advancing Christopher.

"Oh yeah," he said, "You want some and all do ya?"

He was younger than the woman, younger than Christopher, dancing on the spot he stuck his arms out wide in defiance. Come and have a go if you think you're hard enough. He was still talking; "What the fuck's it got do with you? She's my bird, fuck off!" His eyes had narrowed to hate-filled loop holes but in them was an increasing uncertainty as Christopher just kept coming.

The invective got louder, the south London had begun to

55

blend with a hybrid West Indian *patois*. It was noise, chaff, the barking of a dog. The dancing had stopped. The extended arms were beginning to lower. Christopher was close now.

Christopher was in range and the man did as Christopher knew he would. "Right ya cunt!' And threw a right-handed haymaker which Christopher parried, rolling his arm over and under his assailant's, entwining with it and pushing upward against the elbow joint so that it locked and would simply break if pressured.

Christopher unhesitatingly drove the heel of his right palm into the man's nose. The bone broke audibly. He drew his hand back and repeated the action, crushing the cartilage flat. This time he kept his hand there, forcing the man's head back and walking him slowly backwards while he flailed once, twice, impotently at Christopher's right shoulder.

With his head forced, his trachea stretched and the flow of blood from his broken nose flooding his mouth, the man realised he simply couldn't breathe, ceasing any resistance. At that point, Christopher tripped him, releasing him as he sat down hard on the pavement.

Without the pressure of the hand against his nose, the man's head fell forward and, with it, a cascade of blood which flooded down his inked chest and abdomen and began a stealthy dark spread across the track suit bottoms. Drops of blood had already stained the trainers.

He sat there looking at himself almost in disbelief. He raised both arms, briefly, and then dropped them. The impact to his nose had forced involuntary tears which mingled with the blood, diluting it.

His was a look of utter astonishment. A look that managed in a single glance to convey surprise, defeat, humiliation and then, arriving late to the struggle but in overwhelming force, a vision of complete failure. A vision that washed across the expanses of his face like the blast wave from a bomb, snatching away every certainty in its path and leaving him sat there, desolate.

Christopher knew what was going to happen next with the same certainty that had marked his response to the attempted punch. His attacker burst into real tears. Bald, he bawled.

Like an overgrown baby, pink of complexion, eyes screwed shut, he wept with a baby's shamelessness. Loudly, publicly, extensively.

For men of a certain time and place, crying remains a last resort and Christopher still struggled with how easily it came to modern man. So, standing outside the house, he just watched as the machismo disintegrated in the face of abject misery. A cartoon character, pumped up and painted. The attacker's self-regard tied up with his new shoes, he was stranded somewhere between a man and a child who couldn't understand that sometimes grown-ups were right. An infant with the muscles of a man, he'd never been told 'no.'

Scott watched both of them. Christopher was neither triumphant nor pitying. He was detached. Uniforms had arrived by now and were cuffing the man on the floor. The two girls ran towards him, as did the woman, now wearing a blanket and a sweater a neighbour had brought out to her.

You never quite knew. One moment they were screaming blue murder, next trying to hit you with a stiletto for 'hurting my man'. In his days in uniform, Christopher had seen it all when called to 'a domestic' and he watched their approach warily.

He was surprised then when the eldest girl fell into his arms, sobbing her thanks. Sobbing her relief. Truthfully, just sobbing out her sadness. He let her stay there, against his jacket, smoothing her hair, her sister wrapped round their legs, gently hushing them both, his eyes a million miles away.

Scott looked on. Christopher was like a harking back. He had dealt out what could only be described as summary justice. Wordless, confident and determined. No posturing, no exchange of insults, just an outcome delivered. And now he stood there, comforting a child with endless patience and utter tenderness.

"Are you the last of them?" she asked herself. And for a moment she felt like the world had done something terrible to both of them.

Scott and Christopher sat in Francis' office. The events in the street earlier barely warranted a mention between the two men. Scott was rather more preoccupied with it but she had yet to develop their world-weary experience of humanity, nor what dealing with it occasionally demanded.

She wanted to say something but didn't quite know what. She was both impressed and appalled by Christopher's sure-footedness near violence. More, it had made her think about herself. Scott had, of course, seen violence before. Her arrival among detectives had been preceded by time on the beat but that had not yet taught her the insouciant ease with it that Christopher demonstrated.

Insouciant, perhaps, was unfair. He had instinctively known what was coming, read the character of the other man, made an immediate analysis of the situation, acted. Perhaps it would come. She trusted her own training and courage. It was more the aftermath she feared.

The tattooed man was all she disliked in parody masculinity. God alone knew what had been going on before she and

Christopher had stumbled across the half-naked woman fleeing down the street pursued by her own children. Somewhere, in the depths of the nick, someone else was trying to find out.

But watching him sat broken on the pavement in a puddle of blood, tears and indignity, she felt neither triumph nor the righteousness of justice deserved and sentence delivered.

She wondered too about the woman. Why would you keep going back?

Scott wondered whether the downward spiral of thought ever ended or whether it just rotated unceasingly like the grooves on a corkscrew. Would she ever learn Christopher's sense of separation or did that art have a different inspiration?

Meanwhile, he and Francis were mulling their progress, if it could be called that. What all three of them recognised was that they had established very little beyond the inconclusive observations of Ben Le Poirier.

He had seen Christie on the morning of the explosion. She had been walking in a direction that could have taken her to the station but equally to any number of other options. She had nothing but fury and a purse.

Scott had been through the only film footage available of events on the platform at London Bridge in the immediate aftermath of the bombing and it had yielded nothing. Christopher had knocked on doors and staged some kind of reconstruction. Contemporary media coverage had provided no further leads.

That left them with the few living members of the ambulance and fire services and any remaining police officers from the day. Possibly, just possibly, there were some witnesses from among the public or the station staff who might recall something, though how one might track them down without a public appeal the investigation didn't warrant was hard to establish.

59

Potentially hundreds who hadn't either been killed, injured or questioned at the time had simply melted away from the station that day and got on with their lives without their presence there ever having been recorded.

Francis looked at them both. He snapped Scott back from her contemplations by addressing her first. "Rachel, you've done all the reading, where's it taken you?"

She shook her head. She didn't have anything of substance to offer simply because nothing she had seen gave her any cause to confirm or deny. It was possible, entirely possible, that Christie had been there. But probable? Provable? She looked at Sean, hoping to glean from him some clue as to whether he wanted to continue with this.

He looked frankly back at her. If there was battle being fought between his own desires and his detective's instincts, it didn't show. He urged her in neither direction and she was grateful that he looked at her for an opinion and not an affirmation. It freed her.

"If I'm honest," she ventured, "We have a few avenues we can pursue and, if they give us nothing, I don't see how we can carry on. But..." And she paused for a moment while she juggled with whether what she was about to say was a genuinely held belief or born of some other motivation she couldn't quite bring herself to articulate, "I think she was there. I have no reason to say it or believe it beyond a worm in the brain that just won't stop gnawing but I think she was there."

Francis sat back. "That's called a hunch, Rachel. You should be a detective, love."

Scott glanced at Christopher. He was grinning his guileless grin. "Somewhere in all that, there's a compliment."

"It bloody is and all." agreed Francis. "What about you,

Sean?"

Christopher looked at Scott for an unnervingly long time before leaning forward in his seat, his elbows on his knees and his hands meeting in the space between: "I think Rachel's right. We're nearly out of road but she was at London Bridge when that fucking bomb went off.

What happened after, who knows?"

"Well, that's what you're here to find out." said Francis.

"Right. I'm going to get you and Scott here in front of that fella from Special Branch. The one who told his son about the numbers being wrong. He's alive still and, apparently, sharp as a tack but cantankerous with it. His lad, Christ he's not far short of our age, his son, tells me he's never quite got over it. Blames himself. Thinks the Branch missed a trick and should have seen it coming. He's got the anger of the unresolved and can be a difficult old bastard. Let's see if he's got anything to say that might actually help. I'll come with you, I think."

Christopher didn't demur. Francis' charm and powers of persuasion weren't to be underestimated. Instead he handed Scott his bank card. "I've got a job for you," he said. "I want you to call the *Evening Standard*. And then buy a burner."

It had been a long time since Christie had taken a rush hour train and she had forgotten how unpleasant it could be. For a spell, the ceaseless washing of her thoughts back and forward across her mind had inured her to the unwanted body contact, the tense silence and the heaters that oozed warm air into overcrowded compartments in summer and failed altogether in winter.

She had forgotten too, the lengthy stand stills outside London Bridge. The trains jolting into life, creeping forward a few scraping yards and then halting again. A man, surprised by the sudden movement, grasped for the metal luggage racks which topped the seats. His elbow caught Christie on the breast. For a moment, the only sound in the train was his hurried apology and she managed a wan smile by way of acknowledgement.

Someone yawned. No hand went up to their mouth. It was probably trapped.

Christie welcomed another wave of fretful puzzling almost as anaesthesia. A dreadful, creeping realisation had started to take hold of her. For all the sporadic progress of the train, it was taking her away and with each phase of its advance towards London, she felt lighter.

Her intention had been not much more than a gesture. She would change at London Bridge, possibly the terminus over the river at Charing Cross if she were feeling particularly defiant, and then take a return train home. Her brief protest over.

But, seeping into her mind now like an apparition about to materialise, was the most awful thought. Christie did not want to return. She knew what it entailed too. The faces of her three boys wouldn't leave her mind. She could practically feel their anxiety.

Almost by accident she had staged an escape and now she had emerged blinking from the tunnel to find she was beyond the wire with sunlight on her face and the guards none the wiser. Pressed against the fence line were her children, looking for her to wave, then return to collect them.

But for Christie they were melding into the apparatus of captivity. Just as much part of the restraints that kept her pinned in hopelessness as the bullying abuse of the camp commandant. And they always had been. Hostages against her good behaviour. Her parole.

In her mind, she had begun to turn away. She could imagine their increasing franticness. She could imagine the reprisals. And still Christie walked on towards freedom. She let out an involuntary sob. The man who had knocked her mouthed 'Are you all right?' in the still of the carriage. She nodded, not trusting herself to speak.

What Christie wanted to say, more, to declaim was simple: "I am never going back!"

The train started again almost the moment another came past it, heading back down towards the south-eastern suburbs and Kent beyond that. Christie noticed it shower sparks with a brief phut and fizz but her own kept up its momentum now, cutting it only on the final approach to the platform.

Those nearest the windows were sliding them downwards and reaching for the external handles for a quick scape from the claustrophobia of the carriage and to beat the crowds into the narrow foot tunnels that led down from the platforms and out of the station.

It was some moments before the press of passengers had thinned sufficiently for her to feel the pressure release and see a way to alight. She decided to. She would get off, find a café and consider her options. It was clear what, it was now a question of how. The rupture of her decision had released in her an energy and purpose.

It was as she was about to step from the train that she felt the blast. A pressure impact of such intensity that she felt not just as though someone had punched her in every organ but that the fist had been sufficiently hard to reach into her and pummel her from liver to lights.

Christie actually felt her brain vibrate, a conscious feeling of the very fabric of her being humming to a new wavelength, a painful one like a white noise torture. She wanted to grab at herself but her body was held in paralysis by pressure, it squeezed her in its hand almost as though its other was swatting down those around her before the one in which she was clasped dropped her onto the platform and moved on.

It wouldn't stop. This terrible blow to her organs. She'd been hit before. By him. Doubled up in her kitchen while the pain flooded nauseatingly into her abdomen and she fell to her knees. But in the microseconds of the blast she seemed to be being beaten interminably, precisely. Christie screamed. She couldn't help herself. Unconsciousness was coming. Her mind was welcoming oblivion, her heart slowing, slowing, slowing. Stopped.

Rachel Scott had done as she was asked. She had gone to a local shop and bought a burner phone, one unregistered to an owner or address and favoured by people who didn't want to be traced. She had then rung the *Evening Standard* and, at Christopher's instruction, had placed a classified ad.

It was deliberately opaque and a sin of omission in many respects but its request was simple. It read:

"If you were present at the London Bridge bombing in 1979 and have a story to tell, please call this number. Researcher interested in eye witness accounts."

The ad finished with the burner number.

The *Evening Standard* was a freesheet distributed from stands outside London rail and tube stations. It was past its print heyday now, in Russian ownership and repeat attempts to give it influence via editors such as a former Chancellor, a BBC radio chief and the sister-in-law of a former Prime Minister had not returned it to its former glories.

Christopher remembered when it was a newspaper of some authority. Pitted against its rival, the *Evening News*, no self-respecting Londoner passed a newsstand in the evening rush hour without dropping the vendor a coin and tucking it under their arm for the commute home.

The sellers, he remembered, were always dirty from newsprint, swathed in overcoats and cloth caps with a fag stuck permanently to the lower lip as they doled out papers to the rushing office workers.

News at the end of the day, rather than the beginning it had a huge advantage over morning rivals. For developments on big stories, sports results and, in a city devoted to finance, closing prices from the Stock Exchange, picking up the paper was a Londoner's reflex.

Now, it looked what it was. Thin and cheap and commuters simply picked up papers from piles dumped on the pavements by delivery vans. People studied their phones on the way home or used them as radios, each one isolated from the next by their headphones.

For many though, the reflex still held. tens of thousands still dutifully snatched up their copy, glanced at it and left it on the seat for the next reader or cleaner. The older they were, the more likely they were to still to seek the reassurance of a paper or ask for it when perhaps someone in the household came in from a day at work.

It was them Christopher was targeting. Not just because the vintage was right but because he knew people developed a desire in later life to tell their story, almost as though it left some mark of their existence.

The wording was ambiguous deliberately. He couldn't claim this as an official police investigation nor did he want to. The word 'researcher' could mean anything from author to academic. It might also suggest broadcast and he knew the draw television and radio still had on people who wanted to tell a story.

It only took one call. And Christopher was a lucky copper. "Unlucky," as Francis had said, "If you got caught chasing your half-naked missus down the road with grievous intent."

In the meantime, Francis had arranged the meeting with the former Special Branch officer:

"Mick Raglan his name is. He didn't want to do it. His boy had to practically kick the door in. Very sus of the whole exercise. Wanted to know why this all needed raking up again and sounds like he thought he was being investigated for neglect of duty or some such. Silly old sod. What it does mean is we're treading on egg shells. If Sean's small ad only brings up mud and Raglan clams up, that's it, the end of the road."

"Sean, I know this isn't you but, if you have to, I think you're going to have to tug on his heartstrings. He's racked by guilt. Give him a chance to feel he's somehow making amends by helping. If he's got nothing to say, well, fair enough but I want the old bugger feeling honour bound."

Christopher nodded. Scott looked uncertain.

"Don't look at me like that, Rachel." said Francis. "The bloke's dwelt on this for decades and it was no more his fault than yours. We're giving him a chance at some kind of absolution, some kind of respite before he goes to his grave. We all finish this job burdened, love. If I can, I'll lighten the load."

She smiled back. They called her 'love' but these two old hands had given her purpose and belonging in a way her younger colleagues had simply failed to do. She understood too the deep loyalty they shared and the underlying humanity. But Scott knew she would never understand the nature of love, that's what it was, between men.

Michael 'Mick' Raglan had spent most of his thirty odd years as a copper in Special Branch. Set up in the Nineteenth Century to tackle militant Irish republicanism, it had kept its purpose, among others, right through the horrors of the 1970s and beyond.

Raglan had seen those days and the constant efforts to get ahead of the IRA's campaign in mainland Britain. A new blitz where triumph went largely unseen and defeat had the most terrible and public of consequences.

The experience, as he himself admitted, accrued in the mind in screams; of the injured, of sirens and of two wives at the latest reason he couldn't be home for meals or birthdays, Christmas or weekends.

For all that, he had stayed close to his son, one of two, who had followed him into the police force. It was the only reason he'd agreed to speak to the trio who had presented himself on his doorstep now. Christopher, Francis and Scott.

He showed them into his bungalow, walking on still-steady legs through to a conservatory on the back of the house. "Warmer here," he said. Weak sunshine came through the glass as Raglan sat down among the fronds and trailing vines of plants he obviously tended obsessively.

Scott watched him. He looked like he was hiding. He watched her back. "Smart," he thought. Not just the way she presented herself. Clever. A looker too. Made the best of what she'd been given. Scott made him feel every one of his years and very lonely. Because of that, he decided to dislike her.

The two men, well, he could relate to them. Middle aged career policemen. "She," he thought, "is only passing through."

He offered nobody a drink. Just sat there among the foliage, eyeing them like a wounded beast waiting for the hunter to come in and finish it. Well, he'd charge if he had to.

Francis led off, introducing the three of them. Raglan nodded back. Nothing more.

"Mick, thanks for agreeing to see us," said Francis. "We very much appreciate it." Again, Raglan merely nodded.

"We want to ask you about the London Bridge bombing. I know you've got some concerns about why we want to ask you some questions but I promise you this is not any kind of official enquiry. In fact, it's a bit off-book and personal." Raglan relaxed just a little but still said nothing.

This time, Francis did nothing to fill the silence. Scott had detected the rancour and had the wit to keep quiet. Christopher, it was, who sat forward.

"The truth is, Mick, we, I, need your help and I think you're among the last people alive who's in a position to put me out of a personal misery."

This time Raglan's expression changed enough to at least reveal a curiosity.

"Did you lose someone, son?" he suddenly asked. Raglan was estimating his age and concluding that Christopher can only have been a boy at the time.

Before Christopher could answer, Raglan continued almost angrily: "Are you the bloody ghost that's come to haunt me? Well, don't bloody bother. They're here in legions!"

Christopher glanced round the house. Tidy. Quiet. Only a ticking clock. Left alone, he thought, the room must fill with voices of doubt and recrimination.

He moved to soothe the old man. "No, Mick, I'm not here to blame and I don't even really know if I lost someone. I just need some information. A pointer."

"I don't remember anything." Said Raglan.

Francis intervened. "Mick, don't let yourself down." He said, "You sound like some tedious git in the interview room, caught in a house with a bag full of family silver shouting." "I know nuffin!' You know, I know, you're still on the ball. Why don't you let Sean here ask you his questions? You could be a real help."

Raglan mounted his charge: "Don't tell me what I remember! I'll tell you! I remember getting to that station minutes after that bomb went off. Minutes! I saw some kid. Blonde, he was. He'd had his feet blown off and he was missing half his left arm. He had tried to crawl, crawl on his poor little stumps towards his mum. She was lying about ten feet away. He'd trailed blood behind him like someone had dipped him in red paint but he'd died before he could reach her. He must have thought she was still alive. She was looking right at him. But she was stone dead. Stone bloody dead. Her lungs had simply burst.

"All I could think of, all I can think of, is that we should have stopped it. We were running from one explosion to the next, one sighting, one safe house, one meeting, one interrogation, one fucking bollocking from a minister..."

He looked round the conservatory desperately, his hands clenching and unclenching on the armrest of his chair. Christopher realised he was trying to find somewhere to put the frustrated energy of years.

"Mick, Mick," he soothed, "nobody's blaming you."

"I blame me! I do! I blame me like I have done every bastard day since it happened. And it's beyond you, or anyone else, to grant me forgiveness!"

Scott tried not to look at Francis.

Christopher let some of the tension from the outburst dissipate.

"Would you help me?" he ventured again. "I'm not here to grant you forgiveness because you have done nothing to forgive. But, in the end, Mick, you're your own priest. You can do something in the present that might at least put one, possibly two, souls to rest and with them some other ghosts from the past.

Raglan looked at him desperately.

"What, what can I do that can possibly stop all this?" his eyes sought every part of the room in search of a phrase, "this endless noise?"

Christopher paused and then threw him a lifeline. "I think my mother was there that day. Help me find out what happened to her."

The toilet block had probably saved O'Driscoll's life. He had managed to barge and push his way through the flood of commuters to its blind side, away from the train he had just come in on.

He came round dreaming that he was crying out in pain. Screaming in such anguish that he could only be dying or watching someone he loved die in front of him. His ears rang with the force of the explosion and his head, particularly his left temple, hurt badly.

His senses began to restore sound and vision. There was an odd, shocked silence, interrupted by a low and general groaning that grew in volume. He realised that the screaming had been sirens.

From where he lay, he couldn't see the worst of what he'd done. He didn't want to. What he could see was enough. Further up the platform, there were things shattered and twisted. Glass, metal, people.

From the angle afforded him by the block, he could see a

woman looking back down the platform. Her arm was extended as though reaching for something but her glazed stare saw nothing. Nor could he see the small, blonde boy dragging himself towards her. He could hear though. The sound of a wet mop being dragged in slow increments across a floor. It stopped abruptly.

O' Driscoll tried to distract himself by subtly touching his own body. He didn't, as yet, want to be seen to be alive and already there were people moving about. Those who had escaped serious injury were moving among the dead and dying trying to help or comfort. Others staggered blindly. He saw a British Rail cap, its 'there and back' arrows half torn away along with the peak.

A man was using his tie on his own severed leg. Frantically, he tried to staunch the flow of blood as he looked down at himself with increasing desperation. He gently subsided to his left and lay still.

Soon, policemen would arrive. Doctors. Officialdom. He didn't want to get caught up in the inevitable questions and process. There were screams now. Increasingly despairing ones.

His head had been cut very badly and, though he couldn't see it, the gash had revealed the white of his skull. He could feel other cuts of varying severity. His limbs seemed to function and he could feel their presence. The man with the tie had stuck in his mind.

Medics were running onto the platform now. Doctors, nurses in their hats and cloaks and ambulancemen in their grey uniforms bringing stretcher after stretcher from the nearby hospitals, red blankets topping each as they lay them anywhere there was space. They were attempting some kind of triage while police tried to impose order among chaos.

A photographer picked his way ashen-faced along the

platform, pausing regularly to raise his camera and adjust the lens. O' Driscoll assumed he was some kind of official or perhaps a pool snapper from the Press, allowed up onto the platform on the understanding that he shared any images with the various news outlets. He did not want his photo taken.

Those beyond help were being lifted onto the stretchers. A curt nod from a white-coated doctor and they were gently taken up by the ambulance drivers, a blanket pulled up over their faces, before being taken to one of the foot tunnels and laid out in a lengthening line. In no hurry now, they were overseen only by a single British Rail guard.

O' Driscoll saw his chance. His obscured position kept him only in partial view of the comings and goings on the platform. He rolled slowly towards the nearest stretcher. He didn't want rapid movement to catch the eye even among the frantic activity. Only when he started to roll did he feel the pain in his ribs. The slightest pressure as he turned forced the breath from him and he had to stop to prevent himself crying out involuntarily.

He started again but it was too much. He only had to make a matter of yards but the pain of rolling on his ribs could not be endured. Glancing along the platform again to check nobody was looking in his direction, he edged on his back towards the stretcher, a sort of clenched- buttock shuffle that took him within a foot of where he wanted to be.

Bracing himself for the pain, O'Driscoll pitched first onto his front before rolling himself onto the stretcher so that he lay face up. He was panting. The wooden frame had dug into him as he positioned himself. Each breath made him wince until he couldn't help but release a low, agonised growl through clenched and bloodied teeth while his right leg kicked out spastically as though the act itself would provide some sort of release from pain.

There was still no shout of alarm from anyone on the platform, his movements and his cry lost among many, many others. Summoning from himself one last effort, O'Driscoll grabbed for the red blanket and pulled it over his body and up over his face before subsiding gratefully into total stillness and anonymity. He was now just another covered corpse.

He lay there for some time listening to the medics around him, very close now, their muttered instructions trying to hide the worst from the desperately injured as they sought to save life and often limb.

At one point he thought he heard a camera shutter working and focused on restricting his breathing to the most shallow respiration. He heard shouted orders, a sob, the scraping of stretchers being moved. Somebody, somewhere was delivering what sounded like a monologue. A priest perhaps? With his ears still ringing and the blanket over him, the sound was indistinct.

At one point he heard someone shout 'Miss! Miss! Come back, you're hurt!" but the clamour subsided.

Eventually, O'Driscoll felt himself lifted from the concrete. The ambulancemen were gentle even in what they imagined to be death. The jolt was slight as they picked him up and they set him down among the growing ranks of the dead with the respect due a lowered coffin.

Stillness.

Occasionally, he heard another body being added to the line. Then, that too stopped. Somewhere in the foot tunnel, he could hear the faint movements of the guard. O'Driscoll could imagine him, shocked and ill at ease with the company he kept.

When the bodies stopped arriving, O'Driscoll realised he would have to move quickly. Now the injured had been prioritised and dealt with, the process of sending corpses away to morgues would begin.

He heard footsteps and then a man's voice. "You all right, George…?" There was no audible response and he could guess at a careworn nod. "They're going to start coming down for these shortly. Why don't you go and get yourself a quick cup of tea and a fag? You look like you need it and these poor sods aren't going to care."

O' Driscoll heard the scrape of a chair and two sets of footsteps receding along with a staccato conversation. Everyone was in shock. Slowly, he lifted the blanket and looked out into the silent foot tunnel. Body after body stretched out along its length. For a moment, he had to fight an almost Munchian despair. He had done this. Him. He teetered briefly on the edge of an abyss before hauling himself back. Animal survival instinct first. Angst second.

Groaning with the effort, he stood up. Looking for the exit signs, he staggered to the tunnel wall to use it as a support and shuffled down its length. Unable to stand straight, his right arm covering his injured ribs, he mounted a bowed and ape-like run as he neared a way out, stopping sharply as he saw the police cordon ahead. He leant against the wall again and tried to exhale the pain.

Only the agony now was giving him clarity. He could feel an almost overwhelming desire to fall asleep and it was tinged the colour of delirium. Odd flickers and visions of things half-remembered and a dreadful melancholy born of guilt, fear and shock. O' Driscoll felt a loneliness like the last man on Earth.

He looked back down the tunnel at the line of stretchers. He thought of his father, eight- pints brave and a ninth in his hand, a long way from a British soldier but fighting mad.

"If they want me," he would roar, "They'll have to carry me out feet first!" An Irish Falstaff, poet, poltroon and pisshead, the barman laughing and his mates cheering him on to imagined ruddy-faced glories.

O'Driscoll smiled. "You've finally struck a blow for Ireland, Da," he thought, "they'll carry me out feet first!"

And with that he limped back to his stretcher and covered himself again.

Further back down the track, trains waiting to get into London via the wrecked interchange ahead were queued back for miles. Some, the lucky ones, had been brought to a halt at stations. The passengers grumblingly alighted and filtered away looking for buses or taxis.

At Deptford, the guard was besieged by an angry crowd demanding to know when they would be on the move again. Information had not yet been passed down the line. All he knew was that every train was being held at a red signal.

It was a different time. There were no mobile phones. Being sullen and uncommunicative was the default for unionised and state run industries. The 'travelling public' only featured as a concern when a union leader sought to justify his latest excuse to strike.

A woman came out from the ticket office where she had been listening to the radio. She fought her way through the mob to the guard and whispered into his ear. He shook his interrogators off and went to a phone mounted in a small metal box and returned looking grave.

Caught between what he now knew, the gaps he couldn't fill and knowing that some of the people he was about to speak to may have waved off loved ones that morning to earlier trains, he was measuring what to say.

The platform had temporarily quietened under a heavy blanket of foreboding.

"Ladies and gentlemen," he started and then realised his tone was more wedding than funeral. He changed down a register and a gear knowing that adrenaline had made him rev too high. "I'm sorry to inform you that there has been an explosion at London Bridge. It appears on first report to have been a suspect device. A bomb. Details are sketchy but there have been casualties and the emergency services are in attendance. Trains are suspended in all directions. I don't have any further information to give you so I suggest in the meantime you try other means of getting home or to work. I'm very sorry I can't tell you more."

He finished looking slightly defeated. He had friends up the line. He had noticed too that even as he spoke several anxious faces began to look horror struck as the implications sank in.

The sun was up and it was warm now. There was moment of almost somnolent resignation as most people dispersed with the slightly guilty air of people who had misspent their anger on a false premise. It had been like shouting into the grave.

One or two commuters stood on the platform looking anxiously up the line as though out of the slight heat haze rising from the lines would walk some answer to their unspoken question. They looked again at the guard who could only shrug sympathetically. "I'm sorry." he repeated and then sought the sanctuary of the ticket office.

Up those shimmering lines was Jonty Christopher. He had been standing in the stifling carriage for over an hour and was stranded at a junction beside which stood a biscuit factory. The open windows let in a smell of industrial scale baking and sugar. In the developing heat, it was faintly nauseating.

There were no announcements. Merely stillness and a silence interrupted by occasional exhalations and the folding of newspapers. An origami of overcrowding that Jonty had never been able to master.

The passengers had passed the stage of eye-rolling knowingly at each other and sharing the occasional joke with a fellow traveller about the shortcomings of British Rail. "We're Getting There!" went the advertising slogan. "Yes but when?" came the world-weary answer.

Jonty, meanwhile, was left to fulminate. A laval flow of anger ran ever hotter beneath the surface. In it floated dark phrases. 'That Irish bitch of a wife of mine,' 'her whining fucking litter.' A slow-smoking revenge fantasy seeped from vents in an increasingly volcanic fury and a slow trickle of sweat ran down his back and soaked the armpits of his overweight body. It hissed and sizzled on his fury. In his mind, he was already landing the first punch.

If not entirely fled, the shadows were at least confined to the darker corners of Mick Raglan's bungalow. He had emerged, slowly, like an adopted cat from among the foliage of the conservatory and moved himself and his visitors into the house.

The mood was lighter and with a role to fulfil and a sense of purpose at least partially restored, Raglan's sharpness of mind was in evidence. He had been sufficiently aware of his unwarranted coolness towards Scott to ensure he sat beside her as they gathered round coffee he had made and served. She noticed it, a concession to the petty politics of personal power, and made an equally conscious decision to accept the unspoken offering with good grace.

Christopher shared what they had so far, which was little.

Raglan had more.

He knew about the disparity in numbers and conceded that he'd been obliged outwardly to accept it as a miscalculation in the confusion of the moment. However, inwardly, he had never quite come to terms with the explanation.

"Our job was intelligence gathering and then preventative action. Too much time in Irish pubs and pretending to be the GPO," he said referring to the old state-run General Post Office that was also in charge of the telephone system and, as whose workers, Special Branch occasionally masqueraded. "We only turned up at London Bridge in the forlorn hope of nabbing one of these bastards by chance or finding something among the wreckage that could lead us to them.

"It was carnage and it was chaos but it wasn't complete anarchy. The medical people in particular were systematic and couldn't afford to send some poor fucker off to be laid out in the foot tunnel only to find out later they'd been alive.

"I know about the woman who got up off the stretcher. I spoke to the bloke who picked her up. Once that might happen but twice?" He looked up at Christopher at the same time as Scott.

She was too interested in Christopher's response. For the first time he momentarily shed the detachment that had characterised his attitude so far. She could never work out whether it was professional, self-protective or somewhere between the two. Either way, he didn't interrupt Raglan for more details.

He continued: "What's always made me a bit sus about the whole thing was that we never really knew whether we had ever nicked whoever was responsible. A month or so later we broke an IRA cell that had based itself out in Dartford on the

Kent/London margins. They were out of sight there but close enough to the capital to do damage. Half of the six had got jobs at a big local construction firm where they simply became invisible amongst all the other Micks digging a bleeding great hole somewhere or sitting in a crane.

The other two lived without visible means of support and the final member worked in a library and was entertaining himself with a local publican's wife on the side. He found out and, almost certainly out of malice, reported 'suspicions activity.' There's a euphemism for you but, anyway, one thing led to another and nicked 'em.

We went in hard. London Bridge was awful but it had been one of three. We were all aware of the dangers of nicking an Irishman, any Irishman and Birmingham and Guildford proved the point. But we had no choice. Gave 'em the hardest time we possibly could without actually beating the fuckers half to death, tempted though I was.

Anyway, they never bubbled up on anyone else, though we always thought there were more. Had to be. To keep a running operation going on that scale demands resources and they were just too short-handed. Trouble was they knew there going down for life. They had nothing to lose by holding out and giving their mates a free run for home.

Between us and the RUC and Army over in Northern Ireland, we had plants and informers and highly placed ones too but it was rare as rocking horse shit for 'the boyos' on the ground to turn each other in. Once in never out and they were ideological, see. Ireland's curse is the informer. All that old pub song naus they suckled at the teat.

We even put ourselves about among their co-workers. Especially the ones on the sites. The trouble is they were a bit like a football crowd. They might not be in on the hooliganism but they support it from afar. Clammed up if they ever wanted to walk or work again. Lot of talk behind the hand as we passed and spitting on the ground.

Anyway, Friday lunchtimes was the best time to get 'em. Paypacket in by eleven, off down the pub by half past twelve. So we had a couple of boys hover round all the usual spots when they had a few jars down 'em and listened in. I'm talking boys who could pass themselves off as Michael fucking Collins if pushed. Accents and attitudes. You'd never have known.

They never really got anything out of it. Somebody had put the word out. A few quid in the right pockets and everyone stayed off the subject. We did, though, pick up the undertow 'that they'd never catch the other fellas' before it was back to the racing pages and another pint."

Raglan himself dropped into a pitch perfect Dublin accent before resuming.

"Could never nail it down and when the gang we had pinched went to the Bailey they took the rap for the whole lot. Truth is that seemed like job done and we were more than busy enough elsewhere.

I always thought there were at least two more and I think they were there. Could have gone up with it. At least one body was never identified. No DNA in those days and whoever it was has long since gone up the chimney. Could have been that one of them played dead."

Scott interrupted him. "What about the Irishman who tried to hail a cab?"

Raglan's brow knitted.

"Wild goose chase," he said. "It was easy enough to put the word out among the cabbies and I had a few of our boys visit all the usual spots where they stop for tea, fags and bacon sandwiches.

"The driver stuck his hand up within a couple of days. We tracked his would-be passenger down at St Bart's in the City. He'd got as far as the Square Mile before he keeled over. Dazed and confused. Nothing more. Desperate to make a meeting to secure backing for some project or another. The point was, he was completely innocent and not in great shape by the time he was trundled through the hospital doors."

"If the bombers were there," asked Francis "did you have anyone in the frame?"

"Only hunches," answered Raglan, "Nothing firm."

"But we were fairly sure two active IRA members had managed to get in and out of the country on a couple of occasions. Whispers from over the water. The first was a woman called Patsy Kearney. Nasty even by the standards of nasty. She had to be. The IRA was working class and she was supposed to know her place. Her struggle was more than 'Brits out of Ireland.' She was smart. Law degree and radical politics before she took up the struggle with a pistol in her hand and a transmitter in her pocket.

"Proved herself with executions and some Gestapo-inspired interrogation methods. She was prominent and then she wasn't. Fell off our radar for almost two years and I think to go clean-skin while we forgot about her.

"We didn't. She got slotted in an SAS mission in bandit country in the early Eighties. It was hard to question her after that but I doubt she'd have said anything anyway. Die hard. And she did.

"The other one was called Donal O' Driscoll. Unusual in that he wasn't a Northern lad. Proved himself the hard way but, again, disappeared. You never quite knew with the Provos whether they had developed a suspicion. By the 80s, a lot of the more prominent activists were being actively hunted and, to do that, we needed informants. Fed their paranoia no end when one of their own got toppled.

"No suggestion on our side that he was, though the circle of knowledge on these things was necessarily small. But he could be anywhere from a shallow grave to tending his vegetable patch and, even if he's alive, I've nothing more than a copper's itch that he was there. Had the hard arse's hallmark though. You have to be devoted to the cause to do something like that. And he was an ideologue to the point of being fanatical.

"Anyway, point was, both Kearney and O'Driscoll were senior and seasoned. Leadership material and none of the ones we nicked gave that impression. Worker bees. Though they all claimed to be the brains of the operation. It laid a smoke screen."

It was Christopher, because it had to be, who asked the question: "And the woman who took up her bed and walked?"

Scott noticed the biblical reference just as she'd noticed the priestly way Christopher had persuaded Raglan to help. She noticed everything. Particularly when it came to Christopher. He moved between so many things. Entertaining and engaged. Monosyllabic and detached. Copper's copper, king of the canteen and, as she had witnessed, handy in a fight. But, as she had also noticed, he betrayed himself constantly as well-read almost to the point of academic.

Was he religious too or merely facetious?

In the world she had come from, to be anything other than serious was a cardinal sin. But Christopher often gave the impression of finding life faintly amusing even, as now, when dealing with its worst manifestations. Again, she wondered whether it was a form of self-preservation or whether he was hiding a seriousness of intent.

Resurrection, forgiveness perhaps, lay at the heart of what Christopher pursued almost as much as resolution. Did he disguise it from himself or from her, from Francis and from Raglan?

Scott found chasing his mystery exhilarating and exasperating in equal measure. She would end days exhausted by him but ever more fascinated. She also knew she was thinking too much about him.

She glanced at Raglan to find he was watching her. He turned his gaze to Christopher.

"Sean, I just don't know. I spoke to the ambulance driver and his mate at the time. Their description was vague. I've seen the snap of your mum. She was a pretty, dark brunette. Under the circumstances, she probably wasn't looking her best if it was her and those boys caught only a fleeting glimpse. From how she was described at the time, there's a broad similarity and I can't say anything more than that.

"I have to be honest, Sean, it wasn't my focus or anybody else's at the time. We simply had to try and square the numbers and, if not, put it down to the confusion. I was just keen to catch the bastards who did it before they did it again. I'm sorry I can't tell you more."

Christopher nodded his thanks. There was no discernible emotion in him though Francis was regarding him with almost paternal concern.

Their parting, some minutes later, was amicable. Some of the tension had left Raglan as he saw them to the door.

"I hope you find what you're looking for, Sean." He said as they shook hands. Christopher looked him square in the eye. "You too, Mick. You too." Raglan could only smile bleakly.

It was as Scott took his hand that she felt him grip hers tightly. He glanced quickly at Christopher who had set off down the path. "You be careful, love. We're all fascinated by the beauty of ruins. But ruins they are."

Speechless at her own transparency, she followed the two men down the path and back to the car.

The first blow had just landed.

Jonty Christopher had, eventually, arrived back at home having been kept a further hour on the train and then been asked to walk back down the now deactivated electric track towards the station along with hundreds of other over-heated passengers.

It had proven too difficult to reverse so many trains and each would have to be manoeuvred into sidings or wait until they could complete their inward runs and then reposition themselves to provide some kind of service once London Bridge had cleared. That might take hours. So people had been escorted off trains.

It had then taken Jonty a further hour or more to get home involving another sweaty walk up the steep incline from Greenwich towards home. He was no longer a fit man and the heat of the day plus a brief pause in a pub had done nothing to improve his volatility.

It took very little to add a further explosion to the day and the fuse had been lit by the anxiety of Sean and his siblings and the continued absence of Christie. For the first time, it occurred to Jonty that his wife might actually have had the courage to leave and that his edicts on maintaining a deceitful façade to the nature of his family might be betrayed to a relative, a lawyer or a policeman.

The escalation from there had been short and linear and had led Sean to try and protect his younger brothers from the blast.

Inevitably, and not for the first time, Sean had been reduced to covering up and keeping on the move as his father sought to rain blows on him, fists clenched and the full wrath of a weak man's displaced anger unleashed.

It would be the least of it. Worse would come in the combustible silences, the hurled crockery and the lumpen body twitching its toes in threatening disapproval as the boys sought to replicate some sort of domestic routine.

But, for the moment, Sean had learnt something and stored it. The blows were percussive but no longer painful, nor could they be sustained by his father for any length of time. Like a boxer listening to his opponent's breathing, he'd taken a gauge. And he gauged weakness.

At about the same time, Christie Christopher was forced to sit down. She was, of course, unaware of it but she was back from the dead and body and mind were finding life difficult. She had come to in complete blackness and with a horrifying sense both of elevation and suffocation.

For a moment, she genuinely believed herself in the tumult of the afterlife buffeted and pulled between forces that were fighting to claim her as theirs. Had her thoughts been clearer she would have seen the irony. It was not much different to being alive.

Her heart had briefly, very briefly, stopped beating in the immediate aftermath of the explosion. In that suspension between life and death, a doctor had cursorily checked her vital signs and in his haste moved on, her limp form laid gently onto a stretcher and covered with a blanket.

She had swum gently to a halfway point between the bottom of a pool and its surface and there, now in a state of unconsciousness, floated in a form of semi oblivion. Sounds and the occasional shadow dimly penetrated to where she bobbed but nothing more.

As consciousness returned, she felt herself rising to the surface and, with her ascent, a panic-stricken desire to breathe and breathe as deeply as she could.

It was then that she sat up to find herself off the ground and being lifted away neither by angels or demons but two shocked men in late middle age. Christie grabbed at the blanket that had covered her as though her modesty were compromised. She then climbed from the stretcher and, still clutching her red hospital blanket, staggered towards the station exit only dimly aware of the shouts of the men behind her.

Her body hurt. Not just cuts and bruises but the feeling persisted that something supernatural had pummelled her interior, hurling itself against her rib cage and pinballing off her organs in a desperate attempt to leave her body.

For the moment, the bomb, her own physical state was pushed to the back of her mind. What preoccupied her was getting back to her children. Their memory had swept aside all other concerns and she had made the confused connection that what had happened to her had happened to them.

She dimly remembered her half-formed plan of escape though her conscience ached with painful clarity at the thought of it. For the moment though, she had to collect herself.

Unafraid of the police cordon, she wandered up to it, giving some confused explanation of her desperate need to get home. A policewoman made her sit on a bench 'just for a minute' while she went to find someone to help her but the moment she left, Christie rose and shuffled away.

She was now down by the river, having crossed Tooley

Street and drifted among the warehouses and wharves that still lingered there as testimony to a London that had, until relatively recently, thrived on shipping even up as far as London and Tower Bridges. Most were now abandoned, some dilapidated but all were destined to make their owners new fortunes in the building and redevelopment boom whose deep excavations and demolition balls could already be seen.

Like O'Driscoll, she had a feeling of the most desolate loneliness. The warehouse windows gazed down at her like the empty sockets of skulls. She could hear traffic back on the road and the river flowed greenly past on a quick flood tide but for the moment she was as abandoned as the buildings.

Christie fought her throbbing body and stood again. She clasped quickly at herself trying to find the purse she taken with her from the house. It had gone. Panic flooded her. She had to find it. She had to get home. She staggered a few steps trying to retrace her own but nothing would answer. Nothing.

Leaning heavily against a door, Christie shook her head to orientate herself but it only woke the beast within who responded by renewing its assault on its confines, running to the back near her kidneys and then leaping forward with all its force against her abdomen. The pain ran up her body and collided with her heart.

She looked up at the sheer brick wall of the building she leant against. It was a façade now. Through its glassless windows to which clung a few corroded bars, protection for goods long gone, she could see the great pit of new foundations. A smell of brick dust, river and the faint tang of iron giddied the last of her senses.

Christie looked up at the wall again. She had a feeling that if she leaned against the wrong place, it would simply topple into the hole like a child's brick tower. The thought alone made her grasp for something. Her hand found a thin chain round her neck.

One of the boys had given it to her. Sean, she knew. His Communion medal perhaps, yes. The closest he could get to buying her a jewel. She held onto it as though she were holding onto God, holding onto the boys. Then, once again, she subsided heavily against the door.

Later and nearby, O'Driscoll crawled inside a similar doorway. Like a wounded animal, he had sought to limp off and pant his way to the end unmolested. The doorway was dark and smelled of damp. He liked it. It had the feel of the grave and he had accepted the destination from almost the moment the bomb went off.

"If we are marked to die, we are enough to do our country loss." He hissed a smile. Bloody Shakespeare. He couldn't think of a Yeats line and it frustrated him. There wasn't a shortage on the subject of death.

His strength had gone. He'd used the last of it escaping distracted ambulancemen as they loaded corpses and, in another animal moment had instinctively sought the solace of water. He could hear it. Lapping now at a muddy beach he couldn't see from where he lay.

Occasionally a boat would pass and the water would rush more urgently at the shore line as if scurrying to escape.

The old warehouses had been a bonus. He tucked his legs in so that they didn't stick out onto the fractured, unlit pavement and he listened to his breathing. Nothing about it spoke of health.

O'Driscoll could hear someone coming. It was a woman's step. Not the click-clack trot of a woman in heels, just something in its lightness. There was almost a fearfulness to it. A deer creeping into a clearing. The dark perhaps, the desertion. Either way, it lacked a man's bravura. He drew his legs in further as the steps approached.

They stopped right over him. He looked up but in the dark he could barely see. He took in a woman's legs and hands clasped just below her abdomen. She was holding a purse and looking down at him. Of the expression on her face, he could see nothing.

There was silence in the car leaving Mick Raglan's. Each of the occupants was lost in separate but interconnected thoughts.

Up front, Francis was mulling whether his mercy mission had now become a wild goose chase over which he no longer had control. He knew his friend, felt for him, but he understood too that it was in his nature to pursue this to what he increasingly suspected was a bitter end. Francis hoped only that it would come sooner rather than later.

The thought that he had condemned Christopher only to a fruitless physical search rather than merely a psychological restlessness gnawed at him. Again, the aphorism; "The road to hell is paved with good intentions."

Behind, Scott tried not to steal furtive glances at Christopher. She yearned to enquire after him. To touch him. But he seemed more untouchable than ever. As ever, he seemed to sense her mental, she had to admit, emotional, outreach. He turned to her and smiled. One of the boyish ones. Scott tried to focus on a practical response to the increasingly complex problem he presented. A managerial reaction would dampen her emotion however much it was becoming the most exquisite torture.

Christopher himself was a mere façade. He had gone to see Raglan in the shameful internal acknowledgement that he hoped to discover that his mother had been at London Bridge and died there. It was the closest to a full stop he could imagine. He could convince himself that the abandonment had been the unhappiest of accidents. A momentary flight terminated before return.

Raglan's living hell had doubled his sense of shame. Others. The living and the dead. Others. Among them now Rachel Scott. He could feel this affair winding tendrils round her and drawing this woman to the centre of something by which he had been bound for years.

He wanted her there and not at all. Christopher knew his own danger. Shame. Shame for the tearful women in his life. Shame that loving him always came at such a cost. Like greatness there was a price to be paid. But it was seldom the great who paid it.

Like Scott, his mind to turned to the practical. An act of contrition. Harrow hell. Release Raglan, Rachel, his mother, him from its bonds. Solve this, solve everything.

He watched London pass from the car window. She waited to give him her rough embrace. The whiskered kiss of an old and patient woman, coarsened by life but bearing great love. For once, he wanted something softer. Partly for himself, partly as the offering he could give, he turned and smiled at Scott.

Unsettled, she fumbled for the burner phone. Switched to silent for the meeting with Raglan, it had registered four waiting messages. She let it rest between her and Christopher so that he could see it. He reached for it and let his finger gently touch hers. She looked at him and for perhaps the second it took to count, didn't move her own.

They listened to the messages together, Scott and Christopher, Francis having returned to the main business of the day.

What had so briefly passed between them earlier hung in the air without manifesting itself. Both were at a point still within the boundaries of plausible deniability. A smile, the passing touch of a hand. Both everything and, of course, nothing.

In the meantime, they listened first to the frail voice of an elderly woman. She was uncertain speaking to the voicemail service. The lack of someone with whom actually to converse left her hesitant and repetitive. She was also – and reasonably – cautious. Twice she asked who was it who was asking for her memories which, she claimed, had been as a nurse summoned from the nearby Guy's Hospital to help with casualties.

Scott took her details, listening to the message three times to ensure she had taken them down correctly as the quavering voice slowly repeated her name, Mrs Caroline Miles, and her phone number. A landline with a London code.

The second, a young man, gave a rambling second hand account from someone he claimed to be a relative, now dead, who had been a passenger on the train. He was shrewd enough to have taken a clue from the ad and deduce that this was film or TV research and ask whether there was a fee for either his information or any on-screen appearance. Again, Scott wrote down a mobile number but this time given so quickly it was barely intelligible. She used the phone's incoming call notification to double check it.

The third, a well-spoken middle aged man, calmly outlined a series of conspiracy theories at some length culminating in the suggestion that the explosion had been caused by dissatisfied Army officers trying to engineer a coup against the dying days of a Labour government.

Christopher rolled his eyes. The history of the Seventies was a broth of such theories, some to a greater or lesser extent true and often interweaving KGB involvement with Labour or the Unions and former wartime military officers determined to rid a failing Britain of its Communist infiltrators. If only for the sake of rigour, Scott scribbled down the caller's clearly enunciated name and number.

The last message proved the most infuriatingly intriguing. There was a lengthy pause before the voice started to speak. Then, as though courage had been mustered, it began. Clearly scripted, whoever was speaking was plainly overcoming a physical difficulty to do so.

The fact he was reading, and the slightly mistimed pauses, made Christopher think momentarily of Wearside Jack, the man whose tapes falsely claiming responsibility for the Yorkshire Ripper murders, had so diverted the investigation. He was instantly on guard, though the man speaking could have no idea of police involvement and he slowly and carefully left his name and number.

It was what he said that brought both Scott and he to attention. "Hello. My name is…" there was a pause during which could be heard a sound almost like laboured mastication, "Henry. Henry Grumman." Again, a sort of wet hiatus and then: "I was on the train that was blown up at London Bridge." As though gathering himself, the voice stopped again and then took the next stretch in a rush. "I have no idea who you are or why you might be enquiring about that day but I have something to say and I don't believe I have much time left to say it." As though whittling that time still further, there was then a lengthy series of bulldog slurpings and snufflings before the speaker began again. "You see, I think I saw the man who did it." He began to give a phone number before the voicemail cut off.

Scott desperately scrolled the options on the phone. To her relief there was a record of the number. She checked the code. It was a number in Sevenoaks, Kent. Outside London but a prosperous former market town and now a favourite for the well-heeled City commuter. Its large houses, rolling hills and expensive schools spoke of what it was. Wealthy. A legacy of old money and Square Mile prosperity. Through the unearthly noises, the voice fitted and, if what Grumman suggested was true, Christopher had proven once again that he was a lucky copper.

Scott and he decided for the moment to develop somewhat the line that the research was academic in nature with a view to making a retrospective via an independent production company, commissioned by the BBC.

The people they were about to speak to were of an age where the authority of the name still held. The proxy of a production company, now a commonplace in BBC commissioning, was useful in placing a Chinese wall between any curious relatives and a call to Broadcasting House in London or Media City in Manchester.

Until they had filtered the calls and established to what degree they were to be taken seriously, they would leave police involvement unspoken. Christopher rather guiltily handed the job of deceit to Scott. She was presentable, telegenic and a woman. All the things one would expect from a television producer bound to the national broadcaster.

He watched her make the calls, sliding easily into the persona. Her clothes for the day still bore the hallmarks of sober but quality corporatism, just enough individuality to be noticed, not so much as to be considerably individual. Her dark trouser suit was well cut but her colourful blouse stood in perfect contrast. Scott's make up was subtly done and she had pushed her sunglasses up on to her head as they had left the car.

Christopher enjoyed imagining her as an on-screen presenter. He had to stifle a laugh as she dropped her voice to broadcast tone and introduced herself on the phone. "Hello, Mrs Miles? Hello, my name is Helena. I'm calling from Metropolitan Productions. May I first thank you so much for taking the trouble to contact us with your memories of London Bridge. We're so grateful and, of course, it's precisely your human and eye witness recollections of what happened that interest us. Would it be possible to meet and talk at length? I would, of course, be happy to come to wherever is most convenient to you."

Within moments she had secured a meeting at the woman's house two days hence. On speakerphone, Christopher could hear the fearfulness of age evaporating in the warmth of Scott's trustworthy vocal embrace. Instinctively, she knew what reassured.

She took a somewhat different approach with the young man claiming to be a relative of a passenger. She introduced herself in much the same way and to much the same unsceptical effect. However, this time, she quizzed him gently, soon establishing that he was guessing his way into the conversation, venturing experiences and seeing if they matched her narrative. He reconfigured quickly if they didn't, claiming he was only recounting an old man's partial memories.

She realised he was pulling the medium's trick and trying to construct a tale to raise the dead and please the client on the basis of what the client might reveal and desire.

His one point of consistency was pursuit of a fee. Scott held out the unspoken promise of the possibility to keep him talking but it soon became clear that while the foundation of his story may have had a basis in truth, the rest was a confection with money in mind. She reassured him that she would be in touch again shortly and promptly blocked his number.

That left only the man in Sevenoaks. Scott told Christopher off for impersonating him. It was moment of flirtation both of them enjoyed. Mr Grumman would be none the wiser but they were now complicit in the worst sin of a post-humour world;

jocularity. They both felt closer. The Bonnie and Clyde of mild mockery.

She tapped out his number. A middle aged woman answered and Scott resumed her charade as Helena. She soon established that woman on the phone was Grumman's daughter; protective, suspicious and irascible. All Scott's newly discovered BBC smoothness was required to establish a rapport.

The woman, Camilla, exhaled an exasperated "I'm sorry if I'm a little short," she said. Christopher just about suppressed a facetious desire to scribble '4' 10"?' on Scott's notepad.

"My father is very elderly. He is also very physically damaged as he has been since he was caught in the explosion." Scott looked at Christopher and they nodded in time. "He has also had a mild stroke and, although he remains mentally sharp, he develops whims which must be satisfied. I'm grown up enough to understand that this is because he feels he is in a race against time. However, it's exhausting to me and I'm afraid some people have sought to exploit it."

Scott, feeling guiltier by the minute, expressed her sympathies and admiration for Camilla's fortitude at some length. She was aware enough of her own sex's susceptibility to the flattery of suffering to play to it and it brought the desired result.

"You will see what I mean when you meet him which, I assume, is what you want to do. Can I ask that at this stage you do not bring cameras?" Scott reassured her in total honesty that there was no question of cameras at this stage.

"Can you manage tomorrow at two p.m.? My father sleeps later and later and, you will see, preparing him for the day takes some time. By early evening he is often asleep again and I would like you to see him while he is most lucid both for his sake and yours," Scott agreed gratefully.

She ended the call to Christopher's frank admiration. He suspected he had seen a more authentic incarnation and liked it. It was getting late and, emboldened by the conspiracy of transgression, she said: "Buy Helena dinner?"

He looked at her and said rather Bondishly; "I'd rather buy it for you."

Jonty did not report his wife missing. To do so would have been an admission of failure and the carapace of affable, easy, old-hand colonial which had been a lifelong shell to his hermit crab personality could not bear breaching. If asked, he merely said she'd gone to look after her father who had returned to Ireland.

His fluency in untruth talked its way past interrogation he had never found welcome and which in these circumstances posed an outright threat.

His sons were under the strict *omerta* to which they were well used but the stress of a lost mother told and they were asked repeatedly at school whether things were all right at home as their academic performance began to decline and their unhappiness became physically and behaviourally manifest.

Jonty himself became morose, sitting on brood over a developing sense of grievance which said that Christie was an ingrate and an unfit mother. A suggestion that he never failed to reiterate to his children into whose every action he managed to read implicit accusation.

He drank and hit more often. Sean bearing the brunt as he took on more of the responsibility of caring for his brothers and whose head was filled with those preoccupations and the second-guessing of his father's mood, the tensions of which filled the house with the heaviness of imminent thunder.

Moreover, Sean was the lurking threat. The clear and present danger that in some animal way Jonty knew would one day challenge for leadership of the pride.

Till that day, Sean's second brother, Liam, began most obviously to suffer academically, prompting Jonty increasingly to brand him variations on the theme of 'stupid.' More pertinently, the decline had deprived Jonty of the opportunity to boast, the purpose his children largely served. A filling to any empty man.

All of his sons were, at the Sunday lunchtime bar, variously nascent geniuses, musical prodigies, sporting greats, pioneering scientists or naturally gifted in the various arts. A pantheon of which academies around the world would be justly proud. What they were by the time Jonty got in was, of course, markedly different. The highs of alcohol and acclaim were followed by the lows that came with mundane reality, the shame of the fabulist and the retreat of the ethanol coursing the bloodstream.

One of these, at least, could be remedied. When it was, the potion was taken liberally and to much the same effect as Jekyll to Hyde. A horror emerged, hate-filled and furious, careless with hand and worse with tongue and leaving behind it havoc.

There is, though, an inevitable direction in the course of a tyrant and, like the Rake and the Harlot, Jonty was to follow its progress. The moment when the peasants arrive at the gate, the tanks arrive in the suburbs and the coward locks the bar room door finally to confront his tormentors.

He ignored the signs, of course. The increasing scepticism from neighbours at Christie's never-ending absence and the palpable unhappiness of the brothers. The raised eyebrows at school and the failing powers of charm, braggadocio and bluff.

The changes in Sean too he failed to notice. His son was

growing, his fear turning to hatred, his hatred to a stirring. Sean did not fail to notice. Notice that his father was developing the walk which the fattening man confuses with power, arms spread too far at the side, gait too wide. Noticing that his own strength increasingly took him over the line when he had no right to get there, that the power in his delivery sent the ball harder and faster, that the corridor jostling saw more shy away from him than try to nudge him.

Liam proved the catalyst. It was a Sunday. Inevitably a Sunday. The two-hour lunchtime pub slot done, the nation quiet. Boredom, alcohol, the Sunday blues and closed doors. A weekly lockdown with all its attendant symptoms. And Liam hadn't done his homework. Or, indeed, anything else. Not that Jonty cared but it was a chance to humiliate. To have the boy stood before him and scorned. The usual lashes of failure, stupidity and worthlessness. The usual licks of shame.

Sean interrupted a flurry of clips to the head, red-penned exercise books flying like disabled white-winged birds at his sobbing brother. His father, heavy-breathed with fury, paused only to give his eldest son a look that promised nothing more than a place in the queue.

Fear had turned to hatred. Hatred to a stirring.

Liam took his brother's arrival as an opportunity to run. He bolted for the front door and the safety of the street outside, fumbling desperately at the latch as his father pursued him with an open hand swiping at his head and his boot flying at the boy's retreating backside.

Sean watched Liam make his escape. Jonty turned, his unabated fury cheated by his son's quick thinking and quicker feet. He would be outside now, his breath hiccupping and his hand finding the bruises of slapped skull and pulled hair and soothing them with his own gentle rubbing. There was no-one else to do it. He would wander, find somewhere quiet and cry.

Faced now with his eldest, his nemesis, Jonty said, "Right you..." and advanced. The ghost of a smile briefly crossed Sean's lips. He was going to fight and he knew with a certainty that he was going to win.

He didn't wait. He flexed his knees and drove his right shoulder into his father's oncoming bulk using his thighs to provide the force behind the impact. It drove the man backwards onto a door frame. Taken aback and realising he was trapped, Jonty covered up quickly, head down behind his forearms as he tried to collect himself.

Sean didn't want to grapple, he had strength and fitness but his father had the advantage in weight and size. He bounced backwards out of any developing clinch, flung out a left handed jab to test the strength of the guard he faced and watched Jonty almost curl up behind the screen he'd created.

His shoulders were rounded, his face down toward the floor, he had half raised a leg as though somehow this would ward Sean off. It didn't. Sean sent in a long, looping right- handed upper cut straight under his father's guard and into his down-turned face. He sent it in with such force that his father was brought bolt up-right, his shocked face emerging above his clenched hands with a trickle of blood already running from his rapidly bruising nose and his eyes staging a bout between unconsciousness and total, utter surprise.

Sean shaped for a left hook at the now revealed head. He never landed it. Unconsciousness had won the fight in Jonty's brain and he keeled over in slow motion like a drunk torn between gravity and dignity in a long, straight line to the floor.

It occurred to Sean that his father was faking it. He knew

what he'd seen. Cowardice. From the very first moment he'd been driven backwards Jonty had known he was in trouble and had simply sought to hide. Nothing had come back. Nothing.

Sean felt oddly calm. School rules said 'give the fucker a good kicking.' Sean said it was over. He nudged the prostrate body. It was out cold. He felt no triumph. Merely a sense of the inevitable and with it, leaking into the stream of it like a contaminant, a sulphurous contempt.

He looked up. His youngest brother was peering down through the bannisters, clasping a soft toy he was now too old for and looking in equal part frightened, disbelieving and at Sean like the very living God.

Not for the first time, Sean felt as though he was detached, watching himself in a scene over which he had only minimal direction. He went outside and found Liam who had got no further than the space between two parked cars only a few yards away. He took Sean's offered hand, looking at him questioningly and wondering what new miseries waited inside.

Their father came round as they came back in. Staggering to his feet in obvious confusion, he almost fell through the open door repeating only "I've got to go," and weaving away down the path and out towards the road.

Sean watched him go. He knew bullies. Jonty would present himself as a victim. He would present himself as bullied, running to the very authorities he had tried to avoid. And he would do so with the self-pitying righteousness of a Lear.

Sean didn't care. His clarity of mind during the fight had taken him aback. If there was rage, it was cold. He had not thrown the left hook nor delivered the kicks for a reason. His father would stagger into a police station or a phone box, claim that his adolescent son had set about him and that he was desperately concerned for his other children. But Sean knew the score, fair fight in self-defence was one thing, hospitalising the bastard quite another.

They turned up forty minutes later. No sirens, no lights but a white Rover drawn up in front of the house. Jonty was in the back seat looking battered and sullen. He wanted to stay there but the two uniformed coppers made him get out. Sean came out to greet them but they told him to go back in the house if only to keep distance between him and his father.

One came in with him and asked what had happened. He knew anyway. It was the days when policemen knew their beat and swapped notes on its characters. It wasn't the first time they had visited the house to find either Christie looking tear-stained or the kids terrified. It was also the days when they did nothing more than hand out a warning unless someone had ended up in what they then called 'Casualty' at the local hospital.

Jonty had always bluffed his way through it and coerced the complicity of the family. Not this time. Sean looked plain and determined. His brothers backed him up, the policeman squatting in front of them with his hat in his hand while their father stood outside in the misplaced certainty of retributive justice, right there, and on his behalf.

The uniform looked Sean up and down and went through the motions of severity but, as he left, he patted the boy briefly on the shoulder in a gesture stranded somewhere between complicity, congratulation and deep, deep sorrow.

The policemen spoke to Jonty outside. A lecture he briefly tried to counter with a caricature of outraged citizen, the easy recourse of the offended middle classes. The response was unexpected, one of them closing the gap on him in a single pace, the other now behind and blocking any line of retreat, leaning right in and saying something inaudible but unequivocal.

Jonty glanced briefly at the window to see his sons witness his humiliation. He looked as downcast as a boy promised a caning, his face bruised and his eyes full of the sullen sadness of someone unable to see his part in his own downfall.

The police left and Jonty traipsed inside. He had little choice. He glanced at his eldest son. "I suppose you're proud of yourself. In front of your brothers. In front of the street." Sean did exactly as the policeman had done and narrowed the ground, his father stumbling a step backwards, he had no intention in indulging either the self-pity or the diversionary feint this skirmish was designed to provoke.

"Where is she, dad? Where did she go?"

"She's abandoned you, that's where. She fucked off and left us all but you in particular. You kids. We were happy before you but you, you…" he jabbed a finger at Sean, self- righteousness lighting a fire under his now developed sense of persecution and briefly overriding his new-found caution near his son, "You all thought she was fucking great but look at you. This is what that bitch left you to deal with, that's how much she fucking cared."

Sean slapped his face. A left-handed crack which moved Jonty's jaw and transformed the sound into a momentary wet 'clack.' He did it deliberately, he wanted noise, frightening noise, to stop his father's emotional onslaught.

His father eyed the phone. Sean went to the wall and unplugged it with a sharp snatch. He was precociously aware that he was treading a fine line between what he wanted to achieve and what he dreaded becoming, but he knew Jonty well enough to know that having lost the physical battle he would move straight towards trying to cause as much psychological damage as possible.

"I'm going to ask you again, dad. Where is she? I don't want your commentary. A location or 'I don't know.' That's all that's required."

Rubbing his face, a defeated Jonty simply shook his head. "I've never heard from her since the day she left. I can't ask anybody now either. I'd have heard via somebody though, I think, if she'd made contact."

Trapped by his own lies, he sat down casting covetous glances at a bottle of whisky left, with last night's glass, on a bookshelf. One of the boys could clear it up. She was their fucking mother and it was her fucking job. Sean followed his glance and moved it.

He had a mind for song lyrics. Something about 'sipping from the Devil's bottle and he just came in' came unbidden. He didn't want his father drinking himself brave or maudlin. As things stood, Sean was just about in control of the situation and he intended to remain so.

He plugged the phone back in, lifting the receiver from the cradle and listening to the line buzz back into life.

"Phone. Phone everyone now. Ask if they've heard from her."

Sullenly, Jonty started to dial, Sean listening to the dull whirr as the disc registered a digit and then returned for the next, each phone number taking an eternity. He could hear the ringing and imagine the plod to a phone in hall somewhere. Jonty's *bonhomie* sounding hollow as he asked each if they'd heard from Christie. He tried to avoid the obvious questions in response. He may as well have been casting family friends one by one into the void. Few would speak to him again. Lying, like success, is rarely forgiven and most of them were merely having suspicions confirmed.

Sean would do it all again later. In person where he could, just to ensure that they hadn't been sworn to secrecy by his tearful mother. But he was damned if he'd turn up as Jonty's herald. For once, his father could endure the bloody shame of what he'd done to them.

Only Jonty's sister offered him either solace or sympathy. His family had long proven adept at finding mitigation for his behaviour, their capacity for fractious mutual loathing and easy offence dissipated at anything resembling an external threat. In this case, Christie.

Sean could hear her building a case against her sister-in-law and the suggestion, at first insidious and then emphatic with invective, that this was the inevitable and head-shakingly obvious conclusion to a misguided marriage to 'a mad Irish bitch like that.' She offered to come over and look after the boys. Jonty looked to Sean for permission. He shook his head, he noticed the shift in power and didn't want it diluted by an ally to his father who would collude in his capacity for creative fiction. He was in line of fire now and knew it.

The last call made, the older man sat back. He had adopted the mask of a sad clown. A caricature of down-turned mouth, he was short only a painted tear and the comic sympathy of a circus crowd.

Sean felt the contempt start to leach once again into his blood stream. As ever, a pretence, a charade, the cosmetics of being wronged.

"You'll chip in. You'll stay out of our way. The moment we or you can fuck off, we'll do it. Lift a fist or boot to the boys again…" He let the threat hang. They were too many to enumerate anyway, from public unmasking to Sean's right hand. Sean rather thought it was the former Jonty feared most. Tearing down the curtain to find a little man with a megaphone and a smoke machine.

His father cringed on the sofa. Briefly, very briefly, Sean allowed himself to revel in the irony. He turned and left. Behind him, lay a boyhood and the sound of a drink being poured.

They had gone to a local restaurant, up the hill from the station and into Blackheath Village where the choice was evenly spaced out between eateries and estate agents. Christopher remembered when it had been more Bohemian. A sort of shabby gentility, punctuated by bookshops and art suppliers along with shops that sold tangible things like toys and newspapers, fruit and meat. He remembered his brother taking a Christmas job in the butchers.

They'd all had jobs. With the milkman, behind a bar or down at Greenwich market when it still supplied wholesale to greengrocers. Now it was crafts and street food. All changed by time and the flashing towers over the river which had flooded the area with money, nannies and the tastes of women with time and Land Rovers and men on five grand bicycles.

Christopher tried not to bore Scott with his reminiscences. It only accentuated the age difference, of which he had suddenly become acutely aware.

Scott was relaxed. More relaxed than he had seen her. Her confidence was growing and it scoured away the artifice she had created to fit in and to please. He tried not to think so but she was beautiful in her natural colours. It was her turn to smile now and she did so winningly.

They settled at a table. A three-piece band was just warming up at the far end of the restaurant and for a long moment she watched them. She loved the construct of music, the synchronicity of song, built from the first notes until the beat came in behind it and the bass gave the whole thing solidity.

He watched her, enjoying her curiosity and pleasure. They ate and discussed their musical tastes and he let her take the slack by telling him of her life before policing and how her ambitions had run in to the realities of corporate life. Of its demands daily willingly to suspend disbelief and its ironically Communist insistence on blind loyalty, leadership cults and applause.

Mick Raglan had been right though, Scott was not in her *milieu* here either. She was possessed of many of the virtues required for the police; bright, brave and determined but she was with them, not of them. Whether she was aware of it or not, she gave the impression of trying it out. It was in her look and in her demeanour but more, he thought, it was in a sadness at the way the world turned. It was neither *naïveté* nor shocked horror more a dull ache for humanity. Christopher hoped she didn't feel that for him.

If so, she disguised it well. Scott embraced the evening wholeheartedly, ate and drank freely and let herself show by increasing degrees. Christopher liked her more with each passing minute but was increasingly taken aback by the extent to which she lived in disguise.

The earnest seriousness had pushed everything else aside as though it were deadening blanket over what she really was. Was this what she demanded of herself of what she thought was demanded of her?

All of us present a mask to the world, he thought. He had seen its extremes in the killer who, according to his neighbours, was polite and in that well-worn hedge side interview phrase 'kept himself to himself' or the drug dealer and pimp who insisted on describing himself as 'a businessman'. This was more benign, of course, but he felt for a moment as if she were as lost as he and had stumbled into his world as though knocking at the wrong hotel door.

She noticed him looking at him and paused mid-sentence, uncertain whether he approved or otherwise. "Am I talking too much?" she asked. He shook his head. "I was just wondering where you go to when the sun comes up."

Scott eyed him while she decided whether she had just been paid a compliment or vaguely insulted. She paused on a slightly embarrassed smile and opted for compliment.

"Do you think I'm different?" she ventured. He nodded. "Who's the real Rachel?"

She pondered the question for a moment as though it was for the first time it had ever been raised.

"I don't quite know. Perhaps a bit of both. Nature and nurture. One has to adopt a façade of total commitment in the life I had before. You might argue that humour is perspective. They will argue that to be taken seriously, one must be serious. It's practical too. The wrong joke, the wrong time and it's HR and re-education. Or worse. One man's humour is another's wound."

Christopher agreed sympathetically.

"But it's a little more than that. What is it Kipling wrote about 'nor look too good nor talk too wise?'" Scott continued.

"Then you will be a man, my son," said Christopher, filling in the essence.

"Only, I'm a woman and, forgive me if this sounds immodest, hover precariously on the verge of doing both, however unintentionally. Doing one makes other women loathe you and the other makes men feel threatened. I've learned that bland efficiency keeps all parties happy."

"Including you?" asked Christopher, wincing slightly at the implications of what she had said.

Scott looked momentarily crestfallen. She started to say something and then swallowed it back.

"Shall we go?" she suggested.

Christopher honoured his pledge and his preference and bought Rachel dinner. Buttoning up, they walked into the fairy lit street, the fading sound of the band following them as the door swung slowly shut behind them.

They walked aimlessly, slowly, as people do when hoping for serendipity to fill in courage's blanks.

She suddenly turned to him, blocking his path, and kissed him. "You make me happy," she said. "Happy to come to work. Happy to belong. Happy to help. Happy."

Astonished, Christopher's mind filled quickly with confusion and questions, a little delight tainting the reservoir. He was unused to being associated with happiness. Moreover, he was her senior officer, older, fond of her and he didn't want to do her harm.

He opened his mouth and she stopped it with another kiss. Kissing him hard until she felt him relax. She pulled back and studied his eyes, reaching briefly for his cheek and stroking it with the back of her fingers. "Happy," she said again. She took his arm and easily, happily, she walked him towards a pub and one last drink.

Scott pulled into the long u of a gravel drive in a small village just outside Sevenoaks. The house, by contrast, was large, period and very well kept. Wisteria shaded the front door and huge glass windows let in light. She could imagine housemaids making a fire in every room in winter, a permanent job of stoking and dust from a time when coal and wood were heat and the wealthy burnt it in abundance.

She and Christopher had parted the previous evening with one more lingering kiss and a brief clutch of hands. They had decided that it was best if she went alone to see the Grummans. Years in the force had left their taint on him and the upper middle classes could smell it to the much the same distaste as they might the criminal. They were only friends with the chief constable. Best an inspector didn't call.

By contrast, Scott was playing at home. A private school education and a good university had left her used to imposing entrance halls and the distant blue glimmer of a pool sunk into the grounds. Somewhere she could hear the distinctive thwap of tennis balls being struck, quickly, repeatedly as someone responded to the tossed Slazengers of a coach. An elongated 'Goooood!' came from behind a hedge. Scott heard her youth replayed.

A woman appeared, first through the clear glass pane of an inner door and then, busily, at the front door itself. She had an apron on and was drying a cup. Rachel knew her in a second, her mother, her mother's friends, numbing themselves with the anaesthesia of permanent activity, eternal usefulness.

"Women aren't happy unless they're busy," her father would chuckle as the young Rachel's indignation rose to the latest chore he had allowed, or, more accurately, not protested at his wife doing. She smiled at the memory. Perhaps he hadn't been wrong.

"Helena?" she asked.

"That's right. Camilla?" The two women all but embraced. They recognised each other and the rapport was instant.

Not for the first time, Scott pondered on how easily conmen and assassins could thrive. It merely took looking the part to the point of authenticity, questions thereafter became fewer and fewer as the mark transferred the money or the security guard nodded you through. One of us, one of the tribe. She felt, what was the word her father would have used? 'A heel.'

She was given tea in a spacious sitting room, Camilla quizzing her superficially on the nature of the programme Scott was making as she fussed around with the paraphernalia of milk and saucers.

Scott kept her answers breezy but brief. She knew this act for what it was, a cover for scrutiny without direct interrogation though she had the notion that the detail, such as it was, was most likely to emerge only in social one-upmanship or a casual conversation with a cousin or friend in the World Service. Neither posed much threat.

What plainly concerned Camilla more was how Scott would deal with her father. In this, she was direct.

"I'm going to bring daddy in, in a moment." Scott winced slightly at the nursery habits of the upper middle classes. The sting was more acute for knowing she was as guilty. This woman was in late middle age but was still, somewhere, sat with her legs crossed with the one glass of sherry she was allowed when people came round and daddy holding forth at the fireplace. She glanced to her left to find it there, imposing and blackly silent on a warm day.

"He's in good form today, quite lively," this time Scott had visions of a race horse owner meeting his trainer, "but I warn you that you will have to be very patient. It takes him considerable time to articulate anything of complexity and the best thing is to try not to fill the silences. It makes him feel pressured and diverts his thoughts."

Scott nodded obediently, a look of benign shared pain falsely smeared onto her face which Camilla scrutinised for making the right signals.

She softened. "Helena, darling, I must warn you that my father is very physically damaged and it will shock you when you see him. He has lived for years in a state of either pain or anaesthesia and I think he is only now beginning to allow himself recognition of what he has become. Under his heartiness, he is embarrassed. Under his remorseless cheerfulness, he is terribly sad. He is using his last energy on various projects he wants completed before he dies and this is one of them."

She then looked Scott full in the face, taking her hand softly and patting it. "I don't entirely believe you are who you say you are. I don't know why but it's instinct. But the same instinct tells me that your motives are benign and that you will help daddy do what he needs to do before time is up. Would you like to tell me now?"

Scott felt as though her own mother had caught her in a lie about where she was when out late or smelt cigarettes in her bedroom. More, given what she had just been told, she felt ashamed.

Camilla's shrewdness had combined with the most polite frankness to reduce her to little more than a child. Scott had noted the refusal to use euphemisms like 'pass' or 'lose' for her father's imminent demise. He was going to die.

Camilla had the practical robustness of the very last vestiges of her class and age. Kind but unsentimental, dutiful but unperformative, Camilla's forebears came and went under the sun and in places far away, their sons and husbands lay in tombs adorned with county regiment colours and forlorn hope honours while it was their women who soldiered on.

She had kept guardianship of their stoicism and their disarming charm all under the great disguise of a chattering bluffness, while her keen eyes missed nothing.

111

Scott felt utterly unmasked, as though she had just said something very adolescent in the middle of an adult conversation. She could hear her father again: "You're making the great mistake of the clever, Rachel, and thinking everybody else is stupid."

"I'm sorry, Camilla, I'm with the police but here unofficially and my real name is Rachel." She fumbled for her warrant card and, aware of the irony, gave up everything hoping that it would save her the full price of her crime.

When she had done, Scott was again indebted to the older woman's kindness. Camilla smiled and in her most headmistressly fashion said: "There now, that wasn't so bad, was it?" She winked at her to show she wasn't unaware of the tone she had adopted.

Now she was brusque and business like again. "I'm glad it's this way," she said. "We can help two poor men at once. And besides, the BBC has become so terribly left wing." And with that, she went to get her father.

The man Camilla wheeled in was incomplete. That was the only word Scott could think of afterwards. He had lost his right leg, just above the knee. His right arm also had gone at a point just below his elbow. Neither had the prosthetics one had become used to seeing in the aftermath of war in Afghanistan or Iraq, where IEDs had torn the limbs from strong and active young men and left them with bionic replacements, a wan cheeriness and a nice line in black humour.

Perhaps he was too old. Perhaps it was too late. In any event, it was hardly what Scott noticed. Nor too the bulge beneath Henry Grumman's perfectly laundered, sky blue short- sleeved shirt and which, she assumed, helped his body clear his waste.

She did notice the red spotted cravat tied round his neck and it immediately reminded her of one of her father's late life affectations. A film star disguise for a wattle neck. She rather suspected Grumman's covered worse.

She noticed because she was looking at his face which she could tell had once been patrician and handsome and, even now, was topped with a sleek wave of silver hair. It was ruined.

On the right side, was the sort of skin one saw on the faces of burnt Hurricane pilots, pale, mottled and stretched. Most of his jaw had obviously been replaced but it had left him with a sort of rictus like a grinning skull, an impression made starker by a fixed and staring eye which was plainly glass. The left one swivelled towards her in a way she could only describe later to Christopher as reptilian.

Scott suddenly remembered having read in a Sunday newspaper supplement about a hospital, St Mary's, then in the semi-rural setting of London's most south-eastern suburbs and which had pioneered surgery on men whose faces the First World War had destroyed. They had wandered the grounds, unable to present their monster visages to a horrified world but united in the shared experience of what high explosive could do to a body.

It was, of course, what had happened to Grumman. Camilla interrupted her study of this poor, destroyed man.

"Daddy, this is Rachel," she explained no further about where she was from or who she represented, "if you don't mind, I'm going to tell her the beginnings because it will help us get more quickly to what you saw and I think that's most important. Are you happy with that?"

As Grumman nodded, Scott noted how Camilla paid her father the respect of asking whether he was content with the course of action. There was no hint either of infantilising him nor being exasperated by his inability to speak quickly. She plainly loved him very much. Scott again felt humbled.

"Daddy used to work at Lloyds, the insurance market, which is near Cornhill, in the City. We didn't live in Sevenoaks at the time. This was his own father's house at the time while we had one in Greenwich, which was the station from which daddy caught the train on the morning of the explosion. He was slightly later than normal and then there was some problem with the service which meant he didn't take his regular one direct to Cannon Street, his nearest station to Lloyds, because it had been cancelled."

At this point, Grumman gurgled slightly and nodded along in agreement. It was almost, even at this distance, as though he felt he had to explain his tardiness or, perhaps, Scott thought, it was regret that breaking his routine had cost him so much. On such 'what ifs,' minds get stuck and she thought of Sean Christopher. Briefly. Fondly.

The woman continued: "His intention had been to travel to London Bridge and then change for Cannon Street unless by that time he felt like walking over the bridge and into the Square Mile.

"When the bomb went off, he was very close to it. Very close indeed. That he survived at all is miraculous but by dint of the various changes in explosive dynamic caused by seats, other people, the position of the bomb and so on, he didn't quite bear the full brunt he might have done. What he did bear was bad enough.

"My father," and here Scott noticed in the change of noun a change to considerable pride but, she also couldn't help but feel, the beginnings of a eulogy "lost his right arm and leg. Though not immediately, they were amputated later. Ball bearings and other debris tore at explosive speed into his abdomen and some

114

passed straight through him, damaging his organs. The upward force took his jaw, part of his tongue and his eye.

"They couldn't kill him," she said suddenly, angrily, defiantly, "They couldn't kill him though they tore bits off him. And do you know, when they found him, he had put his good arm round the man beside him and he had died on his chest?"

For a moment, Camilla paused, she turned to her father and squeezed his remaining hand, her cheeks flushed with all emotions but, above all, a furious love.

"Daddy spent months in a coma. Several times we were asked whether we would like to let him slip away. Twice, a priest came because we thought he would die anyway. Sometimes, a policeman would appear to see if he could tell them anything. He couldn't, not just because he was in a coma but because he had no jaw and only half a tongue. Eventually, the policeman stopped coming.

"When finally, he came to, he could remember very little though his brain started to function again quite quickly and to a surprising degree of normality. Then there were years, yes, years of reconstructive surgery and speech therapy.

"My father is a very traditional man and a strong one. His own father had survived the war but was haunted by terrible dreams of fighting the Japanese, the effects of which stayed with him for the rest of his life. Daddy watched him combat these demons and do so with commendable courage. It depressed him greatly when he too started to suffer nightmares and flashbacks. PTSD they call it. What it did to him physically made it harder. There are no indignities this man has not suffered. Not a one.

"In all this time, I have never heard him utter a syllable of bitterness nor self-pity, though I have heard him cry out in pain and frustration many times. It is typical of him that, even now, he

115

wants to do something, whatever that may be with what he knows. You'll help him, won't you Rachel? "

Henry Grumman was looking at his daughter, he reached over and stroked her arm with the tenderness one would save for a new-born and he smiled. Smiled to reveal the incongruously pristine teeth an orthodontist had made for him, smiled to show that his jaw was still scarcely mobile, smiled in a way that betrayed his reconstructed tongue and he smiled with a beatific love that made all those revelations seem utterly irrelevant.

Scott looked on. She had no right to cry, though she wanted to. Neither of the Grummans did so. She had no right to usurp their emotions and despised the modern habit of doing so, the piggy back ride to showing you care. But rarely had she wanted to break down so badly.

Her refusal to do so was right. Camilla was watching her. Watching her in a way that suggested she wanted action, not sympathy. Scott had already resolved to provide it.

Grumman himself took up the tale.

"I got on, as Camilla said, at Greenwich. The train was already very crowded and I was resigned to being quite late." He paused whilst his mouth regathered itself for the next effort.

"I was reading my *Financial Times* which, over many years of practice, I had become adept at folding so that it could be read in overcrowded carriages." There was, again, a sort of hiatus while Grumman collected the faculties of speech. Scott was reminded of a young rider, shortening her reins and finding again the stirrups after a challenging jump.

This time, he managed a short canter. "Because of the angle at which I was stood, I could see over my paper and downwards at a man on one of the bench seats. He struck me as agitated. At first I thought nothing of it. In those days train travel could be claustrophobic. It was a common enough joke that British Rail would have been fined if they had transported livestock in the conditions they transported the southern commuter.

"It was also probable that he was late for an appointment and increasingly fidgety at his powerlessness over events. I distinctly remember feeling sympathetic. He was dressed in a suit which didn't quite fit and he looked a little down at heel. I thought he must be going to a job interview that had taken on disproportionate significance. Unemployment at the time was high, very high, and many were struggling."

At this point, his daughter gave Grumman a drink of water which he swallowed to the sound of a gurgling drain.

He began again. "There was a long hiatus outside London Bridge. There often was and particularly if there had been some sort of earlier disruption. During that wait, I noticed that the man was nervy almost to the point of anguish. He caught my eye and I rolled my eyes in a sort of expression of unity.

"I got nothing for my troubles except a look of the most withering contempt. It was a difficult time politically and there was a lot of class hatred about. I was aware I looked what I was and put it down to that. I was prosperous, public school and calm. He was dark, bearded and pugnacious and I'm afraid I dismissed him at that point as just another angry Trot, a Citizen Smith hardly worth taking seriously, and I went back to my paper."

Scott missed the reference to an old TV series but she grasped the point and again waited for Grumman to catch his breath.

He spurred himself on to one final effort. "As we pulled into the station, he started almost to hurl people aside in his desperation to get to the door. He started shouting about being ill. He had an Irish accent and I could place it because my father went regularly to a charming hotel in the west of that country to fish and I often went with him.

"I felt somewhat guilty for judging the man, nobody wants to embarrass themselves in public, so I asked people to try and let him out. Again, I was rewarded with a glance. It was one of hatred. There's no other word for it. Hatred. But it carried with it a sense of satisfied menace. Fleeting but there. Then he was gone and then the bomb went off."

"And you're convinced he planted it?" asked Scott.

Grumman wheezed and slurped into life again. "Quite convinced that he knew about it. He absolutely knew. My daughter tried for some time to convince me that I was fixated but, as my mind has cleared, that conviction has hardened rather than diluted.

"Here," he said and with his good hand he shuffled a piece of paper to Scott. "My poor, long suffering daughter is quite the artist and she has sketched this man time and again to my description until I think she has not just a good likeness but something of his essence."

Scott looked down at the sketch. A man glowered back. He was, as Grumman had said, a little unkempt. She had expected to see a darkly messianic figure, the glint of religiously inspired zealotry beaming from his eyes almost like the cartoon image of a supervillain.

She realised she was making a caricature, a composite of modern experience and the assassins of the past. The man who looked back seemed almost, bookish. His longish hair in an artistic wave and the eyes sad. He looked slightly built, though the sketch showed nothing more of his body than the upper torso. The shoulders of his suit were unfilled by muscle or breadth and the collar of his shirt stood away from a slim neck. The tie's large knot betrayed the era and accentuated the effect of a boy wearing a man's jacket.

"Does it help?" Camilla asked. "It might." said Scott.

Grumman was wheezing regularly and grimacing occasionally. Scott beat Camilla to the inevitable.

"Mr Grumman, thank you so much for what you've told me, it's the strongest pointer we've had so far but I think you're tired now and I would like to let Camilla take care of you."

His daughter smiled gratefully, interrupting Grumman's attempts at polite dismissal of her concerns and his insistence that she should call him Henry.

"You will act on it, won't you?" he asked, almost pleadingly.

Scott grasped his hand and squeezed it. "My word on it." she said.

"And I suspect Rachel always keeps her word, don't you Rachel?" Once again back before the headmistress, Scott nodded penitently to Camilla.

She drove back towards London. Oast houses, pubs and pastoral preservation of West Kent slowly yielding first to the main road and then to the urban sprawl of London's 1930s expansion that had never quite subsumed the rural essence of the capital's far southern suburbs but had scarred their face forever. Ugliness had come like a plague brought from the city.

She resisted the urge to call Christopher straight away. She felt angry and ashamed by what had passed with Henry Grumman and his daughter and perhaps more so for the familial resemblance. Her anger would have shown and Christopher would have felt it, her superior or not.

The sketch of the man Grumman was convinced had been involved in the bombing lay on the front seat. Scott glanced down at it occasionally as she drove. It was clear. Her relationship with

Christopher decreasingly so, forced as it was to occupy a nether world between necessary professional distance and increasing emotional proximity. Scott wanted physical closeness too.

She thought again of what she had just left and felt guilty for pausing, even for a second, on her own desires. They suddenly felt tawdry. Her anger was changing now, its focus less on the embarrassment of being caught in her own deceit but, like Christopher before her, on the realisation of what damage had been done.

Not just to those, there on the day, killed or maimed, but to those like Camilla, Raglan, Christopher and countless others who suffered even now. She pulled over for a moment into the slip road that fed one of those Thirties parades of shops. A dry cleaners, a fish bar, the inevitable curry house, newsagent and a funeral directors.

Above each were flats, the balconies adorned variously with flowers and bicycles, an old roll of carpet or a sun lounger, a trestle of vines climbing up behind it. From the balcony above the chip shop, a crack ran downwards from its metal guard rail. It bled rust into the concrete and a crusty scab of oxidisation had formed where it hung over the street. Beneath, it the pavement was stained brown. Scott felt unutterably depressed. Blood and shit. She'd seen and heard enough of it for one day. For one life time.

Scott started the car and pulled away, chasing off the shadows with the volume button on the radio, she headed back towards the station and Christopher with the bass from the speakers audible outside and her right hand pounding out the beat on the wheel.

She was alive and defiant and suddenly that felt good.

Lewisham nick was modern and had the look of a newly built school. Inside, it had yet to absorb the seediness of overuse and criminality. Scott had worked in worse. Christopher certainly had. Victorian Gothic monuments to the desk sergeant and the majesty of the law, grimy utilitarian Sixties salutes to a brave new post-War Britain.

Only the former had stood the test of time though most were now restaurants with the novelty of cells in the basement or houses prevented by listing from being too radically altered. They would always look what they were.

Christopher couldn't see the attraction, he knew what had gone on inside. Once there had been a station everywhere. People walked, people talked. They didn't any more, not in the same way. Life was outside the home then. On the street. Hanging off the back of a bus. In the pub or the market or the queue at the shop. Strolling bobbies, flexing their knees and saying 'evening all'. He laughed to himself. Next thing the same bobbies would be handing out a hiding to some hard case out of sight at Carter Street nick. That was flats now. Period charm. If only they knew.

He was laughing to himself when Scott came in. Her mood had lifted and she was glad to see Christopher equally light-hearted.

"What's so funny?" she asked in mock aggression.

"When you're older, I'll tell you." he said in feigned schoolyard cockiness.

Well, he thought, he might. "It isn't the job it used to be," was every copper's most boring refrain. It wasn't. For better and worse.

The atmosphere between them was easy, playful. She liked it. So did Christopher but he was always careful not to overdo it when others were around. He had nothing to lose and she had plenty, though Scott seemed strangely unconcerned by the potential consequences.

They worked among the observant and among all the sexual tensions of men and women confined, under stress and united in a shared experience that wasn't easily dissipated or expressed at home. Marriages came and went. More casual relationships died even more cheaply and the working environment had little tolerance for anything either misconstrued or improperly meant.

For the right reasons, a layer of artifice was draped over the infinite variables of human attraction and all of them had to live with the often arbitrary and random results.

He raised his eyebrow interrogatively and Scott filled him in on both the substance and the colour, handing him the sketch of which she had run off copies as she came through the office.

Christopher didn't immediately look at it. Instead, he asked, "What's your feeling?"

"Oh, I've no doubt whatsoever, he means what he says. Take in the all the imponderables of time, memory, injury and, of course, 'the story one tells oneself' as you lie in a hospital bed rationalising a catastrophe and there's a million more questions to be asked but he is convinced. I'll be honest, I am too." She added.

Christopher nodded. "Well, I trust your judgement, it's a question of whether we can trust his." He looked down at the sketch.

"Doesn't mean anything to me but it's before my time and outside my experience. We'll have to get it checked out against the records and let all the interested parties know. Special Branch and so on."

"I might get the boss to do that," he added. "Truth is they'll want to know why we've been sniffing around it and that will take Peter's particular expertise in saying all and nothing at all."

Christopher realised he'd been too informal about Francis. He had a privilege Scott didn't and he didn't want to make her feel the woman in the Long Room, standing at the door and passing a message while the boys had another and roared laughing.

In any event, she didn't seem to have noticed. He looked at her softly. "And how are you?"

"Oh," she smiled, "Just hanging on your praise, obviously."

"Well − obviously − I've rarely seen better investigative policing." He supplied. "Does that help?"

"Only a little. This afternoon was emotionally draining. A bit close to home personally and I didn't enjoy being caught lying. Crafty cow," she added, admiringly, of Camilla. "Worse, I've got to do it all again tomorrow with Mrs Miles."

Christopher nodded and smiled sympathetically. The preceding evening's events hung between them as they looked at each other.

"I enjoyed it," he ventured, not needing to spell out what he meant. "Enough to do it again?" she asked.

"Enough to insist on it."

"Boss, I do believe you're abusing your position of authority but if that's what it takes to get on…" she looked at him coquettishly, tossing her head back and to one side like a star of silent movie melodrama.

"Well, it's either that or you risk a disciplinary!" Christopher looked at her guilelessly as if there was no other way in which the proposition could be construed but as proper process.

Scott couldn't help but laugh.

"Seriously," he asked, "You know the dangers, don't you?"

"I really don't care," she said.

And that really did give Christopher something to consider.

The meeting with Caroline Miles was an easier one.

She was, of course, elderly and age had prompted a timidity which took Scott some time to embolden, just as when they had first spoken, but developed very quickly into a loquacious confidence.

Miles lived in a small ground floor flat in Camberwell, not far from another hospital, King's College at which she had trained and then finished her career a nurse.

Unlike Grumman, She had no protective adult off-spring to guard her. No sign, in fact, no children at all. Her photographs and memorabilia had none of the loving banality of shared holidays, school sports days or the graduation and marriage of a beloved son or daughter.

She came in with a tea pot to find Scott staring at the black and white picture of a notably handsome man in the white coat of a doctor and with a stethoscope strung from his neck. He leaned forward slightly as though speaking to an invisible patient. The artful contrivance of a photographic studio.

Following her gaze, she stooped and looked fondly at the picture before giving a sort of dismissive snort and pottering back out to her kitchen for the rest of the tea things.

When she returned, Miles said: "If he can do that to you now, imagine what he could then and in the flesh. I'm afraid he was too attractive for my own good."

Scott let her continue. She saw the signs of loneliness and isolation. As much as anything, the woman wanted to talk. Between Raglan, Grumman and now Miles, she was being treated to a vision of old age that seemed predicated on just waiting. Waiting for the inevitable while either alone or burdensome.

Outside the window, London teemed by aggressively. On the green, the fractured chaos of urban existence played itself out. Scott didn't know which must be the more frightening in old age. To be locked in or thrown out.

"Yes, all the warning signs were there. Too handsome, too clever. Bad things in a doctor. All this and the power of healing. You can imagine what it induces," said Mrs Miles.

"He was your husband?" inquired Scott.

Miles gave a rueful smile. "Briefly, ingloriously. I'd braced myself for the infidelities. Look at him. There's no sisterhood. He taught me that. Half the girls who had cheered us out of the church were in bed with him either before or shortly afterwards. I always consoled myself that I was at least in possession of the prize." She pointed to a ring on her finger.

"But no, he had ambition. Which as a pretty little nurse I served only while he was a junior doctor and I looked like a good match at the time. Less so as Harley Street beckoned. He left me and unfortunately I still loved him. Always did. I've no regrets. It was a calculated gamble and I'm rather afraid I lost."

Scott could bear no more living examples of the vicissitudes of life and moved the subject on as politely as she could.

Miles was good only for the scenery of that day at London Bridge. Had Scott genuinely been making a documentary she would have given any programme context and colour to an award-wining degree.

Scott noted it, absorbed it, but her mission was detail and of that there was little beyond the horrifyingly fascinating minutiae of death to which Miles, presumably by dint of long exposure, seemed immune.

Scott brought up the issue of the disparity in numbers between those declared dead on the scene and those tallied in the morgues.

"I'm not surprised at all," said Miles. "People bestow on doctors, nurses, policemen and firefighters a competence they rarely deserve except in very narrow circumstances and these were exceptional ones."

Scott tried not to smirk.

"There was simply no way to contain and control everything that went on. People were wandering about all over the place. The oddity of disasters - and I have seen a number – is that some very close to the epicentre will walk away hardly scathed while a man three streets away while be hit by falling masonry.

"This makes forming a picture very difficult. We were under enormous pressure to try and triage but the constant movement, the fact that the police took some time to create an effective cordon around the warren of the station and the compelling circumstances some people genuinely had for leaving very quickly, meant the wash of people was continuous."

"I've spoken to a policeman who was there and he was impressed by the organisation of the medical people," interjected Scott.

Miles smiled. "Well, take my ex-husband. He was very adept at giving the impression of omniscience. It's what doctors do. It's called bedside manner. The danger, of course, comes when they start believing it themselves."

"Is it possible somebody could have been declared dead who wasn't?" Scott tried again.

"Oh yes," said Miles. "For all the reasons, I've explained. Chaos, haste, panic, lack of communication. These were also different times. Organisation and so on were very different. I seem to remember the question of numbers coming up shortly afterwards and nobody on our side was the slightest surprised."

Scott had almost run out of lines of enquiry. It was, of course, difficult to be too specific without arousing suspicion. "Apart from the fact of it, was there anything about that day that you remember as not quite right?"

Miles looked at her quizzically. "Have you something particular in mind?"

Scott thought quickly. "Not really, it's just that ultimately our programme is a journalistic enterprise and any new angle, any new story gives what we're doing a new momentum and a reason to return beyond merely a retrospective."

"I'm surprised anyone really wants to," said Miles a little archly.

Scott paused and then: "I have spoken to a number of people, professional, serious people who have been deeply affected by what happened that day. You seem, if you don't mind me saying, remarkably untouched."

Miles considered the point for a long moment. "In all my years in nursing I have seen many things. The blood and the gore is far from the worst of it. The horrors of lingering death, the desolation of parents condemned to watch their children die by hairless degrees. The hero reduced to trembling fear by the wraiths of dementia. The beautiful scarred and the ugly, and by that I mean the wicked, walk away untouched and smirking.

"Training and habit reduce it to the scientific. It's one half of a coping mechanism."

"And the other?" asked Scott.

"The consolation of philosophy. We are in a game of chance. Deserve seems to have so little to do with it. Fortunately for some, less merited for others. I've simply become..." she searched for a word and her eyes alighted on the photograph of the handsome doctor. She trailed away.

"Acceptant?" proffered Scott.

"Not entirely," said Miles. "I could accept the blindness of the Fates. But we were given God and told he's active, the implications of that are very hard to accept."

Scott got up to leave. She was thinking of Miss Havisham[4]. Everyone seemed pinned to the past.

"Numb." said Miles suddenly. "I've simply become numb." Scott followed her gaze and didn't believe her for a moment. It occurred to her that to this woman no other experience could surpass her one moment of triumph and disaster and it had left her trapped forever.

What was it Christopher always said winkingly when confronted with the dark comedy of the human condition? "There's a lot of it about." And he should know, she thought.

Christopher, meanwhile, was trying discreetly to identify the man in Camilla Grumman had sketched. He was aware he owed a wider duty though equally clear that the enthusiasm for pursuing old Irish terrorism cases was limited by politics being the art of the possible.

For the moment, then he felt able to pursue his identity freelance and light of conscience.

Light, in fact, characterised Christopher currently. His humour had returned. That worldly, irreverent humour that found the ridiculous in most things and which had proven both his blessing and curse professionally.

He bounced through the office with the wistfulness that had

---

[4] A character in Dickens' Great Expectations, she was jilted at the altar and spends the rest of her days in her wedding dress.

begun to characterise him of late all but evaporated. More, his energy had returned and he had applied it with increasing vigour to the investigation.

Christopher looked again at the sketch. It had more life in it than a mere photofit or even the grainy old stills of a surveillance photo. He couldn't help but wonder if some artistic interpretation had flowed through Camilla's hand or Henry's instruction. From the people Scott had described he would be unsurprised if a certain innocent creativity hadn't made a poet of a murderer. It was a desire to transpose personality onto the anonymous author of a deed and that demanded a filling of the gaps.

On the other hand, Grumman gained nothing from making a worthy foe of a train bomber. This was no combat man to man with defeat excused by the skill of a champion who reflected back one's virtues.

None of what Christopher had so far summoned up on his computer matched with the charcoaled likeness in his hand, though some came close, and to get more he would have to ask wider. That came with its own dangers.

He thought about Mick Raglan. They had parted on good terms and he had a clear view of what ailed the man. He picked up the phone, then changed his mind and picked up his car

keys. He wanted Raglan caught off guard. Grabbing a copy of the sketch, he headed off to the secure car park and on to Raglan's bungalow.

Christopher was a rare man in finding driving through London relaxing. He likened it to a war. Long periods of bored inactivity followed by brief bursts of adrenaline and action. In the meantime, he could watch the city live.

He'd long taken his mood from it. Today, in sunshine, it was abuzz. He took pleasure in the passing of girls in light dresses and the sight of people outside pubs, their sociability warmed by the weather. He could feel, even through his car door, the heat of an idling bus engine as it sat beside him at traffic lights.

Londoners thronged the entrance to a Tube station and Christopher remembered an old advert for the Underground which showed people floating towards it like bees to the hive. Some school-age adolescent boys passed, pushing, shoving and flexing, their female counterparts doing what was required and either squealing in mock fright or shouting attention-seeking insults.

He smiled.

He still had the smile on his face as he knocked on Mick Raglan's door and, as was his habit, turned away from it to survey the road. There was movement inside and Christopher turned back towards the house watching a shadow working a lock behind the frosted glass before opening it wide.

Raglan still had all the bravado of an old school police hard man and didn't make any timorous enquiries from behind a door.

He looked Christopher up and down knowingly. "Thought you'd be back," he said, "come in."

"Where's the bird?" he asked. To Christopher's surprise he felt himself bridle protectively. 'Old school,' he reminded himself. And he needed old school help.

"Other enquiries, Mick."

"Shame," he said. "A looker." There was a pause. "And I wanted to apologise. I was rude last time. Out of order. To all of you. Her most of all."

Taken aback, Christopher touched Raglan's elbow. "Don't be so bloody silly, Mick. All forgotten and all understood." Raglan nodded appreciatively before wandering off to the kitchen.

He returned with two glasses and a bottle of Jameson whiskey. Irish with an 'e' as the joke went. 'Old habits' thought Christopher glancing at a clock, it wasn't yet six in the evening. Like Scott, he recognised loneliness when he saw it and despite his reservations braced himself to accept.

He also had the feeling that Mick Raglan was old-fashioned enough to view seeing off whiskey as something of a test of manhood, that he was measuring Christopher's worth. If so, he was in for a shock. Christopher was careful near drink without being puritanical.

More, he'd been blessed with the constitution of a beast of the field, particularly near spirits.

He'd become famous for it. When stress and alcohol had left his colleagues staggering, slurred, pugnacious, lustful or lachrymose, Christopher would walk out rock steady and untouched the following morning, smilingly possessed of the knowledge of what everyone else had done but couldn't remember. His popularity had increased in direct proportion to his discretion.

Raglan seemed to read his thoughts: "Usually have one about this time, you'll join me." Christopher noted that it was less a question than an instruction. He smiled acquiescence. "Come and have a go if you think you're hard enough," he thought.

Raglan sploshed two good measures and passed a glass to Christopher, raising his own and swallowing half at the first pass. He sat back with the satisfaction of a man for whom all was right in the world and looked meaningfully at Christopher who took his cue and saw his shot down in a single gulp of honeyed alcoholic strength.

He didn't look at Raglan but instead shuffled through the various papers he'd brought with him with an artful casualness

131

that, whether he knew it or not, impressed his opponent. He knew Raglan was watching him and, when he eventually glanced up at him, the older man was sporting a grin. "Good lad," he said, "You've sussed me." And he poured them both a second.

Christopher winked back and passed Raglan Scott's notes on the conversation with Grumman. Glasses on, he started to read with a feint movement of the lips which, for a moment reminded Christopher of a reciting imam. It didn't sit well with the whiskey.

"Interesting." said Raglan when he had finished. "Have you got the sketch?" Christopher already had it in his hand and gave it to Raglan, noticing as he did so that the older man had coloured slightly. He thought at first that it had been the sudden infusion of Jameson's but then that it was something more.

Raglan was staring intently at the drawing in his hand. He reached forward and, almost mechanically, drank again, replacing the glass with sufficient force for it to slop a little of its contents over the side and on to the coffee table by his legs.

He looked up at Christopher. "That," he said, "is Donal O' fucking Driscoll. I was right all along."

Raglan had the flush of vindication, of relief and of sheer surprise. He kept looking down at the paper, his lips continuing a sort of monastic recital, a silent chant as though weaving round it something protective lest it should be taken from him. He held the drawing like scripture.

Christopher watched him, watched him become almost young before him, as if the spell wrought wider magic. "Donal O' fucking Driscoll," he said again as though saying it would summon him.

"You're sure?" Christopher was concerned that so strong was the desire on Raglan's part for his hunch to be correct that he might too willingly suspend disbelief.

"Oh yes," Raglan said. "Sometimes we had got surveillance photos, other times old public records or photofits and sometimes these men were not far short of public figures. But O'Driscoll was shadowy. I studied and studied what little we had and this is him. Wouldn't notice him if you passed him in the street, which he relied on. But if you were in our business, well, they were your life's work."

Christopher now sat back. The implications were clear enough. Between Grumman and Raglan they had almost certainly identified the man responsible for the London Bridge bombing. It was not Christopher's primary aim but he fully understood it to be of greater wider concern than his own personal pursuit.

He had to report it and then explain how he had managed to get to the point he had. He hoped Francis would be able to pass it off as a happy accident exploited by good police work. Then it was for his political masters to decide whether they wanted to imperil the brittle Irish peace ensured by the Good Friday Agreement that had finally brought an end to the euphemistic 'Troubles' of Northern Ireland's civil war.

He was pleased for Raglan, of course. It was some kind of vindication and, he hoped, some sort of resolution for him. Pleased too that sleepless justice had woken just in time to finally put someone's name in the frame for the carnage, assuming O'Driscoll was still alive. But it brought him no closer to discovering what he really wanted to know.

"Doesn't help you much, does it?" sympathised Raglan.

Christopher looked at him and, for the second time, swallowed his whiskey in one.

133

Scott and Christopher sat looking at each other in silence. Scott was, for the moment, simply spent by the unexpected complexities of human life. A pragmatist by nature, she had the unaccustomed task of separating her philosophical observations from the task in hand.

She was slowly unpicking the two, as if tearing a gummed label from a rare book or a treasured album she hoped not to damage. It was coming, but slowly. This job, her desire to finish what she started, the seemingly intractable investigation formed a heavy glue and she was determined not to let it hurt this man for whom she felt increasingly strongly.

For his part, Christopher was wrestling down the enormity of their discovery. It was, in itself, a triumph but, a little like his cricket catch of childhood, was a coincidental glory born of self-interest. It had been done but more by accident than design.

This left him with several problems which he more or less cared about.

The first was the politics of explanation, the second the politics of execution. In either case, he felt almost embarrassed by his lack of concern. He had, repeatedly, to remind himself of what had happened at London Bridge and had even gone so far as to view the old news footage Scott had unearthed as though to reinvigorate his sense of horror.

Not for the first time, he battled a sense of detachment. A numbed sense of observing from afar. It had haunted him all his life before suddenly rectifying itself in rushes in which sudden anger, joy, love or terrible sadness would over assert themselves as though someone had unblocked a pipe and bottled up feeling would gush.

He should feel more and less. He should feel what was expected of him.

There were other problems too. Challenges. Opportunities. Scott would doubtless tell him which was which.

Her interview with Caroline Miles had rather served to underline the point that the scene of the explosion had been a porous one. People came and went for some time unchecked. The opportunities for people to disappear and reinvent themselves, for them to have staggered around in confusion, for them to have been misidentified, for them to have done any manner of things was almost infinite and, while all their efforts had been predicated on his mother's presence at London Bridge when the bomb went off, it seemed a possibility rather than a probability.

His thoughts swilled and washed at what that meant. What they left was an unpleasant residue that he didn't want to look at. First and most obviously, if Christie had not been there, where had she gone? How had she managed such a complete disappearance?

Christopher's thoughts went back to his humiliating trudge to the doors of every one of the friends and relatives in whom his mother might have confided. The reiterated questions of his father's phone calls.

It had meant pity and it had meant on occasion an unmistakable *schadenfreude*. Another lesson in the vagaries of human nature when he thought he had learned them all. It had meant too, some love and compassion, of which he was in sore need but to which he was becoming immune. He no longer trusted it. Taking root was the growing feeling that he could only rely on himself.

He knew liars too. He lived with the best and worst of them. None were lying as they shook their heads solemnly or attempted weak smiles which they hoped would be encouraging.

The alternative was that she been on that train and had taken an opportunity to disappear. Again, the same questions. How did she do so with such completeness and why had she made no attempt, none whatsoever, to contact him or his brothers?

He was back outside the last of those doors as it clicked gently shut on him. An icy certainty freezing his heart that she had gone and meant to. It was the quantum of solace that came with realisation. Until now. Until all this had once again risen like a hand thrust from the grave to claw at his heart again.

Christopher felt the blockage clear from the pipe and an awful, desolate sadness inundate his soul. He felt for himself, he felt for his brothers and, suddenly, he felt for all those left baffled by a cataclysm they couldn't explain. One that had maimed or bereaved them forever. An act of God. Or the Devil. And now he could put a name to him.

He looked up to find Scott studying him. Kindly. The care in her eyes was obvious as she watched the emotions swirl and sweep across his face. And, for a moment, he felt another, one he dared not name but which compelled him suddenly to stand and, in the privacy of the room they had commandeered, kiss her passionately.

Rachel looked up at him, clasped the hand he had placed at the side of her head, and simply nodded.

The burner phone, which had remained in embarrassed silence between them, buzzed discreetly.

She found the purse and checked its contents. There was cash still in it, driving licence and the family photo staring out from behind a scuffed plastic window. It marred the pretty Irish face and the smiles of the three handsome boys who surrounded her, the youngest a slight nervousness to the eyes. The one-way ticket jutted from behind them accusingly.

Things were very quiet now. She imagined there would be plenty of bustle back by the railway station but here, among the abandoned warehouses and nascent development, it was increasingly cool and dark. The street lighting was ill-maintained and, here and there, non-existent while electricity was switched off and reconfigured around building work.

The smell of excavation fought with the smell of the river. She could hear it, green and serpentine behind its walls. Trapped between its crocodilian green and the sightless eyes of dark warehouse windows, she had an escalating sense of peril.

A few signs warned of works and a lantern or two flashed the presence of a particular hazard to pedestrians but the dark Seventies of lax standards and dangerous streets gave her the sense of walking among the deadlands. A concrete mixer hung from a crane, swaying gently in the riverside breeze and out of the way of thieves.

Her steps had become more hesitant and she almost felt her way between one puddle of light and the next before changing her mind and deciding that being out of sight might be preferable to seeing.

She became increasingly convinced that someone was there. A feeling less of being hunted than being hidden from though even she knew that atmosphere was bound to induce a certain paranoia, particularly after the explosion.

Becoming increasingly tentative, she had now an unshakable sense of proximity. Is this what it felt like? The deer at the pool, convinced but not so much that it doesn't lower its head again to drink. The feeling of nearness, the sudden rush, the death bite, over.

She trod ever more cautiously. Each foot planted more tentatively, almost feeling her way along the paving stones or the pot-holed bitumen of the road. The odour of lifted tar seeped into the miasma of the river. A long way from home. A long way from a friend. Close, though, to something.

She was in the wasteland. Lethe to the one side, life to the other. She could hear it. Traffic moving on the bridge and the squeal of heavy machinery as the wrecked train was recovered. Beasts nudging aside the corpse of one of their own. Occasionally the night lit with the dragon-breath flare of cutting torches. Here had the feeling of the underworld.

Spirits waiting for the ferryman and the sweet drug of amnesia.

God that she could forget. God that she could return. She was walking among the shadows and the demons and had been for too long.

And then she saw him. Small and broken. His feet just visible in the dark maw of an old doorway. He had drawn his knees up towards his chest in foetal self-comfort. His arm clasped to his side like a warrior protecting a wound, the white of revealed skull stark in the darkness. He seemed dead.

Her shadow spread across him and the primal instinct of the hunted drove him to life, first raising his arms to cover himself and then to try and move. He couldn't. He waited for the strike or the shrill cry of alarm that would bring blue lights and heavy boots. Neither came. She was as faceless as Sister Morphine and him unable to crawl across the floor.

Kneeling beside him, she reached for his head wound and, with a hand cool from the night air, stroked away the hair that had stuck in his congealed blood. As she did so, Donal O' Driscoll slipped into the welcoming arms of unconsciousness, a slight smile playing at his lips.

Peter Francis sat with his back to Scott and Christopher. They sat in front of his desk like miscreants. Not that they had transgressed, or at least not in the context of having, almost certainly, established the identity of the London Bridge bomber several decades after the fact.

He had let them explain before, as was his habit, swivelling away as they concluded. It was an attempt to separate the messenger from the message and had served him well down the years when his temptation had been to hurl a bearer of bad news in to the well like a Spartan king.

He was angry but had no target for it except, perhaps, himself. He had played God and now found his creation had staggered off in an unexpected direction. He exhaled softly.

Something ungodly. More on the side of curse than blessing.

He was now faced with explaining the discovery, the *carte blanche* he had given his old mate and why he was, as Scott might have said, 'off reservation' in investigating and unmasking vintage IRA terrorists. Not that that in itself was the end of his 'challenges.' He smiled to himself. He liked Scott but her tendency to lapse into the jargon of the corporation was irritatingly infectious and he had long thought himself immune.

What Francis had realised was that he was about to delegate upwards − the sure resort of the baffled officer − and delegate an appropriately unexploded bomb.

The Good Friday Agreement did not interdict the pursuit of historic terrorism cases nor the arrest and trial of suspected terrorists. But, over in Northern Ireland a fragile peace rested on the British government letting sleeping dogs lie while simultaneously indulging the prosecution of British soldiers and former RUC officers by Republicans.

That, and he smirked again, 'was above his pay grade' and

he was more than happy to pass the conundrum on. The recipient – someone in Special Branch , someone in the Intelligence 'community,' a politician or civil servant in the Home Office or the Secretary of State for Northern Ireland's office would be less so. Francis hoped they had forgotten his name before it reached any desk marked by the portcullis crest of government. He was nearly out. Not far behind Christopher. And he wanted out safely.

He swivelled back towards them.

"Well, first of all, it's good work. Inconvenient conclusions but good work. We go where the evidence takes us and it's taken us to a significant place." Christopher raised an eyebrow.

His old friend sounded like a press conference and he could almost hear Francis framing things similarly when he told the various interested parties what had happened.

They too would pass it to their superiors in like fashion in a relay race of upward delegation, each taking and giving the ball in a single step just as Christopher's old sports coaches had urged. The long grass beckoned, they all knew it. This would roll there and rest forever in a pending tray, the essence logged in intelligence files but due process mildewing slowly unless it somehow became expedient to back up somebody in Ireland with the whispered knowledge of it.

"You do know though that this now passes elsewhere?" asked Francis. "You'll have to give it up."

Scott and Christopher looked at each other. They were missing a piece, an essential one, but both were increasingly convinced that Christie had passed through the station that day and taken pandemonium as an escape route. It was all that made any sense.

Scott didn't care. She was self-aware enough to know that she had rather taken against the woman. Even her recent exposure to the fickle finger of life in the experiences of Miles and Grumman could not dissuade her that the course Sean's mother had chosen was unforgivable. She cared about the son though. She wanted him and wanted him happy.

Christopher tied several knots of ambivalence together. He felt an emotional distance from the ultimate objective but understood that he had to see this into its grave, a stake through its heart and a crucifix in the coffin or it would rise again and haunt him. He had sacrificed enough of his life to it. It had to die and he felt emboldened by his numbness to whatever he might establish along the way.

Moreover, what united both he and Scott was the copper's desire to 'get a result'. The compulsion forbade letting this go.

Almost as one, they shook their heads at Francis. "Peter, you know we can't do that," said Christopher.

"Sean, you know I can't let you do otherwise." He was emphatic. No greater love is there than a man should lay down his career for his friend and Francis felt he had come close enough.

Christopher coloured. "Look, law of unintended consequences, got it, but you put me on to this, Pete. You've fucking lured me down the alley and now, at the last, won't take your fucking knickers off!"

Scott intervened quickly. "Sir," she said, wilfully reintroducing the fire brake of formality. "Could DSI Christopher take leave?"

"I've got some due and have to take it, or lose it, before I retire." said Christopher grasping at the solution before he overstepped the mark further.

Francis was equally keen to take the high road having embarrassed himself with a step on the low one.

"And do what? You'd still have your warrant card, not off the job yet."

"Go where the evidence takes me!" winked Christopher. Francis had the good grace to blush.

"Give me plausible deniability and don't tell me where that is." Pleaded Francis. Christopher nodded assent. His friend had risked much for him. He knew that and valued it.

"Mick Raglan might be your only route in from here, old lad." Countered Francis "Not much more I can do."

"One thing, sir," interjected Scott. "Might I have some leave?"

Francis looked at Christopher. The old bastard seemed to defy age on occasion. And where its hand had touched him it done so only to add a line where it should be and sketch further at the undeniable allure of well-carried experience. Christopher stared back levelly.

"Really?" asked Francis, though to whom was unclear. Scott filled the silence. "Really." she said.

The two of them listened to the three new messages left on the burner phone. Scott's recorded greeting inviting them to leave details in her breathiest professional broadcast voice. It neither confirmed nor denied, merely hinted.

The first was from the sort of person who can never resist the opportunity to make what they regard as a witty political point. It was deleted immediately. The second was from Caroline Miles. She had nothing to offer but left Miles left an apology for not being able to help further. Scott suspected it was an attempt to re-engage and that its motivation was largely endless days in a Camberwell flat. She made a mental note to call her back, knowing guiltily that she never would.

The third was from a man who claimed to have been working for the railway on the day of the explosion. Scott rang him immediately, both she and Christopher listening in as a strong voice with a London accent answered, Scott adopting her 'Helena' alter ego as they spoke.

The man scarcely paused to question her before giving his account of events that day. Christopher never ceased to be amazed by people's willingness to pour forth information to total strangers. He knew this himself from garrulous neighbours and bored barmen. Silence, closed answers or monosyllabic grunts often spoke to greater effect though often not in the way that was intended. They largely said fear, guilt, hatred or suspicion and trade in those was Christopher's market.

This man plainly suffered from none of them. Christopher could imagine him in some south London pub, holding forth about football or politics, anything really that kept somebody chuckling as they killed time waiting for a friend and bought the old codger at the bar a pint as reward for 'being a character'. Old working London, rarer every day.

Not that Charlie Turner, as he eventually introduced himself, sounded like he was about to expire imminently. He had plenty of what they used to call 'rabbit' or 'old chat', his memories punctuated with the word 'fucking' which he pronounced as 'fackin' for which he would immediately apologise with " 'scuse French, 'scuse French," the phrase always repeated twice.

He was, appropriately, a runaway verbal train and Scott's occasional attempts either to stop him or keep him on track were signals he simply ran. She'd laughed at Christopher's regular use of 'marf London,' his play on words for the famously talkative population south of the Thames, never shy of a word or an opinion. He'd meant it affectionately, she was rapidly falling out of love with it as Turner went on for 'fackin' ever.

Most of what he said, they knew already. If the slaughter of the day had left its mark on him, it was hard to detect. Christopher knew the sort. If you were always at the mercy of life, you were less surprised by its capriciousness. It simply was. And its random cruelties were hidden away under gallows humour or well-told tales. Turner was talking away largely to himself even as they listened.

"Course, the one we all remembered was the poor cow who got off her bleedin' stretcher like she was a fackin' miracle, 'scuse French, 'scuse French, and scared the shit out of the two ambulance fellas. I mean, we shouldn'ta done but we all fell about when no one was lookin'. One bit of hope and humour on a dark day."

Scott finally succeeded in bringing him to a halt. "Charlie," she said, "Did you actually see that?"

"Oh yes, love!" he said, delighted at the invitation to keep talking. "I was just coming up the ramp onto the platform, they'd just started moving bodies down and it was fackin' grim truth to tell. Anyway, I'd been told to go up and start guiding the stretcher blokes down to where we was keeping them all when these two picked one up and she sat up and got off. I honestly thought we were going to have to call a fackin' doctor to the ambulance men, 'scuse French, 'scuse French."

"What did she look like?" ventured Scott.

"Well, I probably shouldn't say this, but she was a cracker. Not at her best like because she had had a nosebleed which she's sort of half wiped away and she'd obviously been cut and bruised but you could see she was a good looking girl. Lovely black hair for all the dust on it and, because she looked so pale, her eyes really stood out. Blue. Beautiful blue eyes. Blood from her ears though, running. I mean, we all laughed, like I said, but it always stuck with me. Beautiful she was but like a ghost. Which I suppose she was, really."

Scott glanced at Christopher who looked like he too had just seen one. Age had suddenly stopped being artful and at a stroke had dashed grey paint at the canvas of his face. He opened his wallet and pushed an old photograph towards Scott. She had seen it before, a Polaroid with its colour bleeding away much like Christopher's pallor as Turner spoke.

A woman stared back, her long dark hair reaching down past her shoulders and piercing blue eyes defying the dying polaroid's attempts to dim them. Scott put the phone on mute.

"Well?" she asked Christopher.

"I think you'd better go and fackin' see him!" he said.

"I think I'd better fackin' 'ad, 'scuse French, 'scuse French!" she answered.

Christopher. Always a lucky copper but – while laughter was restoring his colour – their status changed to 'off duty' the following day and Scott was already heading to her car and Charlie Turner's home in Crystal Palace.

"South London and proud!" shouted Christopher as she left, mimicking the eponymous football team's slogan. He'd placed Turner to a nicety, it was up to Turner to return the favour and place his mother at London Bridge. With her photograph nestled in Rachel Scott's bag, everything depended on the sparky old railwayman and his memory for faces.

Scott headed south. She had rarely thought of the transmission mast at Crystal Palace as a signal for much beyond the forest of aerials sprouting from a million roofs on that side of the river. But suddenly, its Eiffel Tower presence looming ever larger over the London landscape, it had become a beacon for hope, however forlorn.

She watched its navigation lights blinking away, guiding her in, warning her off. She couldn't tell which but she pushed on towards it knowing a shake of the head from the old train guard would end it. But a delighted nod would change everything.

Scott tried to feel something, a sign perhaps, from the woman in her handbag, either fading or glowing like some mystic stone as it neared the magic mountain which spawned it.

Nothing. She lay mute among the tissues and chewing gum, her blue eyes almost supernatural and her silence like the grave.

At the same time, Christopher was on the phone to Mick Raglan. He'd thought briefly of aping Scott and getting in his car but he had no wish to indulge Raglan in whiskey-drinking showdowns, *mano a mano,* in the incongruous setting of the old man's bungalow, each twitching for their tumbler.

Instead, he called, Raglan answering after several rings with the faint surprise of a man unused to his phone demanding his attention. Christopher felt a brief pang of guilt. It was the shock of a lonely man suddenly in demand and it was very obvious.

Consoling himself that he had helped give purpose and some sort of vindication to the old Special Branch copper, he waved away Raglan's immediate suggestion that he come over to discuss things.

"I'm up against it, Mick, and I need your help quick." Christopher explained the changed circumstances as well as the latest lead from Turner.

"I need to find out, discreetly, if Donal O'Driscoll is still alive." He said.

There was a silence. Christopher imagined Raglan like a teeth-sucking car mechanic pulling out all the reasons why the classic over which they stood should never run again before revealing himself as the magician who could spark it up and send it back to the road. The conjuring trick of heroism for the unrecognised, head in a bonnet and only the radio for company.

Christopher let him have his moment, it was more salve to his conscience.

"I could make some calls, Sean. People who know people. All my direct contacts are long gone. I'm reaching back a bit but let's see if we can knock the dust off a memory or two and prompt a quiet dig about.

"Anything else, Sean?" Raglan was back in the game and delighting in being of use. Christopher unashamedly rode the wave of the older man's enthusiasm.

"I might need a guide over the water."

"Fuckin' 'ell, Sean. Freelance native guides to bandit country are rare, tight-lipped and often expensive. I know a few in private security but, for obvious reasons, they're very discreet.

It's well off your manor. What do you want to go over there for? Even now, you'd be as popular as a turd in a swimming pool in some quarters, for being a Brit, let alone a copper, still more a copper of the wrong vintage. You'd stink of it."

Christopher mulled the question. "I don't know at the moment, Mick. Just keep it in your back pocket and have a think but all roads seem to lead that way, one way or another. My mum was Irish in all but name. Looked it, thought like it and saw it as home. If she had wanted to run for sanctuary, somewhere it would be difficult to search for her, somewhere my father's writ just wouldn't run, where better than the old country? If this old guard in Crystal Palace comes good, and she was there, it is, I suppose, a line of enquiry. Nothing more."

"Is that why you're hunting down O'Driscoll?" Raglan

countered.

"Partly curiosity, partly me just shaking the tree. Something might drop out. If I ever needed more proof that there's no justice in this world, that evil bastard on a Provo pension and me and Rachel raking through the human debris in search of the long lost would just about do it."

"Rachel, is it?" Mick smiled down the phone.

"Fuck off, Mick!" Christopher smiled back. And left Raglan to assist him with his enquiries.

Charlie Turner lived in a terraced Victorian house whose front door opened directly onto the street. He opened the door fat and happy to Scott, chattering away as he invited her in. His equally portly wife sat watching early evening TV on a large flat screen that dominated the small sitting room through which they entered the house.

There was a picture of Turner in his railway uniform on a small side table. An executive and a junior transport minister were shaking his hand in front of a modern carriage on which was mounted the nameplate 'Guard Charlie Turner'. An inscription recognised his many years' service to the railway and particularly his dedication to duty on the occasion of the London Bridge bombing. It gave the date.

Turner followed Scott's gaze. "Retirement," he said. "Didn't do much at London Bridge but quite proud of the years on the footplate."

"Footplate!" his wife exclaimed. "On the sick or on the piss!"

She was drinking tea from a mug saying "Glad All Over" and eating biscuits from a plate on the same table. There was a game show on. Loudly.

Turner laughed. "My lovely wife, Elsie." he said "Known for her charm." Elsie just chuckled.

"We'll go into the kitchen," he suggested. "Or she will keep interrupting!" He shot back over his shoulder.

"What? You?" she squawked, taken with her own hilarity.

Turner rolled his eyes good humouredly. The house smelt of overheating and tea towels drying on a radiator. His old guard's hat hung behind the kitchen door as Scott sat down at a two-chair table and Turner manoeuvred his belly round the confines of the kitchen making more tea.

He presented two mugs, Scott's saying; "I support Crystal Palace and this is the only cup I'll be getting this year." His said; 'Class 33 diesel' and bore a picture of an engine. Between them, he placed a shop-bought cake. He patted his belly "Past fackin' caring, love. 'Scuse French, 'scuse French."

Scott smiled indulgently. She suspected she was looking at the three loves of this man's life. His football club, the railway and a nice bit of cake. Add Elsie and it made happiness. She envied him. She liked him.

"You a copper, love?" he asked frankly. She searched his face for hostility and saw none. She hedged her bets.

"Sort of."

He nodded. "Yeah," he said. "Not quite." But didn't push it any further. Instead, he nodded towards her bag. "Show me the photo then."

Scott reached into her bag and passed him the snap. He took it from her with fat fingers but held it by the edges so as not to grease the image. She watched carefully for his reaction.

"Fack." Turner said simply. He didn't even excuse his French.

His eyes had clouded with tears and his free hand groped

149

almost blindly for his tea cup, which he gripped as though for support.

Scott was taken aback. Turner been so remorselessly cheerful and garrulous in his interactions up to now that she'd expected any reaction to be similarly chirpy. Instead, a single fat tear ran down his cheek and he just sat there staring at the Polaroid.

Eventually, he looked up at her and nodded. "It's her," he said. "Pretty as a picture. The only good thing I saw that day. I wonder what happened to her. The poor cow. The poor, lovely cow." And he sobbed.

Scott reached for his hand and gently covered it with hers. He glanced at her unembarrassed. "I never really told Elsie about some of the things on that platform. Always kept it in a box. Who wants to hear it? Every now and then, though, something will shriek to get out."

He looked at the photograph again. "She got up. I'm so glad she got up."

Scott let him cry gently. She guessed it was the first time. All these years on for cheerful Charlie Turner. He deserved his name plate, whatever he said.

Christopher woke before her. They had slept the exhausted sleep of people rescued after a long siege and for whom release had been almost too emotionally exhausting to be pleasurable. Almost.

He lay there with his left hand in the dip between the end of Rachel's rib cage and the rise of her hip and enjoyed the wet press of her against his thigh. She had one leg thrown across him and her head on his chest. He felt its weight and that of her left breast rise and fall with his breathing. She responded with the gentler

150

movement of her abdomen, slow, rhythmic and with the decadent reward of feeling her still slick with him each time she made contact with his body.

Scott had returned with her news uncertain as to how he would respond to the final confirmation of what they had both long suspected, watching anxiously as the moods passed across his face like weather tracked by satellite. Quickly, clouds bubbled up and then passed on, a storm front and then, finally, a settled, almost sunny finale.

He smiled at her and she realised that he had long ago resigned himself to the essential fact. The circumstances were a detail which some instinct had driven him to divine, even in childhood. There was no malice held for the messenger.

Christopher seemed neither disappointed nor overjoyed. The emotions flared briefly and then seemed simply to die.

What it had left them was, for the moment, spent. A battle for base camp which left the summit towering still above them but at least now visible, its peak unshrouded.

They needed to draw breath and into the pause had come the inevitable, long delayed. They had simply and wordlessly left for his flat.

It had not been frantic. The first kiss had prompted an exhalation almost of relief, like a long evening spent at a party at which they had occasionally managed to touch fingers but at which their attraction could not be revealed. Now the door was shut and they were alone.

He had revealed her slowly, curiously, watching her crinkle and rise under his touch and she watching her own responses with equal, slow fascination.

Rachel's body unveiled, Christopher simply stood and admired, she enjoying his scrutiny, enjoying more him parting her, tasting her, his hand reaching again for a breast and she hearing her first involuntary cry as though disembodied.

He could still taste her now, as she could him. After so long, they had simply taken and given every pleasure with unspoken consent. Christopher lay there reliving it, inhaling Rachel's hair and the smell of sex. She surfaced briefly, searching for the reassurance of a kiss and receiving it, before she slept again.

Christopher felt light. Lighter than in years. The woman on his chest weighed nothing. Nothing at all. She fitted.

The next day was their first as lovers. Their heads wouldn't, couldn't focus and, for the moment, they indulged the interlude, replacing the questing of weeks with the joys and terrors of love in transgression, each feeling peaking the other.

They woke late, Rachel enjoying padding his flat, deliberately testing her allure by wearing one of his shirts as she explored and revelling in the private, proprietorial pleasure of making them the first coffee of the day.

Christopher watched her with a knowing eye and duly delivered what was expected of him, ignoring the sound of his shirt buttons hitting the hard wood floor and hoping the world could hear Rachel's cries of pleasure, taking from both of them the burden of confession and revelation.

They clung to each other afterwards, frightened that everybody had. Christopher recovering his courage first and realising that he no longer cared, a fact he proved later by kissing Rachel in the busy lunchtime bar of his local. Nobody but she noticed. The hubbub continued. They were normal. Unremarkable. A fact they celebrated by getting lightly, pleasantly drunk and going home to see if they could once again alert the world to their new-found status as lovers.

The brief, glorious idyll of fresh love. A small, contained world of a flat, a pub and the corner minimart to keep them supplied with the essentials. They spent their money on Rachel's taste in big brand white wine and his in milled coffee and Irish whiskey. Their energies they expended on seemingly endless bouts of lovemaking and recovered them with omelettes, fruit and a shared love of childhood sweets, the wrappers littering the bed until their exertions shook them away. He photographed her, nude, eating an apple and teased her as Eve.

Christopher did daily circuits of body weight exercises. It was habit but also vanity. He had suddenly become aware of the disparity in years. Rachel watched him from the tangle of his sheets and retaliated by making remarks about serpents and the hang of his testicles. He laughed and the necessary tension required to hold press-ups and planks deserted him.

Immunised by relative youth, she allowed herself, for the first time in years to neglect her regular yoga or run for several days.

Both were well aware that this was the temporary Eden of first acquaintance. For any number of reasons it couldn't last but both accepted its transient joys for what they were, as a much needed restorative and reward for a restraint against which both had long struggled. The future, a future, was simply never discussed.

Of the two, it was Christopher who took almost childlike joy in the situation. He toyed with it, revelled in the fact of it, subordinated his customary self-discipline to the sheer pleasure of the moment. It was conscious. He was grown up enough to know what he was dealing with but, watching him, Rachel saw that he was like a child at its first sight of snow. He knew what it was but gambolled unrestrainedly in it. It was love. And she realised he had never seen it before.

Compelled by a sudden sadness, she drew him between her legs, holding him tight to her while he lay baffled in her arms, surprised by her desperate strength, until she relaxed and they began to move slowly together, her stroking at his hair until the pleasure and pain of it proved too much and she shut her eyes and let him finish her.

Lying there afterwards, Christopher began to feel the darkness seeping in. Rachel breathed softly beside him. He couldn't see it but a single tear had escaped her eye and left a salt track down her cheek. The sharp tang of tasting what he had so long missed bit back at him.

The first sparks of an almost incandescent anger were glowing within. She had lived. And simply walked on. It was his soul left at London Bridge.

Reality, of course, had begun to intrude. Between Scott's sudden realisation, and the hammer dropping to the well-primed pan of Christopher's anger, it took only a call from Mick Raglan for the few days of solace to end.

Both had switched their phones to silent in the preceding days. Not by agreement but in the intuitive acknowledgement that they needed to catch their breath. They checked them morning, lunchtime and evening. The burner phone now stubbornly silent and only an inquisitive and speculative message from Peter Francis left for Christopher.

He had gone to make his second check of the day when his phone suddenly came to life in his hand. Buzzing almost from his grasp in his surprise. The name Mick Raglan scrolled across the screen like a news wire. Christopher paused, breathed, answered.

"Mick?"

Raglan's voice was serious. No gentle teasing in regard to Scott, a situation to which he had been alive almost from the outset, nor his usual series of slightly defiant changing room challenges to Christopher.

"Sean, I wonder if you can come and see me. I've got some developments I want to fill you in on."

Again, Christopher paused. He had worked Raglan out long ago. "Not one for the phone?"

"Not at all." It was the old Special Branch caution, rather than a contrivance for another drinking session or the simple need for company. Christopher nodded. Raglan somehow sensed it.

"I'll see you shortly," he said. Then couldn't resist. "Roll over and ask your friend to come along."

Despite himself, Christopher felt more than a little proud. He walked to the bed. The duvet was cast partially across the lower half of Scott's body. She looked up at him curiously. He kissed her mouth, neck and then the nipple of her left breast, before letting his hand flow gently over the curve of her hip. It was almost valedictory.

She too nodded. "To be continued?" she asked.

His hand ran up to her hair and he kissed her fiercely. "Of course." he answered. And he meant it.

They arrived at Raglan's bungalow separately, Scott having had to divert to change and collect herself. Both were past concerned by appearances but it prevented the old man from diverting himself with insinuations and knowing looks.

In any case, both were far more concerned with Raglan's news and evidently so was he. Christopher knocked first and, when Scott arrived some fifteen minutes later, he was welcoming and polite but distracted.

They settled down while their host went through the niceties but the atmosphere was heavy with portent and Christopher could tell he was struggling with framing a message he didn't quite know how to deliver.

He decided to try and make it easier. For all his ways, he liked Raglan, had some sympathy for him and in his perverse manner he had tried to convey to both he and Scott that he wished them well. An empathy, perhaps, for those who might have a second chance.

Moreover, Raglan had obviously put considerable efforts into trying to help. Partly because it made him feel involved and alive but also, and in no small part, because he wanted to.

And that spoke well of him.

"Mick, whatever you've discovered, it's all right. You can tell us. There are few surprises left and I'm far beyond being hurt."

Scott remained impassive. Raglan himself looked at Christopher appraisingly. He was still pin sharp and nothing much escaped him. He exhaled and sat back.

"All right Sean, here it is. I have called in every favour from every former colleague, friend and acquaintance and others many times removed. It has been like stirring the bottom of a long abandoned pond. What rises to the top only makes things darker and you always have the feeling of shadows moving away under the surface. I'll explain why.

"Nobody currently knows whether O'Driscoll is still alive. He was observed and under surveillance for some time and, coincidentally, starting almost a year to the day after London Bridge. He had surfaced in about the safest place possible for an IRA man, South Armagh."

Christopher and Scott exchanged glances. Raglan explained.

"Bandit Country, as a Home Secretary described it in the 70s. Convenient for a quick dash over the border into the Republic and less than an hour's drive from Belfast. A smuggler's paradise and lawless since the days of the Pale. The Army flew everything in by helicopter because the roads were mined so regularly and PIRA had snipers out with American 'longs.' You wouldn't even hear the crack of the supersonic bullet before it disintegrated your armoured vest.

"All the really nasty bastards among the Provos operated out of there and with something close to impunity. Farms, farmland, narrow country roads. Mortars, bombs and snipers. The most dangerous posting in the modern history of the British Army and murderous for the RUC. Ruled by fear and *omerta*. The only thing they feared were the Hereford Hooligans.

The SAS. And not even they all got out alive.

"What better place to welcome back the conquering hero?" said Scott.

"Exactly," agreed Raglan. "Except he wasn't so conquering. He emerged very infrequently. Occasionally seen by one of our boys in balaclavas. He'd limp between farm buildings and sometimes a woman would take him in a battered car to another. We couldn't identify her at the time. Not a known face."

"So was he injured?" asked Christopher. He ignored for a moment the reference to the unknown woman.

"Seems so. And quite badly. A great chunk out of his forehead which looked like a drunk had tried to repair it and with his arm always held close to his side. If he'd been a slight figure before – you remember Grumman's description – he was near wraith-like in South Armagh.

"He plainly wasn't under guard or suspicion. Moved, when he did, either unaccompanied or with a local heavy with whom he always seemed relaxed. The woman perplexed our boys though. A clean skin. They checked the car out but half those farmers were dealing in vehicles, moving them across the border, re-plating them, rebuilding them, all sorts."

"Why?" asked Scott.

"Habits of criminality and an easy pay day as much as terrorist disguise," answered Raglan. The border arrangements, such as they were, made it even easier. Them, fuel and bloody farm animals. Every scam going."

"So the car gave away nothing?" Said Christopher, trying to keep the tale on track.

"Nothing. Anyway, she got pulled over at a roadblock. Somebody was a bit sharp that day and recognised the vehicle off a list as suspicious. An RUC fella asks her if she'd been drinking. Wanted to buy some time without making her wary and, while she's taking the breathalyser and they're running mirrors under the banger, he asks for her licence.

"She passes the test. Just. She had had a drink which was helpful because it stood up the pretext." Here Raglan paused meaningfully, glancing at both of them to see if they were ahead of him.

Christopher, who had thought himself unshockable, was ashen. Scott was looking between then incredulously.

"Yeah. The licence she passes to the copper is in the name of Christie Christopher," Raglan confirmed.

He broke the ensuing silence because he knew that, once the questions began, the thread would be lost and, with it, important details.

"Not long after, O' Driscoll was moved. He was seen briefly near Monaghan over the border and, after that, nothing. Probably moved further into the Republic to keep him out of reach of a snatch attempt. She's obviously sussed it and passed the word.

"It appears our boys in the Branch checked out Christie Christopher and drew a blank. They interviewed your dad, Sean. Said she's upped and left without a word and nobody knew where she was. What he said after that, I'll paraphrase but it boiled down to her being 'a daft Irish bint stupid enough to get tangled up with the Provos on some romantic whim.'

Funnily enough, he never mentioned the domestics but a cross-check with the local Met revealed regular visits. I'm sorry Sean, mate."

Sean just nodded. He looked close to defeat. His armour pierced. Scott did the work or him. "Picture? Description?"

"Well, a couple of long range surveillance photos and, of course, it was in the days before photo driving licences but she looked like a standard issue Mick bird. Dark hair, blue eyes."

"Mick, for fuck's sake!" exclaimed Scott. "Christ, sorry Sean. Didn't think."

"They all look the same to you?" challenged Sean wearily. Raglan didn't answer.

"Accent?" asked Scott quickly.

Raglan took the gap Scott had shown him: "That's a slight conundrum. Irish. Northern Irish. So either she was imitating them or someone was posing as her. Where were her family from, Sean?"

"Sean?" Scott repeated. Raglan noticed the informality but even he realised it wasn't the moment to point it out. Christopher shook his head as though trying to clear it after a good left hook.

"Jesus, I don't really know but the Republic. Not far from Dundalk, I think."

"Not far from the border, either," said Raglan softly. He knew he had to point it out.

"Here it is Mick. The theory you don't want to say." said Christopher suddenly. "My mum went rogue. She was so fucking desperate to get out that she lit out for Ireland, whatever the cost. Jesus, Mary and Joseph and kneeling at all the right moments at Mass, she'd have soon fitted in, picked up the accent and made all the right noises about the 'bloody Brits'."

"Well, I follow the idea, of course." Conceded Raglan, "But with Donal O'Driscoll?"

"My mum disappeared. Completely. She wasn't a member of the underworld nor was she particularly street wise. Simply vanishing was beyond her. She was at London Bridge that day. Who was the one other person who had a vested interest in quietly disappearing from London Bridge and over the Irish Sea where only a bloke with a black balaclava and a gun in his hand was ever likely to come sniffing?"

"Jesus, Donal O' Driscoll!" Raglan coughed.

"One, if not the other," laughed Christopher, bitterly.

"Certainly not the other," said Raglan. "That's a devil's bargain. I don't mean to be disrespectful, Sean, but what kind of a woman would team up with a mass murderer?"

Christopher had to force himself into Raglan's perspective. He struggled with parental respect at the best of times. He noticed the reverence towards mothers displayed by the people he worked with, arrested and questioned. Perhaps they were the one soft-sided thing in a rough-edged world of exaggerated machismo.

He'd seen old school hard men in tears at their old mum's grave side and street-running gangsta's shamed by the dignified chastisement of their church-going matriarchs. Either that or, more often now in the days of the fractured family, it was 'nan'. Black, white and all points between, It was always the same. The equality of abandonment and the ubiquitous need for love.

Christopher re-entered the conversation. "Same sort of woman who'd walk out on her kids and leave them with a complete bastard." He said with quiet vehemence.

Raglan again punctured the silence.

"Neither he, nor she, have been seen in a while. Years in fact. Sean, I know you and I know you'll go now to look. I remembered you asking for a guide. I've found one. Two, in fact, who are working on rewarming some of the surveillance that used to be run all the time. See if they can get a bead. It may be easier than we think to pick up the trail and simply intelligence eyes have been turned elsewhere.

"Some of these buggers hide in plain sight now, after the GFA, and at the age O'Driscoll would be if he's still alive he'll feel he faces nor offers no threat. Old habits die hard though. A tug on the thread, the Church, the Mafia and the IRA. Once in never out. He'll be watched over."

Christopher nodded back. He had a look on his face like God's own vengeance. He softened: "Mick," he answered, "What can I ever do to thank you?"

"You've done enough," Raglan answered. "All I ask is that you remember you have a future as well as a past. It's what you taught me. You're a London copper with all the cock-o'-the- walk habits but you're well off your beat over there."

Raglan looked meaningfully at Scott and then back to Christopher as though the glance would place her directly in front of him. "For Christ's sake be careful." He almost implored.

They had argued about whether she should go with him, of course. Christopher was angry. The first time Scott had seen him genuinely so. She thought it an overdue release and let the waves of it crash and break on her understanding and patience. She was going to go with him and his anger was not really with that suggestion but, for the moment, Scott let him hide behind the pretence of his protective instincts.

Later, he had taken her. It was the only word for it. And she had given over her body to his comfort and fury, trying to hold him, at times almost desperately, but he rose away from her grasp as he thrust at her and then flooded her, once and then again.

She lay in the darkness with him afterwards, feeling like Briseis trying to sate the anger of Achilles. Scott could feel his rage fade to brooding, fade to a simmer. She stroked and soothed at him, at his hair, face and chest then more intimately. If he needed her again, he could have her.

But she had broken him. At least for the moment.

Christopher felt the tension slowly leaving his body. The muscles in his arms and legs trembled slightly as they unwound and he felt his heart slowing to a normal, less painful rhythm. He laughed at himself, his chest rumbling in Rachel's ear as she gently brought him back to life with her hand.

He let her. She liked to do it. Slowly, endlessly, as though the changes in him fascinated her. He found her fascination equally enthralling.

They talked, matter of fact, as she caressed him. The travel arrangements, his insistence on covering the expense of the trip and whether Raglan was exaggerating the dangers. Like two tourists, they discussed what they should read. The facts of the Troubles were complex, both knew enough to know they were hopelessly ill-equipped to navigate them.

Christopher paused suddenly and tried to pull Scott onto him. "No." She whispered quickly. "Just for you." She felt the last of his anger splash her wrist and then watched as he fell into the deepest sleep.

Cloud rolled down from the hills around Belfast. Christopher watched it from the back of a taxi he had taken from George Best airport towards the city centre. It touched the top of the giant shipyard cranes at, yellow among the grey, and occasionally delivered a squall of Harland and Wolff rain to which the automatic windscreen wipers of the car jumped intermittently.

The driver made chirpy conversation to which Christopher felt strangely bound to respond. There was a friendly desperation to it, as though the cabbie wanted to reassure his English passenger that all was well, all had changed. You're welcome. Come back soon.

He looked at the cloud again, it made the view partial. Appearing then obscured. Christopher thought it apt.

The driver chattered on, trying the old local joke about the Titanic. "It was perfectly all right when it left here." Made in Belfast, touched by genius, destined for tragedy. Christopher thought of George Best. "Lot of it about," he thought to himself. If Scott had been with him, she would have laughed. One of his favourite bits of laconic wisdom.

Christopher laughed obligingly and let the cabbie chat on. An odd mixture of fierce local pride tinged with a certain embarrassment. Shame perhaps. The dark past was never far away, like a delinquent relative everybody knew of but nobody mentioned. He couldn't help but see the irony.

Belfast's outskirts became the city itself. Christopher let the driver tell him, again, that the Europa was the most bombed hotel in the world, and saw the new facades mask old scars and an old way of life.

They pulled up outside the hotel. Christopher hadn't been

able to resist. Thirty odd explosions and it had felt like defiance when he booked it. The driver watched him eyeing its modern portico, clean, international, the inoffensive sterility that marked them all. "It's the same the whole world over..." he began to whistle softly.

As though reading his mind, the driver suddenly said: "Are you looking for broken glass and a brick o' soldiers? All gone. And may they never come back." It was an earnest remark, the man's accent falling away almost mournfully and a slight rain in his blue eyes. He was in late middle age. Old enough. His observation was neither challenge nor exhortation.

Christopher looked at him squarely and nodded. "I'm with you." He said. As he paid him off, the driver shook his hand. It was an unexpected and old fashioned courtesy and it took Christopher aback.

He had asked Scott to join him separately and later and now felt vaguely embarrassed by his paranoia. He laughingly blamed Raglan. Here at least, nobody knew him and nobody cared. He was just another tourist, here to see the sights, thrill to vicarious danger, perhaps trace an ancestor. One, at least, was true.

Christopher checked in and settled to the bland comfort of his room. He had three hours before Scott joined him, four before a meeting with the two men Raglan had persuaded to help him search for O' Driscoll. He ordered lunch to be brought up, settled back on the bed and opened a book on Bandit Country.

She came in quickly, her flight delayed and her card key picked up hurriedly at the reception desk. Kissing Christopher briefly, she said: "They're right behind us. We're to meet them in a room two floors down."

The relationship was suddenly very professional again.

Christopher was off the bed and pulling on his shoes and jacket without pausing to question Scott further.

He left first, taking the stairs. She gave him a few minutes and then followed, waiting for the lift to take her down. Simple precautions, agreed with Raglan beforehand, but all they could do under the circumstances. Christopher was decreasingly convinced of the necessity but trusted the advice he was given.

He knocked and was let in. Nothing was said until Scott arrived. The first man was tall, lugubrious and, when finally he spoke, did so in a pronounced Ulster accent. Dressed in a dark suit, he reminded Christopher of a Victorian undertaker, his face frozen in permanent solemnity and, when he spoke, it was with the hushed voice of a man welcoming the bereaved to their pew.

Again, Christopher noted the same old-fashioned courtesy that he's noticed in the cab driver. The eyes, though, were not to be mistaken. In them, were too many thing seen, an implacable hardness that didn't need to announce itself and a shrewd, assessing glance.

The second was different. Small, inconspicuous to the point of considered anonymity. His only distinguishing feature was a cut glass English accent. Christopher was sufficiently experienced not to be surprised but was fighting an urge to dislike him.

There was something faintly contemptuous in his glance. Christopher could take a guess at what he was. Or what he had been. Hours, days, in a covert observation post watching some farm in South Armagh before administering 9mm justice to some bastard mixing fertiliser for a bomb in a barn or rigging out a van to open up on a passing patrol with an Armalite.

He had to respect it and did but he had dealt in the posturing of London's streets too long not to have heard myriad claims of

SAS membership from the drunk hoping not to fight to the drug-dealing doorman. It was in various measures comic, boring and irritating and Christopher knew he was in danger of tainting the genuine article with the laughable fraudulence of others. But he had never joined fan clubs or followed cults and he had no intention of starting now. He'd found most heroes disappointed.

The two looked at each other levelly, the small man eventually smiling slowly and extending a hand. "Not very original but do call me John. I'm sorry about the sneaking around but it's more for our benefit than yours. There are people in this part of the world who aren't fans. I hope you're not among them. I'm afraid I have a habit of appraisal. If it showed, I'm sorry."

Christopher nodded back at him. "Don't worry," he said, "I know the feeling. What did you conclude?"

"Apart from vanity, you mean?" Christopher conceded a smile.

"You're damaged goods. Have to be or you wouldn't be here in pursuit of all this. It's made you unafraid but not demonstratively so. Moreover, under that boyish smile you can back it up. In fact, I think if someone pushed the right button, you're downright fucking dangerous, old lad. Not bad qualities out here, if kept on a tight rein. Peace reigns. All that.

"But you refuse to indulge in 'the game' and, being a good-looking lad too, people are prone not to take you seriously enough as a result. You've hidden behind it all your life and now there's a reckoning. But you're a clever bastard with a lot of experience behind you. I'd be prone to liking you if I hadn't got things off to a bad start."

Christopher gave him the full beam of his smile. Scott watched him deploy it, uncertain whether to allow him once again to melt her or to worry about the facility with which he used it. Peace of mind demanded the former.

"Well, Gipsy Rose Lee," he said. "Your tea leaves or Mick Raglan's fan mail?"

"Bit of both and friends of friends," laughed the other. "Facts as follows, old lad. Most folk out here don't want to go back to the bad old days. An increasing number don't even remember them. Out where we're going to look for O'Driscoll, there's still a few that do but even more who are earning money just like they did and always have done, crime.

"As far as they're concerned, it's different sheriffs, same badge.". It's just their long battle against 'the man'. They'll hide behind the politics to ensure they're left alone to get on with it. Down the lanes that cross the border, in the barns nobody visits, it's still dangerous and a fella with your accent still wouldn't want to saunter into a bar in Crossmaglen and ask for a selfie, a pint and directions. Bandit Country. The capital of. IRA on the town memorial, tricolours on the lamp posts, the republic of South Armagh."

"And yours?" asked Christopher. "You don't sound much like Martin McGuinness."

"Well he was a Derry man and, anyway, a wee fella like me would never get served at the bar." responded John, in an accent purest green.

He had seen the trick done before, of course, but Christopher was still impressed and it showed. John's funereal cohort cracked what was probably a rare grin. Peace reigned. All that.

The early skirmishes dealt with, Scott and Christopher re-rehearsed the story Raglan, or at least an intermediary, had already told their escorts. Neither party minded. The telling of the tale established mutual trust and extra details had John and

167

the Ulsterman nodding at each other knowingly.

In the event, the pair had whittled down O'Driscoll's likely location to three sites based on the most recent sightings, what little was known of his background and on the habits of better known but similar characters.

The first had been way out west where O'Driscoll had been brought up. It had been checked and yielded nothing, both men glad to get back to British jurisdiction and plausible deniability.

The second was also in the Republic. Just over the border into County Monaghan, a short sprint from strongholds like Crossmaglen and in a remote patch of countryside where approach or unusual enquiry would quickly be noticed. A large and well-appointed farm bungalow, finished in a grey pebble-dash had sprung up on a holding long vacant and then suddenly bought and well maintained, its owner hard to trace and determinedly anonymous.

John and his colleague had watched that too. Few came and went, nor was there much sign of agricultural activity despite expensive new machinery in the yard including an impressively sized New Holland tractor juxtaposed with an old tanker on which the lettering was slowly fading. A herdsman led pedigree cattle to and from a modern barn.

"Cover for smuggling, money laundering, more unlikely the old money of a gentleman farmer. Either way, not enough goes on to look like it supports a very comfortable lifestyle," explained John.

"A lot of the boyos in Belfast still live in working class estates and their single luxury is a pint and a punt. Here, no. Smuggling pays. From fuel to hard drugs. If the South Armagh brigade had thrown their arm around a wounded hero, they set him up nicely."

"Jesus," said Christopher wearily, "Further proof crime pays. I thought these boys were all Marx and 'Up the Republic' like good nationalists, or is it socialists? Purity of cause, 1916 and rising again at Easter, all that?"

John laughed, "Well, perhaps some in the leadership. But down South, someone had to pay for all that Libyan Semtex and 50 cal ammunition. They were also claiming every allowance and compensation they could from farm animals scared to death by passing helicopters to fencing when a soldier cut the wire to pass through. Made a nice nest egg and they're making it work."

"And what about the third option?" interrupted Scott. She suddenly felt very English. Her Home Counties tones jarring more here even than they did among the London geezer speak of some of her fellow detectives.

Raglan had mentioned the paranoia. Scott felt hers taking seed as though even speaking would alert someone, somewhere to the presence of 'a Brit' harbouring malice aforethought.

The two newcomers looked at her as though for the first time. She suddenly felt very female too. Christopher tipped her a placating wink. She didn't need it. She'd walked into a realm of dark history where men had been the principle players and to it they had brought their blend of dark and light, horror and heroism. This wasn't her stage and she was glad of it. The play was only ever a tragedy, she thought, and any romance a cruel illusion.

"That's not far from Newry." The funeral director said softly. "Same set-up. Close enough to the border to dash for it, isolated and along friends. A wee lane runs up to it. Only way in or out and there's two fellas forever tinkering with vehicles while the labouring's done by a man who comes in every day from Bessbrook."

"Bessbrook?" she asked, undeterred by their earlier scrutiny.

"A wee town nearby. Was a model set-up a bit like Bourneville in England but linen not chocolate behind it. No pubs or pastors. The former still applies. A butcher, a baker, a candlestick maker and all set around a green. The Army set up a helicopter base in the old mill there when moving by road became too risky. Like Vietnam, choppers and watchtowers. It's quite idyllic again now. Or would be but for the ghosts of massacres past."

Scott chose not to enquire further. She felt blood-drenched and exhausted and Christopher was watching her with concern. She wanted to spit as though she could taste iron in her mouth. It was leaden outside through the hotel window. The mountains and the mist seemed to press in and she felt both depressed and claustrophobic.

"Any reason to think our lad is there beside both places ticking the box for Mr Big's country gaff?" asked Christopher.

John ignored the slightly dismissive implication. "Acting on information received," he answered flatly, imitating a music hall copper. Chastened, Christopher withdrew. Raglan's words were ringing in his ears. "You are well off your manor." Facetiousness remained his worst bad habit.

John relented: "Look, it may surprise you to know that there's still interactions between some of the old parties. Most of them want no return to the past. They'll stop anything that smells of it, even if it means giving us a nod and a wink. A trade here, a favour there.

It was a dirty business then and it remains so. It's one reason nobody wants a truth and reconciliation exercise. It would leave an awful lot of people on both sides very embarrassed and quite a lot more furious. People were sacrificed. Knowingly. You'd be surprised who passed information and why. Navigating that is a maze. Can we leave it that somebody thought reminding O'Driscoll that people knew where he might be could prove helpful?"

"So what's the plan?" asked Scott. She was unaccustomed to seeing Christopher out of his depth. She admired his ability to accept it but she had become used to seeing him as almost omniscient for all the occasional lapses into detached introspection. It disturbed her slightly and she asked as much to stop herself thinking too much as to address the practicalities.

This place shook all certainties.

It was the Dickens character who answered: "John and I are going to split up and keep both spots under surveillance. See if our wee man puts in an appearance. We want you and Sean here to hire a wee car and base yourselves in Armagh city for a few days. It's about an hour away from Belfast here and within striking distance of both farms if we need to get you quickly to either one.

"We noticed you're booked into the same room so I'm sure you won't mind posing as a couple looking at the Saint Patrick trail or some such in the town there. It's their attempt to bring a bit of tourism back. There's a decent hotel and you'll be comfortable and welcome enough, so you will."

Neither Scott nor Christopher reacted to the knowledge of their accommodation and what it implied. Both were secretly quite proud of their burgeoning relationship and its increasing revelation gave them active pleasure. They both felt as watched as watching but let it pass, each trying not to smirk at the other.

John watched them and shook his head. "I hope to God this brings you both some peace and happiness. It's past time this part of the world doled a bit out."

171

A thin band of light sat between the grey of Armagh's slate roofs and a grey and lowering sky. The twin cathedrals of Saint Patrick stared each other down from their respective hills, the one transplanted from an English market town, square towered and provincial, the other Continental, its twin spires like Spanish capirotes spiking up conically cruel like the Inquisition.

They had driven in from Belfast through its semi-rural fringe, tractors and trucks mingling with the cars on the main road, passing Craigavon and Portadown, planned towns and 'peace walls,' before reaching the prosperous suburbs of Armagh and checking in.

Both needed fresh air, Scott in particular looked tired and was increasingly impatient. They left the hotel and walked downhill towards the town. They passed a British Legion hall in the shadow of a fortified police station, its mirror glass and grenade netting still in place, and a steel tower topless like a pollarded tree. Union flags fluttered from a nearby estate.

They found a green and strolled it, pausing at the entrance to an incongruous cricket club and at a war memorial dedicated to the fallen of the Boer War.

Scott took Christopher's arm and rested her head on his shoulder as they walked. She could feel his physical strength through the old thornproof jacket he had pulled on and inhaled

the smell of him and the wax that waterproofed the cotton. Scott felt herself relax, just a little.

He inclined towards her and kissed her gently, blowing away a wisp of her dark hair before he did so. They walked on, Christopher knowing she would talk when the moment was right.

"You seem ready," she said, her head still resting on his shoulder. "Ready for what?" he asked.

"However this ends. I can feel the tension in in you, like you can feel the kill imminent."

"Unfortunate choice of words," he smiled. "But Peter was right. I need this to stop. I'll do what's needed."

She looked up at him and he said: "You look as though you've had enough."

In what he said, Scott knew he was offering her a crossroads. One she could take in a direction that set her free from his cares or keep her bound to him in the hope that they were solved and she could take possession.

She smiled wanly.

"Tired of this." She said. "It's so bloody schizophrenic. An English green and a watch tower. Courtesy and murder. Twin cathedrals staring down at us like we're being asked to make a choice at God's gun point. I hear my voice is shouting even when we murmur to each other and that someone bad is always listening and demanding a declaration.

"I suppose if we went to another part of town, there would be different flags or a different 'tradition', isn't that what they call it? But it will be that same feeling of oppression, of being observed, of lurking unseen danger. It's exhausting me."

Christopher nodded. He felt it too but was uncertain where paranoia ended and reality began. "You'll be quite safe." The woman at reception had said when they asked about things they should see. It wasn't what they had wanted to know but she had offered the reassurance anyway.

Rain began to bead on the wax of his jacket. A fine mist of it. The pale slit between earth and sky had shut between the weight of grey. Scott looked up at it as though standing beneath a shower but made no move to shelter.

"Was it that bad?" she asked. "Was it that bad that she would come here, join this? Especially then. Then, when the soldiers were on the streets and helicopters were in the sky and every hedgerow hid a booby trap and each van a sniper. Sean, could it have been that bad not just to leave you but to leave you for this? I've been here forty-eight hours and it's apparently safe now but I feel the whole weight of it on me. Imagine it then."

She asked it of him with a quiet desperation that he tried to kiss away along with the rain that wet her lips.

"It was like here." he said. "You never knew when it would come. The slap, the punch, the lie. You checked and rechecked everything you did and you tried to live a life not seeing. It was the tension as much as anything. When? How? Why? The secrets and lies.

"The lying was the worst bit. In its way. The constant construction of myths and fictions, the constant building of hope only to have it knocked down again by the reality.

"It left you with the constant feeling that the only person you could rely on was yourself. It crippled your ability to trust or love and it snatched away focus, plans or the ability ever to see beyond the next flare-up.

"My poor brothers still struggle with the legacy. I do, we all do. It never, ever leaves you. A dark shadow waiting to step forward. A gangrenous cut, the poison creeping and rising unpredictably to the surface.

Perversely, you know, he wanted to destroy. Even if it destroyed him. This raging, angry battle with, well, whatever it was that he fought with. It was, I suppose, a civil war. One within a family and, just like here, it was insidious. The damage done not just then but for years and years after. You say you feel it and I say 'I know.' God knows she must have been desperate."

Sean's jaw had set in a way she recognised as the face he

174

adopted when in battle with emotion.

"Disguise fair nature with hard favor'd rage[5]." Scott whispered. He glanced down at her and it was her turn now gently to stroke a strand of damp hair from his forehead.

"What happened to him?" she asked.

"He drifted away. Almost the moment he could. He made two or three explosive interventions from a safe distance. Claims for money. Demands for loyalty. And then he simply stopped. A family friend said he'd moved abroad, somewhere where he could indulge his potentate fantasies. Asia I think. Though he kept moving. Each time he was about to be found out. The same friend told me he'd died. I went to the funeral. Back in England in some dismal civic crematorium. Pretty much him, me and a priest who surely earned his money that day. I only want to make sure they got the right man." He smiled ruefully.

She gazed at him. Another death. "Will this end badly? We're in territory neither of us knows. Is it worth it, Sean? You have me, you know. If that's any consolation. Should we stop?"

He kissed her again. "Rachel, precisely because I have you, I have to finish this. To live like this, with melancholy kept at bay with increasing artifice, with the sense of shame and with the feeling of unworthiness, no matter how much of that you have repaired, I couldn't do it to you. Couldn't impose it on you. Because the plain fact is you don't do that to someone you love."

A discarded cricket ball lay in the wet grass, its scuffed red leather darkening with moisture and the seam stark and threadbare. Christopher picked it up and shied it at some stumps

---

[5] In the instance of the quotes, both Shelley and Shakespeare fall well outside expiry of copyright and are in the public domain while all three, including Beckett, I think fall well within the definition of 'fair dealing' in UK law and 'fair usage' in the US being both fragmentary and answering the following two tests:

standing in the practice nets. The ball hit the ground, bounced and struck them, their heavy metal base trying to hold them upright against the impact, teetering and then just, just recovering.

He turned towards Scott as she digested what he had just told her, "I woke up just in time," Christopher laughed just as the light returned briefly to Armagh and the two cathedrals brooded on heedlessly like affronted Olympians.

They were several days, almost a week, in their hotel before any word came. Days spent studying maps of South Armagh and venturing out in their hire car observing its quickly changing face. Grey estates with their loyalties on display, vast new farmhouses, discreet among the rolling and rugged *bocage* of the countryside. Tiny, hidden lanes and then suddenly across the border without even the realisation, and all within a few short miles.

Together, they climbed the mountain peak of Slieve Gullion. Christopher striding into its mists like some warrior of legend. By evening, he would use the hotel gym, lifting weights and punching a bag. Scott would watch him come in, sweat-stained and intense. He was preparing for battle, as much against the past as any tangible foe. She realised with some sadness that this was how he had dealt with life, a fight for which he was in permanent preparation. She looked out at the cathedrals and prayed for it to be climactic, even if it meant defeat. "Please God," she begged "Set him free. One way or another, set him free." She wanted to add, "And then give him to me," but didn't.

It was as they ordered their evening meal that an encoded message arrived on Christopher's phone. A discreet number one appearing against an app just as a young waitress was extolling the virtues of locally reared beef. He tried to concentrate on her as her accent climbed and descended the scales but she could tell she'd lost him.

"I'll get your wee drinks while you decide." She smiled and headed towards the bar.

Christopher watched her go before glancing at the phone. It was from a number he didn't recognise but he had been warned that might happen. Scott looked casually at the menu while he checked it. He nodded at her just as the waitress returned and placed a pint of Guinness in front of him and Scott's inexplicable taste in commercial white wine in front of her.

"Have you decided?" she asked. Christopher held a forefinger up for the few seconds it took him to drink off his beer in a single draft, placing the laced glass down on the table in front of him. "I'll have another one of those," he said, "And I think you've sold me a sirloin, medium rare."

The girl laughed. "A steak and another pint for a thirsty man. And for you?"

Rachel looked at her and for the first time in days, smiled: "Oh," she said, "I think I've got everything I need." Baffled, the waitress headed towards the kitchen.

They were eating again the following morning when, following the instructions in the message, they arrived at a café opposite St Patrick's Catholic cathedral. Scott was compensating for the previous evening with a sizeable breakfast. Outside it was raining. The long steps up to the church's twin spires shone in the drizzle and, when the door was opened by a customer, the tyres from passing cars hissed wetly.

Condensation clouded one corner of the window from which Christopher watched the scene. A man collected their cups, timing his arrival at the table with Scott hurling her cutlery onto her empty plate. "Need that?" He grinned. Christopher slid a £20 note under a sauce bottle and winked at him just as a silver 4x4 pulled up at the cathedral gates. He and Scott left immediately, hunching against the rain as they crossed the road towards it. The driver released the door locks as they approached.

"Sean? Rachel?" he checked as they clambered in. Both nodded and, wordlessly, the man pulled into the traffic.

They drove for perhaps half an hour, the scenery becoming more and more rural. At one point, they drove slowly behind a convoy of four tractors, before being waved past. A grey bungalow with an incongruous swimming pool appeared briefly behind a hedge, rain puddling the pool cover. A farm sign boasted pedigree cattle as a smell of damp silage and manure seeped through the car's air vents and the local BBC radio station discussed current events just about audibly.

Scott checked her phone to discover there was no signal. She passed it forward so that Christopher could see. He looked at his own. Again, no signal bar.

The driver finally spoke. "Difficult place to get a signal at the best of times." he said. "Undulating country. But the locals aren't keen on towers. They think its surveillance and the PIRA encouraged the notion that masts fry your brain and deform your babies. Best switch 'em to silent anyway. Don't want them going off at an inconvenient moment."

"What a place!" exhaled Scott.

"Ooh, I dunno. Sounds like Surrey to me." quipped Christopher. The driver smiled and the wipers picked up speed along with the rain.

The road was empty when the 4X4 pulled into a lay-by. A non-descript hatchback was waiting. At their driver's instruction, Christopher and Scott got out and went towards it. The sepulchral

Ulsterman was at the wheel. He nodded as they got in but said nothing.

They set off again, the scenery becoming less and less populated and the roads ever more narrow. At one point, they bumped and jolted over a long un-made farm track. Christopher grasped at the hand strap above him as the car's suspension rocked, rolled and occasionally caterwauled.

"Don't they trust you with the 4x4?" asked Christopher. The Ulsterman smiled like death but kept his eyes fixed firmly ahead. Scott, tried not to slide across the back seat.

They climbed for a spell and then, wordlessly, their driver pulled into a small copse just to the right of the track. They all climbed out. Christopher was in his waxed jacket. He had waterproof over-trousers on and gore-tex trail shoes. Scott had on a modern, close fitting waterproof jacket, black leggings and similar shoes. The Irishman inspected them.

"The over-trousers will have to go." He said quietly. Christopher looked at him questioningly. "Walk for me." the man instructed. Christopher took a few steps. The synthetic material sounded like a washing machine turning as one leg contacted with a swish against the other. In the quiet wood, the effect was disproportionately loud.

Christopher nodded and slid the trousers off. Beneath, he was wearing black jeans. He cursed himself for wearing denim in the wet. In the fields beyond the wood, the rain fell continuously.

The Ulsterman returned to the track, checking to see whether the car was visible. Satisfied that it was well-concealed, at least from casual observation, he returned. Almost as he did so, they heard the noise of a diesel engine and instinctively ducked further into the wood.

A tractor eventually rolled slowly, inexorably, by, heading down the slope they had just ascended. Its huge rear tyres threw up clumps of mud and stone. In the cab, its driver turned to ensure the machinery he was towing was still attached as the big farm vehicle hauled its load through a particularly large pothole. Dirty rainwater geysered up as it did so and some crows lifted from the field on the other side. The tractor didn't pause but swept on down the hill, its trailed burden bouncing behind it.

Scott raised an inquisitive eyebrow at their guide. "I don't think he even looked this way, no." he said. "You'd never know anyway. In the bad old days, they were masters of ignoring anyone and anything. Just a whisper, later, in the right ear, that they 'd seen a man moving or a strange vehicle on their land. With that in mind, we'll keep to cover where we can and move quietly and quickly."

They filtered through the copse and emerged on the blind side of a hedgerow that followed the track up-hill. Staying low and close to it, they climbed almost at the jog. The rain accompanied them unremittingly. Christopher felt it running off his coat and wetting the line where its hem met his thighs, soaking the material of his trousers. He bent forward further to try and protect his front from the worst of it, his old field jacket dry, warm and rendering him almost invisible between the field and the hedge. It was a comfort. His jeans less so.

Ahead, Scott moved nimbly and, in front of her, the Ulsterman. At the crest of the long hill, there was a second wood and between it and them the remnants of a stone wall, in which, at some point in the distant past, a gap had been left for the passage of people and animals. Two rusty stains suggested hinges had once held a gate.

Their guide ignored it. He moved cautiously along the wall

below the sightline and quickly rolled over the top of it, before mounting a short, hunched sprint to the next thicket. Scott and Christopher glanced at each other before, one after the other, doing the same.

They arrived among the trees to find a cloudy mist touching the tops. In the fields, the rain hissed among the grass and, even under cover, it dripped through like an ingress. The trio caught their breath before pushing further into the wood, emerging on the other side to find the reverse slope ran sharply down to farmhouse, still some distance away.

The hill was studded with rocky outcrops on which moss clung to every crevice. They ran away to the right of the farm before the last formed a promontory about three hundred yards from a thick tree line which marked the house boundary and which surrounded the buildings on all sides. Another track led from the farm down to a public road on which nothing was currently moving. For a moment, the scene disappeared as a swirl of mist drifted slowly across the hill top.

The Ulsterman took advantage of it to run the three of them to the first outcrop, again, hunched and low, their shoes fighting for grip in the sodden terrain and their thigh muscles straining against the pull of the slope.

They lay among the stones, moving again as another billow rolled slowly downwards, pursuing it not just to the next cover but to the one after that and dropping quietly into the smell of wet turf and rock. Down below, a distant man in a blue boiler suit ran quickly to a tractor and reversed into the shelter of a barn before jumping down and running as fast as heavy wellingtons would allow back towards the out-building from which he had emerged. He didn't look up and the brief sound of the engine had been absorbed by rain and mist.

The run between this patch of stones and the promontory was, perhaps, seventy-five yards. They were now sufficiently low down that the mist had not followed and, instead, wisped by above them in sporadic tufts. Nothing moved below and neither did they. One car and then a cattle truck eventually came past on the road. Christopher could see the long ventilation slits in its side but at this distance no noses press to them searching for air. The car was expensive, silent and incongruous in the rural setting.

The rain came in even harder. An iron grey curtain so heavy that the farmhouse, itself painted grey, became almost indistinguishable against the countryside. The Ulsterman began to move, slowly, cautiously in a squat, extending one leg and then using it to pull his body after him. When his two legs came together, he repeated the action.

Scott and Christopher followed suit, Christopher increasingly aware of his sodden jeans as they rubbed at him.

They reached the promontory. Close to, its structure was not merely a flat rock extending from the hillside as it appeared from above. Erosion and time had hollowed out a section to its rear and beneath. Christopher remembered having seen something similar in Spain, on a grander scale. A relic of another civil war in which neighbour casually murdered neighbour, it had commanded a valley as well as providing refuge.

One by one, they moved into it, the Irishman coming last. Inside, dry, and holding a long monocular, was John.

He was unshaven, looked tired, but he held with him the sense of dangerous mischief that Christopher had detected in him when they had first met. It had been one of the reasons he had been a little suspicious of him. He had worked before with people who thought danger a game from an old war film. They were often cavalier with others.

Christopher had to accept though that people like John were possessed of a deadly and righteous intent which did not necessarily meld well into normal company. The Tom, Dick and Harry, Great Escape persona was almost certainly designed to soften the edges. A disguise and, for him, John had sat for several days in a scrape behind a rock. He repaid him with the warmest smile he could muster. "Another man I owe a good drink to." He whispered. John merely winked a response.

The weather had cleared quite dramatically. The mist had been replaced by a gentle steam which rose from the damp hillside as a strong sun warmed it quickly. Christopher entertained a brief fantasy of stretching his sodden jeans out on the rocks to dry. The very thought made every chafe singe punitively and the denim cling more stubbornly to his thighs like a cold, damp flannel.

He forced himself to concentrate on John who had moved forward and threaded the monocular through a chink in the stone. There was a moment focusing and then Christopher was beckoned forward.

"Same time, every day. With the change in the weather, we may get luckier yet."

Down below, a small car, new but low budget, appeared and drove quickly up the track towards the house. A woman got out. Young, her hair was pinned up behind her head and she wore the white smock and dark utilitarian trousers of the medic. He groped for the modish term. 'Health professional.' A catch-all that told him nothing.

She was shapely. Christopher couldn't help but notice. Her flat shoes detracting nothing from a walk that almost deliberately defied matronly bustle. He focused in a little tighter as she leant in to the back seat and emerged with first one bag and then another.

The powerful lens on the monocular revealed her face with a clarity that almost startled him. As though she would glance up and stare straight back at him through his own spyglass. She had a beautiful, high cheeked and Hispanic face, the strong nose and arched eyebrows sitting below the black hair she had pinned up.

Christopher was not merely admiring the view. He was trying to place her. Local and loyal, a private hireling, or a woman importing her skills to the service of a local health authority. He wanted to know whether she was doctor, nurse or some form of therapist. A tick list that might provide clues as to what he was observing.

She went into the house. After a spell, she emerged again, propping open the door of a large conservatory and waiting there patiently as an elderly man walked slowly but unaided into the sunlight of a decked platform. The woman went in front of him now, mopping the last rain water from a steamer chair on which she placed a long cushion before propping it in an upright position.

The old man lowered himself gingerly into it before swivelling his legs round in front of him. The Spaniard, as Christopher had decided she was, moved constantly, allowing him only the briefest glimpses of her charge as she passed in front of his lens. She opened one of her bags and from it took a blood pressure monitor. Christopher saw a frail arm offered to the band, noticing that the man was wearing a t-shirt. As he did so, an elderly woman emerged from the conservatory, placing tea on a table beside the steamer chair and, after a few words, returning to the house.

Again, she had remained on the blind side of the medic and

by the time Christopher had re-trained his monocular on her retreating form he had glimpsed only grey hair, the sleeve of a grey cardigan and a purposeful walk. He refocused on the efforts of the Spanish woman who was recording the blood pressure and watching the cuff deflate automatically.

She bent down to place the apparatus back in its bag and, in that brief moment, let Christopher have a clear view of the man sat in the chair. Almost as if he knew he was under observation, he rubbed his head against his shoulder, holding the arm straight out in front of him as he did so and obscuring his face. The woman stood up again, just as he let the almost stick like limb drop.

Behind him, Christopher could feel a weight of silent expectation almost pressing him to the eyepiece of the monocular. But he had done enough surveillance to be patient. John squatted beside him, equally insouciant. He was drinking coffee from a flask brought by the Ulsterman and staring with the blank face of the exhausted in the opposite direction.

The therapist now revealed her trade. She stood face to face with the old man, providing resistance to his outer arm, which he was trying to raise. They relaxed and then repeated the exercise half a dozen times before moving on to more stretches and contortions while the woman provided support and instruction. Christopher could just hear her voice but nothing more.

Eventually, she helped him sit back in his chair. Her congratulations on his efforts just about reached the promontory. Deciding he had earned his tea, the therapist moved towards the table to pour it, bringing the drink to him, the old man looked up at her and smiled. He had a neat, grey beard and his still thick hair was swept away from his forehead almost poetically. He looked like a professor of literature albeit one dressed in a t-shirt and sweat pants.

The Spanish woman took his cup from him as he pulled on a light sweater she had given him. He had to raise his arms to do so, and, as his head emerged from the crew neck, he grimaced in discomfort, opening his mouth in a silent cry and in so doing looking straight down the lens of Christopher's monocular.

Christopher waved urgently at Scott who took his place. She gazed down at the decking and at the pair who were having some sort of conversation. The therapist put down her own cup and, suspending her bags from her shoulders, gently touched the man's arm in encouragement and farewell. He looked up at her to smile his thanks and gave Scott the same view he'd just supplied Christopher.

She took her eye away, looked at the group and then directly at her lover. They mouthed it simultaneously, "Donal O' Driscoll."

Voices again drifted up the promontory. Scott glanced back into the monocular. The woman who had brought the tea was walking towards the therapist who was stowing her bags once again on the back seat of her car. Scott again changed places with Christopher.

She walked strongly. A grey cable knit cardigan revealed the blue and white striped collar of a shirt. Her blue jeans led down to the surprise addition of training shoes. Big white soles giving her extra stature as she stood, holding her purse, arms folded across her chest, in front of the younger woman who smiled and then nodded.

Both got into the car. Christopher felt a huge surge of anticipation he tried to control as he waited for the woman to turn towards him. She looked down as she plugged in her seatbelt, toward the driver as she signalled her readiness, towards

Christopher as the car moved off towards the track. He focused hard on her face through the distorting blue of the window, unsure whether he was willing it to be her or willing it to be not.

She kept looking up, kept looking up, perhaps scanning the sky beyond the hills for a sign of the weather to come. Christopher squatted frozen at the lens. And then sat back down hard. Scott took over but the car was hidden now behind the trees and moving fast towards the main road. She watched it pull away, its indicator flashing the shallow turn long after it had made it.

"Cramp!" smiled Christopher to the expectant gaggle looking down at him. It had not been the woman he had both hoped for and dreaded. His explanation for the tumble was in some part true but there had been the emotion of expectation lurking somewhere and he was a little ashamed of it.

His feelings had baffled him. It was a sudden fear of resolution. More, a fear that the answers he sought would not be the answers given. His sense of detachment towards his mother had grown down the years, fuelled as much by his sense of a youth lost and purpose blunted as the constant question 'why.'

Even in the moments when he had philosophised the vagaries of life away, his early condemnation to care, responsibility and guardianship, a sense of failure in some way, robbery in others, he had sought to exonerate this woman. To excuse her.

This latest twist, revisiting what John called COPs, Covert Observation Posts, to see if his mother had taken up with a murderer and a terrorist to escape them all had placed her almost beyond the Pale and his capacity to forgive.

If he discovered her, here, with him, on this farm with all both things implied then the questions once again outweighed the

187

answers and he no longer had it in him to ask further. The fact of it had knocked him backwards. Not the leg he stretched and rubbed almost in consolation.

He shook his head. "Not her." He smiled thinly. "Though it is him."

John nodded as though he had expected it. "She's not here every day. Seems to come and go. There's a village nearby. Not much. Shop and a pub. A sort of café cum post office and a church. She may live there and be an occasional help up here at the farm. It looks to me like she just got a lift into town, possibly to return. She only took her purse."

Mention of the village prompted Scott, "Where are we?"

"It depends which part of the hillside you're on. Down there, our friend just got his physiotherapy in the Republic. Up there, in the wood, you were in the United Kingdom of Great Britain and Northern Ireland. Whichever you look at it, we're in dangerous territory."

Scott eyed him quizzically. "Someone's got to keep an eye on you," John whispered in answer to her unspoken question. It wasn't the moment to pursue it but the jocular brush-off confirmed as much as it denied.

Christopher was looking at both of them and thinking that this woman was no fool. As much watched as watching. He too had put the feeling down to the paranoia the geography engendered but couldn't quell what he suspected.

He moved the subject on. "Who else is down there?"

"Two men. Possibly O'Driscoll's sons. One of them bears a resemblance. The same slightness of build, though less bookish. More inelegantly wasted than Trinity College, Dublin. He buzzed up here the other day on a quadbike. Gazed out over the hillside for a while then slung his can of cider in this direction." John nudged a yellow tin that lay in the corner of their hollow.

"The other is a more physical specimen. Big fella, fit. What they call out here 'farmer's strength.' Looks like his forebears spent a lot of time lifting tractor tyres, fallen sheep and bales."

"And does he?" asked Scott.

"No. Neither of them do. Most of the labouring buses in. One, sometimes two, in an old Japanese truck. This pair are busy but to no discernible purpose. Tinkering with vehicles, moving vehicles and vehicles in infinite variety from quad bikes to lorries."

Down below, the house looked tasteful and prosperous, isolated from the muck and noise of farming in its own almost Italianate compound. A hill beyond and behind rose away and on its crest, cattle flicked their tails and lowered their heads.

In the foreground, the barn into which the tractor had been reversed. Its nose was just visible and the engine canopy raised.

"I've been in, " said John. "Two Range Rovers, a brand new digger and machinery that's never turned a clod."

Christopher thought of certain parts of London, good lifestyles but, as his cynical colleagues put it "no visible means of support." He knew what he was looking at. At least this was discreet. No wrought iron gates and a salon-brown missus in a personalised Mercedes.

A big man emerged from the house and squatted down on the decking in front of the steamer chair. Scott, who was now behind the monocular alerted them to the movement. Receiving no response from the chair's obviously sleeping occupant, the younger man touched his hand gently and then walked towards the barn where the cars were kept.

A Range Rover emerged a few moments later and eased down the track to the main road.

There was complete silence. Christopher guessed the man was on his way to collect the house keeper from the village. He scanned for the other. He found it impossible to believe they would leave O'Driscoll alone. Still nothing.

Suddenly, the slighter man came out of the conservatory. He bent over the sleeping figure in the chair, stood there for a moment or two and then walked lightly back into the house.

Christopher moved to the back of the hollow, stood up and started to walk down the hill towards the farmhouse. He knew he had to move before anybody objected or tried to prevent it and he knew too that the only way he was going to get an answer was to ask a question. And the only person to ask was asleep in a chair a few hundred yards away.

Scott looked on horrified, John with a mild smirk and the Ulsterman with expressionless curiosity. Christopher's jeans were steaming slightly in the sunshine as he walked through the trees, across a gravel drive and onto the trim but mossy lawn that ascended towards the decking. The man in the chair hadn't stirred.

He came round slowly. Christopher was gentle in bringing him round, largely because he had to be. He had no idea what ailed the man and between that and his age, he didn't want a dead interviewee whose silence defined grave-like.

O' Driscoll said a drowsy "Son?" and looked harder at the man sat opposite. Christopher knew what would wake him fast and deployed his accent, slowly, calmly, clearly. "No, my name is Sean and I've come to ask for your help in finding out about Christie Christopher."

He deliberately excluded both his surname and the phrase 'ask you some questions' or the word 'information,' wanting to disguise, just for a moment, the link but not trigger the reflexive silence of a former IRA man.

O' Driscoll was now clear-eyed and looking fixedly at the man opposite. He was considering what he'd just heard. In his brief moment of sleepy vulnerability he had allowed Christie's name to prompt a tangible flicker of recognition in his face. As an experienced interrogator, Christopher saw it, knew it. So did O' Driscoll.

The Irishman countered, "A Brit?" Christopher didn't need to acknowledge the question. "A policeman?" Again, Christopher let the question hang.

Aware he was against time, he came in again. "I'm not here in any official capacity. I want your help. But I do know what you did at London Bridge."

O' Driscoll winced. Whether it was in physical pain or emotional anguish was hard to judge. Again there was a silence.

"Do you know what you're risking sat there?" ventured the old man.

Christopher sighed. He had spent a lifetime being threatened by Mr Big. It had started with his father. "I know where you live? I know where your kids go to school?" he asked.

"Heard it before. Oh, I know what you boys can still get up to given half a chance. Fucking good hiding with a studded bar and a doc to keep you awake right through to the end? You won't even have to drive my body to the pig farm. Mate, it's the same the world over. You're nowhere near fucking unique and frankly I'm past caring."

It was a lie. Christopher felt isolated and vulnerable, the more so knowing Rachel was watching him. He did care. Very much.

But his world weary insouciance registered with O'Driscoll.

191

Men who no longer cared were dangerous. He felt vulnerable too. He conceded a little ground.

"Christie?"

Sean played his card: "She is my mother. She travelled through London Bridge the day you blew it up. And I think you walked out of it with her. She nursed you and it's possible, just possible, that you had some kind of relationship with her."

O'Driscoll sat back. If the intention was to knock him off balance, it had worked. This man knew a great deal, had a very personal reason to be there and had materialised in front of him like an avenging angel. For the moment, he was calm, not to say professional, but for how long he would remain so was surely open to question. If the intention was to trick from him a confession for the station bombing, well, that moment was long gone. It was a sleeping dog politics had long let lie.

All his instincts were to say nothing. Literally nothing. His organisation lionised the folded- arm silence of the know-nothing interviewee and fell upon 'the tout' like the Devil's own. But that was in an interrogation cell where, even if myth and legend suggested lines had been crossed, there was still some notion of restraint. Of the law. As dear as it was transgressed.

Here, it was different. He was old. He was injured. He had never recovered fully from being caught in the blast either physically or mentally. His frame groaned at him daily and, by night, he could hear the screams and see the limbs. Occasionally, one of the big boys of the leadership would pay him a discreet visit, pat him on the back, ply him with Paddy's.

Ostensibly, it was to show they never forgot their own. But it was just as much to ensure he stayed loyal and silent. Being unforgotten was a message of many meanings.

Secretly, when the pain and the pills and the Paddy's kept

him awake, he would have sold his soul never to have done it. Now he feared it would do nothing less than cost it. Death was coming. And he feared it.

O'Driscoll looked at the man in front of him. Something made him want to reach out across the years. Cure one thing, perhaps. Just the one. On the other hand, he was a Brit, plainly a copper and he was on his fucking farm without permission. He sat back. Bide your time, Donal, lad. Someone will come. The boy's upstairs and the big fella will be back shortly.

Then the odds change. In the meantime, perhaps some form of confession was overdue. "I know what you are talking about." Said O'Driscoll.

"I know that," Christopher answered flatly. "I know your role, I know you were there. We also both know that you're hoping for the return of your sons. For clarity, I am not investigating the explosion. I can do nothing to prevent that now. I try to be angry about it. I know I should be. I have seen what it did. How it lingers. But I can deal only with one small aspect. The bit that concerns me most. Did she help you?"

O'Driscoll looked briefly at the sky then back at Christopher, exhaling as though he had just taken a long, long draw on a cigarette.

"As you can see, I didn't escape unscathed. I slid away from right under the nose of the coppers and hid in an old building by the river. I'll be frank. I thought I was going to die. I don't know if you've been at that point but there can be a strange serenity to it. I'm not sure I feel it now." Christopher declined to say anything, certainly nothing that might convey sympathy.

"I was preparing for it. Wanted it. I hurt. More, I was just so tired. The only thing that angered me was that it looked such a rat-like end. I was stupid, you see? Had entertained dreams of

193

going down in glory. The steps of the GPO, martyrdom and a hail of Brit bullets to keep me alive forever."

"The GPO doesn't have steps. Never has," answered Christopher.

"Ah, the vulnerability of you Brits is you've never understood the importance of myth. German Mausers, banshees in the fireplace and rising at Easter," smiled O'Driscoll.

Christopher declined to engage. O'Driscoll looked faintly, very briefly, disappointed. Perhaps in vengeance, he ratcheted the caricature a little.

"A woman came to me."

"Oh please don't tell me you had a visitation, Mother Mary with words of wisdom. There will be an answer I assume?"

"Life and liberty. She saved them both and touch and go in either instance." O'Driscoll was in earnest now. Christopher's joke had been sharp and impatient.

"And it was Christie?"

The man came through the conservatory doors at the run and almost skidded into Christopher who was out of his chair at the first flurry of movement. Since childhood, he had never lost a sense of hyper vigilance and sudden aggression was the stimulus to which it was most alert. He stepped to the left as the man tried to square up to him, an easy pivot off his foot that saw his would-be opponent overshoot and, very briefly, face nothing at all.

"Easy Kevin, son. This man has come all the way from England to ask me a few questions about your mother."

O' Driscoll's talent for explosives had shifted from gelignite to remarks. Kevin had heard nothing but 'England,' 'questions' and 'mother,' exactly as his father had intended.

"Are you fockin' kiddin' me? A bastard Brit, here, asking about ma?" He kept trying to get square to Christopher who

194

simply refused to allow it to happen, stepping away constantly from the man's right hand, keeping just out of reach while at the same time measuring the distance between them.

He watched the man's movements trying to see if he could give away his favoured fist or show a gun. "I think she may have been my mother too," said Christopher. As he had intended, the younger man was provoked into a wild punch with his right hand, Christopher easily slipping the blow as it whistled past and off into the countryside.

Kevin had overthrown and lost his balance.

O' Driscoll noticed it. "Kevin, I think it possible that Mr Christopher here knows what he's doing when it comes to fighting and, fierce as you are, you'll come second if you keep doing that. Leave the fighting to McGuigan."

Christopher, at least, recognised the catch-phrase of the great Monaghan featherweight who had refused to wear the colours of sectarianism. He wondered if it was some sort of code.

"Shall I make a call, Daddy?" The nursery name struck Christopher. A local habit his London roots couldn't absorb. He tried not to glance up the hill where, he hoped, guardian angels still watched.

"No, I don't think so. Your brother will be home soon."

"Kevin is a little raw. We all are," continued O'Driscoll. "That woman you're looking for? I'm afraid she died only a fortnight ago."

It was now Christopher's turn to be off balance. He had expected many things. To be wrong, first and foremost. To perhaps find a woman long dead and in her grave. Or a woman now in old age and tearfully grateful for a chance at reunion, reconciliation, explanation. To have missed, just missed, any of these three was almost more than he could bear.

He remained standing. His instincts for self-preservation weren't so blunted. Kevin was still almost frantic. His displaced emotions driving a frenzy of movement and an internal monologue escaping in little sputs of the word 'fockin''.

"How?" he asked eventually.

"She was old, Sean. She wore out. Like most of us go. Not with a bang but with a whimper." Christopher could see the literature professor in O'Driscoll again.

Kevin started up again. A splenetic tirade that put Sean at the heart of his mother's death. He was here. He was British. Christopher tried to find a resemblance in the angry man boy. He couldn't. Kevin was almost rodent in his ferocity. A coarse face, the face of a son unfavoured either by parent or by nature.

A car came onto the gravel, spitting stones from under thick performance tyres. The larger man got out and walked quickly towards the party on the decking. Of the housekeeper there was no sign.

"Who's this?" he asked O'Driscoll. Kevin erupted in a tirade of invective. For the first time, O'Driscoll lost his temper. "Will you shut up, you silly wee bastard!" The effort plainly hurt and in the moment of rare emotion the accent of his childhood blended briefly with that of the north. Kevin abruptly quietened.

The old man explained to the newcomer, Michael. Michael never took his eyes off the stranger in their midst. For his part, Christopher was equally wary. He was outnumbered now and, but for the watchers in the hill, alone. A wrong move, the sudden production of a gun, and he would simply disappear. Given his predicament, he could rely on nobody even to mount an investigation into the whereabouts of his body. His sudden descent into this morass now seemed impetuous and he was regretting it.

"Is it true, daddy?" asked Michael. "Did mammy produce this?" he nodded towards Christopher who declined to rise to the contempt. He was studying him, trying, like he had done with Kevin, to find, even in a movement, some kind of family likeness. Perhaps, just perhaps, something in the strength, the physical certainty, but nothing he could identify with precision.

On the prospect that he potentially had two half-brothers, Christopher found it hard to focus. Again, he felt the life-long habit of emotional detachment hurling a blanket on any spark of anger, delight, or a confused melange of the two. Besides, for the moment, his focus was self-preservation which, at least, was a talent.

"Mr Christopher here seems to think so. And you know your mother had a life before us."

"Do you have a photograph?" ventured Christopher.

Kevin once again ran to the end of his lead. "Do you think this is some sort of family fockin' reunion that we hand over pictures of a woman like that to a man like you. You can fool this pair but I know what y'are. She's beyond your reach now. You can go fock yerself, so you can!"

O'Driscoll stopped the yapping with a single raised forefinger. Christopher was mildly impressed. For all his physical frailty he was still very much *pater familias*, either through stature gained or by traditions long dead back at home.

"Kevin has a point," conceded O'Driscoll. "Boys, I want you to take Sean here in one of the Range Rovers to see the grave. In the vestry at the church there's a box of Mass cards from mammy's funeral. I was going to have you pick them up anyway. Let him have a read. I think he's owed some kind of explanation. He's come a long way."

The dynamic had changed, Christopher noticed. O'Driscoll

was confident, in charge. To a degree, of course, he was but Christopher was happy to let confidence bleed into complacency and, for the moment, had to contemplate the implications of climbing into a car with his two sons one of whom was over-motivated and the other a physical prospect. He had little choice, however. He had asked and, one way or another, was about to receive.

The brothers looked dubious, O'Driscoll merely nodded an affirmative to the unspoken doubt.

As the group moved toward the car, left with its driver-side door still open in the drive, he said quickly to Michael, "You know the woman in that grave and both of us know why he's

here. I'd prefer this passed off without incident. We none of us need it. But if it's necessary…" he let the implication float between them. For Michael it was tantalising but he answered with a reassuring wink.

With Kevin and Christopher already in the back seat, he climbed in and drove away with neither show nor urgency.

Up on the hill, the trio behind the promontory watched the Range Rover turn onto the main road and head towards the village. As O'Driscoll hobbled into the house, they began to move discreetly back up the hill and towards the wood.

The steeple was a grey and accusatory finger pointing right at God from a green patch littered with the graves of centuries. It stood guardsman straight over the dead. The three men in the Range Rover moved among them undisturbed like crows at a battlefield.

Christopher stood at the grave he was led to. Its brown earth mound was marked only by a wooden cross. The headstone would be added when the excavation had settled. Sexton's tools lay beside it, the old way of pick and shovel and, discreetly parked beneath the trees, the modern convenience of a small, tracked mechanical digger that had done the bulk of the work.

He wanted more. Wanted some acknowledgement, affirmation, any damn thing. She stayed appropriately grave-like. Christopher squatted down and laid a flat hand on the earth. As he had at London Bridge, he wanted communion with the physical, for it to whisper something to inform and reassure.

Kevin and Michael stood and watched, Kevin barely able to restrain himself as Christopher to his mind desecrated the soil. Michael laid a soothing hand on his shoulder but, himself, looked fretful and preoccupied.

"Come here to me, now," he said. Christopher stood and followed him into the church. It was open, quiet and, even here among his troubles, a country's troubles, he felt its serenity slow his heart. Instinctively, he reached for the holy water and crossed himself. He didn't know why beyond a childhood habit. He and God, God the Father, had parted ways among the smashed plates and the unanswered prayers. A child's tears had been met by the great silence. He wanted reconciliation, felt the need among the hushed pews and old incense but something was broken. *Mea culpa.* But the crying boy had been guilty of nothing.

Michael watched him and dipped his fingers too before disappearing to the far side of the aisle to their right. In the stillness, Christopher heard an opening door echo heavily and then the steps returning. Michael held a carboard box in a single large and agricultural hand. His thick fingers took from it a printed sheet which he handed over before moving to a wrought iron stand of candles.

Few were burning. The church was empty. Just two or three little lights in the semi-darkness and a thin trail of smoke drifting

199

heavenward as one guttered. The big man took from his pocket a large wad of notes, two of which he pushed into the little tin box beside the rack of waxy remains. Michael refreshed an entire line of them, adding a dozen, perhaps more, lighting one from the next as a huge sob shuddered his big shoulders. He stared in hope at the altar and then turned and walked out, leaving the main door open behind him.

Christopher waited a moment, moved to the entrance and shut it. The church enveloped him. Sensory overload of all but light. Silence, smell, the embrace of another world. He bobbed before the altar in half genuflection, ensconced himself in a pew and began to read the card he'd been given.

At the top, an old Irish woman gazed from a circular photograph, her vivid blue eyes beneath a witch-like straggle of thick grey hair reminded him of a ship's painted figurehead, a determined guardian against misfortune, a fury, a defiance of the sea, a mother to the crew.

He gazed back at her, meeting her eyes and seeking. The pair searched each other for a long while like some meeting of mythology. Was it she? Was he a lost mariner? It had been so long that his storm-tossed memory struggled to recognise the unkempt figure looking back. He broke the stare.

Beneath, the eulogy read:

'Christie Christopher was, to many, an example to Irish womanhood.

Devout in her belief both in Catholicism and the righteousness of the Irish nation she went further than most in doing that rarest of things and backing her convictions with actions.

Her Christian spirit led her to adopt Michael and Kevin, two orphans of the struggle for a united Ireland and to nurse another in her husband, Donal O'Driscoll, whose deeds in the cause of his country cannot be mentioned here and whose life he owes her.

A spirit and character loved and renowned in our community, she was selfless in pursuit of causes local and national and, like many, her heroism will have to remain obscure for many years to come while those who benefitted from her generosity and her fierceness in defending the right from the wrong will always know what she did for them.

Easily recognised, she spent her later years as some queen of ancient Hibernia, an embodiment of an independence which we all recognise and of which we are all justly proud.

Proud of what she was, proud of what she stood up for, proud to have known her. Go with God, Christie Christopher.'

Sean read and re-read. It had all the bombast of the politically motivated and woven into it the virtuous personifications of a by-gone era. He tried to read past it. Tried, somewhere to find the woman he increasingly dimly remembered. He began to wonder if he too had idealised her. A projection of his wishes rather than the facts.

Once again he looked at the photograph for total, irrefutable affirmation that this was the woman he sought. There was none. Resemblance enough to his memories to suggest it, not enough to confirm absolutely. Age, a new life and poor photography, badly reproduced. All or perhaps none. Only the vivid blue eyes said yes.

Otherwise she was a woman he did not know. He remembered his mother as kind, naïve, increasingly strained by what she faced and, ultimately, broken. This, this… 'emblem' was a stranger in which his only consolation was that she had not produced the pair waiting for him outside in the graveyard.

The big one, Michael, seemed genuinely mournful in the

face of her memory. Perhaps there was the legacy of the kindness he remembered. The other was a tight ball of fiery rage, a comet portending disaster. Stuck 'twixt and 'tween man and boy and would be now all his life.

Had she really lent herself to them over he and his brothers? His anguish almost overwhelmed him. He looked to the altar for solace. Silence. Beside it, in a niche, the Virgin Mary held the dead Christ. "You've got to be kidding me." Christopher half laughed.

Eventually, he pocketed the card, stood and rather reluctantly left the church. He didn't bob this time. Just turned and walked out.

Outside, the rain had started again. It was never far here. He looked for the brothers. They were nowhere to be seen. Christopher assumed they were sheltering somewhere and in his mind's eye could see Kevin sending blue cigarette smoke into the grey from a cupped hand.

He walked to the grave again and squatted beside it, fighting as he did so an almost overwhelming urge to plunge his hands into the wet earth and haul the woman beneath from her coffin. Shake her, shake her until she yielded an answer, shake her till doomsday.

From a damp arched seat, two brothers watched him. A cigarette was thrown to the floor.

"Have you seen enough yet, yer bastard yez?" Kevin came in at the rush, aiming a kick at Christopher's head. Christopher just avoided it, grabbing the man's planted leg in front and above the knee and with his other hand behind the ankle, tipping him onto his back.

Kevin scrabbled quickly for the sexton's tools left beside the grave, pulling from the pile a pick axe which he swung wildly to keep Christopher at distance while he regained his feet.

Michael looked on, apparently willing neither to assist nor prevent the attack.

Kevin came on and met with Christopher's increasing rage. The rage of years. The rage of pain. The rage of questions unanswered and a youth spent wondering. He met a man robbed of childhood and the brief insouciance it brings and a man blighted. And he lost very badly.

As he advanced, plainly struggling with the weight of the tool, Christopher simply stamped his right foot down on Kevin's leading knee, hyper extending it and bending it in a brief backward bow of agony. He screamed, almost disbelievingly, and whilst he did so Christopher hit his jaw cross-ways with the point of his elbow. Dislocation and unconsciousness came together and instantaneously.

"Jesus, Kevin!" Michael was suddenly engaged. He was angry and he was concerned but he wasn't stupid. He came forward more cautiously than Kevin had, hands raised like a boxer, closing the ground between he and his opponent before taking the big man's option and swinging a huge right handed haymaker at Christopher.

It was a bet on power. To connect was to win. But the blow was slow, obvious and clumsy and Christopher slipped it, drilling a left handed upper cut into Michael's now exposed ribs. Christopher heard him exhale hard but not yelp, the man's muscled bulk adding a layer of protection that defied a normally stopping body blow. Christopher immediately added a second and felt Michael's floating rib shift under it.

The big man cried out and dropped his hands to protect his side. Christopher came over the top with a left hook to the jaw from which Michael briefly staggered. Any imitation of a boxer's self-defence had gone, Michael was being hit from too many angles and too powerfully and Christopher simply drove upwards with a final right-handed upper cut that cracked the jaws together and finished the fight.

Michael lay awkwardly on his back, an arm raised in the air as though was pointing out some overflying object.

Christopher stood in the quiet of the churchyard. Neither man on the grass stirred.

He stood like that a long minute. A grave satisfaction filling a void of sentiment. He had heard enough. All his life he had heard enough. He absorbed the silence as the rain fell quietly into the soft earth. There was nothing. He could stay here forever with his two mute companions and the noiseless crowd beneath him. It had stopped. Just for a moment.

"Sean! Oh Jesus Christ, Sean!" John and the Ulsterman were hurrying towards him. He didn't know from where. The peace was broken. "Fucking hell, what have you done?"

They bundled him into the back of the silver 4x4 in which they had been driven from Armagh. Scott was at the wheel and the engine was running. "He's okay!" John answered Scott's unspoken question and she accelerated hard away.

John watched the satnav as Scott drove at remorseless speed into the blind bends and narrow squeaks of the country road. The little flag at the top of the screen flicked from the Republic's tricolour to the Union flag. "Keep going, fast," said John.

They rounded a bend to find the road full of an advancing agricultural fork lift, its prongs at wind screen height for the big 4x4 and a giant black bag of silage perched precariously.

Scott found the miracle of a gateway and barely slowed as she took the space it offered before careering out of it again, the wheel fighting her and the top heavy car doing everything to roll as she struggled to straighten onto the road. She managed to control it and sped on.

The vehicle was very quiet. Christopher stared almost catatonically ahead, the Ulsterman gripping his arm as much in comfort as restraint.

John turned to him, "Sean, we thought we'd lost you and while I have every sympathy for your predicament and reason to thank both you and Rachel for what you've discovered along the way, this has to stop. You've poked a hornet's nest, put us all in harm's way and we'll be lucky if you haven't caused a political incident. You've just committed what could be a deadly assault on foreign soil and while a serving police officer. What's more, if there's a sniff that this is sanctioned you could re-open a bloody war.

"I'm sorry but we're getting you out of here. Under our guardianship, this chase is over. It is frankly past time you reconciled yourself to a situation over which you now have no control. We'll pick up your car in Armagh and then escort you to the airport."

Christopher looked at him and nodded almost sleepily. The conflict in the churchyard had emptied him. More to the point what he had learned had emptied him. Of the two men left behind he scarcely thought except as a drain to a lifetime's frustration.

He suddenly felt able to leave them and her there. He'd lost her years ago. In fact he'd never known her.

Scott eyed him through the rear view mirror. He looked oddly at peace. He had been so keyed up for days that he seemed now to have reached a point of almost serene acceptance. He caught her looking and gave her a slow wink of reassurance. She smiled the faintest smile back.

The rain followed them to the airport but the cloud had lifted.

Scott and Christopher sat waiting for their flight. They had been unable to find one to London immediately and so sat, reflectively, in the airport bar. Somewhere, their escort of John and the Ulsterman lurked. As much to ensure they left as to prevent any pursuit.

Christopher had been unimpressed and less concerned by the lecture John had given him in the car. Under the circumstances, it seemed implausible and impertinent. Though he knew he could never return.

His pursuit had ended first in bafflement and then in sadness. But he had answers and, now, far fewer regrets. His mood was lightening markedly. It was tide that lifted all boats and he and Scott drank their favourite drinks and told their favourite in-jokes. There was, Scott suddenly realised, contentment.

Christopher watched two fully grown men in reversed baseball caps giggling and slapping each other like freakshow bearded children, an effect enhanced by baby-like chubbiness and shorts that revealed dimpled knees. A third, elder man joined them wearing a Bob Marley t-shirt, his belly swelling the word 'wailers' onomatopoeically, as though his tummy button was trapped beneath and singing. He and Scott laughed the disproportionate laugh of the relieved. The men were too busy to notice.

A woman walked past. "You wanna sort yerself out!" she cawed aggressively at someone in a London accent. Even in an airport of many tongues, it stood out. Home beckoned.

"Bet she's in 5C," smiled Christopher. He and Scott were 5A and 5B. "How do you feel?" she asked.

"Exhausted. Raw. Disappointed. But the searching is done and the wondering is done. The truth is I was chasing a mirage, the closer I got the further she became from me. I wanted to confront her though she wasn't the architect of what happened, of course, but in other ways left us the worse curse. To always have our faces pressed to the window thinking we had done wrong. It's easy to rationalise it but it never really leaves you, or at least so I thought. It traps you in a permanent guilty boyhood. There's no consolation in platitudes about the hand life deals you. It scars so deeply when your flesh and mind are so tender.

"The fact that she went on to live such a…" he groped for an adjective and failed, "such a life, tells me only that the offence was hers. We were better off without. I can tell them now. Tell my brothers. Tell my soul."

Scott smiled at him. Her elusive sexuality had returned to her. He wanted her and she briefly enjoyed the knowledge before she kissed him. He ran his hand into her dark hair and responded.

She looked up to find they were boarding.

The cawing woman was not in the seat beside them. Nobody was. Scott reached for Christopher's hand on the armrest and stroked at the wrist revealed by his shirt cuff. She could feel the sinews and latent strength.

John had told her of events in the graveyard and she was unsurprised by them and unperturbed. This was him. She watched him, his eyes shut as he rested his head against the cabin. His handsomeness, which just lately had been dulled by tension and the task ahead, was returning, his eyes had lost their permanent vigilance and had softened again.

Scott realised that he had spent a lifetime burdened by the need to do right. A childhood spent trying to protect and to put things to rights. It explained his choice of profession and the easy shift between humour, humanity and almost Biblical retribution.

It was used sparingly, but it was used. Fire, flood and tempest.

He was as she first knew him. Before Peter Francis had sent him on this quest. Amused by the inanities of this world, its vanities and follies. His facetiousness was back. His refusal to be governed, his pleasure in knowledge and in her.

As for her, she hadn't mastered it. She didn't feel, like he did, that London was a single, living entity, didn't feel its history in everything that he faced, his innate understanding of what drove its inhabitants. "There are no accidents." he would say. More to the point, she had less and less concern for people who were stupid, venal or criminal. Where Sean often found life among them either amusing or mournful, she simply felt... nothing.

He was going back to retire. She to resign. She had him now there were no rivals for his affections. He opened his still young eyes and smiled at her, the boy waved briefly from within, like he'd just seen someone he loved come home.

Sun broke through as they made their approach to London. The loquacious Northern Irish stewardess who had so far shared her views on subjects as varied as craft gin and breast feeding with her section of the aircraft said; "God, will you look at that. It never reaches us at home. It's like two different worlds. The joy of this job is that you see it at all." Her over made-up smile was broad with a natural happiness.

From her seat against the bulkhead, the stewardess winked at Scott at the first bounce of the wheels. "He's lovely!" she mouthed detecting the freshness in Rachel's fascination for the man beside her. It was pure good will to the world, an opportunity simply to make someone proud and happy. And Rachel felt guilty for not loving humanity more while so willingly bathing in this woman's warm glow.

When O' Driscoll had not made the rendezvous, she had begun to suspect. That he had been intercepted, arrested and that a news black-out had prevented her finding out more. In the safe house, the day passed without what she feared most. The sudden rushed entry, estuary accents, English accents, being thrown to the floor before she was given a sly blow or two to welcome her to her new reality. "You, love, are under arrest under the Prevention of Terrorism Act."

Twenty years if she was lucky. She was young and attractive and her vanity didn't like the thought. Her womb ached for what that would cost her. She eyed the automatic left on the cheap coffee table in the back street flat. Her own long cold cup sat beside it.

If they came, she had decided, she'd try and shoot one of the bastards and then herself. But then they all thought that, didn't they? She'd remembered during her training reading something about it. The paralysis of fear. The desperate clinging to life. Dragged away to a cellar to scream under God knows what indignities when all you had to do was take the pill or fire the revolver.

Out where they meant it, out in places where, if you were a woman, they would electrocute and hose you while a gang of men prepared to rape the truth from you, they still never pulled the trigger as the door was kicked in. Life. Hope. Who was she kidding? She'd hurl defiant insults then meekly surrender to a long, long time in a prison. She was bloody terrified.

Nothing. No police cars out in the street. No suspiciously twitching curtains in the flat opposite, no black clad figures scurrying along the rooftops. Silence.

She filled it with the TV. The newsflash. A bomb at London

209

Bridge. More as we get it. Many casualties, including deaths. Her relief, her joy, her worry. Where was O' Driscoll?

By nightfall, she had gone to look. Everything she shouldn't do. But that's love for you. The news had reported no arrests. She had to know if he'd gone up with it. If not, find him, save him.

A mini cab into London. All the trains had stopped. Small talk in a disguised accent. A relative at Guy's Hospital, dying, yes it is sad but very elderly and a relief in a way. "This is as close as I can get you, love." Kind words, a decent tip.

The endless meandering. As close as she dared to the police and the ambulances. A walk through the hospitals, unguarded and unchecked. A few pubs, London moved on, they were full but not of him.

At one point she walked onto the bridge and looked into the oily green of the swirl below.

Then the back streets. From Bermondsey Street and back again to the river. The dark, blind warehouses and the smell of excavation, the City over the water and the glow of arc lights from the recovery at the station behind.

She had peered in and pried, briefly disturbed an elderly watchman in his cabin to find his surprise was greater than hers, and watched a dying rat drag itself towards the water from a fracture in the road.

She found a purse in the middle of the street and, a little further on, a woman lying in a door way. Blood had run from her ears and nose and it had stopped, along with the heart that pumped it, to dry like an iron deposit on her pale face. Her beautiful blue eyes were open, doll-like and unnerving, the more so as the living woman, the searcher, stared back in the same shade of vividness.

She opened the purse. It had some cash, a photograph or two, a single rail ticket and a paper driving licence. A single blank cheque was pushed into one of the slits. Folded for use in an emergency. The woman found a street light and stood matching the name to the driving licence. Christie. Christie Christopher.

She glanced up and down the empty street and returned to the woman in the doorway. Above her towered a great Victorian brick façade. The door itself was nothing more than rotting green wood and, through the iron barred windows, she could see only the blackness of deep works and take in the smell of turned earth, damp from proximity to the river.

She tried the door, carefully so as not to fall through it if it gave. It resisted her. She pushed at its bottom with her foot and felt the swollen wood start to groan against the frame. Again she pushed, daring this time to use her shoulder. Again, it moved. This time she stepped back, drew her knee high and stamped at it while holding the brick work on either side. The door swung open, rebounding off the wall and back towards her, before standing ajar in space.

She looked down now at the bleeding woman in its shelter. One way or another she had to escape this country and her silent companion had so far not been missed. She even looked a bit like her. Taking no pleasure in the prospect, she eased her towards the edge of the excavation with her foot. She knelt beside her and briefly touched her hair. "I'm sorry, Christie," she whispered and pushed her body into the pit. It hit something, possibly iron work, and then she heard it roll.

One of them, at least, was now a new woman. Christie Christopher – the original – had finally escaped.

Fifteen minutes later, she found O'Driscoll. It took all her strength to lift him from the floor of the warehouse. Thanking God that he was such a slight man, she dragged him in stages towards Tooley Street. He groaned with each yard covered, occasionally lapsing into unconsciousness so that he could give her no help by moving his legs. Patiently, she would wait until he came round again before they staggered on towards the main road.

She stood with him draped round her shoulders on the kerb. She had thought of trying a mini cab office. Scarcely legal, the drivers were less fussy and less inquisitive. But she was exhausted now and a wait for a driver willing to take her would mean more opportunities for questions even in late night Southwark.

Black cab it was. Two went by. Assuming the sagging O'Driscoll was so inebriated he would vomit on their back seat, they didn't stop as she waved her hand at them.

It was twenty minutes before a third came. Its light was off but the back was empty and she tried anyway, flagging urgently. The cabbie pulled up and dropped his window. In her adopted accent, she asked breathily: "Look, I know this is a long shot but you wouldn't take me and my boyfriend to Dartford would you? He's had a bit too much to drink and he's fallen over and, honestly, I'm a bit desperate."

The driver looked at the pair of them dubiously, weighing the risk of his cab awash with sick and his conscience if he left this pretty young woman by the side of the road with an injured drunk: "Blimey, you're the luckiest girl in the world, aren't you? I was just going home and guess where I live? Come on then, get him in."

O'Driscoll groaned helpfully as she pulled him onto the back seat, his head cradled in her lap. The driver tsked indulgently and headed south. He was glad of the company but too tired at the end of a long day to hold much of a conversation. Gratefully, she sank back in her seat as London turned slowly to somewhere else. She thanked him and meant it. He'd be getting all the cash in Christie's purse as his tip.

When it had all died down, when O'Driscoll had recovered, they'd make a run for Ireland. In the meantime, she felt her head nod, and slid the window down to fight it.

Sean walked down the hill from where the old general on his shrapnel-gouged plinth still surveyed London with a gimlet eye. He followed the path downwards to meet Rachel who was walking up. She had returned to the City and her milieu. Raglan had been right.

It had been almost two years since, they had returned. A grateful Henry Grumman had been told that he too had been right and had died within three months of the knowledge of it. Mick Raglan lived on, happier and occasionally in touch. Peter Francis had joined Christopher in retirement before instantly returning as a consultant to the force. And since Rachel had resigned from it.

She and Sean kissed as they met. "Did he have much to say?" Rachel asked nodding up towards the statue.

"He's not as talkative as he used to be. I think we don't have much in common anymore. It might be over between us."

"I've always been jealous," she joked.

They turned and walked together towards a favourite pub at the bottom of the park, a ritual now. She slapped his behind with a newspaper.

"Here, brought you this for old times' sake." She handed him a copy of the *Evening Standard* she had brought on the light railway from the Square Mile to Greenwich.

He laughed. The front page was confection, conjecture, apocalypse and outrage. "Read it," said Sean. He turned to the

213

back to look at the sport. Football, in which Sean professed to have little interest though Rachel noticed he always seemed to speak the language fluently with cabbies and barbers. A policeman's art, she wondered, or just his talent for absorption by osmosis.

Three boys were in among the swings as they headed towards the gate. They happily insulted each other and tried acrobatics off the various frames. Sean watched them for a moment.

"Remembering?" she asked.

"Yes," he said, "happily. There were happy times. I'd forgotten."

He glanced down at the paper in his hand and sniffed at it. "Doesn't even smell the same. I used to love the smell of newsprint."

"Christ, listen to you. Come on, a drink, before I divorce you for being curmudgeonly." Sean laughed and dropped the newspaper into a litter bin and, taking her hand, walked on. The paper fell open at page five.

Building Stopped After Remains Found

Work on a major redevelopment at London Bridge was halted today after human remains were found on-site.

The skeleton, believed to be that of a woman in her twenties, was found during excavation for foundations of a prestigious new office and residential project minutes from London's Shard, which it will rival for height as well as striking design.

The remains have yet to be formally identified and cause of death established though it is believed they may have lain there since the 1970s when the site was converted from redundant warehouses.

A medallion, believed to be a Catholic Holy Communion medal was found round the neck and may provide further clues to the identity of the body.

Beneath the story, a picture of a necklace, its pendant blue and green with corrosion, had been captioned. "Medallion may reveal identity after gruesome site find."

Sean didn't notice. He was already in the pub chuckling at Rachel's taste in wine as it was passed over the bar and watching his Guinness settle. A regular hailed them and they fell into brief conversation. Outside, the lights came on, and you could hear the laughter.

GLOUCESTER,
STROUD & BERKELEY

GLOUCESTER, STROUD & BERKELEY

Edward Hayward

Illustrated by Paul Shardlow

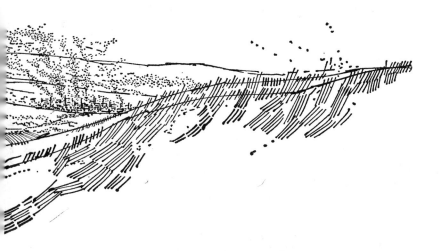

Longman Young Books

LONGMAN GROUP LIMITED
LONDON

Associated companies, branches and
representatives throughout the world

First published 1970

SBN 582 15429 4

The author and publishers wish to thank J. M. Dent &
Sons Ltd. for permission to use the quotations on pages
38 and 58 from the Everyman translation of *Anglo-
Saxon Chronicle* by G. N. Garmonsway.

*Printed in Great Britain by
The Camelot Press Ltd.
London and Southampton*

CONTENTS

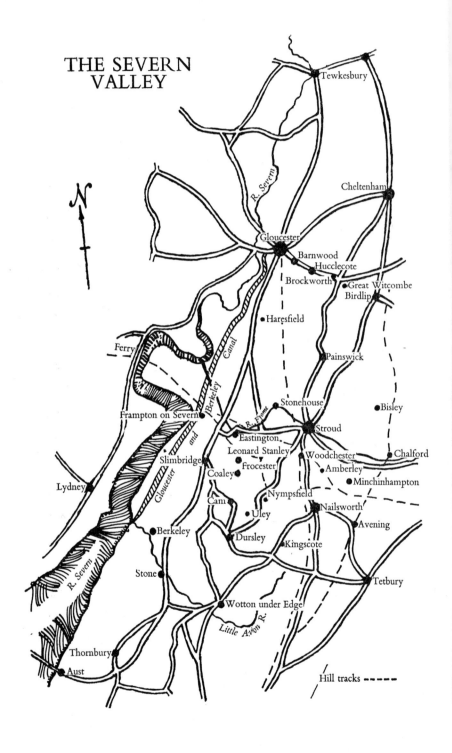

THE SEVERN VALLEY

N

Tewkesbury

R. Severn

Cheltenham

Gloucester
Barnwood
Hucclecote
Brockworth
Great Witcombe
Birdlip

Haresfield

Ferry

Berkeley Canal

Painswick

Stonehouse

R. Frome

Bisley

Frampton on Severn

Stroud

Eastington
Leonard Stanley
Frocester
Woodchester
Chalford

Slimbridge
Amberley

Coaley
Minchinhampton

Lydney

Cam
Nympsfield

Uley
Nailsworth

and Gloucester

Berkeley
Avening

Dursley
Kingscote

R. Severn

Stone

Tetbury

Wotton under Edge

Little Avon R.

Thornbury

Hill tracks - - - - -

Aust

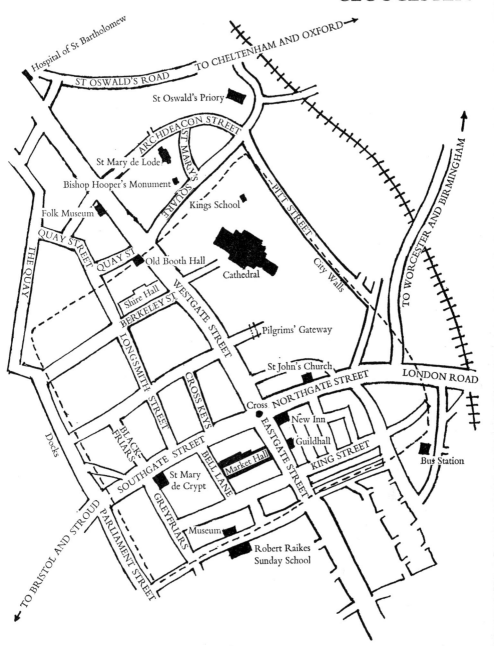

CITY OF GLOUCESTER

Hospital of St Bartholomew

ST OSWALD'S ROAD

TO CHELTENHAM AND OXFORD →

St Oswald's Priory

ARCHDEACON STREET

ST MARY'S SQUARE

St Mary de Lode

Bishop Hooper's Monument

Kings School

PITT STREET

Folk Museum

QUAY STREET

THE QUAY

QUAY ST

Old Booth Hall

Cathedral

City Walls

TO WORCESTER AND BIRMINGHAM ↑

Shire Hall

BERKELEY ST

WESTGATE STREET

LONGSMITH STREET

Pilgrims' Gateway

St John's Church

Docks

CROSS KEYS

NORTHGATE STREET

LONDON ROAD

Cross

New Inn

BLACK-FRIARS

SOUTHGATE STREET

EASTGATE STREET

Guildhall

KING STREET

Bus Station

St Mary de Crypt

BELL LANE

Market Hall

GREYFRIARS

Museum

Robert Raikes
Sunday School

TO BRISTOL AND STROUD

PARLIAMENT STREET

1. THE RIVER

The Severn Vale is the work of the river, and the river began to take the course we know in the warm period after the last of the great Ice Ages, more than 20,000 years ago. The last great advance of the ice probably never reached Gloucestershire, but it came as far south as Shropshire and along the west of the Severn Valley from Ludlow, through Hereford to Usk in Monmouthshire. The river drained away the icy water in the short summer thaws; then towards the end of the cold it must have become fuller and fuller with the melted ice and snow which was never to be replaced.

The rushing water cut deep into the rock in its efforts to get to the river quickly. Valleys, like the Stroud Valley and its tributaries and the Little Avon, must have been formed in this way. When the water reached the wide expanse of the river, it began to leave behind the gravel and mud it had brought down from the high ground. As the last of the water from the glaciers drained away, and the climate became milder still, the river shrank in size and began to flow more slowly. The silt collected along the edges where the water was getting shallower and shallower, and land plants began to spread across it, small plants at first, but later bushes and trees.

The river began to look as it would for many thousands of years, at least until the arrival of the Romans—a wide and rather shallow, muddy stream, still liable to flood the low-lying Vale after heavy rain, fringed on the east by a belt of dense forest land stretching from the river's edge to the foot of the Cotswolds, and up them.

At Barnwood, on the edge of Gloucester, on a bed of gravel that preserved them (and many later remains), have been found

the bones of the early mammals—mammoth, bison, horse, the
woolly rhinoceros and the great shaggy musk ox. Side by side
with these were found handaxes, scrapers and borers made of
flint from the river pebbles, the first signs of man in the Severn
Valley.

The earliest inhabitants were hunters—we know that from
the range of tools that have been found—but we can only guess
exactly how they lived. In the Severn Valley south of Gloucester there have been six big finds of their tools—four along the
banks of the Bristol Avon, one at Barnwood and another at
Frampton—but little else. There are two reasons. First, hunters

have to move with the herds of game, so they cannot collect
many possessions, just weapons for killing and knives for cutting up and preparing the meat. And second, there were probably during this vast period only a few hundred humans in
southern England at the same time. Very likely a small group
of a dozen adults with their children came into the valley on a
summer hunting trip from the south every five or ten years or
so, and camped by the Avon and sometimes on the river gravel
at Frampton and Barnwood. These tiny groups perhaps saw
other humans only a few times in their lives, so new ideas
spread very slowly.

Gradually men began to settle in one place and vary the
game with nuts and berries and the meat and milk from the
half-tamed descendants of the wild pig and the ox they now

kept tethered on the edges of their small villages. We know that by about 2500 BC cereals—mostly wheat—were being grown in a few places in the Severn Valley and along the Cotswold ridges. But evidence of the way these farmers lived is still almost as scanty as of the earliest hunters' way of life. At Toghill, near Marshfield, the tiny, carefully shaped flints of this period have been found at the edge of the Cotswold scarp. At Leonard Stanley, on a bed of gravel along the river Frome, on a site very similar to those of the old hunters at Frampton and Barnwood, there was probably a settlement, because a number of flints have been discovered. And Barnwood itself was still inhabited for some of the year if not all of it. Probably the people stayed in one place only as long as the ground gave them good crops and hunting—perhaps for two or three years or so: then they moved on and cleared more land. But not necessarily very far.

Other finds of the Middle Stone Age, as we call it, have been made at Eastington, Coaley and Frocester, all near Leonard Stanley and all on or near the same gravel bank.

This period was warm and dry in summer and cold in winter: but towards its close (about 3000 BC) a cooler, wetter climate began to take over. The pine forests which had been growing since the end of the Ice Age slowly gave way to oak and alder. And new people came to Britain and brought with them the culture of the New Stone Age.

They were farmers in earnest: they had to be, now that there was less sun to ripen corn and fruit without any effort from man. A number of flint sickle blades for harvesting corn have been found in their tombs. They used heavy, polished axes of greenish stone from North Wales to make clearings in the forest for fields. They had herds of goats, oxen, sheep and pigs, which they seem to have slaughtered each autumn, because they lacked the food to keep alive more than a few of them through the winter. But they were hunters too. They used fragile-looking, but deadly, diamond-shaped arrowheads to kill wild boar, deer and wolf in the oak forests of the Vale and wildfowl along the marshy edges of the river.

We know very little of their lives. But we do know that the farmers of the New Stone Age came to Gloucestershire from Brittany by sea up the Severn and people of the same background settled on both sides of the valley. Up the river, too, came traders from Ireland, Cornwall, Brittany and North Wales with polished stone axes to barter. From our area they fanned out all over England—along the hilltop tracks especially to Wiltshire and Hampshire, and on up the river to Shropshire. The hilltops were easier, quicker and safer to travel along than the valley. There were no marshes to avoid, few streams to ford, and on the open uplands it was much easier to see one's route and to watch for wild animals and robbers. From the time of the New Stone Age at least, men used the river and the Cotswolds as parallel lines of communication, and they were still using the same routes in the Middle Ages.

The biggest clue of all that we have about the New Stone Age farmers and their reliance on the Severn is in the tombs of their chieftains: the Cotswold long barrows. The long barrows, seventy-five of them in Gloucestershire, stretch down the length of the Cotswolds into Somerset. There are more along the coasts of North and South Wales, and up the river valleys of the Usk and the Wye. In their primitive boats these men must have struck out across the widest part of the English Channel to Cornwall, and then either walked across the widest part of the isthmus or rounded Land's End to go on up the river and penetrate into the heart of England. Why they did it we can only guess: perhaps they were crowded out of their own homes and found the nearest land to the north, Hampshire and Sussex, already colonized. Perhaps they first heard tell of their new home when they came to the south-west of England to trade with the Irish and Cornish. Nor do we know how many of them there were—whether they took over the land completely and drove the Middle Stone Age hunter-farmers away, or simply taught them their new way of life and stayed to rule over them. Probably the second is truer, but it does not really matter. Their long barrow tombs—Hetty Pegler's Tump above Frocester, at Nympsfield and Kingscote, on Selsley

Common, at Gatcombe and Avening and Bisley—pay a tribute to their power over the land.

Each barrow is a long, oval mound of turf, covering a pile of stones kept in place by skilfully built dry stone walls. At the entrance—nearly always to the east—the mound curves forward on each side as if to protect the graves not just from intruders but from the sounds of the living world and daylight itself. Perhaps the religion of these people centred on an Earth Mother goddess, and they believed that when they died they were returning to the dark moist womb of the ground as they were carried towards the west into the chamber, just as the sun returned to his mother in the west each evening. Inside the tombs, in the chambers leading off to right and left, were the graves of successive generations of chieftains and their families, their knees bent to their chests in the position of a baby in its mother's womb. They were laid here surrounded by a few weapons and tools, and a few pieces of pottery that would have held food and drink. Often, too, small collections of smooth, beautifully coloured stones and sea shells were left with the dead person—his own private collection—to take with him to the next life. Someone has calculated that there are 5,000 tons of stone in the Rodmarton long barrow. Think of the number of men and the time they would take to collect that much in small pieces, let alone transporting and lifting into place two or three dozen large flat slabs for the walls and roof of the burial chambers. The work involved shows us how firmly in power the chieftains must have been to command such effort.

The New Stone Age men came to the Severn about 2500 BC, and they were still there over 1,000 years later. They herded their cattle, cleared the forests and grew crops, made fine flint axes and the first pottery to be seen in Britain. During that time the barrows were built and used continuously. So strong were the New Stone Age chieftains that even after 1,500 years their influence in the Severn Valley was strong enough to hold back a new group who had already some centuries before begun to take over from their distant relatives in Wiltshire—the bronze users.

The new people probably never took over the Severn Valley completely. For one thing the climate was becoming drier again and the area may not have been able to support so large a population. But for some time, despite the many differences between them, the long barrow farmers lived side by side with people of the new cultures.

The New Stone Age people were smallish, with long narrow skulls. The new bronze users were bigger built and more muscular, and their heads were round. The New Stone Age people were farmers; they used polished stone axes. They buried their chiefs in family tombs and worshipped an Earth Mother. But the Bronze Age people were nomadic hunters. We think that they prayed to a male god of fire and light. Their bodies were often burnt and then buried, normally alone, save for an earthenware beaker with a handle, under a round shaped mound of stone. The beaker in the round barrow at Ivy Lodge at King's Stanley had a whitish film round the inside: this was probably the dried remains of a kind of beer which the Bronze Age man drank.

Although the arrival of the Beaker Folk marks the beginning of what we call the Bronze Age, we must not think that they used bronze and nothing else. Native copper was mixed with Cornish tin to make bronze only in Ireland and Scotland at first. The Beaker Folk got their bronze spears and arrowheads by trading, and they were expensive. Almost all tools and weapons found in round barrows are still of flint, and we have to rely on chance finds for our knowledge of the first users of metal and their trade routes. Two early bronze spearheads were found some years ago on Rodborough Common, near a trackway that ran from the hilltops to the Severn. Four Irish bronze axeheads were uncovered at Westbury-on-Trym, just south of our area. An odd bronze arrowhead was turned up in a round barrow at Minchinhampton.

In Gloucestershire there are many more round barrows than long barrows—350 in all. They appear in clusters, along the hilltops where the long barrows had been built. They often seem to huddle closely to the long barrows, as if accepting that

their occupants, or their descendants at least, still ruled. We believe that the bronze users shared their villages and even married long barrow girls.

One of the Beaker graves at Barnwood was for a man of about thirty. He had a beaker near him, red-brown in colour with the usual patterns scratched round the outside, and a Bronze Age flint knife; a typical Beaker man except that his skull was not completely round—one of his parents must have been of the long barrow people. In another barrow, a long barrow near Bisley, three people were found, a mother, a father, and a young child. The father had a round head, and the mother a long head, and the child's was a cross between the two.

The Bronze Age, first brought to southern Britain by the Beaker Folk, lasted for more than a thousand years. Other bronze users followed the Beaker Folk. Even if we accept that their culture only overtook that of the older inhabitants later than in most other places, the number of round barrow tombs which spread from the hilltops down into the Vale at Standish and Frampton and to the south near Thornbury, shows how numerous the wealthy ruling class must have been.

About 900 BC the climate began to change once more—it became wetter all over Europe, and the low lying areas along the Severn which had been drying out slowly since the end of the New Stone Age became swampy as the river level rose and the river widened. The area round Aust—which was probably an island in Roman times—must have gradually become separated from the eastern bank at about this time. Probably the same change in climate forced certain tribes of red-haired people from the river- and lake-sides of Switzerland and southern Germany to find new homes farther west; between 900 and 700 BC the first of these men—who were later to be known as Celts—came to Britain. It was the cousins of these Celts, the La Tène people, who shattered the peace so suddenly after 300 BC. They were wine-drinking, pork-eating warriors, who fought from light wicker chariots. What made them so terrifying was that they did their fighting with swords and lance tips of a new, hard metal, iron, which their ancestors had learnt to use, probably during raids south over the Alps and into Italy. The La Tène warriors had come earlier to eastern England but had only settled in a few places at first. When they discovered the route across from western France to Cornwall for the trade in tin, and then up the Severn to the iron ore mines that were just beginning to be dug in the Forest of Dean, it seems that they had no trouble in quickly turning the area into a La Tène stronghold.

Stronghold is the word, because the great monuments surviving from their time are the hillforts that they built at strategic points along the hilltops and in the valley. At first they were small—an enclosure, surrounded by a rampart and a ditch, for the huts of the ruler and his family and flocks; this could perhaps house his people and their possessions too in times of danger. Later the whole village began to be housed with its chief in huge forts, often many acres in size—plenty of room for a large number of huts and many head of cattle, sheep and pigs. The early forts had only one line of defences—often they simply cut across a promontory of high ground with the land dropping away steeply on three sides. The first fortifications at Haresfield Beacon are a good example of this.

But about 150 BC a new secret weapon appeared from the Mediterranean—the sling. The sling could throw a small round river pebble or a baked ball of clay about 100 yards—farther than any man could throw a spear, farther and harder than a bow could shoot. You could not hide behind your single rampart and feel safe any longer. A squad of slingers could cause havoc among the people and livestock packed inside. The answer was to build more ramparts—so many lines of defence that the force of the sling stone was spent by the time it reached the living area. The fort at Uleybury had only two banks and ditches but the site was so well chosen that only in one small quarter of the ramparts would the slingers not have had to throw almost vertically into the air.

On a ridge over the river at Lydney stood one of these hill-forts. Here was the reason for the area's importance. It was in the centre of the iron industry of the Forest of Dean. To reach its best markets, however, the iron—in bars shaped to look like sword blades—had to cross the territory of the chieftains on the opposite bank. And this fact was to become the key to the events of the last century before the Romans invaded.

At that time yet another group of invaders began pushing their way westward across England. The Belgae, from what has become known today as Belgium, brought with them heavy wheeled wagons for trade and transport. They made pottery with a wheel. They knew advanced methods of farming. They used coins of gold, silver and bronze. They were head hunters. But most important of all, they came in large tribes of many hundreds of people, with kings and courts and governments.

The first wave of Belgic settlers entered our area from the south. Sheer weight of numbers must have helped them pick off the quarrelsome hillfort chieftains one by one. There were fights for at least two of the forts, at Worlebury near Weston-super-Mare and at Bredon Hill just north of Tewkesbury.

After the settlement, the hillforts seem to have been abandoned, the palisades burnt and the walls pushed down to stop them ever being used again. During the Belgic occupation, the people of the area became known as the Dobunni. It is probable that in giving the people one name the Belgic princes were simply recognizing the fact that the area was already loosely unified. The kingdom of the Dobunni stretched from northern Somerset to the southern half of Worcestershire and included the whole of Gloucestershire east of the Severn. To the west were the Silures, a warlike tribe who could never be friends with the Dobunni. But they depended on each other because it was mainly the Dobunni who passed the iron to the other tribes of Belgic England.

The Dobunni were farmers. Their iron axes and ploughs enabled them to clear land easier and quicker than ever before, and plough the rich heavy soil of the Vale for the first time on any scale. Clearings probably began to appear in the thick woodland along the trading trails to the Severn, by which the bars of crude iron would have been brought from the river.

Bg

One trail led to the Stinchcombe area—it probably came up the hill from the inlet at Berkeley Pill—east and slightly north. A second, which we have mentioned before, came from the river at Arlingham, along the southern bank of the Frome and up over Rodborough Common, or by way of Frocester Hill, towards the upper Thames Valley. And a third, called Portway, crossed the river where Gloucester now stands, mounted the slope at Cranham, crossed the main ridgeway at Sapperton and continued east. The main ridgeway was the great track which ran right down the length of the Cotswolds and crossed the other tracks at the head of the Frome Valley.

In a defensive position near where the four met was the capital of the Belgic kings, Bagendon, just north of modern Cirencester. We know little about any other Belgic settlements in the territory of the Dobunni, so it is from Bagendon that we get our best picture of their lives. It was a wealthy town, because of the iron trade. Traders would have been drawn there from all parts of southern England and beyond. There was expensive red Samian pottery from northern Italy and glass from Egypt. Wine from the Mediterranean came in those non-returnable jars with pointed bases known all over the Classical world as *amphorae*. Tin from Cornwall and gold from Ireland came up the Severn, and copper came down it from North Wales. From much nearer home came lead and silver from the Mendips (within the tribe's frontiers) and, along with the pig iron from across the river, coal.

Bagendon was an important industrial centre. Its metal workers were highly skilled with gold, copper, and tin as well as iron. They used a touchstone, an extremely rare thing in Britain, to measure the purity of metals. They could extract silver from lead, and the quality of their best iron was almost as fine as steel. They made all sorts of objects, including their own type of the brooch that everyone used to fasten their clothes. Near another trackway, the Calfway, which runs along the hillcrests from Leckhampton above Cheltenham south to Chalford and beyond, the grave of a Belgic woman was found at Birdlip. Buried with the woman was a beautiful bronze mirror, engraved on the back with an elegant pattern of crescents and circles, and with traces of red enamel still visible. Perhaps this too was the work of the Bagendon metalsmiths.

At Bagendon the king ruled and his money was minted. The design on his coins was copied from money minted in Macedon in northern Greece. This had started as an ear of wheat or a god's head (Apollo's) on one side and a chariot pulled by two horses on the other. The less civilized British tribes never really grasped the meaning of the pictures but blindly copied the details as if they were part of an abstract pattern. The result is quite incredible! A gold Dobunni coin in Gloucester Museum shows what fine craftsmen the Bagendon metal workers were, and what terrible artists!

The people of Bagendon and their country neighbours we imagine as being unusually well off. They tended their flocks, and harvested their crops. They lived in round, half-timbered huts with stone floors and thatched roofs. They seem to have eaten well—oysters and mussels from the Severn estuary, the occasional gamebird brought down with a hunting bow or sling along the river's marshy fringes, wine from abroad traded for slaves and hunting dogs—and to have been able to afford a good deal of jewellery to set off their woollen clothes. But this wealthy, civilized way of life depended on one thing— the iron trade. Because of its vital importance in the rivalries of the first-century kingdoms, the Dobunni were drawn into the centre of the unrest which was to help bring the Romans to England.

2. GLEVUM

It is probable that the Dobunni, when they fought their way into the Severn Valley from the south and east, had been close relations of the Atrebates, who occupied Berkshire and Wiltshire. But in 15 BC, Tincommius, the king of the Atrebates, became an ally of the Romans; the kings of the Dobunni, who were beginning to feel secure in their new lands, broke their treaty of friendship and joined forces with Tincommius' rival, Cunobelin (or Cymbeline, as Shakespeare called him), an enemy of Rome, who was king of the Catuvellauni, and ruled a kingdom which stretched from the Essex coast up the Thames Valley to Oxfordshire.

Cunobelin's vast, straggling capital near Colchester was probably the most sophisticated city in Britain. When the town of Bagendon was built, it was set out in a similar way. But this does not mean that Gloucestershire became part of Cunobelin's kingdom. From Bagendon, the kings of the Dobunni still ruled their people, and they profited from the trade and protection the alliance brought.

When Cunobelin died in AD 41, the peace of southern England was shattered. His two sons could not keep his kingdom united and secure from its enemies. In Gloucestershire, the Dobunni were split in their allegiance between King Bodvoc, who still ruled from Bagendon, and Catti and his successor, Corio, who ruled in the south. The Romans, in AD 43, took advantage of all the confusion and invaded. Cunobelin's two sons were defeated in Kent and retreated: at the same time the northern Dobunni sent messengers to Kent to surrender to the Roman general. Probably they had been fighting side by side with the soldiers of the Catuvellauni and had been badly beaten. But Corio's part of the tribe, which had not sent its warriors east, was still as strongly against the Romans as ever. And probably when Cunobelin's son, Caractacus, retreated west, he went straight to Corio's kingdom for refuge.

For four years—until AD 47—Caractacus disappears from the history books. On Minchinhampton Common is an Iron Age settlement with deep rock-cut ditches surrounding an area of 600 acres. To the east stand the Bulwarks, which cut off more than half of the promontory from the east even today. Above Amberley is a large living enclosure with plenty of room for hundreds of huts and many hundreds of head of cattle. At Rodborough, on the very western tip of the high ground, is another line of defences. It has been suggested by archaeologists that here, across the line of the ancient trackway to the ford at Arlingham and the iron ore mines of the forest beyond, Caractacus set up his standard and built his Dun—the camp from which he led his resistance to Rome. At Bagendon, only ten miles away, Bodvoc still ruled as king, but his men, since the surrender in Kent, were allowed to carry no weapons. We can imagine Caractacus with his warriors riding out from his stronghold to raid the defenceless land to the east whenever the thinly spread Roman troops were clear of the area. In AD 47 the Roman Governor established a military frontier zone along the line from Bath to Lincoln, deposed Bodvoc and moved his people from Bagendon to a new town, behind the line of the frontier, and called it Corinium Dobunnorum. This was not just to protect them or to try to turn them into civilized Rome-loving citizens of the Empire. Behind the frontier, the Governor could watch them better.

At last Caractacus, if he was at Minchinhampton, must have seen that his time was up. The Roman grip was tightening, and Roman patrols were probably already scouting the uplands to the north as far as Cranham. He had been making friends with the Silures across the river, and at some time in AD 47 he must have slipped away, taking with him his men with their families and flocks, and those of Corio's men who still wanted to fight.

The Romans probably burnt the palisades and pulled down

the walls of the camp at Minchinhampton; perhaps they left a
small detachment of men at Haresfield Beacon to watch the
road to Arlingham, and looked elsewhere. Roman troops had
already penetrated north-west from Bagendon. And at the
foot of the hills there lay the small settlement with the Celtic
name which meant "place by the shining water"—Caer Glou.
The Romans came to call it Glevum; we know it as Gloucester.

The crossing at Glevum was messier and less direct than the
ford at Arlingham, but much more certain. The part of the
river west of the town was then probably a wide shallow
lagoon (the shining water) which the rising tide would have
made a lot wider, but only a little deeper. It was easy to ford,
and a causeway with small bridges at intervals to take the
stream could be built later, as it almost certainly was.

The first elements of the Roman army to reach Caer Glou
probably came from Bagendon on patrol duty when the area
was outside the military zone. They would have been cavalry
—mercenary soldiers from the fringes of the Empire—and they
may have had with them military engineers for the advance
surveying of a road. The road they built does not point direct
at modern Gloucester, but to the first fort at Kingsholm,
slightly to the north of the native village there. We can imagine
that the site had been used by scouting parties for short stays
some time before the first units settled permanently. Roman
troops were trained to set up their camps quickly, always to the
same plan. They carried materials and tools with them as part
of their standard issue of kit, and the first camp, with Caer Glou
on the rise to the south, would seem to us as raw and new as the
timber cavalry forts of Western films, with the ragged cluster
of native dwellings nearby.

Britain east of the Severn was soon at peace again. But to the
west the trouble went on. Gloucester was to become the base
for operations against the Silures across the river, and so
important did the Roman Governor rate the task that a full
legion—only four altogether had been assigned for the capture
of all Britain—was brought out of reserve at Colchester and
sent to Glevum. This was the 20th Legion, the Valeria Victrix,

which had been stationed before the invasion near modern Düsseldorf in Germany.

Now that a full legion had been ordered to set up a camp, the old fort was abandoned. There was a drier, more defendable position on the hill to the south, where the native village had probably been. It was the best site and the native village would have been demolished. In its place rose the turf ramparts of the legionary depot, forty-six acres in area and a mile round the defences. It supplied 6,000 foot soldiers and some cavalry as well with all the facilities of a permanent base camp—the armourers' workshops, the cookhouses, the military hospital, the parade ground, the stores, the administrative offices, the temples, the stables, and the officers' quarters. Roman armies were trained and equipped to supply all their own needs. But whenever an army settles in one place for some time, camp followers collect; at Glevum the ramshackle huts of a settlement began to grow up between the west wall of the fort and the river's edge.

There was probably already a landing place here which had

been used for the iron trade. Now shops and stalls lined the waterfront and ran up the slope—noisy vulgar shops which would have sold cheap drink and cheap meals and cheap souvenirs for the soldiers. Somewhere here too was a pottery which had been set up by craftsmen who may have followed the legion from Colchester. They made fine vases and jugs of shiny buff and brown with a slight glitter of mica dust.

The 20th Valeria stayed at Glevum for nearly twenty years. But in AD 67 it broke its ties with Glevum and moved north to Wroxeter, to replace the 14th Legion which was being withdrawn to the east of the Empire. Some of the potters seem to have uprooted themselves and moved on too. The 2nd Legion, the Augusta, which replaced the Valeria, stayed for only seven years. By then the Roman government felt itself strong enough to break the Silures once and for all, and the Augusta moved again, this time across the river to Caerleon, deep in Silurian territory.

We know nothing of the history of Glevum over the next twenty years, but since the fight against the Silures was a long one, it may well be that the move was only a gradual one, with Gloucester serving as a rest centre, supply base and headquarters of the roadbuilding squads which were pushing the road network up to the advance posts in Silurian territory, and back to Corinium. The roads went upriver to Droitwich, Wroxeter and Chester, too, and down to Abonae, the ferry port on the Severn, near Bristol, which was taking over from Gloucester as the quickest and safest supply route for Caerleon.

The next date we have in Gloucester's history is AD 96. In that year, it officially ceased being a military establishment of the frontier and became Colonia Nervia Glevensium, a new city of the Roman Empire. Setting up colonies, like York, Colchester and Lincoln in England and Colonia Agrippina (Cologne) in Germany, was a cheap practical way of doing a great many useful things. Since Roman soldiers signed on for twenty or twenty-five years, they tended to reach retirement in their early forties, with years of active life left. On retirement they had to be given, by law, some land and some money. All

along the frontiers the government founded colonies—towns
which housed the veterans. It was a convenient way of developing the land, of keeping an eye on the local native population,
and of giving them an example of the superiority of the Roman
way of life. In every frontier area there was always this nucleus
of able-bodied ex-soldiers to be relied on to back up the regular
troops in real emergencies.

Colonies like Glevum were governed like any town in Italy.
They had their forum, their hall of justice and their municipal
offices. They would have had suites of baths, and temples to
the Roman gods, especially the soldiers' gods, Mithras and
Claudius. The citizens could elect four magistrates each year to
attend to justice, tax collecting and public works. Officials of a
colony had a certain amount of independence from the provincial government and the governor; they lived under the *Ius
Italicum*—the Law of Italy—a special law for Roman citizens
that tended to be more considerate and fairer than the *Ius
Gentium*, the law for all the other inhabitants of the Empire.
Like the citizens of Rome herself, the colonists belonged to a
Republic, and like the early cities of Italy and Greece, most men
in them earned their living from the land.

It has been calculated that at any one time there would have
been about 3,000 veterans of the 2nd Augusta living in
Glevum with their wives and children as well as other Roman
citizens—merchants, for instance, and the non-Roman hangers
on—a total of perhaps 6,000 or 8,000 people. The normal
amount of land given to each soldier was about six *iugera*;
common wood and grazing were provided too. Usually the
holdings were laid out in one place, and it has been suggested
that the only level and dry area big enough for the settlement
is to the north-east towards Cheltenham, between the main
Tewkesbury road and the Cirencester road, a rectangle perhaps
six miles by five miles, with the common woodland stretching
up the slopes beyond it. Only one building has been found in
the area so far, the farmhouse at Hucclecote.

This was a small, but well equipped house with a large bathing block. Like most Roman country houses it was built of a

mixture of local stone and half timbering, and it was probably
coated with pink cement on the outside, like houses in Spain
and Italy today.

Apart from its position, the thing which links Hucclecote to
the colony is a roofing tile marked *R.P.G. Pa et Fi. Res Publicae
Glevensium*—Gloucester Corporation! Probably the *Pa et Fi*
were the initials of a pair of magistrates, some time in the
second century AD, and we could date the tile exactly if we
knew more about these two.

The other landmark outside the ramparts of the colony was
the main burial ground, spread out along the high road at the
point where the old road to Kingsholm made its final turn to
the new colony, and along to Kingsholm itself. Here were the
tombs and the altars set up to the dead. The line of graves
reaches almost to Barnwood, the old Stone Age settlement,
still a village in Roman times.

Inside the ramparts the layout of the town is still not certain.
We know that the four modern main roads to the Cross are on
almost the same sites as four Roman ones, and that the side
streets would have run at right angles and parallel to these, but
apart from this we know little. The Forum was to the south-
east of these four roads, with the large bronze statue of a horse-

man in it. The remains of a large public building have been found on the corner of Westgate Street and Southgate Street. There was a colonnade along the front of the building and behind it stretched a floor of flagstones from the Forest of Dean. On the opposite corner (the north-east) the beginning of another colonnade has been found, and on the north-west corner the foundations of a large gate. Perhaps the north-east colonnade was the entrance to the town hall; an enormous hoard of coins was found buried under it—a hoard of small change that could only be the takings of rent and toll collectors or a float for paying the weekly wages of many men: in other words, the town treasury.

Another large building stood in what we know as Westgate Street, a vast building stretching at least sixty yards down the street, fronted by large columns with the elegant leaves and branches of the Roman Corinthian order carved on the capitals. The building must have been as high as the modern Shire Hall —fifty feet at least, and from what we know of Colchester, another colony, it has been suggested that this was a temple to the emperor and god Claudius—the conqueror of Britain and a favourite of all Roman soldiers.

There were at least two other temples. One was at the very end of Northgate Street, dedicated to Mercury, and to his wife Rosmerta: they stood side by side on the altar stone. The other temple, near the south-west corner of the ramparts, was dedicated to Mithras, the Persian god of light and strength.

As well as farming, the colonists and the natives must have earnt their living as shopkeepers and craftsmen supplying the countryside round about with some of the finer things of life —moulds for making clay statuettes have been found in Gloucester, and there is evidence of iron smelting and wine making. And of course there was the earthenware from the Glevum pottery, for those who could not afford the brick-red Samian ware imported from southern France.

Behind the grand public buildings and the cobbled main streets lined with shops were the side alleys, narrow and badly paved. Shops and the houses of the poor were jumbled up with richer homes. The average home centred on an inner court-yard. From the outside the only things to be seen were high blank walls with a few windows and a gate, and perhaps the green tops of a few trees in the garden. Inside, though, there might be an ornamentally carved well-head in the middle of the courtyard, a magnificent mosaic pavement in the main living-room and silver for the table on special occasions. Occasionally, houses even had their own piped water, run from the river Twyver, which had probably been cleaned out and widened to bring it from Robin's Wood Hill for the town's public water cisterns. The family included the servants; they all lived together and prayed together. It was one of the duties of the head of the household to lead the family's worship at an altar somewhere in the house, and these altars have been found. It is possible that the stone head with a very Roman hairstyle (but carved by some native sculptor) found on the site of the Bon Marché may have represented an ancestor one family worshipped.

We can imagine the town developing—the new grand public buildings going up in the first hundred years of the colony's existence: the quay being built to take the increasing trade in stone and iron from the Forest of Dean; the light warehouses extending along the quayside; the wood and plaster houses and shops being rebuilt in stone and tile, and the turf ramparts becoming overgrown with grass and young trees as the ditches outside were filled up with rubbish. Glevum must have grown crowded and prosperous with the peace which followed the move of the military frontier far to the west.

So did the countryside around it. It looked much the same as it had when the first hunters moved across the area looking for game in the Old Stone Age. The river was wider than today, especially in the south. For the most part too, the Vale was marshy and covered still with oak and elm trees. But the Romans were adding to the clearings of Iron Age times. The colony lands to the north-east of Gloucester had been cleared from the forest, and there were farmlands near Frocester, Whitminster and King's Stanley, and in the south near Thornbury. The hilltops were also wooded and in the woods there were all the animals we know today, as well as red deer, wild boar and wolves.

Roman roads boxed in the Vale and the hilltops in a long rectangle. The main paved roads ran from Glevum to Corinium to Aquae Sulis (Bath) to Abonae (Sea-Mills) to Glevum again. But the main roads had been put there to help govern the country: first and foremost they were for soldiers and for government business. Ordinary Romans used the old trackways as much as the natives did, if we can judge by the clusters of Roman and native wayside shrines near them.

The Cotswold slopes and the Vale were farming and hunting country. In the stretches of cleared land corn was grown and often shipped abroad to help feed the densely populated areas of southern France and Italy. Cattle were herded for their dairy produce and their leather. The sheep from the uplands were grown for their fine long-haired fleeces. Orchards of pears, cherries and sweet chestnut were planted too. One crop which we know was grown along the south-facing slopes is grapes for wine.

At first the countryside was left very largely to the natives. A few isolated farms may have sprung up in the first fifty years of the occupation while the legions occupied Glevum and when the Silures were still occasionally raiding the Vale from across the river. But as the frontier moved west Romans came out into the countryside and the native farmers began to realize that they could enjoy the pleasure of living like Romans too. Some villas were large, some were small, but the villa was a Roman thing, a sign that the owners were civilized. There were simple ones, like the one at Frocester, and more lavish ones like Witcombe, but they all had a central dining-room with a mosaic floor and most had blocks of baths (set away from the main living rooms to lessen the risk of fire) where a farmer of the Dobunni, doing well for himself, could take off his clothes and wash himself every evening before perhaps putting on a Roman toga, like his wealthier Latin neighbour.

In the countryside the villas multiplied, especially in the more attractive spots away from towns where the land had not yet all been snapped up and cleared. There is a cluster up the Painswick Valley, another group which took advantage of the views across the Vale from the old Arlingham–Frocester Hill–Bagendon trackway, and more scattered along the slopes above Gloucester. Country life must have been as good as it was made out to be in Virgil's book, the *Georgics*, with plenty of food and drink, the joy of the harvest celebrations, and hunting parties.

The gods of the wayside shrines, some Roman, some native, some from other places in the Empire, presided over everything. At King's Stanley, Nailsworth, Bisley and Lypiatt there were altars to Mars Romulus, the warrior who protected men and their crops from harm. Mercury, the god of businessmen and travellers, and Rosmerta, his wife, who often carries a horn of plenty, were worshipped at Glevum; Silvanus with his hood, his dog and his stick, the god of the richness of the countryside, at Bisley and Cherington. Hygeia, daughter of Aesculapius, god of good health, had a shrine with at least six altars left by grateful worshippers at Leonard Stanley. And there was the goddess who needed no shrine—Sabrina, the spirit of the river.

3. VILLAS

About AD 180, Glevum and many other towns of Roman Britain were walled with stone. The steady advance of the army north into Scotland had stopped twenty years before, and a revolt in the north was crushed by Julius Verus. The tribes to the north overran Hadrian's Wall. Very quickly, within thirty years, there were two more periods of unrest. Hadrian's Wall had to be replanned and rebuilt and many northern forts were reconstructed too. In the panic to save the prosperity they enjoyed, the towns themselves must have taken part in the plans for their own defence.

The wall at Glevum was six feet wide and perhaps twenty feet high. There were gates on each side and towers every few yards. Stone was quarried near Painswick and then brought to Gloucester in blocks, perhaps on rafts down the river Twyver. They cut back the old turf rampart in front and behind to take the lines of blocks for the faces of the wall. Where the ground was waterlogged, they left the stone blocks without mortar so that the water could drain through without causing any damage. The colonists made a good job of it. They were ex-soldiers and most of them had been involved in the building of dozens of stone forts. Much of the wall survived to protect Gloucester until 1643, with repairs and additions.

A hoard of coins has been found buried in a jar under a floor in one of the large buildings near the centre of Glevum. There were 15,000 coins, small ones, but carefully chosen for their fineness. The newest coins in the jar belonged to the reign of Allectus, the finance chief who murdered his master, Carausius, and illegally proclaimed himself Emperor. But Allectus and his men were soon beaten and massacred. Perhaps the Silures took their chance to make a raid in the confusion, and the treasury of the colony was hurriedly buried for protection.

Cities were becoming crowded and expensive. Land prices must have shot up as building space became scarce, and there was no end to the taxes which had to be paid. The years of unrest had badly affected trade and prices rose. Businessmen lived in cities—cities which had recently been fortified so expensively because they were such inviting targets for marauders, either official or unofficial, Roman or native. The best proposition was to move out into the country, invest in a fine house with farming lands tucked out of harm's way, where you did not have to pay inflated prices for your food and drink and fuel and clothing—your land produced them for you for the cost of some native slaves, picked up cheaply at an auction. Rich people, who felt the pinch of town life most and had the money to move, began to leave, often going to villas and land they already owned. The slopes of the Cotswolds south of Glevum was one of the favourite spots for the rich man looking for a country home. The area was beautiful, with good hunting and fertile farming land in the Vale. There was plenty of water, cheap wood and stone for building, and good communications. You could be in Aquae Sulis or Corinium, both extremely fashionable places, in less than half a day if you wanted sophisticated company or a mineral bath for your aches and pains. And if real danger threatened, you could be inside stone town walls just as quickly.

There are no signs of the panic in the countryside. It is not just the number of villas that shows how fashionable the area was. It is their size and elegance too. Nearly all of them had been built seventy or eighty years before, but many were now rebuilt and added to. The large villa at Witcombe, which may well have had something to do with the Colonia, was one of the earliest in the area. Here there were magnificent mosaics; and white marble—the very finest, from Carrara in Italy—was used for cornices and the bases and Ionic capitals of pillars. It was already a hundred years old at this time.

The grandest of all the villas in the province, at Woodchester, shows signs of having had a great deal of money lavished on it at this time. It is not the largest in Britain, but it must certainly have belonged to someone rich, educated and extremely cultured. A Latin, almost certainly, and a connoisseur. Perhaps it was the country residence of the provincial governor himself. Evidence to date the first building here is slight. There could have been a villa at Woodchester along with the others nearby in the second century. But the house we are talking about was constructed all of a piece very likely about AD 230–250.

It is unusual because the rest of the villas in the area are built on three sides of a square with the fourth side walled to form a farmyard or a garden in the local fashion. Woodchester is built on a Latin pattern—and a pattern of the most elegant houses in Italy. It was set round two courtyards; the bathing suite had its own small courtyard, with a portico and what may have been a sun terrace off the outer courtyard to the right. Opposite the entrance to the inner from the outer courtyard, approached along a sort of cloister round the inner courtyard, was a great hall, which almost becomes a third, covered court. Probably the roof of the hall was a light wooden dome standing on wooden pillars set in the four corners. The roof had to be light because it was large—forty-nine feet across—and there could be no central support, because under the dome lay the most remarkable mosaic pavement ever found in Britain. The quality of the design is on a level with the best found in Italy, and only a very few mosaics in Britain can even compare with it.

It seems that a foreign artist came to the area and set up shop for a time in Cirencester, because he laid out three or four other pavements nearby. His wonderful workmanship is one of his trademarks. The other is the subject he chose (or suggested) for each owner—the legend of Orpheus, the god of music, and his power to make wild animals tame by playing on his lyre. In the centre of the design sat Orpheus with his lyre. Round him, echoing the circle of the dome above, were circles of fishes and sea monsters; then birds, a peacock, a dove, a duck, a pheasant, and a fox (to show that they forgot their fear of it as

CG

they listened); and then more animals. These animals are four feet high: a bear, a gryphon, a stag, a leopard, a tigress, a lion, a lioness, a boar, a dog, an elephant and two others which have been destroyed. What a favourite subject Orpheus would have been for a "civilized" villa owner, imagining himself as Orpheus taming the countryside around him! And even more for a governor with a literary turn of mind, thinking of all those "savage" Dobunni up and down the Vale and the Cotswolds in their Roman-style houses, living the civilized life of the Empire which he represented.

The villas and the countryside continued to prosper, but if the towns of the west—Wroxeter, for instance—are anything to go by, the colony gradually began to go downhill. During the emperor Constantius's reorganization of the defences of Britain, he withdrew the Second Legion from Caerleon where it had been based for more than 200 years. It was to be stationed at Richborough on the Kentish coast as a centre for the line of forts protecting the south and east from the growing number of attacks by Saxon raiders. Few veterans, if any, would have returned to Glevum to retire now. At Witcombe, the owners of the villa obviously found it too expensive to keep up as it was. They made the bath block furnace smaller so that it used less fuel. Some of the roofs had collapsed and were very roughly repaired. Rooms at the northern end of the villa were converted into corn-drying granaries and for cooking. At Hucclecote the villa was deserted and then a few years later occupied by new people with living standards which were not as grand as before. The bath block, the social centre for a really civilized owner, was stripped of its building stone to repair other parts of the villa, and the foundations ploughed over. The new owners settled into the living quarters with crude open hearths set in the middle of the rooms. The old central heating system was forgotten.

In the colony and at a number of the villas outside—at Woodchester for instance—there are signs of fires which destroyed buildings that were never completely restored. We know that there was a Roman fleet stationed in the Severn estuary at the time to bar the river route to the Saxon and Irish pirates who were beginning to make raids along its banks, but we can only guess how long it stayed there and how well it did its job. It is possible that the fires began accidentally—the Romans never quite understood the danger of fires—but it is also possible that between the periods of safety, there were times when the fleet was busy in one place and the Irish or the Saxons slipped round them and ravaged the country. It could have been on a raid at this time, perhaps about 380, that a young Roman prisoner was taken from somewhere along the river back to slavery in Ireland, and stayed to become a saint—Saint Patrick.

If this was so, we know that much later he came back to his home and found the area still peacefully settled. And although the owners of the villas were not the grand men they had been, life went on much more prosperously and peacefully along the Severn at this time than in most other places in Britain. Chedworth Villa, high in the Cotswolds beyond Corinium, became a centre for cloth-making about this time, just as the owners of Witcombe began to concentrate more on reaping and drying the corn than on fine living. At Woolaston near Lydney there was another villa whose owner was much more interested in coal and iron mining than in farming and the good life.

There are few signs of Christianity reaching Gloucester. Under Constantine, Constantius's son, it had become the official religion of the Empire. But under a later emperor, Julian, Christians were persecuted again. At Lydney, in a position which must have been very obvious to anyone sailing up the river, sprang up a pagan temple to the god Nodens. He was a god of the river and it has been suggested that his followers might have thought of the Bore as the god moving through the waters. He was a god of healing too, a rival to Sul Minerva and her baths at Aquae Sulis. Perhaps he catered for the retired rich who still lived in villas a short boat ride across the river from Berkeley Pill or Arlingham. Nodens was a great success. Near his temple there was a hospital ward and a dispensary, as well as an inn for pilgrims, a bath block and a large reception hall.

The temple to Nodens was built about AD 370. In AD 406, a certain Constantine, forced, he said, by the army in Britain, illegally proclaimed himself Emperor Constantine III, and set out for France to back up his claim. He took most of the regular soldiers stationed in the British forts, but what is more important, he himself was the last provincial official appointed by the government in Rome. The real emperor, Honorius, told the city and the tribal governments of Britain a few years later that he could no longer be responsible for their defence, and that they must look after themselves.

4. THE HWICCE

Honorius sent his message to Britain in AD 410, and after this our knowledge of life in Britain becomes hazy. But what we do know shows us that it continued to be influenced by the Romans and that it still looked towards Rome as the centre of the civilized world. For nearly fifty years, and possibly for much longer, the local authorities clung to their areas and governed and defended them in the hope that the emperors one day would be able to take over the defence of Britain once more.

We can imagine the citizens of the colony, though no longer ex-soldiers themselves, keeping firm to their military traditions, defending their town and the area round it. Certainly Lydney went on being used long after 410, even if it had to have defences now. And a large number of the villas, like Witcombe and Hucclecote, were still lived in though their owners had barbaric habits and wore strange new clothes. It may have been the iron which made the area important and helped it to survive; apart from Kent it was the most prosperous and settled area of Britain in the fifth century.

For more than a hundred years after AD 420 we know nothing for certain about the Severn Valley. It was a time of legends, of saints, of miracles.

Probably it was the centre of the kingdom of King Arthur. He may not have been a king, but Arthur did exist. And what people think of as his kingdom, the counties on either side of the lower part of the Severn, was a flourishing area with a large population. The Romano-British seem to have moved back into the hill forts for protection, and although they lived much more primitive lives than their grandparents, they were fairly prosperous and traded with merchants from the south who brought them wine from Greece and what is now Turkey. Our area would have been to the north of this developed community, on the fringe, but a piece of a Greek wine jar has been found in Gloucester, inside a Roman house, so the Vale may have been linked to the area Arthur helped to defend.

With one recorded sentence we come back to real fact. The entry for AD 577 in the *Anglo-Saxon Chronicle* reads:

> 577: In this year Cuthwine and Ceawlin fought against the Britons and killed three kings, Conmail, Condidan and Farinmail at the place called Dyrham, and they captured three of their cities, Gloucester, Cirencester and Bath.

Since the 550s, the Saxon advance had been two-pronged.

One group had come across the Berkshire and Wiltshire downs, most likely along the prehistoric trackways and also up the Thames. There is a Saxon cemetery at Fairford, only eight miles east of Cirencester, with the graves of people who died in the 550s, but it seems these Saxons could get no farther west. The forests and the strength of the defenders of the great fortified town of Cirencester would have cut off their advance.

A second group carried on south across the high ground, turning north-west towards Bath. It was this group which was led by Ceawlin, supreme king of Wessex, the kingdom of the West Saxons. They camped in an old hill fort at Hinton Hill, north of Dyrham and waited for battle. They chose their position well. Hinton overlooked the trackway between Gloucester and Bath. They had already cut the main Cirencester–Bath Roman road as they advanced. The armies of the two northern cities now could not use Bath as a base or as a

meeting place. With the host of Wessex swarming over the countryside at this crucial place, the three British armies had to meet in wild wooded country at exactly the same time and place or risk being destroyed one by one. As it turned out, even when they managed this difficult thing they had no time to manœuvre or plan their battle. They were forced to push west and uphill, against an enemy who was well defended, with his reserves coming up behind them from the east. The Saxons won. We know nothing of the fight except that it was the key one for the future of the Severn Valley. The three kings must have had strong armies, but two-thirds of their men would have been tired from a long hard march. Once they were broken, there was nothing to stop the Saxons flooding down into the Severn Valley to pick off the cities one by one. Here is an excerpt from a poem telling what happened to Bath. We can imagine the same things happening when Cuthwin and Ceawlin entered Gloucester and Cirencester.

> Mighty the warshout,
> Many the mead hall
> Of melody full
> Till the strong weird sisters
> Overthrew all.
> The wide walls perished.
> Death consumed all
> Their men of renown.
> Their high fort became desolate heap
> Perished their town. . . .
> And the red hall sheddeth its tiles,
> The treasury roof falls
> Crushed into heaps.
> Earth shrank from the shock.

After the fires had died down Gloucester became almost deserted. A spring outside the North Gate ran into the city and flooded the area to the south and east of the Cross. Very quickly the burnt and tumbledown Roman buildings were covered with a thick layer of rich mud and here, at the heart of the

Roman Colonia, a marshy orchard grew with apple trees and bushes of sloe and blackberry.

The Saxons who settled in Gloucestershire were a tribe called the Hwicce. They held the area of land in the Severn Valley and the hilltops, roughly the same as modern Worcestershire and Gloucestershire, but without the forest. The Severn was a great boundary in the first few years of the Saxon occupation.

The Hwicce would have found the land in a bad condition. Very probably the small native population, who would once have been called Dobunni, stayed on to mix with the new settlers, and many to become their slaves. The large Romano-British farms were desolate, the cleared land overgrown again and the buildings in ruins. The Hwicce would have started their life here in conditions similar to those the Romans had originally found. They had one great advantage, though. They used heavy ploughs with deep cutting blades of iron. They could turn any soil—even the heavy and waterlogged earth of the Vale, and the deep cutting made the lighter hilltop soil more fertile too. We know that some of the villa-owners had these ploughs towards the end of the Roman occupation. The blade of one was found at the Witcombe villa. But they were discovered late, at a time when no more farmland was being cleared, and it was left to the Saxons to make good use of them. Harnessed to teams of six or eight oxen, they could make light work of the newly cleared fields in the Vale, and make the land support many more people than it previously had.

Most of the villages in the Vale, especially the ones with the Saxon "ton", "worth", "ham", and "ford" (Rockhampton, Moreton, Arlingham, Brockworth) in their names, are Saxon in origin. And because they were originally made up of a scattering of houses, with their farmlands in separate clearings in the forest, most of the villages have no green or village street, or centre. They were groupings of separate independent settlers. And because the big iron ploughs they used needed six or eight oxen to pull them, and since, as a rule, each settler could only afford to keep one or two at first, they had to rely on co-operation with their neighbours to plough

the large fields. Living in communities had other advantages
too, with enemies just a boat ride away across the river.

It was the farmers of this time who cleared the Vale and
made it, by the time the Normans came 450 years later, as
thickly populated and prosperous as the hilltops. In many places
one can still see the ridges and furrows of the ploughing strips
first cut by Saxon ploughboys, where the plough cut round and
round a central ridge, piling the earth towards the middle. The
big stretches of woodland were soon being cut back to the
slopes along the Cotswold Edge, with tongues pushing into the
Vale north of Thornbury and along the northern bank of the
Frome to the Severn at Framilode. This was corn country, but
the peasants and their lords had other needs apart from bread.
No village could do without "forest", which is the proper name
for the uncleared land we are talking about. The land provided
rough grazing for animals, especially the pigs which supplied
most of the meat the peasants ate. It supplied them with wood
for fuel and building too. And for the peasants as well as their
lords the forest was important for hunting. So these two
stretches of Vale woodland would have disappeared only very
gradually. We know, for instance, that the southern one was a
Royal Forest used for hunting until after the Norman Conquest
—the Royal Forest of Kingswood.

Most of the settlers struck their roots in new ground, but
they did not deliberately avoid the Roman and Romano-British
farms which we know were so carefully sited and so prosperous. The needs of the Saxon settlers were the same as those of
the Romans—water and wood nearby, good land, good building stone—and the Hwicce had the added advantage of already
prepared Roman building materials to rob from the ruins. At
Woodchester a Saxon church and the centre of a new settlement soon grew up near the villa, and at Frocester the church
was built directly on the Roman foundations of a farm.

To begin with, the settlers were normally independent
farmers, the equal members of a tribe which recognized the
ruler of Wessex as its king. Nobles, the men who led the tribe
into battle and advised the leader, had more land than the

ordinary settlers, but in the early years their style of living would have been much the same. It was only later that a few lucky men collected vast estates which made them much richer than their neighbours.

From the beginning the Hwicce were in a strange position. They owed their land to the kings of Wessex. They spoke the Wessex dialect and carried on their lives just like the other West Saxons. But their lands pointed up the Severn into the heart of Mercia, the big kingdom to the north of Wessex, and Wessex and Mercia were to be rivals for the leadership of southern England. The territory of the Hwicce was a useful route for either of them to use to strike deep into the heart of the other. The Hwicce also faced the Welsh and defended the whole of southern England against them. And, because their territory was valuable with the cornlands of the Vale, the fishing and the trade along the river, and the iron from the forest, they were very vulnerable to attack.

The rule of Wessex lasted only for fifty years, and during this time the Mercians had been growing in power. Cuichelm, great grandson of Ceawlin's brother and now King of Wessex, became very nervous and sent an assassin to kill Edwin, King of Northumbria, who was closely related to the Mercian royal family and allied with them. The assassin only managed to wound Edwin, and when he was well again, he marched south and fought the army of Wessex near Cirencester. Five Wessex chiefs and many of their warriors died and the power of Wessex was crushed for nearly 100 years. The Hwicce became subjects of the kings of Mercia, and they stayed Mercians until the Norman Conquest, 400 years later.

But the Hwicce were considered important enough to keep their own rulers, "sub-kings" or "little kings", as they were called, who were advisers and friends of the Mercian kings.

The first important thing the Mercian link brought them was Christianity. When the Hwicce began to settle in the Vale they had been pagans, and they remained pagan for nearly 100 years. Penda, King of Mercia, did not hate Christians but he feared and hated Northumbria, which was the strongest Christian kingdom in Britain. He fought a battle against King Oswald, who had first brought St Aidan and his monks to Northumbria from the Scottish island of Iona. He had killed King Oswald in the battle, and cut off his hands and stuck them in triumph on two stakes of wood. But only a short time later, Oswy, Oswald's brother, killed Penda, and Mercia became a subject kingdom of Northumbria.

Wulfhere and Peada, Penda's sons, were baptized Christians and introduced the religion their father had refused to his kingdom. Dinna and Ceolach, both Scottish monks, came from Northumbria to begin converting the Mercian people. This happened very quickly. Wulfhere was a good king—Bede the historian says that he made Gloucester a fine city again— and an independent man. His people would have wanted to please him by becoming Christians.

Osric, and his son, Oshere, sub-kings of the Hwicce, were keen to follow the King's lead. Osric gave money to found monasteries at Bath and at Worcester, and in 681 he gave 300 hides of land for the setting up of a monastery at Gloucester too. It was dedicated to St Peter.

None of them would have been as big or as grand as monasteries became later. They were simply the local headquarters of the missionary priests who worked in the surrounding country.

Monasteries in Saxon times stayed very much the property of their founders, who usually chose the abbot or abbess. The abbot was a far more powerful figure than the bishop (who was often only an ordinary monk himself) in local affairs, and the heads of monasteries were often members of the royal family, either men or women. The first leader of the community at Gloucester was a woman—Osric's sister Kyneburga. Brother and sister were buried side by side in "their" abbey.

At first it could not have been a big building. Probably it was made of wood. It was built inside the Roman walls for protection, in the north-west corner, where the modern cathedral stands. To the west because the Saxon settlers began by living in that part of the almost-derelict city outside the walls near the quay. And north because this corner was on the edgh

of the "King's Barton", the marshy land to the north of the
walls which had been drained and cleared by Wulfhere and his
successors as royal land. There were other monasteries, among
them those at Tetbury and at Berkeley. Churches began to be
built, mostly paid for by nobles or members of the royal
family, and usually on their estates. The first church we know
about for certain was at Woodchester, but there were others
founded during the next 200 years or so, at Frocester, Bisley,
Sapperton, Haresfield, Hardwicke, Hawkesbury, Alveston
and Moreton, and by the end of Saxon rule there were at
least five parish churches in Gloucester itself. In many other
places there were priests—though we do not know if they had
churches or simply lived on a lord's land to serve him and his
people. Giving lands to the Church was a sure way of going to
heaven. Within a hundred years or so after the lands of the
Hwicce became a diocese, the Church owned a quarter of it.
The lands of Berkeley Abbey—which later became the estates
of the Berkeley family—were large enough to become a complete hundred, or district, with their own courts and local
government. And St Peter's Abbey itself held 12,000 acres.

For 250 years the Hwicce worked hard. They cleared the
land and grew crops. They began to build the corn mills to
grind the grain. They built churches and abbeys. They fished
the rivers for eels, salmon and lampreys. They began to herd
the flocks of sheep which would later make the Cotswolds so
famous. They began to grow grapes on the southern slopes of
the hills as the Romans had done. But they were not left in
peace. The Vale was far too rich and too important politically
for that.

First it was the Welsh, who were held back unwillingly in
the forest, raiding the eastern bank of the Severn every so often.
The Mercian kings fought them and King Offa pushed them
back through the forest to the dyke he built above the Wye, so
that the eastern shore of the Severn would be secure.

Next it was the Vikings. They had begun to raid the coast of
England in Offa's time, about 780, and within forty years there
were large Viking armies marching about Britain, taking

advantage of the quarrels between the different kingdoms to rob and destroy. The Severn Valley was a perfect target for them. They could sail up the river and beach their longships in any one of a dozen places along the marshy banks. And nearby were rich stores of food in the barns, and plenty of gold and silver in the churches and monasteries. Then they could escape again down-river and make for the Viking settlements in western Wales, Ireland and France. No one could blame the Mercian king, Ceolwulf, for being afraid. At least he did better than Burghred, the previous king, who simply ran away. Ceolwulf tried to buy the Vikings off with the eastern part of his kingdom. In 877 the Vikings were beaten by King Alfred of Wessex near Exeter. Their ships had been destroyed and they had to retreat on foot. They made for the Hwicce lands, where they hoped that Ceolwulf would give them a chance to rest. He had no choice. As they advanced, they burnt the ripe corn standing in the fields. Ceolwulf invited them to Gloucester. They camped inside the walls for the winter. Then, when they heard that Alfred was marching north towards them, they struck south and east again and he defeated them in battle at Ethandun near Malmesbury that Whitsun.

The Vikings still ruled Mercia, but they lost the Hwicce lands. Perhaps it was the bad treatment of the countryside which started the revolt, but very soon Ethelred of the Hwicce, the little king, or Ealdorman as he now began to be called, broke away from Mercia and began attacking the Vikings. His wife was Alfred's daughter Ethelflead, and Alfred joined with him to push the Vikings farther and farther east towards the Danish area of East Anglia. It must have been an exciting time for the Hwicce. Very soon their lord had conquered a huge part of Mercia, a triangle of land that touched London, Bristol and Shrewsbury, and Alfred made him Ealdorman of all of it, with his capital at Gloucester.

The bones of King Oswald, who had been killed by Penda, were brought to Gloucester to symbolize the defeat of the pagans. Oswald was a saint now, and his head and arms, which had been cut from his body, became holy relics in monasteries in Northumbria. Ethelred built a magnificent church for his body almost on the river's edge to the west of St Peter's. The monks of St Peter's must have been furious with envy. The body of the saint brought enormous wealth in offerings. As one man put it, when he saw the church: "It is so decorated with ornaments that it is called 'golden' by the vulgar." To the north of the city lay the royal palace, the "King's holm", and soon the church was named a royal chapel too.

The Witan, the Mercian state council, met in Gloucester. A mint began making gold and silver coins with the portrait of King Alfred on them. And the city became a fortress again, with defences and perhaps with a wooden castle to guard it.

In 910 there was another raid. This time the Vikings of Brittany thought they could take advantage of the trouble King Alfred's successor was facing in Kent with the Mercian army as well as his own men. They probably landed at the inlet at Berkeley, much larger then, and marched off to collect plunder. But on their way back, they were slowed down by the weight of their loot. The royal armies caught up with them after a fast march from Kent. There was a running fight that started at Cambridge where the crossing of the Cam must have slowed the raiders almost to a stop. It finished at Wanswell near Berkeley, when they were almost aboard their ships. There was a massacre and three Viking chiefs died. It may have been at this time that Berkeley Abbey was ransacked and destroyed, because we never hear of it again.

5. THE CITY OF KINGS

In 1005, the Danes, under King Cnut, began another advance west across the ceasefire line that had held firm for so long. One historian has suggested that it may have been at this time that the "Shire" of Gloucester was first founded to organize the men of the South Hwicce to defend themselves.

After a brisk, bloody war, King Cnut met his Anglo-Saxon rival, King Edmund, on the marshy island between the two streams of the Severn west of Gloucester, and agreed to divide the country in two. When Edmund died only a few weeks later, Edmund's half accepted Cnut as king as well, and he became ruler of all England.

Gloucester was an important city to anyone who wanted to be king of a united England. If you held Gloucester you held the Vale and the river and the old Roman roads and hilltop tracks which ran north and south between the boundaries of Wessex at Bath and the boundaries of Mercia north of Worcester.

Edward the Confessor knew this when he met his Witan, his national council, and his three earls, Godwin of Wessex, Leofric of Mercia and Siward of Northumbria, at Gloucester in the midwinter of the first year of his reign. After that, the King spent every Christmas at the Royal Palace in Gloucester and held a "crownwearing", a meeting between him and his people to talk about the affairs of the kingdom. After the first crownwearing, Leofric, Siward and Godwin rode out to punish the King's mother for trying to make a Norwegian King of England in her son's place. It had been decided at the crownwearing that she should lose her lands. And after the crownwearing in 1051, Godwin left with orders to teach the citizens

of Dover a lesson for having insulted a Norman-French noble-
man, the Count of Boulogne, who happened to be married to
the King's sister. But Godwin refused, and collected an army at
Beverstone instead in defiance of the King.

At the beginning of 1051, Godwin, Earl of Wessex, had been
the King's most important subject. He owned huge estates,
including the lands of the derelict abbey at Berkeley, and his
earldom included the Hwicce territory. His daughter was the
King's own wife, and he was the King's. most trusted adviser
But relations between the two men had become strained when,
against Godwin's advice, the King had promised his kingdom
to Duke William of Normandy.

The Count of Boulogne's trouble was not really serious. It
probably came up at that time because the count, through his
wife, the Countess Goda, Edward's sister, owned estates near
Gloucester—at Minchinhampton and Horsley—and the Christmas crownwearing was the time for him, a Gloucestershire
landowner, to complain. But it was the last straw for Godwin.
He had had enough. With him at Beverstone were his two
sons, Harold and Sweyn. Most of England would have been on
his side as the King came to Gloucester again and called him
down from the Cotswolds to answer for his crime. The Anglo-
Saxon Chronicle, the history book of the Saxon period of
English history, describes Danes marching into Gloucester from
the north, part of the army Edward collected in case Godwin
did not obey. It looked as if a civil war was going to begin. But
suddenly the temperature cooled again. Through the good
offices of Leofric of Mercia, the King and the earl met somewhere between their two camps, on Painswick Hill it is
thought, and arranged a truce. Godwin went abroad for a time
but he was soon back again advising the King.

And his advice was necessary, for there had been trouble at
the Welsh border from a Welsh prince called Rhys. Within a
year the Gloucester meeting of the Witan had decided on plans
to beat Rhys. They were so effective that before the Christmas
feasting was over, Rhys's head was brought to the King. Three
years later, after Godwin's death, the Gloucester Witan ordered

Dc

Harold, his heir, to march into Wales after an even more powerful prince. It took Harold three expeditions with his men to bring the head of this prince back. Harold in turn became the King's most powerful subject—more powerful and popular even than his father had been after his exciting and successful Welsh expeditions.

When Edward died he seemed the natural choice for king, in spite of Edward's promise to the Duke of Normandy. At the Battle of Hastings he met William, and with him rode his men of the Shire of Gloucester. We do not know if the Saxon noble Brictric, son of Algar, was there, but we know he did not die on the battlefield as many of his fellow Hwicce did. He was an important landowner, and following William's successful conquest he was present at Westminster to represent the Hwicce, together with Bishop Wulfstan of Worcester, at the new queen's coronation, where he witnessed the official document among the other lords in Westminster Abbey.

William, the new king, did not rush west. He had too much to do near London. Bishop Wulfstan came to him at Berkhamsted and submitted on behalf of his diocese. With Harold, lord of the Hwicce, dead, his promise of loyalty must have been intended as coming from all the people in it, not just the priests. It was a year before William first came to Gloucester, on his way back from capturing Exeter, the town where Harold's supporters decided on a last stand, but very soon after this he began regular Christmas visits, as Edward had done. During one of them, in 1085: "The King had important deliberations and exhaustive discussions with his council about his land, how it was peopled and by what sort of men. Then he sent his men all over England into every shire to ascertain how many hundreds of hides of land there were in each shire and how much land and livestock the King himself owned in the country, and what annual dues were lawfully his from each shire." It was the beginning of the Domesday Book.

At the crownwearing at Gloucester the commissioners for each area were chosen. In Gloucestershire they were to be Bishop Remigius of Lincoln, Walter Giffard, the Norman lord of Stoke Giffard, Brimpsfield and Rockhampton, Henry de Ferrières, a landowner who had been given the job of pacifying the very hostile county of Berkshire, and Adam FitzHubert, who had saved King William's life once and now owned estates in Kent. Very probably William had chosen them (except for Walter Giffard) because they had no lands in the shire and would not be tempted to be dishonest in their work of recording.

The commissioners held court in the main centres in the county, at Gloucester, Bristol, Cirencester, Winchcombe, and at some place in the forest. The representatives of each manor came and were interviewed and their answers written down. The whole survey was complete inside six months, even though the commissioners and the manor representatives had to make long journeys on the wintry roads to get it ready. The records of each county were brought together into two volumes. The Domesday Book is a remarkable piece of work, because we can see from it a detailed picture of each county twenty years after the Normans arrived. It is not a complete picture; it was not intended to be. But it lists the lands which paid tax and the men who paid it, and the number of their tenants who might be called upon to fight in the King's war host. It also tells us who owned each manor, and roughly what size it was, how it made its money, and how prosperous it had been in the comparatively peaceful days of King Edward.

The picture it gives us of the Vale and the hilltops along its edge shows a fairly prosperous area which had almost recovered from the unrest. Walter FitzOsborn, the King's lieutenant for the area, had done his duty in protecting this part of his master's kingdom. Only in a few places were there signs of the chaos of the past twenty years.

The King owned the great manor of Berkeley which Roger de Berkeley held. It had been the land of the Royal Abbey of Berkeley that had returned to the Crown when the abbey was destroyed; it was big enough to be a complete hundred on its own, and it covered a tenth of the shire. There was the central demesne which covered the modern parishes of Berkeley and Stone. At its centre there were the beginnings of the town of Berkeley clustered round the market place above the harbour at Berkeley Pill. It was dominated by Roger's new manor house. The other estates were at Hill, Cam, Dursley, Nympsfield, Wotton, Kingscote, Beverstone, Almondsbury, Horfield, Kingsweston, Ashelworth, Cromhall, Slimbridge,

Arlingham and Ozleworth. Most of them were spread along the fertile valley and the slopes above, and they made their lords the most important men of an important region. The Berkeley estates threaded the county together.

The King's other estates were in Gloucester and near it (Hempsted, for instance) or else they were part of the land of Brictric, Algar's son. Brictric's story was a sad one. His holdings had been one of the largest in the shire. This may have been why he witnessed the Queen's coronation. But the King had little use for him. His great manor at Thornbury of eleven hides with forty-two villeins—tenant farmers—had been given, like nearly everything else he owned, to Queen Matilda. His estate at Wheatenhurst had been mortgaged to Hardinc and his land at Woodchester was so poor that in the demesne (the land he did not let out but farmed directly himself) there were no plough teams. And in our area he was allowed to keep only his large estate at Avening under the King, where there were ten hides of land, twenty-four villeins and thirty slaves, as well as five mills, a large stretch of woodland and a hawk's eyrie.

The other Saxon nobles did much worse, because they lacked Brictric's influence. Countess Goda's land, because she was the old king's sister, became William's and he gave it to the great Abbey of Nuns at Caen in Normandy. Horsley, another of her estates, went to another French church. The lord Ernesi lost the huge wooded manor of Painswick to Roger de Laci, and his Frampton estate was given to Drogo, son of Pons. He was left only with Longney, which was not such a small holding admittedly, with five hides of land and ten acres of meadow as well as the right to fish in the Severn. But there must have been many who lost their lands completely, though usually for less spectacular reasons than Gytha, who lost his in punishment for joining the resistance to William at Exeter.

Apart from the King, the greatest landowner and the one who did best out of the Conquest, was the Church. St Peter's owned the Abbot's Barton—the lands given to it by Osric—and Frocester and Standish. The bishop owned Aust, as well as land inside Gloucester itself; and the Archbishop of Canterbury

held Churchdown and Hucclecote. French churches had been
given Minchinhampton and Horsley, both large and wealthy.
After the Church came the soldiers, from the Earl Hugh of
Gloucester with the large estate of Bisley taking in most of the
Stroud Valley and eleven houses in Gloucester, to Humphrey
de Medehalle, who held one hide with one plough team at
Wotton.

The ordinary people lived on, and the way they lived had
not changed very much since the first hundred years of the
Saxon settlement. The big mass of oak forest in the Vale had
now mostly been cleared, and the number of hamlets had
increased. The only modern ones not mentioned in the survey
were Eastington, which was probably called by the name of one
of its hamlets, Alkerton and Randwick, Thrupp and Cranham,
which would probably all be part of the dense woodland
attached to the other estates in the area, like Stonehouse, Painswick or Bisley. The Vale was a rich corn-growing area; there
was far more acreage of land under corn in 1086 than today.
The river was still as unpredictable and badly banked as it
always had been. The names Moreton ("Mire-town") and
Elmore ("Elm-bank") and Slimbridge ("Slime-bridge") show
us that the New Grounds at Slimbridge were still very far from
meadowland, and the river from Framilode to Elmore was
marshier and much wider than it is now. But if the villages
along the river lost their farmland and their shooting crops
every so often at the time of the spring Bores, they gained from
the fishing. We do not exactly know what the word means,
but there were "fisheries" on the estates at Brewerne near
Gloucester, two at Gloucester itself, at Standish (probably at
Saul), Longney and Hempsted. At Gloucester sixteen salmon
were given each year as the fishermen's rent to St Peter's, and
as eels were eaten and enjoyed and kings were very soon
demanding lampreys as part of their rent from the city of
Gloucester, we can be sure that all these three fish and many
more were being caught for food.

The main luxury of a noble was his wine and even this was
home-grown. There were the vine terraces in Stonehouse in

1086, and only 100 years later a writer tells us how fine the
wine from the vineyards of Gloucestershire is, how it is the
largest wine producing area in Britain, and how its wine is
better than some coming from France.

Salt was the cheapest and strongest flavouring available and
it was also used for preserving meat, vegetables, butter and
cheese. It came from the salt pans at Droitwich, six miles above
Worcester, and it was so important that many estates owned
their own pans, to make sure of their supplies. It was brought
to them on pack horse down the old hilltop routes that now
were called Saltways. It came down the Calfway from the
Cotswold edge above Tewkesbury, through Bisley, Chalford
and Avening, south to Sodbury, and also south from Birdlip,
past Painswick to Stroud, up the Nailsworth Valley to Sodbury, or to Wootton, Thornbury and Rockhampton in the
Vale.

There were about 25,000 to 30,000 people living on the
manors of the shire, and most of them worked on the land.
Apart from the lords, their estate managers, the priests and a
few others, everyone else had a position tied to the land he held
from his lord. At the top of the list were the freemen. They
held their land free from any lord, but naturally they looked
voluntarily for a lord to protect their interests, often in return
for some services, such as helping to plough his land or harvest
his crops.

Only a very small proportion of men were free to choose
their lord—say one in fifty. Most men were villeins or bordars,
peasant farmers who relied heavily on their lord for protection
and justice, for tools and seed. But they could not leave his land
without his permission. They held land and plough-oxen—
sometimes quite a lot of each—and paid for them in goods
from their own land and service on their lord's demesne. The
goods might include honey, as paid by the tenants at Bisley,
usually a large proportion of grain and livestock, and sometimes money. The services included a day's work on the lord's
land at the crucial times of haymaking and harvest, and the
lord's work came first. In the shire of Gloucester, the villeins

and bordars made up about two-thirds of the population.

At the bottom of the scale were the serfs—the slaves. There were more slaves in proportion to the whole population in the shire than in any other area of England—about one in thirteen or fourteen—and at about the time of the Norman Conquest the young port of Bristol was a centre for the shipping of slaves abroad. The great Bishop Wulfstan, the last Saxon bishop to survive the Conquest, spent several months there preaching against the trade which was frowned on by most men and forbidden by law before the Conquest, but it continued for some time before Wulfstan put an end to it.

The slave's life was not always as hard as it sounds. There were eight serfs on the land of St Peter's Abbey at Standish—perhaps two families—and ten more at Minchinhampton. These slaves were the property of their master, to be bought and sold as he wished. But only a stupid master starved or ill-treated a slave, because he wanted the most work possible from him. Slaves had to be fed two meals and two loaves of bread a day by law. They had Sundays and feast days off and they could keep anything they were given or earnt in their spare time. If they saved enough they could buy their freedom, though for many freedom was hardly worth the expense.

There were few other members of the county community. There was a group of potters paying rent in the manor of Haresfield; a band of clay among the layers of stone that comes to the surface in the slopes between Haresfield and Harescombe seems to have been where they worked. There is mention of two reeves—estate managers—and twelve Frenchmen, probably the camp followers of the Norman lords, and one Welshman, who were villeins. There were also two swineherds, and strangely enough only two smiths, neither of them working in the Vale area. But the largest number of non-landowners were the priests: fifty-three of them.

Most of these would have lived where there had been priests for many years, and although the commissioners note only a few churches, we know there were others which they did not record. Most Saxon churches were of wood and have rotted away or burnt down, but Bishop Wulfstan, among all his other good deeds, replaced many wooden altars with stone ones and built new churches on his own land.

One more important set of landmarks in the countryside were the mills, more than 250 of them. A corn mill was expensive for the lord to build, and so he made it a rule that his tenants had to use it and pay his miller for the privilege. Once it was built, though, a mill was a profitable part of an estate. Its income equalled that from sixty acres of good land every year, that is, about 6s. on average. In the Vale itself, streams were shallow and moved slowly, but on the slopes, and especially down in the valley of the Frome, there were profitable mills every few miles along the strongly flowing river.

The towns that Domesday mentions were small and not towns at all by our standards. Winchcombe was called a borough, and there were "burgesses"—men who were the free citizens of towns or who earnt most of their living by trade— at Bristol and Tewkesbury. There was the market too, at Berkeley. But the only "civitas" or city in the shire was Gloucester itself.

The population of Gloucester was between 2,000 and 3,000 people—the size of, say, Stonehouse or Thornbury today—and no settlement in the shire had more than 700 or 800 inhabitants. The Saxon settlement at Gloucester had been along the quayside to the west of the Roman city walls at first, and later had grown back from the river and up the hill. It had nowhere else to go, because there was an area of marsh upstream and the walls came close to the river bank downstream; the main channel of the river ran much closer to the west of the city than it does now. The Mercian palace was almost certainly derelict by this time—there is a story that the crownwearing at which Domesday was approved was held in a hall of the abbey. The Saxon fort had been knocked down on the orders of William FitzOsborn, William's lieutenant, and a new Norman castle was rising on the same land. We can only guess what it looked like from the other Norman castles which are still standing in the area—Chepstow, Usk, or Goodrich. As a key royal fortress it would almost certainly have been built on the pattern of the oldest parts of the Tower of London or Dover Castle, a tall wooden, square keep-tower with buttresses on the sides, and with corner towers and an entrance on the first floor. In the bailey round the keep other buildings would have sprung up— stables, kitchens, perhaps a hall, a chapel and so on—and beyond, a wooden stockade and a moat fed from one of the streams running into the river. At the same time William FitzOsborn repaired the Roman walls. They had been neglected for 500 years and apart from natural damage—the effect of 500 frosty winters on the mortar, or the constant washing away of the foundations by underground springs—stones had been taken from the walls by the Saxon inhabitants for other buildings, such as St Oswald's and St Peter's.

By the standards of the time, Gloucester was a grand place. In 1153 St Oswald's Abbey, the old royal chapel, was given by the King to the Archbishop of York and he began to rebuild it in stone. Just before the Norman Conquest Bishop Aldred had taken much of the land St Peter's owned to pay for the setting up of the new church province of York when he was appointed its first Archbishop, and he left it so poor that it only had two monks and eight novices. But Abbot Serlo, the first Norman abbot, fought to get the land back and wheedled new estates from the local Norman lords as well. He then set about repairing and rebuilding the abbey, although he probably only had to add towers and a nave to the rest of the late Saxon church to put it in order. This may have been made necessary after a raid on the royal lands in the shire by William d'Eu, lord of Stonehouse, the year before. If it was, the abbey was having a hard time, because only twenty years after the new church had been consecrated in 1100:

At Lent-tide the Abbey of Gloucester was burnt while the monks were singing the Mass and the deacon had begun the Gospel. Then came the fire to the tower and burnt all the monastery and the treasure therein except a few books and three mass robes.

You can see what may be the marks of this fire on some of the pillars in the nave to this day. And then, in the 1170s, while Bishop Roger was singing High Mass, the west tower collapsed as he came to the words of consecration and it was only because the people were crushed together close to the altar at the east that no one was hurt.

St Mary de Lode

The people usually worshipped not in either monastery, but in their parish churches. St Mary de Lode, by St Peter's Abbey gate, was the senior church. It had been in the middle of the Saxon city. "St Mary de Lode"—"the ferry" because it was by the ferry across to the town Ham, the common grazing land of the city on a marshy island across the main stream of the Severn.

Gloucester was a royal centre with its castle and its crownwearings. The King owned more than half of it himself. The nobles of the county all kept houses there, partly for rent, partly for their own use as residences when the King was in council, and partly, especially in earlier times, as a refuge in times of unrest. The other houses were owned by businessmen.

Gloucester may have been involved in the wool trade; it was certainly the centre for the finest iron trade, and iron manufacture probably went on too. The dues from Gloucester to the King were thirty-six pounds, 720 iron horse-shoes and 100 bars of iron for making ships' nails. Other dues were twelve measures of honey and the annual gift of lampreys, which reveal the area's rural aspect—Gloucester was small, and the countryside came right up between the houses, especially to the east. Yet it was still one of the most important cities in the kingdom, as events were to show.

6. THE KEY TO ENGLAND

The Domesday survey tells us much about Gloucester as a royal centre in the southern borders or Marches. But it tells us nothing about the bridge west across the river. The Romans found an easy ford at Gloucester, and they probably built a long causeway over the shallows with two or three small bridges for the bigger branches of the stream. But the passage over the Severn was to be supremely important for the next 600 years. Gloucester was on the route to South Wales. It was the centre for expeditions against the princes of South Wales, and the base for the Norman lords colonizing the wild lands along the South Wales coast, especially Glamorgan and Pembroke, and on the route to Ireland. Gradually it came to hold the key to the success or failure of revolutions, because the holder of Gloucester and its bridge could decide whether the armies of the Norman Marcher lords, once they were settled in their new lands, could join up with their allies in England against an enemy. It is interesting that the small Domesday entry for Wales is included in the Book directly after Gloucester itself.

The English kings were in the shire as often as ever, though the regular Christmas crownwearing became less frequent after William's death. It was in 1092 that William II, William Rufus, as he is usually known, spent Christmas in Gloucester. After the crownwearing, he rode south with his court, perhaps to hunt in the Royal Forest south of Kingswood. But at Alveston, along the main Roman road, he became very ill. He was brought back to the comfort of Gloucester, but everyone thought he was dying. He wanted to make his peace with the world before he left it and the bishops gathered round him suggested that he should appoint a new Archbishop of Canterbury. When any bishop's place was vacant, the King pocketed the income from his land, and for three years now the King had greedily taken the huge amount of money the Archbishop received. On the first Sunday of Lent, Anselm, the Abbot of Bec in Normandy, a good man who later became a saint, was chosen. He did not want the responsibilities of the job, but the bishops dragged him to the King's bedside and wrenched his fingers open so violently that he cried out in pain. The King stuffed the Archbishop's staff into his hands, and officially he became Archbishop. Anselm was carried to a nearby church—probably it was St Peter's—the bishops singing the Te Deum in thanks and Anselm shouting that he was not the Archbishop. As he wrote later to his monks at Bec, after he had accepted his new position:

> It would have been difficult to decide if madmen were dragging along someone sane, or vice versa, except they were chanting and I was pale with pain and amazement, and looked more dead than alive.

In Stephen's reign, the constable of the castle, Miles, son of Walter, had inherited from his father the title of constable of England. He was also sheriff of the shire and lord of the Honour of Gloucester, and half that of Brecon, which meant that with Pain Fitzjohn, the other lord of the Brecon Honour, and sheriff of Hereford and Shropshire, he was officially in control of all the lands along the Welsh border. He was a powerful man, and well liked in Gloucester. Like Robert, Earl of Gloucester, he supported Matilda, Henry I's only child, against Stephen of Blois, his nephew, because of an oath he had sworn to her while her father was alive. But when Stephen came to the throne, Miles did not look for trouble. In May, 1138, Stephen visited Gloucester and the citizens greeted him as they did all kings (how they must have become used to them!) with speeches and processions. Even after Robert of Gloucester had raised the standard of revolt the same summer, Miles did not move. Only when Matilda herself arrived in England the following year did Miles go to her at Bristol and, as a writer of the time says, "begin filling the place of a father to her". His first advice was that she should move to the much stronger city of Gloucester. Here her supporters gathered, as Miles's men raided the surrounding land for supplies. The local lords either submitted freely to her or were tortured until they agreed to: if they still refused they were killed. For the next year or so Gloucester was one of the capitals of England, the base of an army that Miles occasionally led out for raids, plundering up and down the Vale. And Bristol was England's second city.

In February, 1141, Matilda's army beat Stephen's at Lincoln;

although he fought fiercely with a sword and a battle-axe till they both broke in turn, he was knocked down by a stone, brought to Gloucester as a prisoner in chains, and thrown on his knees before his cousin Matilda. Matilda set off on a triumphal progress round the country, but she was arrogant, and no one took to her. Her tour turned into a hell-for-leather gallop back to Gloucester and safety; she entered the city strapped to a horse litter, exhausted. Things looked grim, but Miles still supported her. Finally, two years later he was wounded at Flaxley while hunting in the forest and was brought back to Gloucester to die. When Robert also died soon afterwards, Matilda gave up and fled abroad.

Henry II, who followed Stephen on the throne, must have dreaded the unrest which Stephen had to deal with. One of his first concerns was to strengthen his position in that part of the country which had most troubled his predecessor—Miles's shire of Gloucester.

He built a bridge with a fortified gateway across the Severn at Gloucester to encourage trade with Wales and Ireland to pass through the town. He permitted the merchants of Gloucester to travel up and down the river with their cargoes of wood and coal without paying tolls.

But most important of all, Henry gave the city its first charter, the royal document that laid down its rights and its duties to the King, and confirmed the fact that the King was its only master. Henry needed Gloucester's loyalty, and he thought that he would get it if he made it prosperous and independent of the powerful lords of the shire. Every growing town fought hard for a charter, because there were fewer taxes to pay and less interference in what really mattered to the townsmen, the growth in trade. Sadly for future kings, Gloucester's loyalty remained doubtful. But evidently the people under King Henry and his successors, Richard the Lionheart and John, did prosper. The tax records showed that a number of trades began to develop very rapidly at this time. And the fact that in 1194 Gloucester had one of the earliest halls for the use of its business-men, the Guild Merchant as they were called, shows how strong the growth was. There was iron manufacture—particularly weapons and armour of all sorts—which naturally took advantage of the nearness of the forest iron and the wood to fire the furnaces. Swords and spearheads, bows and shields from Gloucester helped the Normans kill their enemies in Ireland, France and the Holy Land as well as at home, and iron clamps and rods made in Gloucester reinforced the delicate stonework of the new abbey at Westminster when it was built a century later.

Another important industry was weaving cloth from the local wool brought in from the Marches, and down from the Cotswolds. At the time of Domesday all the mills in the country, powered by the fast flowing streams along the edge of the hills, ground corn. But in 1185, we hear of a new sort of mill—a fulling mill. Someone must have discovered what the

Romans knew, that in the Cotswolds were layers of a sticky wet clay called "fuller's earth" which dissolved the natural grease in the wool. If you mixed it with water and stirred the cloth round in it by a water-driven machine the process was very much simpler.

Henry thought that he had secured Gloucester, but wanted to make sure of the Vale too. He saw his answer scattered along the entire length of the Vale—the holdings of the lords of Berkeley. If the lord of Berkeley were a friend, if he were safe in his head manor, then no one in the Vale could move against the King.

The royal manor of Berkeley had been handed at the Conquest to Roger, Lord of Dursley. But his successor in Henry II's time had supported Stephen, and Henry was Matilda's son.

At Bristol, Robert FitzHarding, a businessman, had lent Matilda and her son money and had showed them friendship. Now he was rewarded with the vast estates of Berkeley, provided he built a castle there. There had probably been a fortified house or even a castle on the site before the new lord's time. A "small castle" stood at Sharpness at the time of the Domesday survey, but it was a royal fort which was meant to guard the river together with another on the opposite bank at Lydney. And since the Conquest "Berkeley" had moved from the place where the Saxon abbey had stood at Wanswell, to the island of rising ground just above the quay at Berkeley Pill, which would soon be crowned by the new castle.

The deposed lord would not take his loss lying down. He retreated to Dursley, his other main estate, and caused Fitz-Harding a great deal of trouble, until at last the King persuaded them to join their families by a marriage between their children. It was probably FitzHarding's son, Maurice, who was in charge of building operations. It seems he was a keen builder, but his father was a businessman and never moved to Berkeley from his affairs at Bristol.

The new castle had a round keep with an entrance on the first floor and a fore building to protect the steps up to it. To the south-west there was a "bailey", a courtyard, protected by

EG

a ditch and a moat. The entrance to the bailey had a double gateway, and on the other side was a small postern gate with a drawbridge. It was the only castle between Bristol and Gloucester, and just as Henry wanted, it was the key to the Vale.

Berkeley Castle, the keep from the forecourt

Henry's own short reign was a period of calm, except for the constant toing and froing of armed bands raiding the Welsh. The next King, Richard I, spent most of his reign locked up in a castle abroad. His brother John, who came to own the lands of the Earl of Gloucester through his wife, was trying to take advantage of the situation by plotting with many people, including the Welsh Prince Rhys ap Gruffydd.

Gloucester Castle was put in first-class order, and when John started a revolt, the sheriff had orders to raise 450 footmen and forty archers for seven weeks to defend the town for him. In the following year, Gloucester got a second charter, just to remind it where its loyalties should lie. The constables of the castles at Gloucester and Bristol and the lord of Berkeley would all have come out for John if his revolt had not ended too soon. But the royal authorities nipped it in the bud and

Roger de Berkeley lost the income from his lands for six months as a punishment.

John was Earl of Gloucester, and Gloucester was loyal to him, but when Richard died and John became King, he forgot his old friends. He divorced his wife, the Lady of Gloucester, to marry someone richer and grander who soon became tired of him and hung her lovers' favours on her bed to taunt him. He put her in Gloucester Castle for that, and made one of his relations, Engelard of Cigoigné in Normandy, constable and sheriff. Engelard was cruel and he took far more than the usual number of bribes. He was one of the few foreigners whom King John promised would be exiled when he signed the Magna Carta at Runnymede. John's reign was a succession of broken promises; if he had not died suddenly in Gloucestershire trying to crush a revolt among those who had once been his friends it is doubtful he would have kept his crown.

Everyone heaved a sigh of relief when he died. As he had been in Gloucester with all his barons holding a council in the late summer, the Abbey of St Peter's was a natural place for the new King, Henry III, to be crowned. Unfortunately a short time before his death, John had dashed across the country to get help; while he was crossing Lincolnshire, his baggage train with the crown jewels took a short cut across the fens, got caught by the tide and was completely lost—and Henry, only nine years old, had to be crowned in the Abbey with a plain circle of gold.

His regent, William Marshal, the Earl of Pembroke, anxiously asked the nobles to support him. The King swore on the Gospels and the Abbey's holy relics that he would obey the Magna Carta and behave lawfully. There was a High Mass, and the King put on some red robes that looked suitably royal. They all feasted and next day the barons swore their loyalty to him.

Henry, or rather his regent, was as good as his word. Within a few months he had organized a court of six independent judges to tour the country and put right all the unpunished wrongs of John's reign. They sat first at Gloucester, from dawn to dusk, seven days a week for about a month. In the shire of Gloucester alone there were nearly 500 cases brought before them, and more than half of those were murders, or brawls that had led to a killing.

Gloucester was Henry's favourite city, it is said, and this is not surprising when one thinks of the part it played in the promising start to his reign. But it was twice the centre of trouble too. There were three full-scale military expeditions against the Welsh princes in his reign, and plenty of smaller raids; as usual the base for recruiting and assembling the soldiers was the shire of Gloucester. The lords of the Marches, as the border lands were called, were powerful generals who were used to living by the sword, and their interests as well as their families were woven together tightly in their attempts to keep the Welsh at bay and their English neighbours off their lands. Only a stupid king would have tried to weaken their control of the area because they knew their job and they did it well. But the Marcher lords owned lands on both sides of the frontier and their interests were not always the same as their King's. And when they moved against the King—the de Clares of Gloucester, the de Bohuns of Hereford and Brecon, the de Valences of Pembroke, the Mortimers of Hereford and Shropshire, the Giffards of Brimpsfield, the Cliffords of Frampton and sometimes the Berkeleys—his whole kingdom trembled.

In the 1260s Gloucester was in the middle of a revolt. The King had appointed one of his Frenchmen, Matthieu de Besille, constable of the castle and sheriff of the county. The constable and the sheriff were responsible for law and order in the city and the shire, and the sheriff collected royal taxes everywhere outside the city boundaries. The local nobles were afraid that a foreigner just would not understand the delicate balance of power locally and act with a high hand, and they felt he would try to take more tax than he was entitled to. So, without more ado, they elected a local man, Sir William de Tracy, their sheriff. As he sat at one of his first official functions at Gloucester, Matthieu and some of his men pushed into the room and dragged him from the dais and through the streets to

the castle. Sir Roger de Clifford and Sir John Giffard besieged
the castle at once, but it was so well defended that they would
not have captured it except for one piece of luck. In the confusion inside, some of the prisoners got free and let Sir Roger
and Sir John through a small gate into the courtyard. They
were then able to batter down the door of the keep with ham-
mers and axes, free Sir William and despatch Matthieu as a
prisoner to Wales.

This was only a small event in a very large revolt, led by
Simon de Montfort, Earl of Leicester. Gloucester was a key city
and when the rebels finally lost it, they lost the revolt too,
though it was to change hands twice before then.

Edward I's reign, like the early part of Henry's, was a time of
peace for the Vale, except of course for the constant expeditions into Wales. Edward II, however, was a weak man, bullied
by his wife and his friends and in no time signs of a new revolt
were apparent.

In 1314, most of the lords of the shire had ridden north to
fight the Scots. The English army was badly beaten in a battle
at Bannockburn, and of the lords who went, Maurice de
Berkeley and Sir John Giffard (old Sir John's son) were
captured and Gilbert de Clare, only son of the Earl, was killed,
"by a score of Scots lances" it was said. The de Clare name, the
most powerful in the shire for 200 years, died out, but there
was another family trying to take its place—the Despencers.

Hugh Despencer and his son, also called Hugh, were
doing their best, with the King's agreement, to take the personal land of the de Clares, together with large parts of the land
of the Earls of Gloucester, by a mixture of bullying, lies and
dishonesty. Most of the other nobles of the Marches were
affected by this manoeuvre, and they knew they had to stop it
if the King would not. When they raided the lands of the
Despencers, the King became angry. He had the lands of the
Berkeleys seized and Sir John Giffard's castle at Brimpsfield
pulled down.

Now the revolt became open. Sir John buried his fortune,
4,000 coins of silver, in a jug and rode off into Wales, taking

with him all the cattle he could find. Before he went, he ransacked a royal baggage train that rather foolishly passed Brimpsfield on the Roman road from the King's headquarters at Cirencester on its way to the royal castle at Gloucester. The King advanced and captured Maurice de Berkeley, but the rest of the barons retreated north and he caught them with their backs to the narrow bridge at Boroughbridge in Yorkshire. Hereford was speared by a Welsh soldier from under the bridge as he tried to force his way across. The rest were stopped by the hail of arrows from the King's men on the other side and captured. Sir John Giffard was brought back to Gloucester to die. Some said he was hanged and cut in quarters, but probably he was simply beheaded.

In 1325 the King's wife, Isabella, and her son, Prince Edward, landed in England. At last the opposition to Edward had a leader. Edward, terrified, fled west to try to collect an army in the old recruiting city of Gloucester, but his luck was out. Isabella and Edward were close on his heels as he fled to the Despencers at Bristol and on to the Island of Lundy, but he was driven back to the mainland by bad weather. Isabella and her lover, Mortimer, captured the King and imprisoned him at Bristol until an escape plot was discovered.

Isabella had given the Berkeley lands back to Thomas, the son of Lord Maurice who had died in captivity at Wallingford, and now she looked for a favour. In April, 1327, the King was brought to Berkeley by night, in thin clothes and with a crown of twisted hay on his head in mockery. They made him shave off his carefully curled pointed beard so that he was less recognizable, and he was given a rusty helmet full of cold water to do it. The story is that Edward, a sensitive, timid man, burst into tears. Edward was a nuisance. He was not only weak, but dominated by evil men. Mortimer decided that the only way out was for Edward to die, even if he had to be assisted. Sir Thomas de Gournay and Sir John Maltravers were ordered to "look after" him.

The King was put in a damp room with a pit-full of rotting carcasses near him. He was not strong, they thought, and the

damp and the decay would soon kill him. But it did not. The
Queen sent his guards a message in Latin that she had deliberately given two meanings. It could mean: "Do not kill Edward:
it is a good thing to be afraid." Or else: "Do not be afraid to
kill Edward: it is a good thing." In that way she made it quite
clear what she wanted done, but if ever she was accused of
ordering his death she could say that it had all been a terrible
misunderstanding, or that the two knights had done it against
her will.

The King lived on, writing some beautiful poetry, praying in
the chapel of St John the Baptist with his confessor, the
Dominican friar Robert, and eating a great many pigeons and
eggs to judge from the castle accounts. Finally, one night late
in September, de Gournay and Maltravers became impatient.
They suffocated the King with a pillow. The following day
they got some burgesses from Gloucester and Bristol to come
and see the body and persuaded them that, as there was no
mark on the body, the King must have died of a natural attack
of some kind. His body was embalmed by a wise woman
and laid in the chapel until they could make the funeral
arrangements. The King lay in the chapel for seven weeks before
plans were finally ready.

At last, in November, his body was brought from Berkeley
to Gloucester in a wagon draped in black canvas. It took two
days for the journey, and the monks at Standish, one of the
farms belonging to St Peter's, looked after it overnight. At
the entrance to the city it was met by the monks of the abbey
and a procession of all the citizens escorted it to the abbey
where it was buried by the high altar.

People who die tragic deaths have a way of becoming
romantic heroes. Very soon the weak, irresponsible King
Edward became one of them. Very quickly people began
praying at his tomb in the abbey of St Peter's. The tomb looks
very beautiful even today—the alabaster statue of Edward is
one of the finest ever made in England, and a very early
example of portrait carving. When medieval people went to
pray at someone's tomb, for the dead person's soul and their

own, they left an offering, even if it was only the price of a candle to burn in front of it.

Inside six years, pilgrims to the tomb had brought in enough money to rebuild a large part of the abbey church. As well as offerings of thanks, there were gifts of land or money to pay the normal small fee for prayers or a Mass to be said by a monk for ever, in the name of the person who gave them. And so, suddenly, the monks of St Peter's found themselves with huge amounts of money to spare.

7. MONKS AND PRIESTS

We last looked at the abbey at the end of the rule of Abbot
Serlo. His new church had been consecrated in 1100, and by the
time he died there were a hundred monks at the abbey. Gradually, like any living thing, the abbey buildings and the abbey
inhabitants changed. Serlo's Norman nave remains, and the
vaulted roof dates from Bishop Cantelupe's time, the 1240s.
The choir, and most of the west end of the church, was built in
the 1300s and the lady chapel in the 1400s.

Serlo had left the community in a good state. But over the
next 150 years, the monastery and the whole diocese with it
ran gradually downhill. By 1251, there were debts of 3,000
marks—£2,000—and the monks were trying hard to bring in
some extra money by running the abbey as an hotel. In the
previous 100 years, many new parish churches had been built in
the Vale in stone and there were some new monasteries as well.
The Berkeley lords provided the money and lands for two of
them, at Kingswood and Leonard Stanley, and Miles of
Gloucester gave the land for a third to the south of Gloucester,
to rehouse the monks of Llantony priory in Wales who had
suffered from raids by the Welsh princes.

Monasteries and their monks were much closer to the world
and its inhabitants in the Middle Ages than they are today. The
abbot and his monks were landlords and farmers who lived
very much like other men and shared their interests. They
worked long hours but they lived well. In 1301 the Archbishop
of Canterbury ordered that the Abbot of St Peter's should
not have more than five attendants or twelve hunting dogs.
And every monk had the chance of becoming the abbot of his
monastery. As monks, even poor peasant boys could become

Norman nave, Gloucester Cathedral

the managers of one of the abbey's rich estates, like Standish or Frocester. At St Peter's, and the other monasteries too, a poor novice was at the bottom of the pyramid, which might lead him up to the dizzy world of international politics as an ambassador or a royal adviser, or into the world of scholarship as a famous writer or thinker.

Part of the monastery was set aside for study. In the bays round the cloister the monks sat reading the works from the library—mostly commentaries on the Bible or the lives of the saints—and composing new works, often more lives of the saints or new commentaries on the old, and illustrating and decorating their work with beautiful coloured drawings. In 1283, John, Lord Giffard, paid for the foundation of Gloucester Hall at Oxford, where promising monks of St Peter's could continue their studies. Thirteen brothers went. Some monks, including Abbot Wigmore, were embroiderers. And the monks helped the master masons and their apprentices on alterations and decorations to the abbey buildings—including the magnificent south transept which we will hear about later. When the Archbishop limited the abbot's style of living, he also ordered the monks to stop their games of chess and dice and their archery and crossbow practice.

But there cannot have been much time for these. The castle at Gloucester could never have provided comfortable accommodation for visiting royalty. A royal castle was a place for defence not a setting for a royal court. Gloucester Castle did have a "king's chamber", but when any royal business had to be done in Gloucester, or when kings came to stay, it was to St Peter's with its ranges of bedrooms, its well filled store-rooms and its many meeting halls that the royal party often turned for hospitality.

In March 1349, the Great Plague—the Black Death—arrived in England, at the south coast port of Weymouth. Very quickly it raced across the whole of the country, to Bristol and Gloucester and then back across the Cotswolds to Oxford and London. Men died everywhere in their thousands; no one knows how many. They blamed on the plague the desperate shortage of working men during the next hundred years and the greater demands these workers were able to make for more money and a freer life. Twice the government tried to stop wages going up. And twice the demand for workers was so great that landlords broke the law and paid more to make sure they had men to plough their fields and bring in their crops. During the reign of Richard II, the government tried once again to impose its will. The peasants became angrier and angrier. Naturally they did not want the King to prevent them earning more. And because the anger made itself felt most in London, Richard II held a parliament at St Peter's Abbey, well out of harm's way.

Parliaments provided the new royal means of getting money by summoning the powers of the land together and asking them to agree to be taxed. One of the most profitable taxes was on wool, and from time to time parliaments were held in Gloucester, perhaps partly so that the important sheep-owning lords could attend. But in 1378, parliament had different work to do. For nearly four autumn weeks, from eight o'clock in the morning, the lords sat in the new hall of the abbey and the commons in the chapter house, first of all to agree to the wool tax (£6,000 was the final amount fixed) and then to try to stem the tide of rising wages and prices and stop the growing revolt. There were fewer MPs then, and the King himself stayed at Llantony Priory on this occasion, but still the abbey had to accommodate 400 or 500 men. The abbey registers tell us what happened, and obviously the writer was more than a little indignant:

> The rightful occupiers of St Peter's were obliged for some days to take their meals in the dormitory, both on flesh and fish days, and their dinner was prepared in the store-room. All open spaces were so crowded by persons coming to the parliament that it looked more like a fair than a house of religion. The grass plot in the cloister was so trampled down with wrestling and ball playing that not a vestige of green was to be seen on it.

The Abbot of St Peter's was the most important churchman in the county, and the richest property owner as well. Pilgrims went to Hailes Abbey to venerate the speck of the Most Precious Blood of Christ that the monks there guarded—and this is the origin of the proverb "As sure as God's in Gloucester"—but the Abbot of St Peter's was the host of kings and parliaments, the most important citizen of the key city in the west, and the

assistant to the bishop himself. Yet the abbots were often local
boys, if we can judge by two of their names—Walter Frocester
and Adam de Staunton.

Monasteries lived mainly for themselves. They offered men
the chance to save their own souls by living a perfect life of
work and prayer. They did teach and help the poor and the
sick, and very often men retired to them at the end of their lives
to prepare for death. At least one of the Giffard lords did this.
But although most of the monks would have been good men,
there were no saints among them, at least in the rich monasteries of the Severn Vale. The tithe barn at Frocester tells us

Tithe barn, Frocester

why. If you look at it, nearly 200 feet long, and think that this
was to hold the harvest from the lands farmed by the monks
and only a tithe—a tenth—of the crops of the farmers they let
land to, and that this was only one of the thirty-odd manors of
St Peter's, you can see exactly why the life of a monk was a
worldly one, even if it was a respectable and upright life too.

There were other newer orders of monks who worked much
nearer the people, especially among the teeming life of the
towns that were growing everywhere. The new orders were
the friars, monks who were so poor that even the houses they
lived in had to be owned by someone else, usually the towns
where they worked. The best known of the four orders of the

friars was the Franciscan, a group of men who followed the teaching of St Francis of Assisi. The three largest orders had houses in Gloucester and another had one at Wotton. The friars went out among the people to teach and preach wherever they could get an audience. Because they were as poor as the poorest people themselves, and because religion was so much a part of everyone's life, they usually got a good crowd at the preaching crosses on the street corners in Gloucester and in the villages round about.

However poor the friars were, the Church remained rich. Families could die out, or have their lands taken from them, but the Church went on and on, as generations of men gave it gifts in thanks for answered prayers or to make up for a sinful life.

In 1327, when Edward II's shrine began to bring in rich new offerings, Abbot Thokey began the hundred years or so of rebuilding which gave the abbey almost the appearance it has today and turned it into a landmark in the history of English architecture. The architects and master masons of the kingdom had made a breakthrough in architecture. In the late 1320s, the works at St Peter's was the first really big contract which gave them a chance to show off their new style.

We do not know who its masons and its designers were. The abbot after Thokey, John Wigmore, was a skilled carver and he could have had a hand in it. But it may be that the greatest architect in the land, William de Ramsay, the King's own chief mason, gave his advice on the work while he was in the city attending to the castle and the walls. Certainly the style was up to date and exciting: the designs of many other buildings in the west—the chapter house of Hereford Cathedral, the choir at Tewkesbury Abbey, the cloisters of Lacock Abbey in Wiltshire and the church of Ottery St Mary in Devon—show that architects were influenced by the new abbey and tried to copy it.

The south transept was rebuilt first, then the choir and the east window; after that the presbytery and the north transept, and last the cloisters. The delicate stone tracery covered the heavy Norman stonework like a cobweb and formed a perfect frame for whole walls of brilliant stained-glass. The treasure from pilgrims was large, and it supplied a great deal of the money for all this. But the £136 for the glass of the magnificent east window came from Lord Bradeston, constable of Gloucester, who was the lord of two of Maurice de Berkeley's manors, and the lord of Berkeley's great friend. The story is that the window was built as Lord Bradeston's own tribute to the Englishmen, especially the men of the shire, who had died in the great Battle of Crécy in France in 1346, and as a great prayer of thanks for the victory won there. The picture shows the hymn of praise after the coronation of the Blessed Virgin Mary, with her Son, and all the company of heaven, the apostles, martyrs, saints, kings and abbots. Along the bottom are the shields of the King and the lords who fought in the campaign in France. The names read like a roll call of the Marcher lords. The Arundels of Stonehouse, Thomas de Berkeley; Thomas de Beauchamp, Earl of Warwick; William de Bohun, son of the Earl of Hereford; Lawrence de Hastings, Earl of Pembroke; Richard Lord Talbot, lord of Painswick; Sir Maurice de Berkeley; Thomas de Bradeston of Bradeston and Stinchcombe.

It was the largest stained-glass window in England and was made by Thomas Glasswright, a craftsman of Gloucester, whose workshop was near the river. Perhaps it made his reputation, because we find him a few years later in London, working on some new windows in Westminster Abbey. And how he deserved it!

Thomas de Bradeston was a wealthy man. But even so, £136 was something like £5,000 in today's money. It was an expensive tribute, and it showed how much wealth there was in the land of Gloucester.

8. A MEDIEVAL CITY

When we last looked at the day-to-day lives of men in the shire, it was with the help of the Domesday Survey. In fact, by 1200, the lives of working men had not changed a great deal since then. There were still villeins and bordars and serfs, though fewer serfs and more villeins now. They still lived in hamlets, though they were less scattered and isolated. Land was still being cleared at a tremendous rate and the lords along the river began to drain the marshes for more. Probably the walls and the drainage channels along the river were built by men serving under the Berkeley and the de Clare lords during peacetime. While there were many mouths to feed and labour was cheap, the clearing of land went on, and the lord now always made sure that new land was held directly from him and not subject to the law of the hundred. And when the King threw open the old Royal Forest of Kingswood, the local barons moved in to divide it up.

The thirteenth century was a time of tremendous development. While royal Gloucester was getting its bridge and its first two Charters from Henry II and John and the first hall of the city's Guild Merchant was going up, other lords tried to make a success of towns on their own land. Towns brought trade, and the more trade a town attracted, the more profit a lord made from the tolls and the dues. Of course, to attract traders and craftsmen you had to offer them good terms, a low rent, a good deal of freedom from services to the lord and a good site. And the more profitable a town became, the more insistent it got for a charter to break its ties from you altogether, and the more trouble it caused. This was why the village of Berkeley had to wait 300 years after Domesday to become a proper town, because the Berkeleys could not bear the thought of trouble so near. They allowed a market at Newport on the main road instead, but it never really became profitable.

Thornbury had to be pushed. It was on a by-road as Berkeley was, and like Berkeley it was a great feudal centre of the de Clare family, the Earls of Gloucester. But Richard de Clare, who was Earl in the 1250s, announced that anyone who came to build a house and settle would have the same rights as the burgesses of the prosperous little town of Tewkesbury, and only then did it begin to grow.

At Domesday there were four towns with burgesses in the area: Gloucester, Bristol, Tewkesbury and Winchcombe. But by the time of Henry III there were tiny settlements trying to become towns at twenty-four places in the county, including Painswick, Dursley, Thornbury, Wotton, Berkeley, Wickwar and King's Stanley. Some succeeded. Some failed. King's Stanley never really developed at all, despite its position on the Rodborough to Arlingham road.

A town was for trade and manufacture. Now that men had more money they could sell their surplus grain or let out their spare land for money and spend it on luxuries in the towns. Once a man managed to buy a piece of land in a town, a burgage lot as it was called, he became part of an exclusive club that looked after its members and tried to stop others enjoying its benefits. In Gloucester the burgesses elected their own leaders, called reeves. Only burgesses could be elected to the Guild Merchant, the society that controlled all trade and took a large part in the town government. The Guild Merchant members paid a large share of the town expenses, and in return had the right to buy and sell in the borough without paying tolls. Strangers not only had to pay tolls, but they could only buy or sell at the Bothall, the market hall in Westgate Street. And as the Guild Merchant saw that all traders kept to the rules and gave honest measure, we can be sure that they were particularly strict with outsiders.

After 1250, the boom began to slacken. Cleared land was abandoned or turned over to pasture or orchards. The farming villages that had earnt their living from the poorest soil grew smaller, and some disappeared altogether as peasants moved away. There was less ready money about, and the smaller towns suffered too. Even Gloucester, which had been so prosperous, began to decline. This was partly because the Guild members were too keen on what we would call today "restrictive practices"—they left no freedom for new men with new ideas to use them and make themselves rich. It was also due to the growth of Bristol based on the wool trade.

There had always been a wool trade in Gloucestershire from Roman times, and medieval Gloucester was a trading centre for wool from the Cotswolds and the Welsh hills. It had its own cloth industry as well. But because of the strict guild regulations, and because of the drop in demand for land for growing grain, more and more lords were turning to the profitable wool trade for their income and the weavers moved out of the city to where the wool was. Most of the weavers settled along the valley of the Frome, and the trading centre of the area, Strode or "the scattered place", a small outlying part of Bisley parish, began to grow. This took a very long time. The medieval trade guild of the weavers of Gloucester did not die until 1629, more than 250 years later, but Gloucester became poorer and poorer and Bristol replaced it as the capital of the west.

There were many reasons why Bristol won, but probably the most important was the river Avon. We know that the Severn was shallow with jagged rocky reefs across it, particularly between Oldbury and Berkeley. The sailing channel was narrow and winding, and the tides and current were, and still are, strong and treacherous. More and more of the wool was being sold to merchants for direct shipment to south-west France and Italy. The city of Florence grew great on the wool and the partly finished cloth from the Cotswolds, longer and finer wool than any other in England, except perhaps for the fleeces from Hereford. At the peak of the weaving industry in Florence, 100,000 cloths were being made a year (Gloucester was producing or selling about 450, and Bristol about 3000 or 4000 at roughly the same time). When the Italian merchants discovered the fine English wool, they snapped it up, but to carry big cargoes all the way to Italy they needed big ships and a good harbour for them, and the Avon at Bristol was far better than the Severn forty miles upriver at Gloucester.

So Gloucester declined, but the landlords flourished. At one parliament in Edward III's time, it was agreed to let the King sell one-fifteenth of the county's wool for that year to pay for the French wars. The collectors gathered from the Berkeley estates alone forty-seven sacks of 364 lb each. The lord of Berkeley who gave these forty-seven sacks must have had about 100,000 sheep. A little earlier, John de Gamages, an abbot of St Peter's, had sheep flocks of 10,000. And by far the largest proportion of sheep in the county were in the hands of small landowners—the villeins and bordars who had managed to buy small pieces of land and turn themselves into free peasant farmers.

Sheep farming offered a prosperous living. In the 1420s, Lady Elizabeth of the Berkeley family married the Earl of Warwick, who was head of the government in England while King Henry V was fighting the campaign which led to the great victory at Agincourt. Her account books for 1420 still exist to show how prosperous life was in a great house. On 2nd March, a Sunday, forty-six people sat down to dinner at Berkeley Castle, including the vicar and his curate, five knights, two valets, two pilgrims and two charcoal burners. That evening at supper, there were thirty-eight.

On that day the household consumed 146 large white loaves, 100 fresh herrings and 80 smoked herrings, and drank $10\frac{1}{2}$ gallons of red wine and 68 gallons of ale. This was a day during the fasting time of Lent. Usually there were oxen, sheep and pigs, as well as wildfowl from the Severn marshes and lampreys, eels, sturgeon and salmon from the river itself. And each day at the bottom of the account is the food for the countess's pets, her greyhounds and the pet bear—the Earl of Warwick's badge was a bear chained to a wooden staff.

But the accounts show signs of another side of the countess's life. She had no brothers to carry on the Berkeley line, and another relative, James Berkeley, was quarrelling with her

husband over the Berkeley inheritance. James was happy to
allow her twenty-three manors, but she wanted all of them.
Earlier in 1420, the Earl had seized Berkeley Castle from James,
who stayed on in the district to cause trouble. Early in 1421,
James occupied the rectory at Wotton, where one of the
Berkeleys' favourite houses was. The Earl called in fifty-three
of his soldiers to the castle in case of attack. But he was called
away on state business, and some months later the countess had
to go to Walthamstow on business too. She went in her usual
style with thirty-two attendants, and nearly seventy horses to
carry them and their baggage. She took two weeks to reach
Walthamstow, stopping almost every evening at a Warwick or
a Berkeley estate. On the way back, though, James's men,
travelling along the trackways and Roman roads from Cirencester and Tetbury to Wotton, shot arrows at her party and
shouted insults, and she was forced to take a different route
home.

The quarrel went on for fifty more years, long after Elizabeth, James and the Earl were dead, and there had been a siege,
a long law case, and a heavy bribe to the Duke of Gloucester
from James. At one point a poor sheriff's messenger had been
forced to eat his master's summons to one of his parties, seal
and all! Finally, in the spring of 1470, James's heir, Lord Lisle,
agreed with Elizabeth's heir to fight it out. They decided to
meet at Nibley Green, halfway between the castle and the Lisle
headquarters at Wotton. The Berkeley army was 500 strong.
There were not just the local retainers, but men from Maurice
Berkeley's estates at Thornbury and from the forest.

At first light, Lord Lisle's men were up and armed and on the
move down the slope from Nibley Church. As they gathered
speed and neared the Berkeley lines, a volley of arrows stopped
them almost dead. Lord Lisle had his visor up, shouting orders.
An arrow struck him in the face, and as he fell a forest miner
moved in to stab him through one of the chinks in his armour.
His men turned and fled back up through the woods, dying
along the way. The Berkeley army did not bother to follow
them very far. They soon turned off to Wotton to smash the

windows and the panelling and furniture at the manor house
and to rob it of anything they fancied. Lord Lisle left no son:
his wife was about to have a child, but the shock was too much
for her and it was born dead.

The straggling untidy brawl at Nibley Green was the last
"private" battle in England. The "public" Wars of the Roses
hardly touched our area, except at the very end. Henry VI's
wife and her son, Prince Edward, were fighting another king,
Edward IV. If they had managed to cross the Severn to their
Welsh allies on their way north from Devon they might have
beaten Edward. But a Beauchamp descendant of the Earl of
Warwick held the castle at Gloucester and the bridge was
closed to them. They were caught from behind at the narrow
bridge over the Avon at Tewkesbury and defeated heavily.

Edward's brother, Richard Duke of Gloucester, had been one
of his strongest allies. He received huge estates in Yorkshire and
Cumberland as a reward for his part in the victory. When he
became King, twelve years later, he remembered the city that
had played such a part in Edward's victory and his own. In
1483, Gloucester received from Richard, now King Richard
III, a charter which made it an independent self-governing
city, answering to no one, not even the Abbot of St Peter's,
but only to the King. There was to be a mayor and a council of
twelve aldermen, elected by the burgesses. The mayor was to
have a sword bearer and four mace bearers to walk with him in
procession to show off his importance. He was responsible for
the defence, law and order and the taxing, as well as for the day
to day affairs of the city; the city area was now to include a much
bigger circle of rich farming land, from Corse Lawn and Wainlode Hill in the north to Harescombe in the south. It was a
magnificent present, and it should have been the making of
Gloucester, but it came too late. We heard earlier how rapidly
Gloucester's trade was dwindling. It was not long before the
mayor was writing to Henry VII that:

The great costs and importune charges we have to sustain in
the reparation maintaining keeping and repairing of the

great bridge over your water of Severn thereby which all
your liege people in that part of this your realm have their
several passage, course and recourse into Wales and the
Marches of same, which bridge, walls gates and towers be
now very ruinous and have great need of reparation and are
like to fall in desolation.

From time to time over the last hundred years and more that
cry had gone up, and for the sake of the safety of the kingdom
it was answered as soon as there was money in the royal treasury
to repair the defences. The trees and undergrowth were cleared
from the town ditch and the streams that fed it with water were
made to flow again. The friars, who used a tower on the
south wall as a classroom, and treated the part of the wall that
ran through their grounds as their own, had to be made to
move, and the fishing weirs that jumbled up against the castle
on the side overlooking the river dismantled. The towers and
the battlements were built up to their proper height with
expensive newly quarried stone, and iron straps and heavy
baulks of timber had to be paid for by the city authorities to put
to rights the half-dozen gates, big and small, together with
their portcullises and wooden bridges. But then, when the
emergency was over, the young trees soon grew again, the
ditch quickly became clogged with rubbish, and the salmon
once more had to look out for the putts just downstream from
the town quay. But when Gloucester refused to let the Queen
and Prince Edward through before the battle of Tewkesbury, it
was no longer much more than a large provincial trading city,
which catered for the needs of the people in the country round
it. The bridge, the reason for Gloucester's existence, was in a
very bad way. It was more than 350 years old when Richard III
granted his charter and for all that time it had been in the care,
not of the city authorities, but of the Hospital of St Bartholomew, a monastery that stood in Lower Westgate Street near
the present bridge. Henry III gave it lands, and medieval
businessmen who wanted to give an offering to God which
might help themselves too, left much money to the Hospital to

help with the repair work. But the bridge and the causeway ate up an immense amount of money. St Bartholomew's simply could not afford it, and in the 1450s there were four members of the Hospital travelling round the country trying to raise money without very much success. When Henry VII came to the throne he did not help much. He left it to his son to build another new bridge—one which was to last 300 years.

The Roman population of the city we can guess had been 6,000 or so. In the late 1400s there were only 4,000 people in the city, and they spread outside the walls the way the Romans had done. People packed themselves much more tightly into fewer houses then, and we must not think of Gloucester as being built up as it is today. The four main streets, following the line of the Roman streets, would have been lined with tall, half-timbered buildings of three, four or five storeys—with shops on the ground floors—all jostling together and leaning drunkenly over the roadway. But you only had to turn the corner down one of the narrow side alleys that often began in passageways through the buildings, to find that the burgesses and citizens had another side to their existence.

There were cowsheds for cattle, stabling for horses, as well as barns and granaries. The burgage lots, the long thin strips of land that were the holdings in towns, were only built up at the front; behind they might be cultivated or used for grazing. If you walked a few yards out from the centre of town, the houses quickly became lower and more spaced out, with barns end on to the road and patches of green grass in between them. On the southern side, at the bottom of Southgate Street, on the quietest side of town, the land on each side of the street, behind the straggle of houses and inns and farm buildings, was almost all orchard, belonging to the Blackfriars and Greyfriars. And it was as much a part of a tradesman's day to see that his cows were led down Westgate Street to the Ham, the common town grazing land on the Island between the two branches of the river (it is still called "the Island" today), as to set out his wares each morning in front of his shop.

The centre of town was the High Cross. It was a tall angled

stone building surmounted by a crucifix, and underneath was an open arched arcade with lead water spouts let into the walls. There were steps leading up to it. The Cross was all things to all men: a place to do business, to meet, to gossip; a place to hear the news, the royal proclamations, or a sermon from a friar; to fill the water jars, or to take shelter from the rain. It was also the best begging pitch in the city, and the place to stand with a white paper dunce's cap on your head and a lighted candle in one hand, in penance for your sins. From the High Cross ran the four main streets, each with a character of its own. Southgate Street, as we have seen, was the quietest, on the road to Bristol. It was a street of inns and religious buildings. Five churches or monasteries and three large inns catered for the passing trade and the pilgrims to Edward II's shrine. Somewhere here, too, was the town pillory.

Most of the Jews had lived in Eastgate Street before they were sent to Bristol with their belongings in the 1290s. They had had a school and a synagogue there, and they must have played a big part in Gloucester life, especially in business. In the Public Record Office in London there is a document showing what money the Jews of England paid Henry III in taxes for part of 1233, and the Jews of Gloucester are prominent on the list.

Northgate Street was the shortest of the four, but it had two important buildings in it, the New Inn and the Cordwainery. The New Inn was one of the three inns owned by St Peter's which the monks enlarged to help house the pilgrims coming to Edward II's tomb. They found it not only easier than putting them in abbey buildings scattered round the town, but much cheaper too. At the New Inn, the Ram, or the Fleece, the pilgrims paid the monks for their stay. When the pilgrims stayed in the abbey houses they could claim the hospitality of the abbey, and paid nothing. The other important building in Northgate Street was really part of the busiest section of the town, the business and manufacturing area round the corner at the top end of Westgate Street. It was the Cordwainery, the group of open fronted shops and stalls where leather goods— shoes, saddles, bags, hats and so on—were made and sold.

The New Inn

At the Cross, at the very top of Westgate Street, the noise was loudest and the traffic at its busiest. From the earliest times, the market place had always been where the road was widest, with a line of stalls straggling down the centre of the road from the Cross. Then the stall-holders began to build more permanent buildings to house their goods, and by the 1450s, there was a block of houses and shops in the middle of the market. On one side were the shops of the mercers, the cloth merchants and the hat makers, next to the stalls selling herbs and fish. On the opposite side, nearly at the corner of Southgate Street, were the butchers' stalls, with the slaughterhouse in the middle. On this side of the road worked the little cluster of goldsmiths who made jewellery and religious ornaments. Very probably they were working on the ancient site where the royal mint had stood for 350 years from Saxon times until the reign of Henry III. There was a bakery near here too, but it was not a large one. People ate huge quantities of bread every day, just as they drank gallons of ale—the accounts of Lady Elizabeth, the Earl of Warwick's wife, shows us that—but nearly everyone baked their own. It was considered wasteful to buy at the baker's, except for elaborately shaped loaves on special occasions, or spicy cakes sold at Christmas, Easter, Whitsun or during the Midsummer Fair.

Behind the bakery and the goldsmiths' and butchers' houses was "Smith Street" where the ironsmiths had their shops. Perhaps here too was the bell workshop that cast iron bells for many medieval churches in the county.

Two more buildings stood in the middle of Westgate Street, the King's Board and the Church of the Holy Trinity. The King's Board was the butter market, where the milk, cheese and butter were laid out on wooden boards. And just below Holy Trinity, where the Shire Hall is today, was the Bothall.

The Bothall was the headquarters of the Guild Merchant, as well as a town hall and a market where people from beyond the town walls could sell their produce. This was a natural arrangement, because it was the powerful members of the Guild Merchant, the businessmen, who controlled the business life of the town and were also members of the Common Council and the court. There was a house where the royal stewards lived at the top of Southgate Street, but it was not to come into its own for another 150 years as the new Town Hall, or Tolsey.

At first sight, the life of a medieval town looks chaotic.

People loved noise and bright colours, and enjoyed being in crowds. The happiest time of all for the Gloucester people was the week of the Midsummer Fair of St John the Baptist, when there were processions and feasts and strolling players and foreign merchants.

The streets were narrow and dirty and disease ridden, and there was the constant risk of fire. But the Guild members and the town court at least tried to tackle all the problems in their town. To begin with they controlled trade so strictly that, as we have seen, they frightened it away. They made sure weights and measures were fair, and fixed the price of bread and beer. They fixed the tolls for goods coming into the town, and saw they were paid. They ran the fair and the markets, and saw that market tolls were paid, and that no unauthorized buying or selling was done outside the market. For the safety of the citizens, they made sure that no houses were roofed with thatch for fear of fire, and saw to it that no one carried a weapon inside the walls and so be tempted to cause bloodshed. At the time of the Black Death, they tried to stop all contact with Bristol, to prevent the plague spreading, and they made sure that anyone who caught a dangerous disease, and especially anyone who became a leper, left the city to live in one of the leper hospitals the monasteries ran outside the town walls. In time of war, it was the members of the Common Council at the Bothall who saw that the young men were trained, armed and ready, and the defences in good repair. And for anyone who broke their rulings there was the lock-up in the North Gate, or a spell in the pillory in Southgate Street.

Just below the Bothall, Westgate Street became Bridge Street. In fact there were three bridges: the tiny Hambridge, by the town Ham, the great Inner Bridge, called the Foreign Bridge, with shops and watermills built along it, and the Westgate Bridge itself, with its fortified gatehouse. In Roman and Anglo-Saxon times, the river was a number of shallow streams running through marshy grassland. The main channel ran close to the town near the church of St Mary de Lode and St Oswald's monastery. The quay was here, and along the

water's edge grew up the earliest part of Anglo-Saxon Gloucester with St Peter's Abbey and the royal palace of the Ealdor-
men of Mercia behind. But this old channel began to silt up,
and by the end of the 1400s the main stream ran along the outer
channel. The channel crossed by Westgate Bridge and the quay
was moved down-river to the deeper water near the castle
walls. Although Bristol had passed Gloucester in the size of its
trade, Gloucester was still a thriving port, because medieval
roads were so very bad, fit only for trains of packhorses. At the
top end the brewers collected the water for beer. Lower down,
there were steps where the women did the washing, and near
the bottom was a big rubbish heap where all the butchers'
waste was burnt.

Everyone must have known everyone else in Gloucester,
particularly the men who worked in the same trade. Very early
they began to form themselves into guilds of their own trade.
There were guilds of mercers, joiners, shoemakers, metal
workers, tailors, barbers and many more, though the most
important of all was the Weavers' Guild. These trade guilds
each had their own officers and entrance fees, their sets of rules,
and their little customs. In the Tanners' Guild, for instance, each
new master was crowned with flowers when he was elected.
Each guild had certain rights in the town, such as attending the
mayor with their banners on important occasions.

But the guild's main purpose was to protect its members in
times of trouble, in sickness and death, and especially against
anyone else who wanted to take away their livelihood by new
methods that were cheaper or quicker, or by bringing in new
workmen from other towns.

9. REFORM AND REVOLT

Gloucester in the 1450s had 4,000 people. There were eleven parish churches—one for every 400 people—six monasteries and three hospitals run by monks. The Church owned almost two-thirds of the property in the city. There were also seven stone crosses at places where people met, where the friars could preach and the people could pray.

It would not have seemed strange to a citizen of Gloucester that the Church was so powerful—about one in ten citizens would have been clergy of one sort or another anyway. There were four churches clustered round the noisy business area of Westgate Street, and far from being aloof from religion, it was often the businessmen who remembered God most often and most generously in their gifts of money and land. The guilds maintained chapels in churches where they heard Masses for the good of the souls of dead members and where they kept candles and silver lamps burning in honour of the guild's patron saint. The tanners had a chapel in the church of St John the Baptist near the North Gate, to their saint, St Clement, and the weavers had one dedicated to St Ann in St Michael's Church at the Cross. Religion entered everything from birth to death, at work and at play. It was as natural for the medieval citizens of Gloucester to slip into their church to pray as it would be for us to walk to the corner shop. There did not have to be anything "special" about religion, reserved for Sundays. It was a normal, natural, unremarked-on part of life, and it had been for many hundreds of years. Although priests were often greedy and ignorant, the Church was the only comfort for millions of poor people.

In July 1535, Gloucester was preparing to welcome a royal

visitor. It was a visit which would have made the wiser of the citizens aware that the Church as they knew it was in great danger; King Henry VIII arrived on a royal progress with his wife, Queen Anne Boleyn. Henry wanted a son, but his first wife seemed able to give him only a daughter. When he had asked the Church to allow him a divorce to marry again, it refused. So Henry decided to make himself its head; then naturally, it accepted his divorce and allowed him to re-marry. And now, by King Henry's side, riding towards Gloucester was his new Queen. The Reformation in England was about to begin.

But on the afternoon of that summer Saturday, there were no signs of the changes that were coming. The mayor and the aldermen rode out to Staverton Bridge in scarlet gowns and velvet tippets to meet the royal party. About a hundred burgesses in grey followed them. After the speeches of welcome, and the kissing of the town maces, the party returned to the city and at the house of the Whitefriars outside the walls near the modern bus station, they stopped again to meet all the clergy of the parish churches in their finest vestments, led by the assistant bishop. The bishop himself was an Italian living in Rome as Henry's ambassador to the Pope.

The King and Queen kissed the cross the assistant bishop held up and then they rode on, through the North Gate, wheeling right at the Cross to the abbey gateway, where they were to stay. The abbot and his monks met them and they kissed the cross again before they were shown to their apartments. They stayed at the abbey for three days, riding out to hunt in the woods round Painswick and Coberley and coming back after dark, lit the last few hundred yards of the way by groups of citizens with blazing torches. And on the next day, Wednesday, they left again, travelling south in a leisurely way to spend the next few days at the priory at Leonard Stanley, and at Berkeley Castle and Thornbury Castle.

Henry knew very well how wealthy the Church was. He only had to look round him during his stay at St Peter's to see it. The last parts of the abbey as we know it, the great tower and the lady chapel, were still less than 100 years old, and the stone and the paintwork gleamed brightly. He would have discovered, if he did not already know, that the monks (there were only thirty-two of them) were the lords of more than forty manors, with hundreds of servants working their land and running the rambling domestic buildings of the abbey that have now mostly disappeared.

Within a year, he was beginning to "reform" the smaller, less powerful monasteries and the friaries and selling their buildings and land, first to pay their debts and then, if any money was left, pocketing the profits himself. St Oswald's was one of the first to go. The Anglo-Saxon royal abbey that had been a rival to St Peter's itself, now had only seven monks and a small amount of money coming in from its three manors.

The royal commissioners were polite, but very firm. They made a list of the possessions of each monastery and then the chief commissioner talked to the monks. The King was the head of the Church in England, they were told, and he wanted the monasteries to be reformed. When a monastery was too small to carry on, it was to be "reformed", that is, closed. The monks were perfectly free to become ordinary priests or move to other monasteries of the same order. Five at St Oswald's decided to remain monks, and they were moved.

Many of the small monasteries all over England were slack and badly run. Often they were deeply in debt—the Grey-friars in Gloucester had long since rented or sold off most of their land, and they only had a few onions and some wheat in their larder at the time they were "reformed". The real pickings were in the great monasteries, like St Peter's, and they must have known that before long their turn would come. At Kingswood they were taking precautions. In 1535 Thomas Reading, the prior, sent a book to the King telling him he agreed that Henry was the head of the Church of England and asking him to "close up the eye of justice and open the eye of pity to me and the religious men of this house who have no succour except in your evangelical charity". It must have been very embarrassing for Prior Reading that one of his monks at about the same time preached a sermon saying how much he disagreed. The Pope in Rome was still the head of the Church, the monk said. He was quickly packed off to London as a prisoner.

The Archbishop of York, the protector of St Oswald's, wrote to Thomas Cromwell, asking him to make it an exception, as a special favour, but even his influence did not help save it. Kingswood had no such friends. Very soon the commissioners, led by the Bishop of Dover, were making their rounds once more, to survey, to report. In February 1538, Kingswood became one of the first of the larger monasteries to go. It was a year before the commissioners, who had a great deal to get through, got to Llantony, and another year before the thirty-four monks of St Peter's itself accepted the King's will, and gave him their monastery with all its lands.

There had been monasteries in Gloucestershire for nearly 1,000 years. But nearly all the monks went quietly, with grants to buy themselves a house or a small piece of land, and sometimes with a job to go to. Edward Bennet, one of the assistant sub-wardens at St Peter's, got £13 6s. 8d. (several years' wages for a labourer), and he became the vicar of Badgeworth. Robert Dursley, a local man (to judge by his name), was still living quietly in Gloucester on his pension ten years later. And William Bewdley, the Abbot of Kingswood at the time it was closed, not only got £50, but was made vicar of Hawkesbury, married and became a father.

Gloucestershire, the new head of the Church decided, was to become a diocese, and its cathedral was to be St Peter's Abbey, renamed the Cathedral Church of the Holy Trinity. St Peter, the first Pope, was not a suitable saint to watch over one of Henry's "reformed" cathedrals! And the bishop and his staff, very naturally and conveniently, were to be the abbot and the core of his staff. They would hardly have had to move from their rooms to make the change. As it happened, though, at the last moment, the abbot, William Parker, died, and the next senior churchman in the county, the Abbot of Tewkesbury, got the job instead.

At the beginning, the Reformation in England just meant a

change of landlords for most ordinary men. They went on
going to Mass and Confession exactly as they always had. The
parish churches looked the same inside with the images of
saints, silver lamps and candles always burning and the walls
brightly decorated with religious paintings. You can still get
some idea of how colourful the decorations of churches must
have been from Berkeley Parish Church today. But there was
another side to the Reformation, a much more important one.
The reformers wanted people to cast off certain beliefs and
worship in a different way. They "protested" against the old
ways of worship, which they said were based on greed and
ignorance, and which had no justification in the Bible. For
these early reformers—"Protestants"—the reading of the Bible
was very important. But the Bible was in Latin, and the Church
was keen that no unofficial translations were made that might
include errors to be misunderstood by ordinary men. One of
the chaplains to the Berkeleys, a priest called John Trevisa, had
translated it in the mid-fourteenth century into Norman French,
which was not exactly the language of ordinary people, but it
was understood by nobles, and it was used for all official
documents. And another translation was made by William
Tyndale, born at Nibley or Slimbridge, into English this time,
in 1524.

Gloucestershire was one of the counties where the new ideas
caught on quickest. Some historians believe that the weavers
were among the strongest believers in the new ideas because
they could often read books propped up against the loom as
they worked, and they were free workers who had no lord to
answer to in matters of religion. And, of course, in Bristol and
Gloucestershire were some of the most prosperous groups of
weavers in the country.

Until Henry VIII's reign, the Church managed to confine
these dangerous ideas to one or two small areas. William
Tyndale was burnt for his views, and many poor people in the
county were made to do penance for theirs. But after the
Reformation the atmosphere changed suddenly—too suddenly.
The first bishop, John Wakeman, did what he was told by the

Bishop Hooper and the tower of Gloucester Cathedral

King. But the second, John Hooper, was a man marked out for trouble. He had been a monk, perhaps at the house of the Blackfriars at Gloucester. He had fled from the King's agents to Switzerland disguised as a sailor and there he had met many of the greatest thinkers among the reformers and studied the scriptures and their writings. He began his appointment as bishop by refusing to take the oath and refusing to wear rich vestments, and he went to prison in London until he eventually changed his mind.

He was a kind of churchman that Gloucester had never seen before. Anyone could come and speak to him or eat a meal with him, even the poorest. But the Church had suffered from neglect over the past twenty years, and he had a great deal to do. The priests were lazy, ignorant and bad: Robert Whitfield, the priest at Elmore, apparently had a lover; the vicar of Uley was always drunk; William Newport, vicar of St Owen's in Gloucester, an ex-monk of St Peter's Abbey, used sorcery on one occasion to find a thief. Thirty-one priests, Bishop Hooper discovered, did not know who had devised the Lord's Prayer, and the people were worse.

John Hooper worked hard to make the priests and the people good Christians again. He examined all his priests to find out just how ignorant they were, and toured the county hearing cases of bad living and handing out punishments generously. All the gold and silver and rich hangings in the cathedral were taken away, except for one chalice and the bells. All Latin books and the statues of saints were destroyed. It may have been at this time that the carvings in the cathedral were deliberately damaged, and the figures from the niches on Slimbridge church tower taken away.

There were to be no candles or bells or ceremonials during services. Everyone had to go to church once a week, or be punished, and one member of each family had to attend prayers every other day. To ease temptation, inns were to be closed at service time. The priests were to study hard; each parish was to buy copies of the English translation of the Bible and the priests were to teach their people from it.

Bishop Hooper was the hardest working of all the bishops in England, and the strictest. When Henry's daughter, Mary, came to the throne, she brought back the old religion just as suddenly as her father had got rid of it. Because Bishop Hooper had worked so hard, and held his views so strongly, he refused to change and was one of the first of the Protestant bishops to suffer. After his trial for heresy in London, he was brought back to Gloucester to die. On the way, at Oxford, Sir William Kingston, the lord of Painswick, and the stepson of the man who had bought the old monastery lands of Leonard Stanley, met him. He had already changed his religion to keep his life and his lands, and now he came "with tears in his eyes" to persuade Bishop Hooper to do the same. Hooper could not agree. He spent his last night in a house in Westgate Street, and on the following cold February morning he was led out to be burnt outside the main gate of his cathedral, watched by the people he had loved so much.

Six other people were burnt in Gloucester in the five years of Mary's reign; one of them, a boy called Tom, was blind. When Elizabeth, Mary's half-sister, succeeded her, the official religion changed back again, but the sickening list of burnings did not stop. Although Gloucestershire was a Protestant county, there were a few Roman Catholics who, in turn, died for their faith. Two of them—Thomas Alfield, son of the headmaster of the cathedral school, and Thomas Webley, a young cloth dyer's apprentice—were tortured in the Tower of London before they were hanged at Tyburn Tree.

In the hundred years after Bishop Hooper's death, Gloucester became poorer and poorer while Gloucestershire became richer and richer. This was caused by the cloth trade, and although different governments had passed laws to stop the move from the cloth towns into the country, the clothing manufacturers of the Stroud area were so prosperous and so well established that in Queen Mary's time the government made a special exception for them. And when the trains of pack horses loaded high with wool and cloth set out for market now, they went to Bristol or London, not Gloucester.

Gloucester was as loyal to Queen Elizabeth as any other city in England. When she visited the city during a stay at Sudeley Castle, the corporation paid the troupe of the Earl of Leicester to put on a performance in her honour, and the Earl of Sussex lent his bear, at a price, to dance "before Mr Mayor". The Queen made Gloucester an official port—which meant that merchants could export goods directly from Gloucester Quay to places abroad. She was trying to make Gloucester a prosperous city by encouraging trade, but it was no good. The burgesses of Bristol objected to the Queen's minister, Lord Burleigh, saying that "Gloucester has always been a creek of Bristol"—which was unkind, and not strictly true. Luke Garnons, a draper and a mayor many times over, went up to London to plead for Gloucester, but Bristol had become a much more important city and Burleigh had to recognize this.

The 1580s and 90s were hard times. There were several bad harvests and corn prices rocketed. Poor people starved. They could not afford bread and they robbed the corn ships at the quay. The city even put a chain across the river to force the captains of the corn ships coming upstream to sell their cargo at a fixed price in Gloucester. But when physical danger threatened, Gloucester turned out in force to face it. In 1588 the Armada came sailing north towards Plymouth, and orders went out from London to put the city and the county on the alert, ready to meet the invaders. Gloucester and Tewkesbury clubbed together and found £440 to fit out the bark *Sutton* to join Lord Howard's fleet in the Channel. Up and down the county the men answered the muster, took down their rusty swords and drilled on the village greens. Just outside the South Gate at Gloucester the archery butts must have been busier than ever before with the apprentices and their masters practising in every spare moment. In the forest, the cut timber waiting to be used in the shipyards of Lydney and all over England, had to be destroyed, to prevent it being captured. And in almost every parish, bonfires were built on the highest hill to warn against the invasion. There were beacons on Frocester Hill and Haresfield, and the Gloucester Beacon was on Robin's Wood Hill. The city paid two men to tend it, and built a hut for them; they kept watch night and day for many weeks. Two more men were to ride from parish to parish to give the alarm the moment Haresfield Beacon was lit, to bring the terrible news of invasion from the south.

Every year for many years afterwards the people lit bonfires to celebrate the defeat of the Spanish Armada. Elizabeth was a popular queen, but one of the reasons why everyone rallied round to beat Spain was because they were afraid that the Spanish would force Elizabeth to make Englishmen Roman Catholics again.

Gloucester was a "Puritan" county. The "Puritans" were not simply men who believed in freedom of worship and in sober, quiet clothes and behaviour. They were the businessmen who were annoyed at the government for interfering with the cloth trade, and blamed it for the slump which began at the end of Elizabeth's reign. And they were the men like squire Henry Stephens of Eastington, who sat in Parliament and saw Elizabeth's successors, James I and Charles I, acting against the wishes of the taxpayers, and wasting money on military expeditions and luxurious living. There were also the grave, religious men like Alderman Pury of Gloucester, who would have seen the royal family as a group of foreigners, leading lives of pleasure and idleness and dabbling in Catholicism.

In Gloucester, Bishop Miles Smith, a great scholar, spent most of his time in the library. He was a member of the committee that translated the Bible into English—the Authorized Version; it was he who wrote the long introduction at the beginning. He was interested in nothing but his books. The cathedral was almost falling down when William Laud, a favourite of the royal family, was made dean.

The dean was completely in charge of the cathedral, and the bishop by tradition almost a guest when he entered it. Laud did his best to change things to his own liking without consulting Miles Smith. He had the church furnishings put to rights. He made some of the cathedral staff spend an afternoon every week tidying up the document room, where all the precious documents of the cathedral were lying on the floor in a mouldy heap. He made the boys of the choir school attend early morning prayers. But worst of all in Miles Smith's eyes, he gave orders on his first day as dean for the altar table to be moved from the middle of the church, and up some steps at one end of the choir, to the place where it is today. He also had some rails put up in front of it to keep out the dogs. This was a sign to the Puritans that Dean Laud did not share their views on religion. He might even be a secret Roman Catholic! Bishop Smith was so disgusted that he said he would never enter his own cathedral again. And, as far as we know, he did not, for nearly ten years until he died.

Dean Laud's time at Gloucester helped to prove to the people what they had always believed about the government and the royal family—it was trying to ease back into use a much more Catholic attitude to worship.

Richard Capel, the rector of Eastington and an outspoken preacher and scholar, resigned his living over "the Book of Sports"—a government attempt to encourage leisure activity on Sunday after church. All Puritans felt as he did—that any worldly pleasure was wicked—and the answer of Gloucester corporation was to pay a lecturer, a learned Puritan, to preach long sermons twice a week, on Thursday mornings and on Sunday afternoons. Many other places were doing the same, but John Workman, the choice of the Common Council, was a particularly acid-tongued man. From the pulpits of the churches of St Michael and St Nicholas, he told his audience, seated and quite deliberately wearing their hats to show they held the church building in no special reverence, that the number of steps a man took dancing was the number he was taking towards hell; that the government of the Church was evil; and that holy pictures and ornaments were unlawful. This was all directly against the views of Dean Laud, who had now risen to become an archbishop. What made it even worse was that in front of the King, Charles I, Mr Workman had prayed for the safety of England's Protestant rivals, Holland and Sweden.

It was a sign of the times. All over the country there was deliberate defiance and hatred for the King. When he had John Workman tried, in spite of the fact that his living as vicar of St Nicholas had been taken from him and he had been forbidden to preach, the Common Council of Gloucester voted him his lecturer's pay "whether he preach or not".

10. FOR KING AND PARLIAMENT

The country was moving towards war, and Gloucester, like most of our area, was naturally on Parliament's side. In 1640 only a very few extreme Puritans wanted to fight their king, but everyone found himself forced to take sides, and the citizens of Gloucester and the cloth men of Stroud and Wotton and Dursley faced the local gentlemen, who barricaded their houses and declared themselves for the royal side. By the standards of Europe, the Civil War was very gentlemanly. The English countryside had not seen war for more than 150 years. One writer at the time says that no living person as far inland as Gloucester had ever heard the shot of an artillery gun. But the chief reason for the gentlemanly progress of the war was the lack of men and money on both sides. The Gloucester garrison's pay was always late. There were only a few guns and a little gunpowder because there was neither cash nor time to buy them. The Gloucester garrison consisted of two regiments—1,500 men—and there was no one to spare to guard prisoners. You simply let them go, hopefully having made them promise that they would never fight you again. The garrison not only had to guard the city itself; it was responsible for the countryside as far as Tewkesbury, Monmouth, Berkeley and Cirencester. A few precious men had to be spared to occupy country houses to stop the Royalist garrisons at Berkeley, Beverstone, Cirencester and Sapperton House from raiding, and to make sure that trade carried on after a fashion, that food could be harvested, and that taxes could be collected in the name of "the king and parliament" to carry on the war.

In the middle of 1643, it looked as if Parliament was about to lose. A series of battles had been lost all over the country and the

war committees in London were in confusion. The King was in
the south-west with his better drilled, better equipped and
larger army. He had captured Bristol easily, much to his own
surprise. London lay ahead to the east, and Gloucester to the
north. If he went north he could join the Welsh army being
raised by Lord Herbert. Gloucester would be the meeting place
and the springboard for the march to London and victory.
Surely, Gloucester would not resist now Bristol had fallen . . .?
But Gloucester did resist.

In February 1643, the King's nephew, Prince Rupert of the
Rhine, asked the city to surrender. Dennis Wyse, the mayor,
prayed for time and said he would not surrender his city to a
"foreign prince". The city was desperately training men, buying weapons and gunpowder, and storing provisions for what
they knew was going to come. In charge was twenty-three-
year-old Colonel Edward Massey, a soldier of fortune who had
offered his services to the King and then left him when he saw
too many favours being given to Roman Catholics. He was a
brave fighter and a good leader, and for two and a half years he
was to fight Parliament's war in Gloucestershire with perhaps a
quarter of the men the King commanded.

He was not deterred, although for most of those years he
could only say he controlled a few miles round the city and the
rich farming land to the south protected by the Slimbridge and
Eastington garrisons.

For the rest of that spring and early summer of 1643, with
the royal army at Bristol, Edward Massey fought bravely. He
captured Sudeley Castle guarding the vital route north to the
friendly cities of Warwick and Coventry. His men stabled their
horses in the chapel and chopped up their meat on the communion table. When a Welsh army moved up to Highnam
Court at the western end of the Westgate Bridge, Colonel
Massey could not face them alone. Sir William Waller had
the nearest reinforcements, and was busy holding off Prince
Maurice and Prince Rupert. They were raiding west from
Cirencester into the Stroud Valley and "they took away cloth,
wool, yarn, besides other goods from the clothiers about

Stroudwater to the utter undoing of them and theirs". But Colonel Waller—they called him "night-owl"—stole away one night late in March and rode hard for the ferry at Framilode with his men; they crossed the Severn, coming up to the Welsh trenches from behind. At dawn, Massey and Waller attacked together from the east and the south and before they knew it they had 1,600 bewildered Welsh prisoners of war to look after. They were herded into St Mary de Lode and Holy Trinity and "fed on turnip tops, cabbage leaves or any such things for ten days", before being sent back to their homes.

But as the summer went on, the King made up his mind. On 5th August, his cavalry had reached Berkeley, the scouts reported. The next day, a Sunday, despite the strict beliefs of the Puritans, everyone was working feverishly packing the crumbling medieval walls with earth and river mud. Horse patrols were still going out through the defences to scout and skirmish. On Tuesday, 8th August, the King reached Berkeley with the infantry and artillery; on the 9th they camped at Prinknash, and on the 10th, in the fields of Tredworth, between Robin's Wood Hill and the South Gate, the bulk of the King's army, 30,000 men, formed up. Somerset Herald, and another herald, dressed in their gold and scarlet tabards, rode into Gloucester to read a proclamation at the Tolsey, by the High Cross. It asked the citizens to surrender their city without bloodshed.

Sergeant-Major Pudsey and one of the citizens rode out to the King with the answer. It was short and to the point. "We, the inhabitants, magistrates, officers and soldiers within this garrison of Gloucester unto His Majesty's gracious message return this humble answer: that we do keep this city according to our oaths and allegiance to and for the use of His Majesty, and do accordingly conceive ourselves wholly bound to obey the commands of His Majesty as signified by both houses of parliament, and are resolved by God's help to keep his city accordingly."

Everyone knew that the key phrase was "as signified by both houses of parliament". The citizens inside believed that they were loyal, but that they had to resist the King's evil advisers who had led him astray. As Sergeant-Major Pudsey returned, the little cluster of houses outside the north, east and south gates went up in flames. None of the King's men would be allowed to use them as cover. But the King's sappers cut the lead water pipes that supplied the city from the springs on Robin's Wood Hill, and Gloucester was under siege. There was very little powder, and no money to pay the troops, and very soon the mill streams that turned the cornmills would be blocked. But the citizens went on as if very little unusual was happening.

On the very afternoon of the start of the siege "women and maids wrought in the Little Mead [one of the town meadows by the river] in the very face of some horse in fetching in turf for the repairing of our walls". All through the siege, the city's cows, more than 200 of them, went out under guard to the town Ham to graze, and when the weather was right, those who could be spared went haymaking. The King's guns bombarded the city nearly every day, and Colonel Massey's headquarters at the old Greyfriars monastery was hit several times, but no one seemed too scared. On one day, the King's gunners fired 150 shots, but they were nearly all too high, and there were only three casualties, a man, a woman and a pig. In fact, it was said that most casualties were caused by people becoming curious and going up on to the ramparts to peer at the enemy.

The citizens went to church as usual, though they forewent their long sermons in order to help fill yet more houses near the gates with earth as defence against gunfire. Drinking water was pumped up from the Severn. Horses worked the cornmills, and the army master-gunners built a gunpowder mill which turned out a precious three barrels a week, and a forge for making gun parts and musket balls from scraps of metal. The soldiers were boarded, sometimes unwillingly, with the townspeople, but they were hardly ever at their lodgings. Nearly all the men lined the ramparts day and night for the whole three weeks, snatching what sleep they could at their posts. Outside, the King's army, 30,000 strong, concentrated with their big guns on the north and the south sides. Lord Ruthven, the commander, had his headquarters at Llantony, and the King lodged at Matson House. Prince Rupert, in charge of the cavalry, remained at Prinknash.

The Royalist plan was simple—to dig the trenches closer and closer, under cover of the artillery, and to break holes in the defences until it would be easy for the infantry to climb over the top, and charge the gaps to let in the rest of the army. They focused their attention on the south-east corner, where the Central Library now is. It was the defenders' job, every so often, to go out, kill as many of the trench diggers as they could and bring back their picks and shovels, to blow up their trenches and tunnels and to immobilize their guns. Then the besiegers would have perhaps three or four days of work to do all over again. The longer the city held out, the better was the chance that Parliament in London could send a relief column to drive the King away.

After three or four days of battering, the south wall was beginning to show signs of collapse. Musketeers inside had been hard at work picking off the King's gunners despite the basket-work barriers built up round the earthen square artillery redoubt, but very steadily the wall was crumbling. The miners had moved forward with their trenches, and they were already draining the water from the town ditch—a disgusting job, because it was still the only town rubbish dump. And already, where a gap was appearing, they were throwing wicker hurdles across the muddy moat to give a firm footing for the attackers when the order came to charge. Inside, in the old Greyfriars orchard, the defenders were patching up the holes with basket work and bales of wool, and packing yet more earth behind the walls.

It was a Saturday evening, the 19th of August, when the first attack was expected. All day the batteries on the south and east had been firing. This was the day when the pig was shot, and some soldiers cooked it for their dinner. One cannonball fell down a chimney in Mr Hathaway's house and landed in the kitchen fireplace as three women were sitting warming themselves, but no one was hurt. The defenders built a breast-work across the orchard as a second line of defence in case the Royalists got over the walls, and that night drummers beat up the alarm all round the city. But the attack when it came was a feeble one.

All the next week the King tried to bring the action to a quick end before Parliament pulled itself together and acted. A fire burnt one night on Wainlode Hill, which was to have been a signal to the city that help was on its way. But inside, every-one realized that this was a trick.

The next evening: "They shot likewise great fireballs, and great stones out of their mortar pieces which did little hurt and killed none. They shot from their battery at Llantony above 20 melting hot iron bullets, some 18 lb, others 22 lb weight; in the night we perceived them flying in the air like a star shooting. Most of them fell into houses and stables where hay was."

But they went through the hay so fast that they started no fires. And when one "fireball" landed in a bedroom in the house of Mr Cornelin the apothecary, his family and servants simply poured buckets of water over it until it was cool. Alderman Pury's son, Captain Pury, was ordered to climb the cathedral tower and show some lights, to tell everyone in the countryside around that Gloucester still held out. And although "the enemy vexed thereat levelled some shot at the tower one whereof came close by Captain Pury, as he was looking towards Llantony, who for all that continued the burning of his lights until the moon was fully risen".

All that week too, a second attempt at the south wall was being plotted by Prince Rupert. He was spending a great deal of his time in the trenches with the forest miners in the King's service. With the help of Dr Chillingworth, the classical scholar, they were remembering what they could of sieges in Greek and Roman times and building galleries over the trenches to protect the workers and mines and tunnels under the walls. One of the mines, under the East Gate, was nearly finished when a sergeant and five men slipped out through a side gate, lifted up the board that covered their tunnel, and dropped in a hand grenade.

But by the end of the second week most of the mines were packed with powder and ready to be blown. Later in the same night, when Captain Pury was guarding the lights, the weather broke: rain poured down, the tunnels were all flooded and collapsed, and the powder was soaked. Two weeks' work had been wasted.

Three days later, although the mining and the galleries had begun again, spirits rose inside the city. Two messengers slipped back from Warwick. They brought news that the parliamentary forces were on their way. In every London church preachers were demanding action. The country could not let Gloucester down, they said. It was the turning point, and suddenly Parliament began to believe that it could win. The trained bands of the City of London had been drilled, and four new regiments were raised almost overnight. So many horses were taken from the farms that there were none left to bring in the harvest. The shops had all closed until the news of the relief of Gloucester was announced. The London army had paraded on Hounslow Heath before moving off west through the harvest fields.

The going was slow and the royal garrison at Oxford caused them trouble. The weather had turned cold, but they could not light fires at night and give away where they were. At last, on 5th September, they reached Prestbury Hill, and saw the city below through the drizzle, with the leaden curve of the river beyond. The last of the King's troops had just left, burning their huts as they went. The two young princes, who had spent the last three weeks locked in a room at Matson and carved their names in the woodwork to pass the time, were now bundled into carriages for the muddy climb up the hill to the friendly comfort of Painswick. But there is a story that when one of them asked when they were going home, their father told them that now they had no home to go to.

Gloucester and the Parliamentary cause were both saved. The London trained bands were heroes of the hour. But the war was not over yet. The "trained bands" were not regular soldiers. They were apprentices and working men and they wanted to get back to their families and jobs now that the jaunt was over. They stayed for only a few days, and then Colonel Massey and the Gloucester garrison were on their own again. They still had their pay owing to them, and powder and food were scarce. Sir William Vavasour for the King drove a parliamentary force at Painswick back into the church, burned down the door and threw in hand grenades. A plot to betray Gloucester into the King's hands was only discovered through the honesty of an officer of the garrison who was asked by his relative, on the King's side, to help.

But the Parliamentarians knew they could not lose now. Beverstone Castle fell, while its commander was away courting a lady. Malmesbury and Tewkesbury surrendered too; very slowly, the whole of Colonel Massey's area was cleared except for Berkeley Castle and its garrison of horse and foot from Ireland. In the parish register at Slimbridge is this entry— "Lieutenant Harris and Richard Taylor, both soldiers shot at Berkeley Castle. They were buried the 8th September, soldier like with the drum and two peals of shot on the north side of the church." Slimbridge had been garrisoned, and its men had been fighting against the castle for three years. But now the colonel could concentrate on it, and late in 1645, two years after the Gloucester siege, 1,000 men from Bristol arrived to join him for the attack.

They rushed the church, firing as they went, and shot the lock off the door. But only when they began to haul small artillery guns to the top of the tower where they could fire directly over the castle walls, was Sir Charles Lucas, the commander, forced to surrender.

It was over. The Puritan Parliamentary party had won. The King was executed, and his son fled abroad. A huge hole was blown in the wall of the keep at Berkeley to make sure it could never be used as a fortress again.

But for nearly fifteen years few supporters of Parliament were happy with their victory. In the end even Edward Massey, now a major-general, grew tired of the new Commonwealth of England, and went to join the future king, Charles II.

Hauling the guns up the tower of Berkeley Church

11. "HANDSOME MILLS" AND "LOW-BUILT COTS"

Like the other cities of England, Gloucester sent its address of welcome when the new King, Charles II, was crowned in 1660. And when Parliament was recalled, Sir Edward Massey, as he had now become, represented the city. But Charles was no fool. He remembered his stay at Matson House and the wet and slippery journey up the hill to Painswick nearly twenty years before. Gloucester's new charter cut the city area in half. The South Gate, in a terrible state, was pulled down and the walls were allowed to crumble.

The wool trade in the city was now almost a memory, but in its place was a completely new industry—pin making. The bell foundry, owned by the Rudhall family, continued turning out bells for almost every county in England, and for churches in the colonies too. The knowledge and experience of the Gloucester metal workers, dating from medieval times, must have helped to make pin-making a success. In the 1700s and 1800s, the population rose slowly from 4,000 to 7,000; and 1,500 of these worked in the nine pin factories that traded not only with London but with Spain and America too. Gloucester became a typical sleepy little cathedral city, a little more industrialized than many, but without the big smoky chimneys and the slag heaps of industrial cities today. The "factories" were mostly large old houses, like the present Folk Museum in Westgate Street.

The cathedral and its community had passed through a frightening period. Bishop Goodman, Miles Smith's successor, had supported the anti-Puritan beliefs of Archbishop Laud, and Parliament had imprisoned him for it. His palace had been ransacked, and in the heat of the Civil War, when the county signed a petition for all bishops to be abolished, a number of enterprising men had decided that cathedrals would no longer be needed; they actually began to knock St Peter's down to sell the stone, the wood and the lead. Luckily the aldermen listened to their town clerk, John Dorney, who had lived through the siege and wrote a diary of it. They stopped the workmen to save "this, the city's greatest ornament". But after this it settled down behind its high walls to a hundred years of calm. Some of the Puritans stood out against the return of the Church of England, but most accepted it, or attended the new licensed "nonconformist" chapels that were being established at Berkeley, Dursley, King's Stanley, Nailsworth, Painswick, Stinchcombe, Uley, Wickwar and Wotton. They became tolerated as part of the system, and even the Catholics were not hounded now as they had once been. Only the Quakers were persecuted by everyone.

> On the 16th day of the third month 1660, at Nailsworth, there came a wicked man, with others with him, with their swords drawn and their pistols cocked, and lighted matches in their hands into the meeting, and laid hands on one Friend and had him before the Mayor of Gloucester, who said to the marshal he should take him away, and set a strong guard of musketeers to look to him.

In Stroud Museum and at Elmore Court are similar paintings of a green valley with trees and houses along the slopes and a river at the bottom. On the slopes are painted long rectangles of bright red. The pictures represent the valley of Stroudwater about 1790, and the red rectangles are lengths of cloth, freshly dyed, and laid out to dry. Ever since the monks and the medieval lords had begun to herd sheep and the weavers had been moving from Gloucester and Bristol to the freedom of the countryside, Stroud, Dursley and Wotton had been growing. Any weaver could enclose land and build a home on Minchinhampton Common. There was plenty of first-class wool to be had locally. The damp air suited weaving beautifully—it made

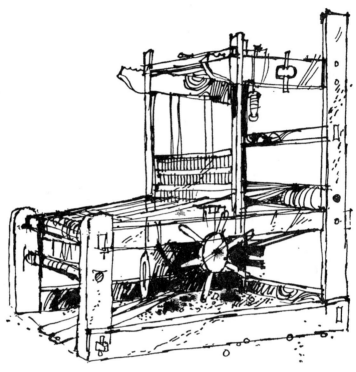

Hand loom

the thread springy. There was fuller's earth nearby to wash out
the grease and plenty of fast water to drive the fulling and dyeing
mills. And the water was so soft that the colours it produced
were strong and pure, especially the reds. In the County Record
Office is the dyers' book for 1794–1804, used by Messrs Marling
and Evans, clothiers, of Stonehouse. In it are samples of dyed
wool—scores of them—with the recipes and names for the
different colours: bat wing, red ratt, Paris dirt, and a brilliant
blue, drake's back. The woad plant grew well near Wotton,
Painswick and Stroud. It gave a blue dye that was used for
making blacks and the famous Uley blues. And it could be
mixed with the yellow weld—a plant that grew in the fields
of stubble during the autumn and winter—to make green.

The heavy clay of the Vale produced fields of enormous king teazles with hooked spiny heads that were fastened to wooden frames and used to comb away the loose fibre from the cloth and raise the nap. Everything necessary was on the spot.

The clothiers flourished. Their wills show how wealthy they had become. In 1545, William Haliday of Rodborough paid £42 in tax alone, when a labourer would have been lucky to earn three or four shillings a week. These rich men built magnificent stone houses in Painswick, Wotton and in Nailsworth as a mark of their success. Often you can see them today, with a loft in the gable end for storing wool, and a garden at the back long enough to stretch out a broadcloth—twenty-eight yards.

In 1610 a record was made of the men in each parish and what they did. It was made to show how many owned weapons or could turn out to fight in an emergency, but it also shows us just how many people were involved in clothmaking. In the Stroud Valley there were 746 men concerned in the wool trade. At Nailsworth, 25 of the 30 noted worked in the trade. At Upper Lypiatt it was 48 out of 61. At King's Stanley 80 out of 142. At Dursley there were 53 cloth workers, and at Stinchcombe the lord of the manor was a clothier. At the same time there were only two or three clothiers in Gloucester.

It was said that it took thirty men to finish a cloth for the market. At the top end was the clothier. He bought the wool and paid spinners to spin the thread, weavers to weave it, fullers to clean it and tuckers and dyers to dye it and give it a finish. Then the clothier sold it to the merchant who took it to market at Blackwell Hall in London, to Bristol, or to inland market towns. Very often the clothiers were weavers or fullers with some savings put by, who invested their money in some wool and could only deal with one cloth at a time. The risks were always very great. There might be no demand at the market, and usually the clothiers paid the workers and the wool merchant out of the sale money. The clothier might be left with a useless piece of cloth and no cash to pay his bills. Many men, even the big clothiers, were ruined very suddenly like this. But often, too, especially in times of war, the demand for cloth was tremendous; even today, the regiments of the Guards dress in uniforms of Stroudwater scarlet.

Clothiers who were lucky could become very rich, and by the 1700s the richest were as cultured, as well established and as important in the county as any of the gentleman farmers. They employed architects to build them grand new country houses like Frampton Court, built for one of the many Clutterbucks, or a little later, follies in the new romantic fashion like Rodborough Fort. They dealt in hundreds of cloths, and had invested in the most advanced machinery in existence to finish the cloth.

A long way below the gentlemen clothiers, sometimes a little above the smallest clothiers, were the weavers. It took two or three weeks to weave a broadcloth and besides the master weaver there was a journeyman and his wife and children to help. The weavers were independent men. They owned their own looms, and they worked them in the downstairs living-room of their own cottages. Occasionally you can still see the cottages, with long large windows which the weavers needed to see to do their work.

A weaver could earn good money, especially in the prosperous times of war in the 1680s and 90s. The Government made sure there were never more weavers than work by limiting the number of looms each weaver owned, and insisting that he served his seven years' apprenticeship. The Justices of the Peace fixed prices for cloth too, depending on the fineness of the weave. In good weeks a master weaver could earn 10s. in the 1750s and that was not bad money. But the weavers were independent men and they stuck to their old-fashioned ways. The clothiers brought in more and more machinery to speed up fulling, dyeing and finishing, but up to the 1830s the weaving was still done slowly on old-fashioned wooden looms. As the eighteenth century wore on the fixed rates became worth less and the clothiers could not pay more. Weavers had once been prosperous and independent men. Like Samuel Dansell of

Bisley, they owned not just their house and looms but land in the common fields and cottages too. But in 1806, when Parliament enquired into the woollen trade, someone gave evidence that "there is not one family who has as much land as this room". For much of the time the weavers bore their lot. They could do little else. But in times of slump the prices they were offered for their work could not keep them alive and they took action.

In 1727, for instance, Mr Thomas Roberts, a clothier, had organized the local clothiers and made them promise not to pay the legal fixed price for their weaving, and because many of the weavers had nowhere else to turn, they signed agreements to take less money for their work. A letter, badly written, but quite clear in its message, was dropped mysteriously in the courtyard of Mr Roberts' mills. "This is to give notice to all weavers not to put their hands to any paper made by Mr Roberts or any other clothier, if you do, we the weavers of each parish are fully resolved to meet in a body and car him on the wooden horse and throw him into his master's mill pound, where he signed the writing. As for you clothiers, we think it not worth your whiles to trouble yourselves with any such thing if you do be it to your peril though it is our desire to be quiet." It was an ugly situation. Another clothier, Mr Ellis, had to destroy the contracts in front of the weavers' leaders in the end, because they had refused absolutely to do any more work and returned their yarn to him.

In 1756 the situation was even worse. The Justices of the Peace, who were mostly landowners, knew nothing of weaving rates. They fixed them at up to 21s. each week per loom—a master would get about 10s. 6d. of this, by the time he had paid his assistants. The clothiers protested. They could not pay the rates, they said, and the weavers did not need them. They only spent their wages on drink and let their gardens run wild instead of growing vegetables. For six weeks, while the Justices were deciding what to do, the weavers grew more and more angry, and the clothiers bought guns and mounted guard over their own houses.

On 11th October, 1756, the clothiers met in Stroud, very probably in the saloon of the George Inn, which was in the High Street. It was agreed that the leading weavers should attend. The clothiers knew the weavers were so stubborn that they would have to consult them, but two or three thousand turned up, some from as far as Kingswood. The clothiers, scared for their lives, agreed to hold a regular committee on rates of pay. The weavers, who had hoped for an immediate settlement, were furious. They tried to burst into the room,

and the clothiers fought to get to the back window. Although the room was on the second floor, some dropped to the ground outside before the weavers saw what was happening and blocked their escape. But before any blood was spilt, a body of the friends and servants of the clothiers forced their way up the stairs and rescued the frightened men in the room. The insults and the threatening letters went on. Some weavers refused to work for lower than the legal rates and for those who did there was the constant terror of a knock on the door that meant a gang of strikers, come to remove the shuttles, to destroy the tools and to damage the cloth on the looms. Six companies of infantry were drafted into Stroud. Their commander was General James Wolfe, soon to distinguish himself in Canada. Very quickly the outward calm was restored and the weavers one by one gave in and returned to work, in greater misery than before. The larger clothiers began making tremendous profits out of the army contracts for the war against Napoleon, and very soon their old-fashioned equipment, in long low sheds, could not cope with the demand. There was little level space to build. The only possible direction was up, and up their new mills went—four storeys or more—magnificent structures of stone with iron pillars and arches, echoing the elegant building styles that graced the fashionable city of Cheltenham, or the workmanlike stone barns of the Cotswolds. Inside them was new machinery, some of it imported from the north, and more and more of it driven by coal fired steam engines.

No one thought industry was ugly then. People only saw the power of the machines and the ingenuity of their inventors. The church organist at Stroud was moved to put into rhyme the romantic feelings many people had about the view from Rodborough Common:

> With handsome mills this craggy dell doth teem,
> Where engines work by water and by steam.
> High on the mountain cliffs large houses stand
> Appearing awful yet secure and grand.
> The poor mechanic from his low-built cot
> Looks up, contented with his humble lot.

The organist chose to ignore the horrible truth about the mills. For all their magnificence they stand as memorials to the hundreds of cloth workers whose suffering increased as the mills grew higher. After 1756 the weavers rose in earnest three more times, but they were doomed. Against the law of the land —a law nearly 300 years old—first gig mills (for raising the nap), then shearing machinery and finally, in 1835, power looms were installed. Then, with peace came a slump. The weavers suffered terribly.

The weavers are much disturbed. They are wretchedly off in bedding, I have seen many cases where the man and his wife and as many as seven children have slept in straw laid on the floor with only a torn quilt to cover them. Sometimes I have had occasion to search the houses of some weavers on suspicion of stolen yarn and I have witnessed very distressing cases: children crying for food and the parents having neither food nor money in the house or work to obtain any: I have frequently given them some money out of my own pocket to provide them with a breakfast. These men have a great dread of going to the poor houses and live in constant hope that every day will bring them some work. I have frequently told them they would be better in the house and their answer has been "we would rather starve". I consider this wretched state stunts the children in growth and causes a great deal of sickness and I have often dropped in at mealtimes and found them eating of potatoes with a bit of suet.

That was the constable at Minchinhampton in 1839. The weavers had risen for the last time twelve years earlier. In the court records of the Assizes held at Gloucester, we can read of William Pickford, 20, who "on the sixth day of June, 1827, riotously assembled at Stroud and committed a violent assault on William Camburn by throwing him into a pond and at the peril of his life continuing him therein for a long time. And also charged with having on the fourth day of June at Stroud with sundry other persons to the number of 3,000 upwards riotously assembled before the woollen factory of Messrs Henry, Peter and Geo Lingard Wyatt and used threats to do the said Geo Lingard Wyatt some bodily harm."

William Pickford was sent to Northleach Penitentiary for one year. But in many ways he was lucky. At least in prison he would be fed. A factory worker of Nailsworth, George Risby, had 12s. 6d. to feed his wife and eight children. Once he had paid his rent, and bought coal, candles and soap, he had left enough for five pounds of bread per week for each of his family and nothing else. He said that he was so weak that he could not walk to work properly. For the last time the army had been called out against the cloth workers at Chalford and Dursley. Many people left the valleys for good, some to work on the railways, and many more to seek a new life in Canada or Australia. The local parish councils often sent them at their own expense. It was cheaper than paying them parish relief for ever. Seventy left Uley in one week, and in the summer of 1837, the parish of Bisley sent sixty-eight poor parishioners to Australia, with a Bible and a prayer book each.

A government commissioner, Mr William Miles, was despatched to look at the tragedy. He put up at the Old Bell Inn in Dursley, where the cloth workers' leader, Timothy Exell, sought him out. They "held open court" on the grass in Chalford Bottom and Mr Miles heard the evidence of thousands of weavers. There were 1,135 weavers who testified that they had 1s. 8d. a week less to live on than the criminals in Horsley House of Correction. It was the same story all over the country, and it was a terrible report that Mr Miles submitted. The clothiers suffered from the slump as well—143 firms closed in the fifteen years after the peace treaty of Vienna was signed in 1815. They were not entirely to blame for the misery of the weavers. They were not quite the ogres they might sound from what has just been said; some of them had real sympathy for the poverty and distress they saw around them. But their time had come too, and the cloth trade at Stroud was dying fast. The wool towns of Yorkshire were beginning to overtake the industry of the Stroud area in size and wealth, and in misery too.

The clothing workers were independent men and they showed it in their religion. As the cloth centres in the valleys of the Frome, the Cam and the Little Avon had grown, so did the congregations of the Non-Conformist chapels. In the 1750s, there were about 300 Non-Conformists at Cam alone, and forty years later the local vicar at Uley reported to the bishop that a new chapel had been built to seat 400 to 500 people. The clothing trade was not where the churches were and the church did not try to cater for them. The parish of Stroud was still very hazy in most people's minds—"situated in the parish of Stroud, or Bisley, or one of them", someone wrote in the 1730s.

The Church of England allied itself with the country gentry and left others to care for the souls of the industrial workers. The clergy of the local parishes must have felt it beneath them to visit among the untidy scatter of dirty churs—alleyways—that were the backstreets of the busy little town of Stroud. At first it was the older Non-Conformist groups, especially the Baptists, who filled the gap. But in the 1730s, there were new voices. George Whitefield, the youngest son of the landlord at the Bell Inn in Gloucester, had acted in plays at the Crypt School and had left wanting to become a professional actor. But then his mind had taken a serious turn and he went to university at Oxford instead. Oxford at that time was a sleepy place of good living and little learning, but George joined a small group of students who were taking life earnestly. Their leader was John Wesley, and because of the way they behaved, they came to be called "Methodists" in fun by the other students. They went without food frequently, and prayed for hours on end. George became worn out and ill, but when he returned home to recover he persuaded a group of religious minded people in Gloucester to join him, and the group "quickly had the honour of being despised at Gloucester as we had been despised at Oxford".

It was not long before he was ordained a priest in the cathedral—the Methodists still thought of themselves as members of the Church of England—and he began a wandering life as a missionary to the people the Church had neglected in the West Country. He already knew the Stroud Valley well. For two months he had been a curate at St Cyr's Church, Stonehouse. He said afterwards, "It is the pleasantest place I ever was in". But his main gift was for preaching. People still enjoyed long sermons on Sunday afternoons, and the sermons of John Wesley and George Whitefield were very exciting and completely new. Dr Johnson called George's preaching "wind and fury" and many people laughed at his crossed eyes and called him Dr Squintum, but in Bristol his visions of hell and heaven made a girl so excited she was hysterical for five days. He regularly collected crowds of thousands in the open air, because most clergymen thought he was a dangerous man to encourage, and refused to let him borrow their churches.

His diary tells us about his preaching tours:

April 14: Lay at Stroud about three miles from Chalford. Preached in the fields belonging to the inn at nine in the morning, to about 600 people.

April 15: After dinner went to Stonehouse being invited thither by the minister as well as the people. It rained all the way going thither, but not withstanding that, I believe 3,000 souls were ready to hear me. The church not being large enough to contain a third part of the audience, I preached from a very commodious place on the outside. And though it rained the whole time, yet I did not observe one person leave his place before I had done.

July 1: Preached in the afternoon at Randwick church. The church was quite full, about 2,000 were in the churchyard, who by taking down the window that lay behind the pulpit had the conveniency of hearing. Many wept sorely. After Evening Service, I hastened to Minchinhampton Common, where to my great surprise I found no less than 20,000 on horseback and foot ready to hear me.

George Whitefield calculated that he preached 1,800 sermons in his life. Usually he preached twice a day. He brought to Gloucester and the clothing valleys a message of hope, and the promise that God looked after the poor as well as the rich. Part of the Puritan belief had always been that learning was important for a godly man. Learning began with reading the Bible and understanding God's word, but it did not end there. Education was a prize that the clothing workers valued, and many of them, like Timothy Exell, had taught themselves and were extremely learned.

Some of the workers earned a little extra money by teaching a group of children as they worked at a loom or the spinning wheel. John Twining had a school in his cottage at Sheeps-combe, and so did William King, a card maker at Dursley. But education was very haphazard. If you lived in Stroud, there was the charity school. In Wotton there was the Grammar School and the Bluecoat School. And in Gloucester there were the Crypt School and the Kings School. But most children had to work hard, and there was neither the time nor the money to learn to read and write. In 1816, a certain meeting took place.

The Fleece Inn at Rodborough had always been a favourite meeting place for the mill owners and clothiers. On 18th April, they gathered to protest against some proposals that Parliament was considering, to limit the number of hours children were forced to work, and to stop children under ten years of age working at all. A committee of local clothiers, including Mr Shepphard of Uley and Mr Hicks of Eastington, was asked to present the clothiers' case. In a printed petition sent to Parliament they said that in the Gloucestershire factories:

> Their time of work never exceed twelve hours in the day. That by early and moderate employment they are brought up in habits of industry and good order instead of being left to run wild, as would be the case if the proposed measure was to take effect. . . . Sunday Schools are established where the children of working people are encouraged to attend. The cleanness, civility and good order of children where factories are established is most evident when contrasted with the other parishes of the neighbourhood.

The schools they were talking about were not exactly like the Sunday Schools we know, though they were run by religious men and they did include some Bible study. Their main aim was to give some general education to the children of poor cloth workers who had to work all the week.

It was a Gloucester man who first put Sunday Schools on the map. Robert Raikes was the editor of the local weekly newspaper, and he was also an extremely religious and kindly man. He got the idea walking one Sunday in St Catherine's meadows, near St Catherine's Street. It was one of the poorest

Robert Raikes

quarters of the city, where many of the pin makers lived; he saw the ragged children with nothing to do playing on the waste land and he decided to help them. Almost before his first Sunday School was open, it was bursting at the seams. And soon there were five more in Gloucester and others in Painswick, Woodchester, Stroud, Stonehouse, Nympsfield and Tetbury. It does not sound an exciting way of spending a Sunday to us, but then a little education, even just being able to read and write, might make all the difference between starvation, with a body twisted and crippled by too much hard work in a cloth factory, and a job as a junior clerk, perhaps, with easy work and food in the larder at home. For those first Sunday School children, Mr Raikes' idea meant a wonderful opportunity.

12. AN END TO SMALLPOX

Although it was such an amazing sight, and so important nationally, the Stroud Valley and its clothing industry was only a small, untypical part of our area. The mills and the cloth workers' cottages that spread up the valley sides quickly gave way to deep countryside as they do even today. The prosperous clothiers, the Shepphards, the Playnes, the Hickses, and most of all, the Pauls, liked to think of themselves more as country gentlemen than as factory owners; and as a hedge against the ups and the downs of business they bought land to fit them for the part.

The countryside of the Vale and the Edge was an idyllic one in the eighteenth century. The long process of the change from corn growing to pasture and fruit growing, which we saw beginning in the 1250s, was almost complete now; where the local farmers did not want to change over, they found they were being forced to do so because the soil was tired out after centuries of cultivation, and the size of the harvests was beginning to drop. There were probably fewer people living here by 1800: many may have gone to work in the mills at Stroud or Wotton or Dursley. The life of those who were left was one that the romantic aristocrats affected to envy and imitate. It was a life of "honest toil" amid beautiful surroundings, a land rich in the good things of life—the ripening apples and pears with cider and perry squeezed from them by a patient blindfolded horse working an old stone cider press; grapes and apricots ripening against the warm stone of cottage walls. There was creamy milk and butter from the herds of dark brown Gloucester cattle; big orange cheeses sold each month under the stone arcades of the market at Berkeley; sides of beef and pork fed on the lush grass and the orchard windfalls; wild asparagus from Thornbury; edible snails round Cranham; fruit from the hedgerows in autumn; rabbits and hares from the fields and wildfowl from the marshes and the New Grounds; pike, perch, tench and sometimes a trout in the Frome, the Cam or the Little Avon. And products of the river: eels, lampreys, lamperns and elvers; small sand dabs and sea fish; the occasional sturgeon; and above all, thousands of fat silver salmon, caught in the wicker engines, with a net, or an old-fashioned fish spear.

Mending an eel wheel

But the picture was only partly true. For the ordinary people life was far from romantic. Most cottages had earth floors and little furniture, and were very damp. Even today, many houses in the Vale are flooded regularly, and people along the river have chest complaints and other illnesses caused by the damp air. For the majority of working people, money was scarce.

I G

Bread and potatoes made up the main part of every meal, sometimes with a little cheese or salty fat bacon, or perhaps a poached rabbit or eggs, and a few boiled nettles or turnip tops. They had cider to wash it down, supplied by the local farmer, or once in a while, a mug of tea. Work for these people was long and monotonous, with only an occasional break—the harvest supper being one, with plenty of food, including roasted meat, and plenty to drink. And always there was death looking over their shoulder, carrying away perhaps one in every three or four children before they grew up.

For the gentry, life was much freer, but often as tedious. The men spent long weeks looking after their lands; the women, who did not even have that diversion, wrote long letters to each other, taking all day to write, and filled up books —like the large long leather-bound notebook that was kept in succession by several women of the Clutterbuck clothier family—with recipes and cures and passages from books that had caught their eye. But the "county", as the group of gentlemen of the county and their families were known, provided a cure for boredom and loneliness.

The "county" was a sort of large family. They played together—at the races, at subscription concerts in the Shire Hall, at balls in the great houses, while taking the waters at Gloucester Spa or Cheltenham, or at the hunt. They often went to school together—at the Kings School in Gloucester—and they were nearly all related by a network of marriages. They even voted together, with or against each other—they all managed to take sides in the great election battles between the Beaufort party and the Berkeleys. They sat together on county committees and associations, and talked agriculture, literature, medicine. And from day to day, they met on the court bench as Justices of the Peace. When they went up to their town houses in London for a season in the world of fashion, there was the Gloucestershire Society to attend. It had originally been founded to finance poor boys to become apprentices in London, but by the 1780s had become a dining club where sometimes fifty Gloucestershire squires sat down to dine together.

The "county" was prosperous and a little over-pleased with itself, but it knew its responsibilities. There was Sir George Onesiphorus Paul of Hill House, Rodborough, who owned mills and had an income of £2,500 a year. And he spent it too! We have to multiply this figure by at least ten to show how well he lived and how little Sir George had to worry about from the world around him. He was an engineer and inventor who designed, among other things, an ingenious new machine for raising the nap on the cloth in a decorative pattern of knots. This made his competitors more prosperous as well as himself. At the same time, and much more important, was his work as a Justice; he was clear thinking, firm and conscientious, but with a strong feeling for his fellow men.

In 1777 a reformer called John Howard toured the prisons of Gloucestershire and found them in a terrible state. The old castle, at Gloucester, the part that had survived the siege, was the county gaol. It was almost falling down, with broken floors that could not be washed and no proper way of keeping prisoners in. They lived cooped up together in a room eighteen feet by fifteen feet, and slept with their manacles fixed to one long chain. New prisoners had to pay "garnish" to buy drink for the other prisoners—and anything above the bare minimum of comforts the gaoler had to buy for prisoners in the town for ready money. There were outbreaks of smallpox and typhus— gaol fever—as well as the other illnesses caused by bad food and dirt and damp—but the sick were simply moved upstairs to smaller rooms.

Horrified, Paul did his best to put things right. After a great deal of petitioning he managed to have a new county prison built at Gloucester, and completely new "houses of correction" constructed, including one at Horsley. He even wrote the rules for them himself: prisoners were to be given good food—meat twice a week and cheese once—and clean straw for their mattresses, which were to lie on iron bedsteads. There was to be no strong drink, and no pets. Prisoners had to wash each day, and attend chapel before they began work oakum picking, or in the tailor's shop. Because of the work of Sir George Paul of Hill

House, one of the "county", the prison system of Gloucestershire became noted all over England as a model of the new thinking that was going on regarding the treatment of prisoners.

In many other ways too, the "county" showed that its talk and its thought were not only on farming and hunting. In 1781, the Three Choirs Festival was founded to cater for its musical tastes, as a change perhaps from the rather bad amateur playing in the evenings at country house parties. There were also many local historians, amateur and not so amateur, from John Smyth, who wrote about the Berkeleys before the Civil War, through Atkyns, Rudder, Rudge and Fosbroke. Richard, one of the Clutterbuck family, was completely blind, but still recognized the importance of the Roman objects the workmen were digging up in the old graveyard at Woodchester, and tried to stop the gravedigging before any more damage was done to whatever was underneath. That was in the 1680s. Ralph Bigland, an importer of Dutch cheese from London, married a Frocester girl in 1737 and became an adopted member of the "county"; he wrote, among others, a book about the books on Gloucestershire.

But the most important and well-remembered of all the local gentry was Doctor Edward Jenner, who was born and died at Berkeley, and who loved his county all his life. He was a perfect example of the best members of the "county", not quite so rich as Sir George Paul or the Berkeleys, but part of their world. Dr Jenner, like the rest of them, spent his summers at Cheltenham in a hired town house taking the waters. He had his accomplishments: he could play the flute and the fiddle. He went on the long walks to which nearly everyone was addicted. He spent mornings at a time on the round of visits the members of the "county" were expected to pay on one another, and whole afternoons writing the graceful, longwinded letters one was expected to write. He took part in the endless round of charitable works which ladies and gentlemen felt it their duty to do. Two mornings before he died, he was at Cam arranging for some firewood to be delivered to old people. But above all, he loved to explore. Cabinets of curios had an important place in the drawing-rooms of Edward Jenner's time: they occupied the mind and the conversation when today's news had been reported and talk was flagging. But Jenner's collection was enormous—more like a private museum—and it gives us a good clue to the restless curiosity that led him to great discoveries. He wrote a poem about it.

> There's an encrinites' head, a cornu ammonias,
> And marquisites fit to adorn an Adonis
> Fine corrals, all fossil, from Woodford's grand rock,
> And granites from Snowdon in many a block
> Hippopotamus' bones and a great alligator
> And things most surprising thrown out of a crater;
> All changed into flint are an elephant's jaws
> The mammoth's vast teeth and the leopard's huge paws.
> There are beautiful agates washed up by the fountains
> And crabs that were found on the tops of the mountains.

Most of his exploration was in the rich county where he lived. He wrote about it all in his journals, and in his letters to his medical teacher, John Hunter, in London. There was his study of hedgehogs, and the dissection of two stranded dolphins by the river; an essay on the migration of birds, and years of experimenting with and watching his particular interests, cuckoos. But he was a doctor, and his observation and curiosity led him to discover a strange fact that stuck obstinately in his mind. If you had cowpox, you did not catch smallpox. A famous doctor had worked out that one in twelve of the world's population died of this terrible disease. Once it struck an area, one in six of the people who caught it were doomed to die. There was no cure, but there was a prevention, of a sort. Children were deliberately inoculated, infected that is, with a slight attack of smallpox by means of a knife cut and a little pus from a smallpox pimple. Once they had recovered from the resulting slight attack of the disease and the terrible spots had healed, they could never catch it again. The idea had come from the East: millions had been inoculated all over the world, as had

Edward Jenner himself. But it was a dangerous risk. Sometimes the disease took in earnest, and the patient died. And, of course, the pus only remained active for a few weeks, so inoculation could only be given during an epidemic. Dr Jenner realized that no one had ever been known to die of cowpox, even though the symptoms, the pimples and so on, were very similar. As cowpox was much more frequent, especially among the cows in the rich Severn dairy country, it was also easier to use for inoculation.

There were setbacks at first. It appeared that cowpox inoculations didn't always prevent patients catching smallpox; but then he realized that there was more than one disease called "cowpox", and to give the right inoculation, you had to be able to sort out real cowpox from the diseases like it. Once he had done that, the next stage was to try to give smallpox to people who he was sure had had the real cowpox. The first was Joseph Merret, a gardener working for Lord Berkeley. Then he tried it on Sarah Portlock, who had had smallpox twenty-seven years earlier, and John Phillips, a shopkeeper in Berkeley. He inoculated fifteen people, farmworkers, farmers and town dwellers at Berkeley, and not one caught smallpox when Dr Jenner tried to give it to them. At last he felt he was ready. In his notebook he wrote:

> Case 16: Sarah Nelmes, a dairymaid at a farmer's near this place, was infected with the cowpox from her master's cows in May 1796. She received the infection on a part of the hand which had been previously injured by a scratch from a thorn. A large pustulous sore and the usual symptoms accompanying the disease were produced in consequence.

And then:

> Case 17: James Phipps. The more accurately to observe the progress of the infection, I selected a healthy boy of about eight years old for the purpose of inoculation for the cowpox. The matter was taken from the sore on the hand of the dairymaid [that is Sarah Nelmes] and it was inserted on

the 14th May 1796 into the arm of the boy by means of two incisions each about half an inch long. On the seventh day he complained of uneasiness in the armpit, and on the ninth he became a little chilly, lost his appetite, and had a slight headache. During the whole of this day, he was perceptibly indisposed and spent the night with some degree of restlessness, but on the day following, he was perfectly well.

James Phipps became a walking exhibit. He lived to a ripe old age, as a gardener looking after Dr Jenner's beautiful secluded garden running down to the churchyard. They tried to give him smallpox twenty times, but never once did he catch it, in all his hundred years.

The news of the discovery swept Europe. Jenner's new treatment was named "vaccination" after the Latin word for a cow. Doctors all over Europe wrote to Jenner asking for amounts of cowpox fluid to vaccinate their patients. The Emperor Napoleon heard of the miraculous discovery and sent Dr Aubert to England despite the war to find out about it. The first child to be vaccinated in Russia was named Vaccinoff by the Emperor's mother and given a pension for life. Two of the sons of George III, the Duke of York and the Duke of Clarence, were commanders of the army and the navy; not only did they set the fashion by asking for vaccinations in their family but they ordered that every soldier and sailor who had not already had smallpox was to be vaccinated. One of Jenner's friends, Dr Marshall of Stonehouse, was chosen to join the Mediterranean fleet as "vaccinator". All round the Mediterranean, people had heard of the vaccination, and wherever he landed—in Gibraltar, Malta, Naples and Egypt—Dr Marshall gave quills full of the fluid from the arms of his cowpox-infected sailors to the authorities. In Sicily, whole villages came to be treated, herded along by the parish priests, with a crucifix at their head.

Twenty-two children with cowpox were put aboard a Spanish ship that set out to carry the vaccine to the King of Spain's Empire round the world. The vaccine went to India between two glass plates sealed with wax, and it reached

America too. In England at least two dozen vaccination stations were opened, and every week Dr Jenner himself spent one day vaccinating the poor country people free of charge in the old rustic summer house at the bottom of his garden at Berkeley.

Dr Jenner became famous. Foreign universities gave him degrees. Cities made him their freeman. Learned societies in London met to hear him speak. He even had a letter from ten Red Indian chiefs to thank him: "We shall not fail to teach our children the name of Jenner, and to thank the Great Spirit for bestowing upon him so much wisdom. We send with this a belt and string of wampum in token of our acceptance of your precious gift, and we beseech the Great Spirit to take care of you in this world and in the land of spirits."

He could have earnt far more as a fashionable doctor in London. But he preferred life in Berkeley and the countryside he knew, among his friends and relatives. He was far happier at a meeting of the Convivio-Medical society in the Fleece at Rodborough than attending a presentation at court. Two days before he died, after he had walked to Cam and back, he set out to attend a school-friend, Mr Ellis, who was dying. The next morning, they found the doctor unconscious and dying himself, the notes on Mr Ellis carefully complete on his desk.

13. RAILWAYS AND CANALS

During the sixty years before Doctor Jenner's time, the countryside had been changing. The common fields and the strips that the Hwicce had first ploughed a thousand years before were becoming private farms with more or less square fields surrounded by miles of new stone walls and hedges. It suited the richer farmers to have a block of land instead of scattered strips and patches; by bribery and persuasion and threats they managed to get most of the poorer men to see their point of view, and accept a field or two in compensation for their strips. It was all part of the revolution that was to make English farming the most up to date and scientific in the world, but in the process the villagers who had worked side by side on their land for centuries and enjoyed a say in the community, now found that the farmers suddenly belonged to a different class and they had become for the most part just hired labourers.

The enclosing of the village fields and the commons took a very long time. The first enclosures were taking place in Henry VIII's reign. Parts of Coaley and Frocester, Thornbury, Charfield, Quedgeley, Oxlynch, and Frampton Cotterell were fenced in, sometimes by force, and the squires turned them over to pastureland or hunting parks.

Most of the Edge was enclosed in the fifty or so years after the Civil War, and much of the Vale too. Mr Marshall's *Rural Economy of Gloucestershire* tells us that in 1789 "except some common fields towards the upper angle there are not perhaps a thousand acres of arable land within the district". Because the "modern" farmers who pushed through the enclosure agreements in each village grew grain only to feed their horses and to make their beer, we can be sure that most of the Vale was the enclosed dairy land we know today.

Enclosures, especially "towards the upper angle", were going on into the 1860s, but still a few corn strips of the common fields survived. At Upton there were common fields in 1897, and at Eastington they were planting strips with corn up until the First World War, using a spade instead of a plough, and planting by hand with a dibber.

The towns and villages were changing too. The three town gates of Gloucester that had not fallen down after the siege had to be pulled down in the next century. The central island of buildings at the top end of Westgate Street were so tumble-down that they were demolished in the 1740s, and with them went the Kings Board and the last part of Holy Trinity Church, its beautiful tower. They cluttered the streets, which had to be wider now that more and more carriages were using them and the packhorse trains were disappearing. The bridge, too, the one Henry VIII had built, was about to be replaced by a brand new affair designed by that expert engineer, Thomas Telford.

There were brickworks at Frampton in the first part of the nineteenth century, and at Stonehouse a little later. There was still plenty of stone nearby, but many people, including most of the contractors who built new houses in and around Gloucester, preferred bright red bricks, which were cheaper and easier to use. And when they built the mills at King's Stanley in 1813, they used iron for the pillars and arches, and even for the ornate round window frames. Most of the new bridges were of red brick and iron too. Iron mills were in full swing at Framilode at this time turning out all the "modern" metal castings people clamoured for.

In the 1830s the Lamb Inn at Dursley was knocked down to make way for a police station. Earlier, during the weavers' strikes and revolts, the cavalry were brought in to keep order, but no one liked them. They upset the local community even more than they protected it from harm, with their drunken brawls and their love affairs with local girls. The Dursley cavalry unit caused just this sort of unrest and in the parish records are a number of petitions asking that they might leave. Local people formed Voluntary Associations to support the work of the parish constables, and it wasn't until in the late 1830s that the county police force took over.

Another new development in the 1830s was the first appearance of the National Schools. Most of the school buildings you can still see in the parishes of the Vale and the Edge date from the 1840s and 50s, but the schoolroom, just one class usually with its tiny playground and the schoolmaster's house, became a landmark in the village. And though they are often empty today, we can imagine what an impact they originally made. Children still had to help with the harvest in the summer, and many could only find time to learn to read and write at the evening and weekend classes because they were needed on the farm or in the mill. But within fifty years most country people could read and write and do simple sums.

In the 1830s, too, Stroud and Dursley were lit by gas for the first time. The Gloucester Gas and Coke Company had been in operation for nearly fifteen years, but it provided only 150 gas lamps for the whole of a very busy and growing city—there were none at all in the Greek- and Roman-style streets of houses in the new suburbs of Brunswick Square, Wotton, Barton Street, and the area round the Spa. Now a new company promised to extend the benefits of the industrial age to this part of Gloucester too.

The biggest change of all came in what we call communications. In 1770 you could travel from Stroud to the Bull and Mouth Inn near St Paul's in London in two days, by way of Oxford. By 1795, you could do it in one long day—the coach left the Golden Hart Inn at three in the morning and reached the Belle Sauvage in Ludgate Hill at ten that evening, but it was a hard, tiring journey. William Marshall, the writer on agriculture, wrote in 1789 that the Gloucester to Cheltenham road was "scarcely fit for the meanest of their Majestie's subjects to travel on and pay for and much less suitable their Majesties themselves to trust their own persons upon". He was right. A number of Acts of Parliament had been passed to put the roads to rights. You paid your money at a toll house, the keeper opened the gate, and in theory the road ahead was well kept up with the toll money. But the Cotswold roads were notoriously bad, and the way from Stroud to Chalford took a whole day. You went along the top Bisley road, and dropped down the deep slope to Chalford, or you wound along the valley side, up each tributary valley and then back to the main valley once more until you reached Chalford. To get from Stroud to Cirencester and on to London was a lot easier. The new toll road had been opened in 1751, up Rodborough Hill and past Minchinhampton. But still the narrow roads along the valley were only really passable by packhorse. And when in 1814 the Turnpike Act was passed, providing a road to take the present route through Chalford, there was so much opposition to it that the road engineers had to order the workmen to pull down the walls and hedges by night before the contracts were signed so that nothing could be done about it. The toll companies were very happy to collect their money, but not too keen to spend it.

Mr Marshall, when he was so rude about the roads, was talking of a visit King George III made to Gloucestershire in 1788. Sir George Onesiphorus Paul was asked to make arrangements for the royal party to visit his brother Obadiah's mills at Woodchester, and on the way they stopped at Wallbridge in Stroud, to watch a barge pass through the lock into the new canal downstream towards Framilode. Canals were still a bit of a novelty. This one had been at work for a dozen years, bringing coal and bricks upstream and taking hay, corn, stone and timber down to the Severn and the cities of the west and the Midlands. It was fed with water from the river Frome, and for sixty years the mill owners had prevented plans for a straighter, deeper Stroudwater in case it took power away from their water mills. But for two years now an engineer, Robert Whitworth, who had learnt from the great master himself, James Brindley, had been wrestling with the problem of extending the canal and crossing the highest point of the Cotswolds to join the Severn with the Thames and London beyond.

A year later, the canal was ready. From the lock at Wall-bridge it wound upwards, past the mills lining the valley to the little inland port of Brimscombe, where the barges were off-loaded and their cargo reloaded on smaller vessels for the steep climb to Sapperton. Then on, the mills and the weavers' cottages getting fewer and fewer as they passed through lock after lock, until at last they reached the final curve before the classical stone portico of the tunnel mouth came into view, buried deep in the green of the countryside. King George had come to the tunnel opening in the winter of 1789.

It was the wonder of the age. It was two miles long and it had cost £245,000 to cut through the solid rock. It was so well supplied with water that it stayed full even though the section

King George III opening the tunnel at Sapperton

at the highest point would have drained completely dry in three hours without extra water supplies. At Sapperton the horses were unhitched from the traces and the boatmen took over. They lay at the bows, one on each side, and pushed the barge by "walking" along the sides of the tunnel. It must have been four hours before they came gratefully out into the air again, once more in deep woodland near Coates, for a rest and a drink at the inn there.

For a time there was canal mania. Canals were planned—and often dug—to connect everywhere with everywhere else. After all, barges moved goods quicker and easier than any carrier's wagon. The biggest in England was planned to run from Berkeley to Gloucester, to replace the shipping that had almost given up the river Severn for good in the 1720s. But although customers flocked to the canals, and they were busy with traffic, they had cost so much that many years passed before they began to make a profit. Both the Thames and Severn and the Gloucester and Berkeley (which they had to cut short by two miles and join to the river at Sharpness to save money) were always in difficulty in this way. And then just as they became profitable concerns, they were given a blow that killed one and nearly killed the other.

Already in the 1820s there was talk about "railroads". In the 1830s, they began to form companies and collect money to finance them. The railway age had begun. Its king, Isambard Kingdom Brunel, the engineer of the Great Western Railway, was a hard riding, hard working man who drove through his apparently hare-brained plans against all advice and showed he was right.

His plans for the west were laid out. From the depot at Swindon the main lines, seven feet apart, strode towards Bristol, getting nearer every day. At Swindon there was to be a branch line to Cirencester, and on to Gloucester through the Stroud Valley. The problems were tremendous. Money was short and although the railway companies sent letters to local gentlemen, quite a few replied in the manner of Mr Charles Owen Cambridge of Whitminster House at Wheatenhurst:

"With respect to myself becoming a purchaser of shares, etc., I think it would not become one at eighty years of age to be dealing in adventurous speculations. . . ."

Even more objected to the noisy dirty locomotives crossing their land. When Mr Brunel was planning the line from Bristol north to Gloucester a petition was sent from Dursley saying that the railway "interferes with private and ornamental property" and that the plans were "a wanton invasion of their (the petitioners') rights". When a railway employee called on the local gentry at Cam, to ask how they felt about the coming of the railway, he marked the vast majority on his list with a shaky, frightened "dissent". But the railway was surging forward and nothing could stop it. The gangs of Irish navvies attacked the Cotswold limestone a mile from where Mr Whitworth's men had begun, and to save time they started the tunnel at the other end as well. And along the Golden Valley they built viaducts with great baulks of timber to take the steam locomotives.

In 1845 the line to Gloucester was finished. The stations were built to look like the local houses of 300 years before, in soft honey coloured stone. 1845 also was the year when "railway mania" overtook the country. There were six schemes for lines in our area. Two of them were to connect Bristol and Gloucester and Birmingham and Gloucester. Mr Brunel had been called in to plan the first and very naturally he had planned it on Great Western specifications, since it was to have joined the Swindon line at Standish. It was to have the safe, fast, seven-foot wide track that only the directors of the Great Western could afford to build. But as for the Birmingham and Gloucester. . . .

For nine years railway travellers came to loathe Gloucester. On their way from Bristol to Birmingham they had to change at Gloucester from a seven-foot gauge train and cross the platform to a narrow gauge (four feet eight and a half inches) train to take them on to Birmingham. It was all part of the Gauge War, a very serious battle between the railway companies, and in the end Brunel and the Great Western lost to the cheaper, more widely used four foot eight and a half inch gauge track. But while the break of gauge at Gloucester lasted, children were lost, luggage was left behind, precious parcels were smashed and everyone became furious. In *Punch*, Mr Thackeray, the novelist, wrote articles as from Mr James Plush, the cockney footman, about "that *nashnal* newsance—the break of gage".

And in the *Illustrated London News*, a correspondent put it perfectly:

KG ·

Smash, dash splash crash,
Fowling scowling howling growling
Tearing swearing devil-may-careing
Rushing crushing, ladies blushing.
Crockery breaking, babies shrieking
Boilers steaming, parents screaming
Earthly Pandemonia seeming
O the Gauge, the gauge,
The Break of the gauge,
The *Crack* improvement of our age.

In 1854 the Great Western railway admitted defeat and began to add a third rail to its tracks to allow the narrow gauge trains to use it. The irons of the narrow gauge went straight through from Birmingham to Bristol.

The railways were a tremendous boon to ordinary people. In 1851, when the Great Exhibition in the Crystal Palace in Hyde Park displayed the riches of the world for anyone to see, the railways ran excursion trains. It cost 5s. return from Stroud or Brimscombe, and 6s. from Gloucester provided you took "no luggage beyond a carpet bag". The cheapest admission ticket to the Exhibition was 1s., and 6s. was roughly what a farm worker could earn in half a week. But the 5s. fare was far cheaper than the cost of a seat on the stage coach, and during that summer of 1851 many people who could never have hoped to travel farther than Gloucester had a glimpse of the biggest, richest, most powerful city in the whole world. The trains were fast—some even faster than today's. They were comfortable and cheap, too, and they brought Gloucester, Stroud and the Vale almost on to London's doorstep, and to the very edge of modern times.

14. TOWN AND COUNTRY

In the early years of the nineteenth century, it seemed that Gloucester was on the decline. Everyone hoped that the Spa, just outside the old North Gate, might bring Gloucester the riches and the royal patronage that Cheltenham had found. But Cheltenham was an elegant and modern city, and Gloucester was a jumble of medieval half-timbered shops and houses, far too damp to attract the rich families, either of the county or of the kingdom. No one wanted to spend their summers in a ramshackle city that had seen better days, a city that had slums, and earned its living largely from making pins. But after the Berkeley Canal had been opened, and when Gloucester became an important rail junction where the lines from the north to the south-west and London to South Wales crossed, the city began to attract businessmen and new factories opened. One of them made railway wagons and signals. Another built slate fireplaces and painted them with enamels to look like marble or rich wood, for richly furnished Victorian parlours. Another began as the timber dealing business of Moreland & Co. and became a factory producing "England's Glory" matches made from the wood brought up the Berkeley canal from Scandinavia. The ship on the matchbox was H.M.S. *Devastation*, the last word in engineering in 1879. She was not a large ship, but she was one of the first to have electric light, and perhaps this is why Mr Moreland chose to decorate his matches with the *Devastation*—they were supposed to be as up to date and well made as the latest ship in the Royal Navy.

Stroud must have been an exciting place between 1800 and 1900. The number of woollen mills was going down all the time, and the ones that survived did so only by modernizing fast and specializing in the finest, most expensive cloths. But Stroud, far more than Gloucester, was a Victorian city.

The Victorians were very sentimental about the legendary poor boy who, by his own efforts, became a rich and respected member of society, and Stroud was a little like that. In 1832, as a mark of its importance, Stroud was made a parliamentary borough, with its own members of parliament. Many of the churs, the narrow alleyways of the medieval town, had been swept away, and rows of severely classical shops and houses were rebuilt, especially down the hill from Rowcroft and from George Street south towards where the railway would soon run. The suburbs and large houses in the opposite direction, towards Paganhill, began to develop. The grandest of them all was Stratford House, built by Mr Joseph Watts, the prosperous owner of Stroud Brewery.

It was not just the clothiers who benefited from the boom of the Napoleonic wars. Others prospered from the money they had to spend. The new rich began to demand better food and finer goods than the tradesmen were used to supplying. The George Inn moved from the High Street to King Street and became a larger and finer establishment. Several watchmakers had moved into the town, and there was even a resident art teacher for a time soon after the turn of the nineteenth century, who taught the daughters of the local gentry how to draw and paint in water-colour. There was a theatre too, in Bedford Street, and the famous actor Edmund Kean acted with the company there and married one of the actresses in the parish church. But the greatest Victorian building in Stroud is still the Subscription Rooms, by the Cross. Built in 1833, it provided a social centre for the richer clerks and tradesmen as well as the clothiers. They were called "Subscription" rooms because, in the spirit of the times, private individuals subscribed to pay for them, for the public good. There was a reading room, a billiard room, and meeting rooms for lectures on all the controversial issues that faced thinking men in that age of science, the reign of Victoria. There was a debate between a local clergyman and one of the richest local gentle-

men, who had become a Roman Catholic. Catholicism was all
the rage among university students and fashionable young
ladies, but the solider citizens frowned on it as it became more
and more established in Protestant Victorian England. There
was also a lecture and discussion upon the subject of evolution,
shortly after the publication of Mr Darwin's famous book,
The Origin of the Species.

The other little towns were growing like Stroud. Nailsworth
and Dursley both began to grow prosperous again after the
slump of the 1820s and 30s. There was a branch railway line to
each of them, and they helped new industries to take over from
the wool factories. At Nailsworth there was pin making, brass
finishing and stocking weaving, and a new cattle market. The
businessmen of Nailsworth built their own Subscription Rooms
in 1852 as a mark of their growing success. At Dursley, from
1867, the prosperity of the town grew with the success of
Listers, an engineering firm which had been founded by the son
of a mill owner who had fallen out with his father.

While the towns were becoming modern, the countryside
stayed much the same. One historian has calculated that in
1801 half the people in Gloucestershire still worked on the
land. By 1901 only one-sixteenth did so. But those who were
left changed their way of life very slowly. Farm labourers were
left out of the general rise in the standard of living. This was
especially true in Gloucestershire, where many still lived in
primitive cottages, and had only bread, cheese and fatty bacon
to eat. When you look at the little cottages in Eastington,
or Slimbridge, or Randwick, remember that they were usually
home to mother, father, and perhaps ten or fifteen children.
There were rats, and damp, and floods, and dirt. The men and
the women worked for the whole of the daylight hours, and
they often started long before and finished long after. On
many small holdings, the farmers still used the breast plough to
turn the furrows, and harvested the corn with sickles or scythes.
In June the pubs were open at six in the morning to serve the
men who had already done two hours' thirsty work in the hay
fields; in hay time, too, the blacksmith was up and about at

two to begin the grinding of the scythes, so that not a moment of working light would be wasted. For these poor people life was not just hard, it could be unexpectedly tragic. Everyone expected that one or two children in each family would die before they grew up. Rickets and tuberculosis—"the consumption"—worms, ringworm, fleas and lice: all these the ordinary people accepted as part of their lives. In the Eastington area people took their illnesses to the wise old woman who lived on the way to Nympsfield; they trusted her rather than the doctors, and she was cheaper too.

There were other disasters. In 1879 the schools postponed their summer holiday until early September, waiting for the harvest to ripen. But slowly it dawned on people that the corn was rotting in the fields. There would be no harvest that year for the schoolchildren to help with. And it wasn't just the grain that failed. Disease spread quickly through the sheep and cattle, and they died faster than they could be buried. Many labourers must have found themselves without jobs, and many of their masters must have been ruined. For these people there was only the workhouse, breaking stone or making pins, in a place as near to a prison as the Guardians of the Poor could make it.

There were a few pleasures, though. In the evenings the alehouses were full, especially after a good harvest or a successful cattle market when the men had money in their pockets. There were about a dozen pubs in Eastington alone, in the front rooms of poor earth-floored cottages; they served mainly cider: gallons of it every week. The young people in Stonehouse met every night under the only gas lamp in the village, like moths round a flame. And there were high days and holidays, and Sunday, when almost everyone went to church or chapel. The church was still the grandest place most people had been in, just as it had been for villagers in the Middle Ages. Here the squire, the doctor, the Justice of the Peace, the rector and all the wealth and power of the parish met each Sunday with their workers. There was singing, and music from a small orchestra or a mechanical barrel organ in the gallery, and during evening service the church was lit with more candles than the labourer would use in a month. And once or twice in the summer the parish might hire horse drawn brakes to go off to Malvern or Portishead for a sniff at the world and a picnic tea. In the summer most things stopped for the harvest. There were cricket matches and harvest suppers and concerts by the local brass band as well. In the autumn boys and girls found ways of slipping away from school to follow the Berkeley Hunt across the fields. At Christmas there were carol singers and mummers. And once in their lifetime there was the greatest show of all—the Diamond Jubilee of Queen Victoria in 1897, with concerts and pageants and a holiday from school, and memorials of the event set up by some local bigwig, like the Eastington water fountain paid for by Charles Hooper, the local mill owner.

What strikes us most about the lives these people led is that they were not so different from the lives of their ancestors in the reign of Elizabeth I or Edward I. In the bustling towns, especially the young ones like Stroud, there were new buildings and new ideas. But two miles away there were families with names like Guinnell and Heaven and Clutterbuck who had lived in the same village as far back as records stretch, in the same way and with the same narrow view of the world.

15. MODERN TIMES

In 1914, Britain became caught up in a war with Germany. It was a different sort of war from any that had happened before, because everyone in Britain was involved in one way or another. Of course, there was no fighting in England, but it was the part that everyone was forced to play in the war which finally broke down the settled life in the countryside that had gone on with only gradual changes since the time of the Saxons. The young men flocked to join up because war for them was a colourful glamorous thing and they felt that Britain was the greatest power in the world and bound to win. The *Stroud News* reported that the day war was declared there were crowds of men round the Post Office, anxious to hear news of the war and to find out how and when they could join the army. When the first trainload of army reservists pulled out of Stroud Station bound for Gloucester and the regimental depot of the Gloucestershire regiment, crowds turned out to cheer them as they went. In all the parishes around, the men formed drilling-companies to prepare themselves for the day they would join up. The first one was at Amberley. There were recruiting offices in Stroud, and the *News* recorded that in the first week there were forty recruits from Amberley, twenty-three from Stonehouse and thirty from Painswick. Cainscross did not do as well, and the editor said so disapprovingly. Many men in the county joined the Gloucestershire regiment. It was a regiment with a magnificent history, and the men of the Vale were proud to join it. But the pride of the regiment and the bravery of the recruits was not enough to save them from death. The First World War was the bloodiest in history, and the best regiments often fought in the most dangerous places and suffered most.

Over and over again the battalions of the Gloucestershire regiment, their ranks full of newly trained recruits with new equipment, marched proudly to the front and within a few days were destroyed almost completely. At the battle of Ypres, only a few weeks after the war had begun, 1,026 Gloucesters began the fight and only 100 survived. A year later, at the Battle of the Somme, the first battalion lost 900 of its 1,000 men. And so it went on.

Many families had all their sons at the war, and one by one they were killed or badly wounded. It was like trying to fill a colander with water. But those who did survive brought home more knowledge of the world outside than any generation before them. They had seen big cities, and foreign countries. They came to realize that life at home was poor and monotonous, and never again would they be content with it as it had been.

At home, things were changing too. There was more money around. Girls were replacing the men in responsible, well paid jobs, and they enjoyed their independence. At the beginning of the war, the yard of the Midland Railway station at Stroud had been turned into a sale yard where agents bought horses for the army. By the end, an airfield had been laid out on Minchinhampton Common manned by Australian airmen. In 1916 the electric lights had to be dimmed for fear of an air raid, and by the end of the war people whose parents had lived in earthen-floored cottages were flocking to the Empire Cinema or the Picture House in Stroud to see the latest newsreels from the front.

The Second World War brought ordinary people even more into the front line. Gloucester suffered only a few stray bombs, and Stroud saw almost no action at all. But just as in the First World War, local factories had been hard at work turning out uniforms and machinery for the war effort. One factory above all was now desperately important—the Gloster Aircraft Company at Brockworth. Just before the war it had been building Gloster Gladiators, sturdy little fighting planes with two sets of wings. These old-fashioned aircraft were used as second line

Lc

Gloster Meteor Mk I

fighters when war came. But they fought the modern German aircraft all over the world. When Malta stood alone for Britain in the Mediterranean Sea at the darkest time of the war, the only fighters available to beat off the German and Italian planes were three Gladiators that local people nicknamed "Faith", "Hope" and "Charity".

By the beginning of the war the factory had begun making Hawker Hurricanes, one of the greatest fighters of the war. Gloster Aircraft built 1,000 Hurricanes in the first year of the war alone. But the Germans were trying to destroy the Royal Air Force to clear the skies for an invasion, and during the summer of 1940, in the Battle of Britain, all the aircraft factories in the country could not keep up with the terrible destruction. It was quite usual for Hurricanes to leave Gloucester on Monday or Tuesday, and be back by Friday for repairs to gaping bullet holes. Gloster Aircraft would have made a first-class target for German bombers, except that the Government had ordered the different departments to be sent to work in towns and villages for miles round. They worked in halls and garages and even department stores, but nowhere was there a workshop big enough to be worth bombing. The bombers passed over to South Wales and the Midlands, using the spire of Bisley Church as a landmark, and Gloucester and Stroud escaped the suffering of Cardiff and Coventry. But the German bombers did drop some bombs, and twenty-six people died in Gloucester.

Most people worked hard for the war effort, sometimes fourteen hours a day. At night, they often put on tin hats and uniforms and joined the Home Guard or one of the

organizations helping the police and the other emergency services. When Gloster Aircraft was supplying Hurricanes to keep
back the German invaders, invasion was very near indeed. The
Home Guard, the part-time soldiers and the others, trained
hard because they knew they might be helping to defend
Stroud and Gloucester from the German army in a very few
weeks. They dug trenches and set up road blocks. On Minchinhampton Common they built rows of concrete posts to stop
enemy gliders and aircraft from landing. Every town and village had its own Invasion Committee and a secret, bomb-proof
headquarters, where the commander could organize the resistance. At Gloucester it was in a cellar under the Guild Hall, and
at night, when there was more danger from the bombing, it
moved out to a school in the suburbs at Tuffley. Each Invasion
Committee kept an Invasion Book to give the defenders on duty
information about stores of food and arms, details of the secret
telephone lines and the plans for defence in case the invasion
came. Each defence area was allowed one big training exercise
to test its defences. The "Battle of Stroud" took place in the
spring of 1942. But most of the time the work of the Home
Guard, the Air Raid Wardens and the Fire Services was much
more boring. At the beginning there were defences to be prepared and air raid shelters to be dug. One was right outside the
Subscription Rooms in Stroud. People not only had to be fitted
with gas masks, but also persuaded to carry them always. A
register had to be kept of all people living in each street so that
it was easier to identify casualties, and no one liked giving the
information. They were afraid that they would be made to take
refugees from the big cities if they said there was plenty of room
in their homes: people resented the refugees who were pouring
in by their thousands from Birmingham and the towns along
the south-east coast most threatened by invasion. Usually they
were young children, who came with only a little luggage and a
label tied to their coat.

As the war went on, the threat of invasion dimmed. Some of
the defenders moved to the south-east, to help out the local
volunteers where there was still an emergency.

At Brockworth exciting things were happening. A secret new plane was being built, code-named the E.28. Experts had begun work at the very beginning of the war, and now, on a May night in 1941, it stood in Crabtree's Garage at Cheltenham, ready for its first flight. A German bomber force was passing overhead and splinters from anti-aircraft shells were thundering on to the roof above. In the darkness of the blackout inside the garage, a group of men were examining the plane by torchlight. One of them was an official inspector, making sure that the new aircraft was airworthy and safe to fly. It scarcely seemed possible that it would be—it had no propeller, and a completely new type of engine. The following day this first jet aircraft did fly, successfully. From then on, the engineers began to design a jet fighter. Much of the work was done at Moreton Valence Air Station, and within three years the first Meteor jet fighters were being delivered to the Royal Air Force, in time for the last chapters of the war.

More and more soldiers in strange uniforms and with foreign accents appeared in the streets of Gloucester and Stroud, and the older men and the apprentices in the factories like Tylers at Brimscombe were working even longer hours at a new project that made their hearts leap! Gliders! Plywood gliders to carry these American, French, Polish, Dutch as well as British soldiers, to the invasion of France that would drive back the Germans and win the war.

And then one day it was over. Gloucester and Stroud both became a milling mass of people hugging and kissing each other. And that evening, in Stratford Park, they found some coloured lights and broke the blackout regulations to dance round the bandstand under the stars.

A Working World?

The Thames and Severn Canal has gone. The broad gauge has gone. The cloth mills are nearly all closed. Farm machinery has long since replaced the patient lines of haymakers and harvesters, the teams of horses and oxen. Few people eat lampreys now, and much of the milk they used to make into

Double Gloucesters now goes to Cadbury's factory by the Berkeley Canal at Frampton. Few people walk the footpaths to work—the factory car parks are full. The grounds of Rodborough Fort are a camping site.

Already, before the war was over, the newspapers were talking of the great new developments that would take place when peace returned. The river Severn would be spanned by a great bridge, a bridge that would make the ancient ferry at Aust close at last, and a new network of motor roads, "Motor Ways" the writer in the *Citizen* called them, uncertainly, was to criss-cross the country. It all seemed very hard to believe. Of course, these things never do happen as quickly as the planners hope. It was more than twenty years later that the great Severn suspension bridge opened, and the motorway, the M5, is only being built now (1970), alongside the line of the Roman road, to join Birmingham, Manchester and Glasgow beyond with Bristol and Exeter.

In the meantime, Stroud and Gloucester have become bustling, modern towns, with supermarkets, boutiques, Chinese restaurants, and parking problems, for all the world like miniature Londons. Gloster Aircraft has now been swallowed up by a much larger company, but before it closed it produced a number of advanced aircraft, ending with the Gloster Javelin. Now, instead, the factories round Gloucester turn out two million ice lollies and several million ice creams a year; they produce millions of miles of nylon thread, and 200,000 concrete railway sleepers annually. They build church pews and steel barges, huge presses for making car parts and paving slabs, and those giant machines that turn old cars into blocks of compressed steel. They make composition floors, and special grinding wheels and parts for bridges and milking machines. And they still produce matches by the million with H.M.S. *Devastation* proudly steaming on the front of the box.

Gloucester is growing outwards. New estates stretch well beyond the bypasses in some directions, but the medieval centre, neglected for centuries, has died. A few of the old church buildings survive if you look for them among the ugly

factories and piles of rubble, and if you walk down any alley-
way behind the main streets and look up, you can see that some
of the old buildings are still there, although their façades have
been carefully hidden.

The plan for the new centre is a brave one, as brave as the
Roman plan was when Glevum became a colony. Strangely
enough the site the modern planners chose is the place where
the Romans built the new forum for their city, as archaeologists have only just established after 100 years of wondering.
You cannot call Gloucester a beautiful city—yet. But it is
obviously a prosperous one, and one day, when the worn out
buildings have been replaced and the worst of the traffic
diverted, it may become a pleasant place to live in once more.

The problems of Stroud were much more than those of
Gloucester in one way. All Stroud's eggs were in one basket.
In the 1700s, when there was a cloth slump, the town trembled.
Today there are still six cloth mills, with names as old as the
industry itself—Playne; Strachan; Marling; Hill, Paul. They
make some of the finest cloth in the world, and their order
books are full. Lodgemore Mills still sells the scarlet uniform
cloth to the Guards regiments, just as they provided the
cavaliers with cloth when the Golden Valley was no-man's-
land between Royalist Cirencester and Parliamentary Gloucester.

But Stroud's wealth comes from the scores of small firms,
and the few large ones, up and down the valleys, who concentrate in high quality, high value goods. "Light industry" is
what they call most of it, meaning anything from dashboards
for Minis to fittings for the liner *Queen Elizabeth II*, as well as
umbrella parts, knitting needles, garden gates, plastic egg
boxes, rush matting, curtain rails and paper bags. Stroud
factories, like Daniels', make the machinery used in other
factories. The most advanced gyroscopes and steering equipment are made by Sperry's in Stonehouse for guided missiles,
ships and tanks.

Even deep in the Vale, there are many changes. Elvers in
their millions are sent all over the world from Epney. Thorn-

bury is almost a dormitory suburb of Bristol. And the New
Grounds have become the Severn Wildfowl Trust.

Soon, very soon, the motorway will snake south from
Tewkesbury past Gloucester, Whitminster, Cambridge and
on to Bristol. Overhead the prototype Concorde flies from
Fairford to Filton in a few minutes, the journey that took the
earliest Anglo-Saxons thirty years and more to make. Across
the fields and up the slopes march the power lines and their
pylons. They spread out from the new nuclear power stations
at Berkeley and Oldbury, a source of power so great and so
mysterious that it touches the limits of our understanding. And
there, crouched over the river like two great animals drinking,
are the reactors.

The story began with the river and it ends with it. It created
the Vale and the Edge, and it took part in the dramas played
out on them. The power stations make use of it, the bridge
builders have spanned it at last. But still, when the moon is
right, the bore comes up, the banks overflow and the river
claims its own again.

BIBLIOGRAPHY

FINBERG, H. P. R., *Gloucestershire—The History of the Landscape* (Hodder & Stoughton, 1955).

FULLBROOK-LEGGATT, L. E. W. O., *Anglo-Saxon and Medieval Gloucester* (Bristol and Gloucester Archaeological Society, 1950).
Roman Gloucester (Bristol and Gloucester Archaeological Society, 1968).

HYETT, F., *Gloucester in National History* (Gloucester, 1924).

LEVINE, I. E., *Edward Jenner* (Blackie & Son, 1962).

PAINTER, K. S., *The Severn Basin* (Cory Adams & Mackay, Regional Archaeologies, 1961).

RYDER, T. A., *Portrait of Gloucestershire* (Robert Hale, 1966).

WATERS, B., *Severn Tide* (J. M. Dent, 1947).

WHITE, H. C., *Gloucester Story* (British Publishing Company, Gloucester, 1947).

WILSHIRE, L., *The Vale of Berkeley* (Robert Hale, 1954).

INDEX

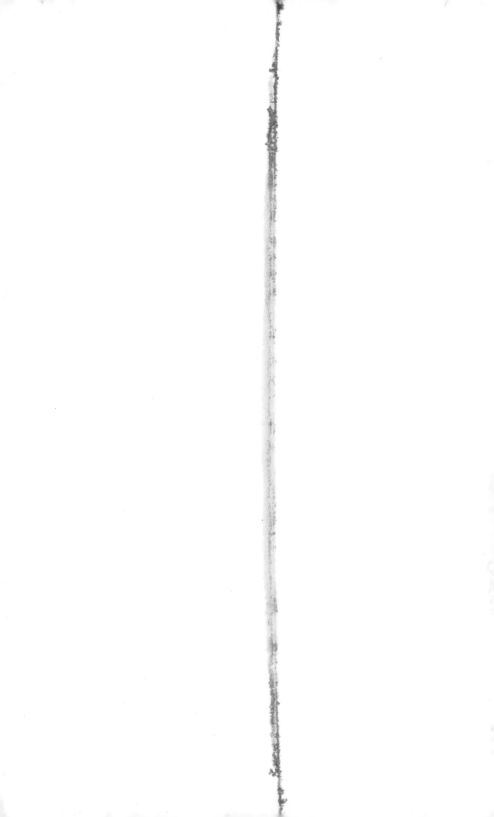